Pairs

By D.W. Richards

PAIRS

Copyright © 2010 by D. W. Richards

All rights reserved. No part of this book may be reproduced, stored in a retrieval system or transmitted in any form or by any means without the prior written permission of the publishers, except by a reviewer who may quote brief passages in a review to be printed in a newspaper, magazine or journal.

First Printing, 2010

All characters in this book are fictitious, and any resemblance to real persons, living or dead, is coincidental.

ISBN: 978-0-9867380-0-5

It is the purpose of art
to heighten the mystery

Part I

*The clouds have landed
While I slept,*

*Suspended breath,
    All is possibility.*

Chapter 1

You remember Gavin McKay? Come on now. Gavin, Gavin McKay. Oh, for the love of God. Gavin: Ned and Alison's boy. They lived in that odd, jigged-up house at the end of Cedar Brooke. Has a sister. What's her name? You know, the red-haired one. Has a name like some kind of flower. Rose? No. That's not it. Help me out here, some kind of flower. Petunia? Nope. It's right there on the tip of my tongue. Quiet now, I've almost got it. Hyacinth? No, it wasn't Hyacinth. Strange, I can see her plain as day. I call out her name to say hello. I'd call, I'd call, Iris? No, that's not it. Just a minute, I'll get it yet. Joy! That's right. Joyfulness McKay, she was cute as a button. We used to call her a summer flower. Born in the scorching heat of July. Oh, that was a blistering hot day. Much like today, actually. Her poor mother's water broke right in the middle of the produce isle at Sobeys. Dropped a basket of Granny Smiths right onto the floor. Not a big fan of the Granny Smiths myself—gives me cramps.

Summer flower. We're talking some thirty odd years ago. Where has the time gone? She ended up marrying one of the Stevenson boys. Tom, I believe. Works down at the General as a technician of some sort. No, no, I'm thinking of his brother. Tom works at Weatherby's Clothier. Where Jake McAllister bought his tie. Only owns the one. Got it for his wedding. What a day that was. Rained like the dickens. I've been to happier wakes. You can't blame his parents, of course; the woman was his teacher after all and had a bun in oven.

Gavin was the best man. Thin fellow. Oh for God's sake, he was in one of your classes or some such at the Mount. Had that nickname. Right. So you remember him then? Well, he's dead.

Chapter 2

After hanging up the phone, Kayley lay in bed reflecting on her grandmother's news. Fondness and guilt, both half-forgotten, lined the passage back to her university days with Gavin. She couldn't recall if she had ever known his name, she only remembered him as Spaz.

PAIRS

Through the close-knit channels found only in small towns, her grandmother had been informed that there was something for Kayley in Gavin's will. However, there would be a delay as his estate had been frozen. Her anticipation about the possibilities churned feelings more associated with an impending exam than with curiosity over an expected gift. Perhaps because that was usually the form in which his gifts had tended to be delivered.

Gavin had encouraged her writing and had introduced her to the great women of literature. He had his favourites. There was Sappho the romantic poet, whom he would quote from time to time. And, of course, there was Sidonie-Gabrielle Colette. He saw her recurring theme, of women turning to other women as a result of the pain in loving men, as gender neutral. In the larger picture, she wrote of a universal abyss of conflicting desires.

Kayley wondered if Gavin would be disappointed in her, given that her literary career was stalled at writing greeting cards, and hoped he would understand that life had simply gotten in the way.

***

Summoned by a firm knock, Kayley stood in the foyer of her townhouse chastising herself while unlocking the deadbolt. She had forgotten that the carpenter was coming that morning. Her four-year-old daughter, Terra, upset by the fog, remained very close.

It had been a morning of mayhem. Starting with the call from her grandmother, their normal routine had entirely unravelled. She hadn't had time to get dressed or pull up her hair or even check her appearance in a mirror. Before opening the door, she reviewed the first impression she was about to present. Dirty housecoat, serpentine springs of blond hair, morning breath, and likely, she suspected, a new big and sore-looking zit, one befitting her morning, somewhere very obvious.

When she finally opened the door, the surprise of the moment left her temporarily speechless. Adam had come at the recommendation of her friend Helen. Kayley couldn't recall his exact relation to Helen, a family friend or cousin of some sort. She had agreed to meet him as a favour, or so she had thought. Upon beholding him, Kayley reconsidered her original take on the arrangement. It was definitely Helen that had done the favour for her.

Kayley had on more than one occasion, but only after splitting a bottle of wine, shared with Helen her penchant for red-headed men and nicely cropped beards. And there he was, delivered to her doorstep: her own fit and trim Highlander.

She speculated that Adam was likely in his mid-twenties and therefore thought him a little too young for her to seriously consider as dating material, but she allowed herself the acknowledgement that he would definitely be a nice distraction while he was around. She had to laugh at herself for wondering if he worked with his shirt off. But as Kayley soaked in her first impression of him, the guilty pleasure of her tiny infatuation suddenly, agonizingly, crashed into the recalled calamity of her own appearance. She could hear the bagpipes wheeze to silence.

"Kayley?" he asked.

"You must be Adam," she replied, unsure of whether she had been gawking.

"That I must."

"Come in."

Kayley stepped back to the foot of the stairs leading to the second floor, making room for Adam in the tight foyer. After entering, he extended his hand in greeting and breathed in the aroma of coffee coming from the kitchen.

"I'm a little sticky," she responded, while assessing the tackiness of her fingers and glancing down to Terra. "We had a bit of a juice incident."

Adam smiled and looked down toward Terra, who partially hid behind her mother, but pushed aside her ringlets of red hair for a clearer view. He crouched to her eye level, and Terra moved a little further back. Adam stroked his hand apologetically along his beard as a speculated explanation.

"No. No," Kayley said. "It's not you. Waking up to fog has thrown her off. Normally, Terra would be doing laps and offering to give a tour of her playroom."

"The fog?" he asked Kayley, before repeating his question to Terra. "The fog?"

Terra didn't initially respond, but with gentle encouragement from her mother, stepped into view, nodded, then retreated.

"The fog makes her anxious," Kayley explained. "Our doctor figures that it is along the same lines as being afraid of the dark. She believes that Terra will probably grow out of it."

"Fog," Adam said to Terra, "that's just a grownup way of saying the clouds have come to visit." With the encouragement of Terra's sudden interest, he continued. "They see us all the time, but from far away. They're curious and sometimes come down for a closer look, and to play."

Holding her mother's hand, Terra stepped out in full view and thought about this surprisingly reasonable explanation. Her confirming glance alternated between Adam and her mother. Terra liked clouds. Assured by their expressions, Terra concluded that it made perfect sense and repeated Adam's insights to her mother, as if Kayley had just arrived and missed this important piece of information. When Terra was done, a light went on for her and she gave Kayley a befuddled look, which Kayley interpreted as either *Why didn't you tell me?* or *Shouldn't you already know this stuff by now?* A laugh bounced from Kayley as she nodded at her daughter. Although triggered by her daughter's behaviour, her joy in the moment lay not only in the humour she had found in the childlike easiness of Adam's solution, but also in the release of a long-standing concern.

"Adam is right," Kayley said.

He was right, Kayley thought when she looked at him. Fog was just a grownup way of saying that the clouds have landed. It was that simple. He seemed a little older to her than her initial mid-twenties guess. Kayley caught herself in content admiration, then soberly wondered how long she'd been smiling.

"Sorry to have to ask this," she managed, "but do you mind if we just finish off with breakfast? We're running a little behind."

"Sure. No rush."

Adam enjoyed the idea of extending their time together. After removing his boots, he followed Kayley's waved invitation to join them. Within the small confines of the available floor space, he could have almost reached out from the foyer and grabbed the chair at the head of the table without ever moving.

"Coffee?" Kayley asked, while assisting Terra into her chair.

"Sure," Adam replied as he sat down.

"I'll just get Terra settled."

The glass table and four chairs were all that could fit between the window wall at the front of the townhouse and the short jut of lower cabinets that denoted the threshold of the kitchen. Although Adam sensed a definite vibe of spent anarchy, he felt a personal serenity as he observed the interaction between mother and daughter.

He watched Kayley while she went to the kitchen and rinsed her hands before mixing water from the kettle into a bowl of dry oatmeal. After adding a touch of milk, she poured a glass of juice and returned to the table with her daughter's breakfast. A faint aroma of cinnamon trailed behind her, settling around the bowl when it was placed on the table. Extrapolating, Adam wondered about the kind of person she was. It was a question that caused a rewind to his initial surprise when he had opened the high wooden gate leading into her front yard.

Cement patio stones leading up to the entry were grey-black with age and speckled by mould. With the passage of time they had shifted slightly out of level alignment. Midway up the path was a concrete bench, which had settled into a fixture. The fog added a weight of antiquity, an illusion of ruins. In that setting, the sorry condition of the stunted vines and drooping stocks had created a vision of a bygone glory, a secret garden left unattended due to a change in fortune.

"If you don't mind me asking? What happened to your garden?"

"I am what happened to my garden," Kayley replied, with a tone of defeated acceptance. She spoke to Adam from the opposite end of the kitchen, with her back to him, as she poured his coffee.

"Cream and sugar?" she asked.

"Black is good."

Adam stood up and remained by the short run of cabinets beside the table, waiting for the hand-off from Kayley. During the exchange, they both became very conscious of their close proximity. A moment made awkward because Adam had assumed that Kayley would be returning to the kitchen, but in fact she was on her way to join them. She peered up to him, relaying her intent immediately.

"Sorry. Yes. Of course," he said, feeling like a hapless barricade.

Adam went back to his chair and Kayley sat across from her daughter, happy to see her settled down.

"You're what happened to your garden?" he asked.

"Take a look around," she replied. "Not a houseplant in sight. I gave up a long time ago. Yet every year, Helen goads me into trying my hand at growing vegetables, and every year, I wipe out a wheelbarrow load of plantings. The tomatoes never had a chance."

"She can be very convincing," Adam said.

"Hence the career in pharmaceutical sales."

"You're going to grow lots and lots of tomatoes," Terra said between spoonfuls of oatmeal.

"Thank you for your encouragement, Mouse," Kayley replied.

Helen had provided Adam with mere snippets of Kayley's story but they had been enough for him to agree to her request to donate his labour, to do the work at cost, and to never let Kayley know. What Helen had not prepared him for was Kayley's attractiveness. Blue-grey eyes, wavy blond hair currently in the cutest case of bed-head he had ever seen, and evidently, even through her bathrobe, she was pleasantly zaftig.

Adam assumed Kayley to be a contemporary of Helen's, given that they knew each other from university, and therefore would place her in her mid-thirties, but to him she appeared younger. However, he had long ago given up on guessing the age of a woman based her appearance, preferring to reserve judgement until he heard the woman talk, listening for what she had to say and how she said it.

"Thanks for your patience," Kayley noted, appreciatively.

"Actually, this is nice," he replied. "A slow ease into the day."

Kayley reached to her daughter and softly stroked her cheek. "Yes," she agreed, "it is nice to ease into the day slowly."

"How do you know Helen?" she asked.

"Three degrees of separation, sort of. Well, two degrees anyway. Helen is the stepsister of my cousin Henry. Her mother married his father. They were both in their early twenties when it happened, so they're not really that close. No animosity or anything, they're just not tight. Anyway, he was a math major and during his studies he met a woman named Daleesha who was doubling in physics and biochemistry. Uber-brain."

"I know," Kayley said. "I've met her."

"Really?"

"Kind of a three amigas thing with Helen, Daleesha, and myself."

"No shit," Adam said, then glanced at Terra and winced in apology. "Sorry."

"That's a bad word," Terra noted.

"Terra, he apologized," Kayley pointed out, and she smiled at Adam. "So, you were saying."

"Henry and Daleesha lost touch after graduation," he continued. "Totally unrelated, Helen got to know Daleesha later on through her job in the pharmaceutical industry. At one point Helen was a kind of liaison with the universities."

"I know," Kayley reminded him, through a subtle grin.

"Right. Three amigas."

"Sorry," she said buoyantly, then briefly glanced at her daughter. "We won't interrupt anymore."

"In a nutshell," Adam summarized, "when Daleesha decided to give it all up to open a daycare, she was in the market for a contractor to do some renovation work. In passing, Helen mentioned it to Henry who immediately thought of me. I told my boss and, well, you know the rest."

"You do big jobs like that and you took on my basement?"

"That wasn't a big job. And that was my boss. I'm kind of her site-manager slash foreman. This is a little side-project for me. I take them on if things are slow."

Adam never liked to lie, even halfway. He tended to blush. Yet this time was different. Although he had told a bit of a fib, he didn't feel the least bit dishonest.

Chapter 3

Henry opened his eyes to find Michael sitting on the edge of the bed with his back to him and stretching silently. He lay watching the movement of muscles in Michael's shoulder blades and down his arms, trying to convince himself that he felt something more than admiration.

"Good morning," Henry said.

"Sorry. I didn't mean to wake you," Michael replied, peering back over his shoulder. "I should be going. I'm opening the store."

Michael leaned in, bracing himself on his arm toward the centre of the bed, and lightly kissed Henry on the lips.

"Mind if I shower?" he asked as he pulled away.

"And then put on your *morning after the night before* duds?" Henry teased. "It makes perfect sense."

They traded smiles before Michael stood up and went out to the hall. Henry remained in bed, pondering etiquette. He concluded that offering breakfast, while perhaps a demonstration of his nouvel arrivée status and maybe showing him to be too eager, would be a nice gesture. But then he heard it. At first he doubted his senses and sat up to gain a clearer earshot. His fears confirmed, he slumped despondently back into the mattress. His body had suddenly become a dead weight. Breakfast plans were abandoned in favour of sharing a quick coffee.

Henry stared up at his bedroom ceiling, his mood deflated. To bide his time, he visually connected the petrified drips of the popcorn stucco overhead into caricature images. His apartment was in a turn-of-the-century building that, except for the misguided addition of the cottage cheese ceilings throughout, had managed to keep most of its original charm. Henry would often gaze at the ceilings and wonder about the course of reasoning which led to the conclusion that defacing them would be a good thing. However, he was currently too depressed to speculate, so he just let his mind doodle amongst the dots.

For him, the cheerful humming emanating from his bathroom was nothing short of belligerent. He had held such great hopes. But they were gone, scrubbed away with the vigorous dental scouring noise that seemed to saturate his apartment like a dripping faucet on an otherwise peaceful morning, a veritable mosquito in the tent.

He was numb with disappointment. For the first time, dating hadn't felt so emotionally one-sided. The flattery, the small gifts, and the subtle, yet important, thoughtful gestures had made his decision feel right. And to further reinforce his certainty, and much to his surprise, Henry had discovered an additional benefit that he had not foreseen: the absence of any guilty-by-gender undercurrent, the background drone of male stereotypes through which he had always found himself filtered. It had been so pervasive and constant that he had forgotten its existence until it was no longer present. Like the blackout's cessation of the eternal electric murmur, the silence was startling. Magically, he had been freed from his socialized reflex of apologizing for being a man, and the harsh scrutiny of his masculinity.

From the beginning, everything had been wonderful. Relaxed, because the precarious walking-on-glass feeling he experienced with women wasn't there. He was free to fully enjoy all the nuances of those first dates, a smooth progression that had led naturally to the sexual encounter of the prior night. Henry's first such experience. And even though the sex, while not unpleasant, was definitely going to take some getting used to, he had been prepared to endure because everything else had held such promise.

Michael returned to the bedroom wearing only a white bath towel around his waist. His swimmer's build and full head of jet-black hair, still damp, didn't quite affect the eye-candy impact with Henry that it might otherwise have had on someone more allured by the male physique. Yet Henry did experience the pleasure of being in the company of someone attractive. Michael dropped his towel to the floor, where he left it as he gathered his clothes. Henry glanced down at the damp clump of terrycloth sloughed onto the hardwood and felt a further sense of insult. The coffee was downgraded to an expedited farewell.

"I'm sorry to rush you along," he said, "but I'm meeting a friend shortly."

"At this hour of the morning?" Michael asked. He had taken a seat at the corner of the bed, his attention divided between Henry and the task of putting on his socks.

"To go shopping. For a new tie, before the stores get crowded."

"Out and about this early on a Saturday? Don't let any *sisters* catch wind of it or you'll have your gay card revoked."

Henry smiled. A self-described parvenu to the subculture, he still found humour in the pat responses. The idea of a gay card also held an air of exclusivity, which he wasn't opposed to.

"You'll be *out and about* on your way home," Henry replied, coyly.

"True. But I will be doing the walk of shame to get to work. A permissible exception, commendable really." Michael smiled a mischievous grin—humourous, contented, and propositioning.

The moment rekindled in Henry the attraction he had felt at their initial meeting. The lure of Michael's charisma and confidence when he had caught Henry's eye and playfully redirected his attention to the young man behind the bar who had been so suggestively polishing the ceramic handles of the draft tower. Until Michael's smile, *suggestively* had merely registered with Henry as *conscientiously*.

However Henry's sentimentality was brief. Self-preserving alarms came alive in a rush of memories, a highlight reel of all the relationships where he had ignored the early warning signs. The playback was not in chronological order, nor was it ranked by severity. Rather, it was Henry's personal level of astonishment that dictated the sequence. Moments that shared an emotionally debilitating chill. Each was a tiny vignette, as small and piercing as a bullet.

The Christmas morning when he opened a sample pack of miniature bottles of cologne, none of which he had ever heard of. Six nondescript testers the size of his thumb, cradled in a flimsy plastic display that had been coated with gritty faux velvet. What Henry had come to refer to as the ultimate last-minute *I don't know you* drugstore purchase was given to him by his first live-in girlfriend. Henry knew that her choice was not the outcome of some type of forgivable shopping phobia. He had witnessed her agonize for two months and make several trips to the mall in her search for the perfect present for her friend. By comparison, he felt slighted. And in retrospect, he also felt foolish. Henry saw it as an indicator that spoke volumes about their future together, an indicator that he had chosen not to heed.

"I'm off then," Michael said. He was confused by Henry's disposition. The wonderment, the après glow, was gone. Calcified and deadpan.

"I'll walk you to the door."

Michael's attraction to Henry had been immediate. Henry wasn't model material, a little too short and his sandy-brown hair a little too thin, but still handsome. He had a wonderful smile and beautiful, expressive green eyes that gave his face fascinating character. There had been something puppy-dog about the way Henry had been sitting at the bar. Michael had believed that everything had been going well, but somehow things seemed to have changed since his stint in the bathroom. Henry was unusually distant. Michael, while baffled as to the reason, had a gut feeling that he was being dumped. He wasn't upset—for him it was really a game of numbers—he was just very confused. Michael felt better off for the experience of meeting this curious man, if only because of getting a really great blowjob out of the deal. It was all in the meticulous attention to detail that only someone with a Type A personality could achieve.

Henry stepped out of bed, grabbed his robe from the back of the door, and followed Michael into the entry hall. Henry was determined to be strong. It was farewell. There was an exchange of glances that Michael couldn't decipher, a peck on the cheek, and then Henry was alone. Down but not out, he was determined not to surrender to the obvious. Henry retrieved a pad of lined paper and a pen from his beloved William IV writing desk of flamed mahogany that he displayed in the foyer. He had many cherished things throughout his apartment, all positioned to create the greatest impact.

After placing the pen and paper onto the coffee table, Henry made himself a small pot of tea, opened the living room drapes, and sat against the arm of the couch. The couch was on the long wall across from the elegant electric fireplace and oriented lengthwise to the pair of large double-hung windows through which he was gazing during his morning contemplation. In the summer they would be left open, along with the transom on the back wall of the dining room, allowing the heat to be carried out on the cross-breeze.

The city beyond his apartment was still asleep, curled up in a thin blanket of early morning fog that the sun was already showing signs of burning off. A wistful reflection, foreign but comforting, brushed through Henry's thoughts and was released in his quiet, meditative whisper.

"Clouds have landed while I slept."

How in his wildest imagination could he have foreseen such a thing? If there had been any warning, there would have been an intervention. Henry reviewed his trail of logic over and over again, but always returned to the same indisputable fact. There are some standards of social decorum that are so widely accepted as to border on being universal.

Just because his mouth was all over Michael's genitals the night before, did not in any way extend an invitation for the man to borrow his toothbrush the morning after—because *that* is gross.

Defiantly, Henry took up the pen and paper and set out to make a list of the pros and cons of homosexual dating. In his effort to argue the strongest case possible, he pulled not only from his own limited experiences, but also from the lessons he had gleaned while listening to the anecdotes, gay and straight, of those who had confided in him.

Pro

more approachable / friendlier

more affectionate / romantic

reciprocal spoiling / greater participation

more generous

more attentive / aware?

more courteous

more gracious / appreciative / realistic?

no simplistic (narrow?) definition of masculinity / stereotyping

no sexist remarks

no double standards

no badgering with unsolicited advice

fewer dating and relationship rules

less argumentative / less confrontational / calmer?

Con

gay men have a male body

And there it was, clear as day and in his own handwriting. The nays had it by a landslide. He felt absolutely deflated and wondered how many entries into the priesthood had come as a result of similar lists. Even worse, Henry reluctantly conceded that the exercise had not been required. The realization was emotional. He was not gay. In a wallow of self-pity, Henry pondered his life's fortune and arrived at the cynical assessment that the universe had it out for him and therefore he, of course, would not be lucky enough to be a homosexual. Not even the slightest morsel of bisexuality resided within him. That loophole did not apply.

Chapter 4

Kayley was in the habit of cleaning the breakfast dishes immediately after she and Terra were done. It was a routine that clicked on without her realization, leaving Adam to observe the ritual in silence. Helen had forewarned him about her friend's obsessive-compulsive tendencies. Framed within that caution, he took pleasure in Kayley's almost mechanistic approach, one that emphasised a refined efficiency of motion. For Adam, the sheer fluid orchestration made every minute of the additional postponement worth it. He smiled visibly when the nickname Helen had for Kayley popped into his mind, for at that moment he fully understood: *Mom-bot-o*.

Terra patiently remained in her chair the entire time, knowing the high price for gumming up the gears. However, she didn't have long to wait. It was an expeditious process, honed to fall well within the patience tolerance of a four-year-old.

It was only when Kayley was retrieving Terra that she knew she had delayed Adam even further. Her apologetic countenance was met by Adam's pardoning smile.

"Sorry," she said. "I just like to get things away. A *do it now or it may not get done* approach."

"Gave me time to finish my coffee," he replied, as he stood up beside her. After his final sip, he placed the mug onto the table. It took everything Kayley could muster not to rinse it out.

"I don't know how much Helen has told you," Kayley said, walking hand-in-hand with Terra as she led Adam from the table into the kitchen. "I'd like to renovate my basement. Nothing fancy. But nice."

The eternally closed entrance to the basement of Kayley's townhouse was located near the back of the kitchen, situated across from the fridge. While waiting on Kayley to open the door, Adam took note of the fridge and found the bareness peculiar. In his line of work he had been in the homes of many young families. He had found that the fridge was generally the display area of their child's artistic achievements. However, nothing about Kayley impressed him as being pell-mell, so he didn't count her out as a proud parent. He simply assumed that Terra's accomplishments were elsewhere, neatly presented and likely catalogued.

"Nothing has been done down there," Kayley said, as she opened the door to the basement. "Construction-wise I mean. My studio is down here and so is the laundry and Terra's play area."

Kayley reached through the doorway and flicked the light switch. It was as dim as a mine. There was no direct illumination within the stairwell itself. Ambient light came up from below. Its source was primarily from the two small casement windows on the front wall of the basement.

The stairs had been painted with the same glossy wet-clay colour as the cement floor. The air was redolent with the old tinder fragrance of dry wood. To Adam's relief, he didn't feel any noteworthy amount of dampness.

When they were below the support beams, he could see, through the bars of two-by-fours that flanked them, a single glowing light bulb on each side of the staircase. He was overcome with a need to help Kayley. To transform the cell into a comfortable, welcoming space.

"A blank canvas," Kayley said when she had reached the floor. She felt a childlike excitement about the impending renovation, of having a small dream coming to fruition.

Kayley looked down to her daughter to explain why Adam had come to visit. It was then that Terra's patience registered with Kayley. Terra was standing quietly and holding onto her mother's hand while they waited for Adam. Kayley speculated that her daughter might also be a little enamoured by their guest.

Upon joining them, Adam took a quick overview of his surroundings. In one dark corner at the rear of the basement was the laundry area. Huddled against the opposite corner of the back wall was Kayley's studio. It overlooked Terra's play area and a low shelving unit lined with bins, each faced with a cartoon pictogram of its contents. The final corner, Adam surmised from the *best efforts* stacking, was for general storage. Spurred on by Adam's unspoken but obvious assessment, Kayley apologetically acknowledged her over-simplified appraisal.

"Okay. Not exactly *blank*."

"Where are you going to store your stuff while I'm working?"

"I was kind of hoping to shell-game it. Move it wherever you weren't."

"Ah."

Adam wandered the basement, checking the foundation and giving a quick inspection for signs of water damage and mould. "*Before I built a wall I'd ask to know what I was walling in or walling out*," Adam said to himself in a quiet voice.

"*And to whom I was like to give offence*," Kayley added. "'Mending Wall,' by Robert Frost."

"My father always says that before he starts on a project," Adam explained. "Helen said that you write greeting cards."

"I draw them, too."

"Mommy draws pictures of me," Terra said.

"Really? Neat," Adam said in a child-friendly tone as he glanced in their direction.

"I'm on a bird, and a cloud, and a oo-no-corn, and an island with a friend," Terra said. Driven by the excitement to share, she slipped her hand free from her mother's and walked quickly to her play area. For Adam's benefit, Kayley mouthed the word unicorn. He smiled and nodded.

"And you can just make stuff up to say on these cards?" Adam asked Kayley.

"It's my calling."

"Just like that?"

A verse jumped fully formed into her head as she watched Adam move about the basement, tracing his hand along sections of the wall and tapping spots along the joists.

Roses are red

Violets are blue

You are a hottie

And I look like poo

"Sometimes just like that," she said. "Sometimes a lot longer."

After retrieving a few of her mother's drawings, Terra brought them to Adam. Regardless of their merit, he was prepared to give a show of awe. He had not been expecting their quality. Each was a piece of fantasy art worthy of framing. His favourite was of beautiful, red-headed Princess Terra and the oo-no-corn.

"Ever think of writing comics or graphic novels?" he asked, without raising his eyes. "These are incredible."

"See," Terra said, "I'm on a cloud."

"Yes, I see."

"Comics? No. Never even crossed my mind."

PAIRS

Gavin had frequently commented on the rarity of her talents. Not merely each taken separately but the bundling together in one person. She had always dismissed his praise as exaggerated sentiment intended to instill the confidence he felt she lacked. However, from Adam and in the wake of Gavin's passing, it seemed genuine and believable. She was flattered.

"You should," he replied. "They're not just about superheroes, you know. And they're not just for kids. There are adult comics, too."

"Adult?"

"Not like that. Real stories. I read them all the time."

"You do?"

"I'm dyslexic. They are a little easier on me."

He looked up from the sketches to find Kayley staring at him blankly. Her enigmatic silence left him feeling a little exposed and defensive.

"They're not just for dyslexics. Fully functional adults read them, too."

"Oh no. Sorry," she said, appreciating how her lack of response could have been interpreted as snobbish and dismissive. Perhaps, she admitted to herself, because there may have been some pretentiousness in the mix of her thoughts. "I was just wondering if I had it in me to do it."

Adam blushed, smiled self-consciously, and handed the drawings back to Terra, who returned them to the bin with the pencil on the front. He recognized that he had no reason to have jumped to his conclusion. She had been nothing but decent since his arrival. Kayley watched the flow and ebb of his blush with tender amusement. The moment left her in a diatribe with herself over her foolishly escalating crush. *He would never*, *he is too young*, and just plain *wow* were tussling.

"Or a picture book," Adam said. "You've probably already read a ton of those."

"It never occurred to me," Kayley confessed.

She wondered about the coincidence of Adam's suggestions in light of her grandmother's call, a reminder from beyond the grave advising her to listen.

"It will be about me," Terra said.

"What will?" Kayley asked.

"Your book."

"You think so, do you?"

Terra nodded and then looked to Adam as if she were requesting some grownup corroboration to this obvious fact that Mommy was, for some reason, questioning. The silent request caused Adam to laugh.

"You've already got some of the artwork done," he said to Kayley.

"In sports, don't they call this being double-teamed?" she asked.

"I don't know," he replied. "I'm not really into watching sports. Women, cars, gadgets, action movies, and beer, yes. Armchair warrior? No."

Kayley could only conclude that she was very obviously still in bed, peacefully asleep and happily dreaming. Her day had yet to start. Her carpenter had still to arrive. He would be a grubby, sexist ogre of a man. The mere sight of him would send her daughter from the room screaming in terror.

"Really?" she asked, trying to ensure that all the cooing syrup was strained from her tone before speaking. Hearing herself, Kayley judged that she had managed to sound innocently curious.

"I'm a member of a secret society of guys that don't follow sports."

"Are you, now?"

"I'm strictly Orthodox. Not even the playoffs."

An unchecked giggle percolated aloud from Kayley. There was a pleasant sound in the laughter that made Adam want to hear it again, but he couldn't think of anything humourous to say. Kayley didn't know how to interpret Adam's grin. She was a little worried that she could be coming across like a schoolgirl, or worse, like the woman going squirrelly for companionship that she actually was. She quickly sobered the course of their conversation.

"I was thinking," she said, "that I'd like to make the laundry area its own separate room and just leave everything else open."

Adam glanced down and panned across the floor in the direction of the catch-as-catch-can storage piled in the corner in front of the laundry area. His eyes then moved slowly up to the ceiling and travelled a sight line from one bulb to the next before returning to Kayley.

"Flooring of some sort would probably be a good idea," she said, appreciating the hints. "And I was also thinking about a deep storage closet. And quite a bit more lighting."

"Seems like you've got everything covered," he replied. "I'll put some options together."

Kayley crouched down in front of Terra and made a broad sweeping gesture, directing attention to the entirety of the basement.

"Adam is going to make this like the rest of house," Kayley said. "Nice painted walls, a nice floor, and lots of lights so it won't be so dark."

Terra's flat response of indiscernible emotion or thought confused Kayley. If it had to be labelled, Kayley could only read *perplexed*.

"And big windows," Terra eventually said.

"Sorry, Mouse, we can't change the windows," Kayley said.

"Big windows for drawing."

Kayley was lost for a response. She stood up and looked at Adam. He sensed her concern. It seemed that in Terra's mind the windows were an absolute fact. More set than the mere wall of concrete and pile of earth that were the real obstacles. Adam stepped closer to Kayley.

"Maybe you could paint some big windows," he whispered. "You'd never have bad weather."

"Maybe," Kayley said, studying her daughter.

Chapter 5

Henry was not generally in the habit of doing his laundry on Saturday mornings. Truth be told, he was not generally in the habit of doing anything before noon on the weekend. Yet he needed to do something to occupy himself and, to his chagrin, going to the laundromat was the best he could come up with. It didn't require any significant depth of mental commitment, yet was more stimulating than the test pattern on the television or the infomercials of equivalent thought-provoking merit. A desire to be around people that he didn't have to engage with socially helped to nudge him along. He got dressed, gathered up his half-empty duffle bag of dirty clothes, and left.

The hall outside his apartment, as with each floor, was actually a continuous terrace that threaded past all the doors and looked out upon the open expanse, of aviary proportions, around which the building had been constructed—architecture from a time when HVAC concerns didn't weigh in on the design. In the summer, residents would open their apartments' transoms, the narrow windows of leaded glass that overlooked the building's interior. This allowed for the cross-breezes upon which cooking odours would occasionally swirl gently into the great piazza.

A central chandelier hung, like a massive pendulum, from a single chain that ran down from the ceiling for nearly five stories, ending above the lobby's fountain, which had long since been converted to a tiered planter. The prosperous village aesthetic was of a different age—romantic, innocent, safe, and neighbourly. It was Henry's wonderful bubble in time. He loved his apartment.

At the back of the building, the stairwell corkscrewed around the elevator shaft. The elevator itself was small and old and Henry found it to be far too reminiscent of a dumb waiter to ever seriously consider using it. He took the stairs down to the polished terrazzo of the ground floor and strolled past the fountain to the vestibule of the main door. There was resonance in his solitary steps, soft echoes that the acoustics of the lobby made homey.

The entrance to Henry's apartment building opened out into a lush courtyard. A pathway of stone led through the foliage, under a cluster of overhanging branches, toward a tall, wrought iron gate. It was an inner-city ravine that the morning mist had given a romantic mystery. At the gate he toyed with the idea of driving, but decided that the stroll would probably do him some good.

PAIRS

After a contemplative journey peppered by bouts of self-pity, Henry arrived at the cracked slab of grey asphalt that was sandwiched between the side of Unicorn Books and the back of Ultra Comics and served as the laundromat's parking lot. If there had ever been distinct spaces, all evidence of it was gone. Henry was at once happy and sad to see it empty. He wanted company, but didn't want to fully surrender his solitude.

The entry into the laundromat was a glass door that was set within a long wall of floor-to-ceiling windows. As he got closer, he could see through the mist that he was not going to be entirely alone. A solitary figure, which looked to be a woman, was sitting on top of the counter. When he opened the door he recognized her immediately. Lindsay. She was sitting cross-legged in a white T-shirt and faded jeans.

The smells within were familiar to Henry and did not quite instill in him the sense of cleanliness alluded to by the building's purpose. Detergent and bleach were unable to fully mask the odours Henry was certain he could detect: the dirty mop, the residual trace of stale hampers, and the washed-out crotch pong from the pubic hair that had become affixed to the numerous lint traps. Henry disliked laundromats.

Lindsay worked as a waitress at an all-night diner that he frequented after his periodic nights of restrained debauchery. During the past few months of his cautious foray into what he had initially perceived as the gay underground, the diner and Lindsay had become somewhat of a mainstay. A group of regulars at the bar Henry tended to favour had introduced him to their ritual of a final pit stop before heading home.

Gay life had proven to be a lot less surreptitious then he had originally imagined, and a lot more fun. Evenings of interesting conversations, karaoke, dancing, and singing around a piano were made all the more enjoyable by the complete absence of fun-stifling macho crap. Sometimes there was pretentious crap, but it never amounted to more than a few quips. If he were asked to choose, Henry would say that the shallow, skulking sexuality he had thought he would encounter was actually what he had left behind in the singles bars of the straight world. He didn't know if he could ever go back.

Lindsay was a reminder of the good times and, conversely, a symbol of the decision he faced about his future. She had served Henry and Michael earlier that very morning.

To those who met her, including Henry, Lindsay was a beautiful woman of an ambiguous age that fell somewhere between fifteen and thirty. She kept her dark hair short and often had it spiked. Her face, while having soft contours, had a boyish quality of gorgeous androgyny, and her body, almost in spite of its generous feminine curves, was clearly solid and youthfully athletic. She exuded an undeniable sexual charge that had once resulted in a member of Henry's group joking about a fantasy he had of Lindsay ravishing him with a strap-on. The plausibility of the scenario had left everyone at the table, including Henry, in hysterics.

Circumstances reflected in her. A change in the mood of her surroundings would result in this tempered veteran warrior of the night shift suddenly sparkling with childlike appreciation.

When Henry had arrived at the laundromat, she had been too engrossed in her schoolwork to notice him. Her book rested in her lap and a three-ring binder lay open beside her. Normally very attentive, she was lost in the mysterious hieroglyphs that were algebra. She was frustrated and despondent. Although not quite at her usual pre-test *really what does it matter in the grand scheme of the universe* fallback position, Lindsay was questioning her decision to be in school.

Sensing her preoccupation, Henry worked without interrupting as he separated his laundry and then loaded machines with the sorted piles. Periodically he would glance in her direction. He always found attractive people, particularly women, pleasing to watch. Oddly, if he became consciously aware of his enjoyment of a woman's beauty, he would berate himself and the doom of cruel fate.

It was finally his unintentional sigh that caught Lindsay's attention. There was a familiarity to it. Her head pivoted in his direction. His presence lightened her mood. Henry's dry and subtle humour, sometimes unintended, had endeared him to Lindsay.

"Hey Henry. When did you get here?"

The sincere warmth of her welcome had pushed aside his bitterness at a universe that had given him every reason to be homosexual, only to torment him with his own orientation. But the reprieve was short-lived.

"I take it the date didn't go too well," she said.

"It went fine," he replied, in a tone of voice that entirely betrayed the lie.

"Well, unless you're cleaning your only set of sheets for another round, I'm sticking with it didn't go well."

It was odd yet comfortable for both of them to be talking outside the setting of the diner. The artificial facade of employee and client was absent. He was Henry and she was Lindsay and nothing in their acquaintance was lost in translation with the change in setting.

"Sorry," Henry said, pointing toward the algebra textbook in evasive redirection. "Don't let me interrupt."

"I need a break anyway."

"A break?"

"I need whatever it is you need when something is beating the hell out of you and you don't want to deal with it anymore."

"A break," Henry agreed as he strolled toward her. "From what?"

"Overall? School. This morning? Algebra."

The idea of Lindsay in school surprised Henry, and he wondered, as he had done from time to time, about her age.

"What's giving you grief?" he asked.

"Overall? School. This morning? Algebra," she replied. "Keep up, would ya?"

She smiled at him to emphasize the lighthearted intention of her teasing, and revealed the slightly out-of-line upper incisor that she was self-conscious about but which Henry had always found charming. Unconsciously, he grinned in response.

"I mean in particular," Henry said. "Maybe I can help."

"Are you kidding me? You get this stuff?"

"I teach that stuff, and other stuff like it."

"Sweet!"

In her excitement, the childlike facet of Lindsay was captured in her beaming smile. She uncrossed her legs and with a push, vaulted herself off the counter in Henry's direction. When her feet hit the floor, Henry's attention was immediately drawn to the taunt bounce under her thin cotton T-shirt. During his briefly refocused interest, Henry was certain that he could pinpoint the exact location of both nipples, a detail that reinforced his conclusion that she was not wearing a bra.

To stop Lindsay's enthusiastic charge, Henry directed her to stay put with his upturned palm. When he was beside her, Lindsay placed the textbook on the counter. She stood close to him, eager for any type of knowledge osmosis. Henry had a brief struggle with the distraction caused by the close proximity of her *unfettered* breasts, but after stepping away to allow for more personal space, managed to focus on the text. In doing so, Henry cringed at the self-indulgent bounce admiration he had just allowed himself.

"Grade eleven?" he asked.

"Yep."

"And you work night-shift at the diner?"

"Well, all the university professors were busy, so I got the job."

It took a second or two for Henry to catch on to Lindsay's tangent thought. He looked at her and chuckled before correcting her.

"Sorry. I meant aren't you a little young?"

"Nope."

In response to a nearby buzzer, Lindsay excused herself. She retrieved her laundry basket from under the counter and filled it with warm clothes from the dryer. Lindsay dumped the contents beside the textbook and folded as Henry scanned through the first of her assigned problems.

It took him a few passes before he formulated the approach to the solution, as his eyes would move off the page, in a self-chastising slide, toward Lindsay's stacked undergarments. Thongs and panties, some with phrases like *You know you want it* written across the back or *While you're down here* scrolled along the front, stylized in rather handsome embroidery that Henry had also managed to make note of. Quality never escaped him.

Lindsay caught Henry reading her underwear and felt a little embarrassed by the implication she thought it made. She didn't want Henry getting the wrong impression. Her experience with gays at the diner was threefold. They were good tippers. They were great fun. They could level razor critiques. She was concerned that her underwear might trigger the last.

"A friend of mine bought them for me," Lindsay explained with an attempt to seem nonchalant. "She thought they were funny. When I get down to the funnies, it is time to do laundry."

"Oh," Henry replied. His quick glance below Lindsay's waist telegraphed his curiosity.

"*A hard man is good to find*," she said, pointing to her hip. Henry thought her tone to be almost apologetic.

"Funny," he said, without appearing to see the humour.

Lindsay misunderstood the reason behind his lacklustre response. She thought he had found her kitschy panties immature. However, he wasn't focused on the wordplay at all. Rather, Henry was very busy berating himself over mental images of her body.

Chapter 6

Henry seemed to have a way of imparting the mysteries behind algebra that left Lindsay feeling a glimmer of hope. It was as if he could sense when she was having difficulty and would then provide seamlessly corrective guidance. While not exactly clear, things were definitely clearer.

"You know," Lindsay said, glancing up from the problem she was working on. "If you ever want to give up your career as a man-hunting barfly, I think you'd have a great future as a teacher."

"Being a barfly is more rewarding. Stay focused."

"Algebra is all left-brain. I have a whole other lonely hemisphere that's spent the morning with its thumb up its ass."

"So it should be accustomed to that by now."

"You're quick," Lindsay replied, without looking up. She smiled and shook her head at the ease of her own defeat. And as always, was in awe of the speed of Henry's wit and his wonderfully unaffected and even delivery.

"All the slow teachers get eaten alive," he said.

Lindsay's calm but relentless drive to understand was inspiring to Henry. He wasn't sure if he would have it in himself to deal with the same level of frustration for such an extended period. Henry saw in her an unshakable, single-minded tenacity that could not have been taught. He reasoned, once again, that it had to have been forged.

In spite of her frequently childlike zest, he suspected that her life had not been an easy one. Occasionally, at the diner, when she was tired or a customer was out of line, Henry had gotten the tiniest glimpse down to her foundation, and placed her soul's age somewhere between a tireless five and a very sober one thousand.

When Lindsay finally took a break, she noticed that they were no longer alone. She blinked to regain her distance vision. Interspersed amongst the dryers that lined the walls like oversized portholes and the narrow islands of back-to-back washing machines, she noted familiar faces. A disparate group gathered from both sides of sunrise. Other creatures of the night like her, and a small collection of industrious, foreign student day-walkers. Outside, the fog had dissipated, the discarded wrapping of a beautiful summer's day. The sun was flooding in through the large panes of glass. She stared through the windows to the awakening city, unhurried. Lindsay glanced at her watch, a metallic and chunky timepiece suited for a man but sized to fit her wrist.

"Break," Lindsay said, sliding her answer in front of Henry. "My brain is full. Both sides."

"Okay," Henry said, before giving her a sympathetic smile of encouragement. "I have to throw some stuff in the dryer anyway."

Borrowing Lindsay's pencil, he glanced over her solution, placing check marks where applicable and circling errors. He smiled and handed back the pencil before heading off to retrieve his wet clothes.

"Well done," he said.

"Well done? But I got it wrong."

"Yes, but you did so in a very logical and systematic way," Henry noted, while peering into the washing machine. "And besides, it was only partially wrong."

"Is that like being kind of pregnant?" she asked, sarcastically.

The disappointment was evident in her tone. With his wet clothes held out at arm's length, Henry walked to the dryer and wondered about Lindsay's choice of a comparison. She picked up on his speculation instantly.

"Which I'm not," she said.

"It's not like being kind of pregnant," he reassured, while loading the dryer. "It's like being partially correct, only the opposite."

Lindsay had been far too taxed by problem solving to have given Henry, the man, much thought beyond his tutoring. However, no longer engrossed in algebra, she now had the cognitive resources to process the significance of an observation that she had held on pause. Henry had rolled the pad of his thumb in his nostril while talking to her. Not a full-on pick, but she was confident that she had witnessed definite nasal penetration. It was an unconscious habit that Lindsay associated strictly with men, and more specifically, straight men. Although she was very confident that it was exclusively a male quirk, she was not nearly as certain that it was limited to just the heterosexuals. Yet the incident stood out in her mind as an anomaly.

Lindsay had not been offended. She remembered it as a habit of her father's. A recollection she swiftly followed with an incisive reminder that clarified, if only for her own sake, her *real* father.

"You've been a great help, Henry."

"Thanks," he said as he inserted his coins into the dryer. "It's nice to have someone who actually wants to try and learn."

"So you don't think I'm a lost cause?"

"Far from it, I think your biggest problem is psyching yourself out. You're defeated before you've started."

"Can we do this again?" she asked. Lindsay turned her back to the counter and hopped up into a sitting position.

"Laundry?" He teased.

"No, smartass, tutoring. I can pay."

"Sure," he said, returning to the counter. "But you don't need to pay."

"Well, I have to do something," she said. "It's only fair. I know. I can muck out your place."

"There is nothing to muck," he stated, in a matter-of-fact tone.

"You're muckless?" Lindsay asked. Unsure if it was the muck or the place that was absent.

"Indeed I am."

"No one is muckless."

Henry's confident air had enough indignation sprinkled in to clearly relay a reprisal for suggesting otherwise.

"Okay then. The muck-out is out," she said.

She slid off the counter and stood in front of Henry. In such near proximity she became very cognizant of his gender. He was a head taller and much broader. As she had done in the past, Lindsay made note of his flat stomach and the wisps of chest hair peaking out above the top button of his shirt. She could smell hint of the cologne he had been wearing on his date, Dolce and Gabbana. Although she knew he was gay, Lindsay had to concede he was also definitely male.

"So what actually did happen on your date?" she asked, after she began to pack her books.

Henry's response was not immediate. He considered his answer, crafting the perfect meld of truth and lie. The least amount of *fact* required in selling the *fiction*.

"Role confusion." He attempted to give his tone casual authority in an effort to suggest such occurrences were common and trivial. Unfortunately for Henry, Lindsay tended to ignore subtle nuances of inflection.

"Role confusion? Like top and bottom role confusion?"

"Something along those lines."

"Shouldn't you have that sorted out before knocking boots?"

"It just never came up. And it's not like we planned to knock boots, it just happened."

To Henry, Lindsay seemed rather bemused by the current tack of their conversation. He was not completely confident that she wasn't having fun at his expense. While that did factor into Lindsay's motivation, she was also genuinely very interested.

Wrapped within her street smarts, Lindsay possessed the blunt innocence of a child that, at times, caused her curiosity and concern for others to be viewed as invasive or suspected as denigrating.

"So were you a couple of pitchers or a couple of catchers?" she asked.

Lindsay was bent over her bundle buggy, loading it with her books and laundry. Henry wasn't certain if he was prepared to dignify her question with a response, but was adamant that he wasn't about to speak to her backside. His silence interested Lindsay. Without entirely having completed her packing, she stood and found herself privileged by Henry's *we are not amused* air.

With loose reins on her smirk, she explained, "You know. In case I have a chance to hook you up. I see a lot of cute gay men at the diner."

"Thank you, but no."

The suppressed fluster in his voice was more than Lindsay could take. Unable to restrain herself, she finally smiled and wrapped her arm across the top of his shoulders. She gave an affectionate hug that resulted in her breast pushing up against his arm—a positioning that was not lost on Henry.

"Don't be so serious," she said. "I'm sorry."

"You're right," he confessed, "It didn't go well at all. And I'm a little sensitive about the whole thing right now. Sorry. I overreacted."

"You're a handsome man," she said, as she withdrew her arm. "There are a thousand guys out there just waiting to get to know you."

"Thanks."

Lindsay kissed Henry on the cheek and backed slowly toward the door with the buggy in tow in front of her. Henry watched as shadow slowly erased her features the closer she got to the contrasting daylight. Lindsay stopped when she remembered her need for Henry's help, appearing to him as an hourglass sunspot. Cool and magnetic.

"So can you help me out?" she said, in a voice loud enough to draw the attention of the other patrons.

"Of course."

Lindsay dug out her binder and pencil case and waved Henry over in order to exchange telephone numbers. She tore off a section of lined paper, wrote down her number, gave it to Henry, and scribbled his on her hand as he dictated it.

"I'll call you and we can make arrangements," she said as she tossed everything back into the buggy.

"Sounds good. If I'm not home, just leave a message on my voice mail."

"I really appreciate this, Henry."

"Hey, it's what I do."

"Well, you do it better than anyone I've ever known. You've really found your calling."

Before opening the door, Lindsay smiled at Henry, a gesture he could not quite discern due to the brilliant backlighting. Lindsay interpreted his failure to reciprocate as a testament to how truly awful his date must have gone. She felt a need to shore up his spirits.

"A hard man is good find," she said as she rolled up her hip and pointed to it. "Only a matter of time. And I'll see you soon."

Lindsay continued to tow her buggy in front of her as she pushed back against the entry door before stopping astride the meridian between the laundromat and the asphalt.

"And I will pay you something," she said. "I won't take no for an answer."

She released the door and brought the buggy in front of herself as she crossed the parking lot. Henry watched her as far as the sidewalk before he decided to return to his laundry, an intent that was delayed by a surprising discovery. All eyes were upon him. Some were chastising, many awestruck, and from a shapeless, stringy-haired beldam, there was a look that Henry was loathe to interpret as coquettish.

"Or," he said to the group, confident that he had accurately gauged their consensus, "the services I am providing are as a math tutor."

They remained unconvinced, and waited for Henry to explain away any and all inconsistencies in his story.

"The hard man comment was merely in reference to," he began, but trailed off when he considered the burdensome task of explaining the implausibly interlinked events that had led up to her farewell. "Fine, I'm a gigolo."

He despised laundromats.

Part II

Nothing to purvey,
Or reveal,

Save myself

And the garden path
Down which I walk

Alone

Chapter 7

Hello dear. How is my Kay? And Terra? You always catch me at a good time. Been making strawberry jam all morning, just letting things soak now. I'll be taking a few jars to the Sisters of course. Put a little rum in one for Sister Margaret. Suppose I'll have to make some scones now. I've got them spoiled. Done just in time for raspberry season. Serves me right for putting things off. Strawberries did well in the chest though, not a touch of freezer burn.

Nothing from the Gavin fella's estate eh? Geez Louise, didn't we hear about it at the start of the summer? Must be coming on two months now. Lord almighty, you'd think it was an Irving that had been taken off to the marble orchard. Speaking of crossing over, I think I'm starting to smell old, Kay. I notice it now and then. Always had the nose. Your grandfather said I was part bloodhound. Sure your scent can change with age, everything else does. And I smell old. Reminds me of my own father: sourdough, rawhide, and dust. Put it in an ionizer and sell it as wisdom. He was a good man. Threw out every piece of fabric he had come in contact with. Gave the carpets to the Church.

Dating yet? Don't "Oh, grandma" me. Time to get back at it. I don't want to see you get in the habit of being alone. You're too young. And that little girl of yours is too busy finding the world to make time to fill in, so don't ask it of her. I know you've got friends, Kayley, but that is not what I'm talking about and you know it. Don't let that deadbeat ruin you for life.

Carver's lad, Edison, was asking about you. Not that you should give him the time of day, but just to let you know the boys here remember you. Growing up, that Edison slept more hours than a cat. Probably still does. At the best of times he doesn't do enough to break the Sabbath. Always been an "It's the early worm that gets eaten by the bird" sort, if you get my drift. He's handsome enough, but sweet Mary and Joseph, is he daft.

I'm at Carver's the other day and feel the need. Carver, of course, only letting me know that the power's off 'cause Edison was working on something or other. Well, imagine my surprise when I find Edison on a stepladder he had straddled over the toilet bowl, hands all in the wires of the exhaust fan. Holds out his hand as if he thinks I'd shake it. Another time, I tell him. Daft. He stared at me as blank as a fresh piece of slate. I said, "Edison, you know when you flush the toilet the spray goes ten feet into the air." Still nothing. Daft. "Son," I said, "the ceiling is only eight." Stone stupid. Reminds me of that saying. Every time you think about how dumb the average man is, just remember: by definition, half of them are even dumber than that.

Sorry dear. What did you want to talk about? Really? That's music to my ears. Tell me about him. Adam you say? Oh, don't go hedging your bet now. Everything is maybe until it's happened.

Chapter 8

Daleesha's Georgian-inspired home followed the same central hall layout of Kayley's townhouse, but on a much grander scale. If the townhouse were a seed planted in the ground and tended to for centuries, it would grow into the giant redwood of Daleesha's manor.

A former residence of a dentist, the only competition for stately impression in the neighbourhood was a family-operated funeral home three blocks away. A rival that Daleesha appreciated, for it anchored the wedge in zoning that had allowed her to convert the second and main floors, as well as the entire backyard, into a daycare.

She had left the third floor, where there had been some attempt to hold true to the original architecture, as living quarters. The Historical Society was by no means appeased. Daleesha could not have cared less.

Kayley parked her car on the street to leave the driveway clear for parents and guardians. She walked with Terra into the opened garage and climbed the four steps of the old block of solid concrete to the side door. Without knocking, they stepped into the small landing that served as the intersection of the kitchen entry, basement staircase, and garage.

Helen was in the kitchen pouring a cup of coffee. Alerted to the arrival of Kayley and Terra, she took a second mug down from the cabinet as she greeted them.

PAIRS

"Hello ladies. Daleesha will be back in a minute. She has temporarily taken on the role of scullery maid."

"Hi Helen," Terra said, as she followed her mother's lead and wiped her feet on the bristled mat.

"When did you get here?" Kayley asked.

"Fifteen, maybe twenty minutes ago," Helen replied. "Daleesha and I were just talking about the Lost Boys project she's organizing with Henry when she got called into duty. Funny, Henry and I live in the same city and it is Daleesha that brings me up to speed on his activities.

"Lost Boys project?"

"Well, that's what I call it anyway."

Taking both mugs by the handle, Helen faced the table but stood aside for Terra's charge past her toward the cinema room. She was headed for the door to the backyard and, ultimately, the swing set.

"Think she's glad to be here?" Helen asked as she went to the table.

"You think?"

Helen placed the mugs on either side of the cream and sugar service. "Apparently, boys have been showing a steady academic decline over the last twenty years and the two of them are somehow involved in searching for the fix."

She sat and waited for Kayley to settle into her chair before starting on her friendly cross-examination.

"So?" Helen teased, after sipping her coffee. She was parlaying the certainty she felt into some harmless fun, an intention that she made no attempt to conceal.

Kayley was focusing on the cream and getting her coffee to the perfect colour of caramel, and offered only a brief upward glance of acknowledgement to Helen's inquiry.

As always, their conversation was completely unfazed by the controlled anarchy coming from their surroundings. The kitchen itself was understood to be off limits. Designed to blend industrial prudence with homey nuances, it was a large space that served as both cookhouse and parlour. Everything involved with food preparation had been chosen with factory efficiency in mind. The non-essential furniture and fixtures, such as the table and the chandelier suspended from the ceiling twelve feet overhead, reflected Daleesha's personal taste, which blended Gothic and Baroque filigree and frills. Safe within this main-floor bastion, Daleesha had left the large original window of clear leaded glass above the basin sink. She enjoyed how the bevels refracted the light of the morning sun.

Helen's artificial demureness relayed exactly the message she had intended. Kayley knew instantly what, or rather who, the overtly innocent question was in reference to. She smiled and remained fixed on Helen while framing her answer. In the silence, Kayley contrasted herself with her friend, as she was prone to do. Helen was wearing a tailored business suit. Her hair, soft strands of dark goldenrod, flowed from a central part about her shoulders. She exuded confidence, a person very comfortable in her own skin. Since first meeting her at university, Kayley had felt that there was a constant glimmer of mischief in her hazel eyes. At times it was all the difference between finding humour from Helen's torment and feeling malice. It was her charm that let her get away with behaviour that few others would even dare to attempt.

"You set me up," Kayley replied.

"You're welcome."

Daleesha entered the kitchen from the doorway leading to the front of the house. She was carefully holding a cloth that had become saturated to capacity as a consequence of soaking up a larger-than-expected spill. She was a slender black woman with a statuesque build who dressed practically when in her daycare role of owner, matriarch, warrior, and diplomat. Helen and Kayley had only ever known her with short hair. Both women had reasoned that with a face as beautiful as hers, she would be foolish to add a distraction. Daleesha walked to the sink and stood with her back to them as she rinsed the cloth.

"How old is he?" Kayley asked Helen. "Twelve?"

"How old is who?" Daleesha asked, over her shoulder.

"He's legal, dear," Helen replied. "That is all that matters."

Beyond the kitchen, strands of calm adult voices could be heard weaving clearly into the welter of squeals, laughter, and the small, rounded words of children.

"Do tell," Daleesha said, after dropping the cloth into a bucket labelled *dirty*. She washed and dried her hands before resting back against the counter.

"Helen here is trying to fix me up."

"And?"

"He's very handsome," Kayley admitted reluctantly.

"*Brevior saltare cum deformibus viris est vita*. Life is too short to dance with ugly men," Helen said. She sat back in her chair, perched an arm atop the backrest, crossed her legs, and smirked.

"But?" Daleesha asked, after noting Helen's self-congratulatory posturing.

"But," Kayley said. "He is twelve."

"Twenty-something," Helen corrected.

"*Something*?" Kayley asked.

"Five. I believe."

"Twenty-five?" Kayley asked rhetorically. She repressed her wince at the news. Seven years in the difference. With ridicule as her ink, Kayley penned her personals ad. *Seeking much younger, handsome, ambitious man that wants to be saddled with single mom whose life is stagnating.*

"Think of the sex," Helen said, sounding adrift in possibilities, before springing back to the conversation with conviction. "I'm positive you're his type."

"How do you know his type? Exactly what type is that? And do not say *Rubenesque*."

Helen sipped her coffee at a considered, nearly ritualistic pace in order to buy herself some time. She was aware of Kayley's body image issues. Yet she was not entirely sympathetic. Helen had a small streak of jealousy that she concealed from herself as impatience. She was impatient with Kayley and her inability to see that men were interested her.

"I have my ways," Helen said. "He likes full-figured women."

Kayley wanted it to be true, but was cautious. It felt safer to dismiss Adam as too young rather than risk being hurt. However, she couldn't deny her attraction and thought Helen awful and wonderful for arranging the meeting.

"Your ways? I bet you do. You're shameless," she said.

"Dear, it is way past due to get the plumbing checked. How long has it been?"

Kayley didn't answer. Not as a matter of avoidance, but because, to her mortification, she couldn't honestly recall. She refused to accept the memory lapse and forced herself to roll back the months, and months, in search of the last time she had been with a man. Daleesha, sensing a need to rescue Kayley from her obviously disconcerting immersion, threw out a question.

"Does Mr. Handsome have a name?"

"Adam." Helen and Kayley said in unison.

"Helen recommended him to renovate my basement."

"Adam. Adam?" Daleesha asked Helen, as she made a gesture that indicated her surroundings.

"One and the same."

"Oh 'Leesh," Kayley said, concerned in the wake of her disheartening revelation that she had become a charity case, "don't tell me you were in on it, too?"

"No. But you could do a lot worse. He is a very nice man."

Outside the kitchen a wail of injustice rose noticeably above the joyful din. An affront had been made and retribution was sought, erupting into tiny voices quarrelling for turf and trade, all the while escalating toward an ultrasonic pitch.

"He really is a nice guy," Kayley agreed. "Terra even seems a little smitten with him. Within five minutes after arriving, he had her settled down about the fog. He said that the clouds had come down to play."

"I knew I liked him," Daleesha said.

The stubborn screams gave way to the soothing voice of a woman coaching, guiding, and stating. Soon, the commotion dissipated into the contented simmer from which it had come.

"And he said something else. He suggested that I try my hand at comics or a picture book."

"Comics?" Helen asked.

"You'd be a bit of a trailblazer," Daleesha said. "I think females are few and far between in that industry."

"One step forward for the ladies," Helen said.

"He said that they weren't all about superheroes," Kayley noted. "But still."

"The Kay-a-nator: single mom by day, cougar by night," Helen said. "You could draw yourself with a huge, and impossibly gravity-defying shelf of cleavage."

"Like I'd want supplementing," Kayley said, while she underscored her bosoms with a pass of her hand. "Although, gravity-defying would be a bonus. Oh! And I could have a wasp-like waist."

"Throw in a showgirl's butt and legs and women the world over would despise you," Helen contributed.

"Wouldn't they. What could my crest be?"

"A soother. It's applicable to you *and* to your alter-ego," Helen replied, which resulted in Kayley's feigned gasp of theatrical offence.

"Actually, Kay," Daleesha said, choosing to realign the direction of their conversation. "He might be on to something. It would be nice to see a female heroine that wasn't some hyper-masculine Alpha male stuffed into a hyper-feminine shell."

"Soft on the outside," Helen said. "Crunchy on the in."

The design and creation of greeting cards felt as temporary as a summer job to Kayley, but the idea of writing comics and children's picture books struck her as a career move and that didn't sit well. It would be an admission that she would never be a novelist. Daleesha read her misgivings.

"Kay," she said, "I know greeting cards are what you are doing until you write your first manuscript, but couldn't you be doing comics and picture books just as well?"

Their conversation stopped when the kitchen door opened. A young woman focused on Daleesha and smiled apologetically in a non-verbal request for assistance. Daleesha gave a *duty calls* glance toward the table and followed the woman out of the kitchen. Kayley and Helen watched her leave, remaining in silence after the door shut. It was a departure that triggered a shift in Kayley's thoughts—loss.

"Gavin's passed away," she said.

Helen was unable to tie in how the news related to her and stared impassively. Kayley, although bothered by the response, understood. Her own had been very similar, which she viewed as being the greater shame.

"Spaz."

"Ah," Helen said after making the connection, and then "Oh" when the significance sunk in. "When? How? Who told you?"

"My grandmother phoned me. Gavin had a stroke."

"God, Kay! He's our age."

Helen quickly recognized the depth to which Kayley had been affected and reached out to her across the table. Their hands squeezed together and Kayley forced herself not to cry.

"How are you doing?" Helen asked.

"I think I'm still coming to terms. Am I so cold? Should it take this long?

"There's a lot of history, Kay. A lot to work through."

Chapter 9

"If you're not interested in her, then why do you want me to check her out?" Adam asked.

He was sitting on the couch, gazing out the window of Henry's apartment. It was propped open by a book, Colette's *La Vagabonde*, allowing a summer breeze perfumed by the flowers of the Goldenrain tree in the park across the street to wander in. Disengaged from his own fidgeting, Adam was slowly spinning on the side table a bronze torso of a woman the size of a pop can.

Henry was in the kitchen amused by the smell of eggs Benedict that wafted through the open transom above the kitchen sink. It was a brunch his neighbour reserved for particularly *adept* overnight guests.

The sound coming from the felt pad on the statue's marble base as it buffed the oak tabletop during the legless pirouette was unmistakeable. Henry speculated that, in addition to dyslexia, his cousin also likely had an attention deficit disorder.

"You know my feelings about dating," Henry replied.

Henry's final encounter had been uneventful affair. He had found himself at restaurant table sitting across from an unassuming but pleasant woman. They had been introduced through a mutual friend and co-worker. While watching her work at her slice of Black Forest cake, he stewed on the prospect that she would be expecting him to pay for their meal. In his wandering thoughts he leafed through his experiences, every slight ever done, and arrived at a parallel between dating women and restaurant desserts. Both were tempting on display, but generally overpriced, frequently disappointing, and always rather bad for him. His social life had ground to a halt that night.

If he had been honest with himself, the inevitability of that outcome would have been readily apparent. A man that is put into a slow burn every time he reads articles written by women on the topic of dating will likely experience excessively long stretches of bachelorhood.

"And, to be clear, I don't want you to check her out," he explained to Adam. "I just want you to guess her age. I'm curious more than anything."

Adam remained silent but rolled his eyes. He was not a believer in mere curiosity. There was always a motive. In Henry's case, at least for that morning, Adam was correct. Henry wanted Lindsay to be in her twenties. Twenties would be fine. It would be enough to offer a faint glimmer of possibility. He only needed that faint glimmer and he would be content.

"And leave the bronze alone," Henry said.

Adam had lost track of his actions, but, under the prodding of Henry's disapproval, he caught himself. He looked over to the autonomous hand that was leisurely spinning the statue, as if winding the mainspring of a giant, ornate clock. He pulled his arm back and stood.

"Got it. You're not interested." he said, on his way to join Henry. "And you'll date again when hell freezes over."

Adam stopped in the hallway and leaned against the doorframe of the bathroom across from the kitchen entry. "Maybe you should give guys a whirl," he said, half in jest.

Henry kept his thoughts on the topic of homosexuality entirely to himself. It was a conversation that he felt, if ever to occur, would be the chaser to several belts of Scotch. He waited in front the steaming kettle, ensuring that it had come to a full rolling boil, before he poured the hot water into the teapot that sat resting on the white enamel of the stovetop.

Lindsay and Henry had developed a routine over the course of several weeks. They would meet on Saturday mornings at his apartment and share a small pot of tea before jumping into her lesson. He had initially offered to alternate between her place and his, but Lindsay had appreciatively though flatly declined. Henry had sensed apprehension, which had surprised him. Although curious, he didn't want to be intrusive.

"I'm terrible at guessing a woman's age," Adam said. "How old does she seem?"

"Seem? In what way?"

"The way she acts, the way she dresses—that sort of thing."

"That's the mystery," Henry said. "She's a mixed bag of goods. She seems anywhere from five to a thousand."

"Well, at least you've narrowed it down. You know, you could always ask her."

Henry acknowledged Adam with an arch in his eyebrow as he moved from the stove to the fridge. It was an action that prompted Adam's looping question, and around the reel it went once more.

"Why do you keep that thing? There was this breakthrough a couple of decades ago. You may have heard about it: frost-free. Hasn't everyone else in the building gotten one? Just ask."

"You know why. I don't want my landlord to raise my rent," Henry said as he retrieved the milk and closed the door.

"Over a new fridge? Seriously, has he raised anyone else's?"

"No."

Adam wasn't sure if he felt protective of Henry or was frustrated with him or if he simply wanted to goad a confession out of him. Adam knew Henry was confrontation-averse, practically phobic.

"You really are a weenie sometimes," Adam said. It was a comment that Henry chose to ignore completely.

Henry decanted milk into a small Denby pitcher and placed it, along with the matching sugar bowl, onto a tray before returning the carton to the fridge. After glancing to the stove's clock, Henry warmed three cups under the tap, dried them, and set them onto their respective saucers. All three handles, under which he had tucked a teaspoon, were angled to the right after being positioned on the tray.

Not that Adam minded one way or the other, but there were occasions when he questioned which side of the fence Henry was on. Tea service was one of them. It was the blur between gracious snobbery and effeminacy that Adam couldn't really get into focus. Although there was nothing in Henry's manner that Adam would describe as feminine, there was such a landslide of circumstantial evidence that he couldn't help but wonder—anecdotes and traits that, if listed out, Adam would attribute to a woman.

"Actually, you might be interested in Lindsay," Henry said, as he carried the tray in the direction of the hall. He stopped in the kitchen entryway across from Adam. "I'm pretty sure she is single."

"So you know her status but you don't know her age?"

"I suspect her status. I have no clue about her age."

"Well, when you grow a set of nads and ask her age you could throw in the question about her status."

"Far too forward, on both counts."

"Wimp," Adam said.

Henry rolled his eyes in a good-natured dismissal of Adam before he gave a quick side-nod in the direction of the living room.

"Anyway," Adam said, following behind his cousin, "I'm kind of already interested in someone. I think it's a long shot, though."

"You're interested in someone?" Henry asked, on his way to the coffee table. "Who?"

"I'm doing reno work for a HSM. Actually, I'm going there right after I leave."

Henry was in the process of placing the tray onto the coffee table. He looked at his cousin in search of elaboration. The acronym was unfamiliar.

"Hot. Single. Mom," Adam responded.

"How long has this been going on?"

"Nothing is going on. I can't ask her out while workin' there. If she said no, it could get real awkward. Fast."

"I assume then that you are speeding things along so you can pop the big question?"

"Actually," Adam admitted sheepishly, "I'm a little worried that she'll shoot me down, so I'm stretching it. And my boss is really starting to ride my ass. To be fair, she's been great up until now. Her own sister is a single mom, but I'm her right hand and this is peak framing time."

"Who is the wimp now?"

The call-buzzer sounded with the short refrain that Lindsay was in the habit of using when she dropped by for tutoring. It was metered to the musical phrase "Shave and a haircut, two bits," which she had picked up from the movie *Who Framed Roger Rabbit* and which Henry had only ever previously associated with the musical *West Side Story*. However, his thoughts now immediately sprang to Lindsay.

"She is always on time," Henry said, and then added appreciatively, "and she returns phone calls."

He left the tray on the table and slipped past Adam on his way down the hall toward the foyer. He struggled with an internal, last-minute debate on whether to inform Adam that Lindsay was not in the custom of wearing a bra. He wondered if it would give Adam a fighting chance at a mature greeting or whether it would just implant an overwhelming temptation into his head. Grudgingly, Henry decided to give his cousin the benefit of the doubt.

"Lindsay rarely wears a bra, so don't stare."

"Dude, give me some credit. It's not like I haven't seen a few sets in my day."

"Sets? Oh this is going to go real well."

"Just let her in."

Adam was standing in the living room at the entry into the hall. He was watching Henry in the foyer, sensing his hesitation as his index finger hovered in front of the speaker button.

"Really," Adam said, "I know this is important to you. She could be naked, oiled down, and arriving with her twin and it wouldn't faze me. You'd think I was gay. I do have some adult moments."

Less than comforted, Henry hit the call button and invited Lindsay up. Normally he would have left his apartment door ajar for her to let herself in. However, he felt pressed into doing some preparatory scouting. Henry stepped out into the hall and waited by the handrail for Lindsay's entrance into the lobby. After exiting the vestibule, she caught sight of him and waved. T-shirt. No bra. Henry waved back and returned to his apartment.

"Eyes front and centre," Henry said to Adam.

"I'm not fifteen."

Henry went into the kitchen to retrieve the teapot, flustered because he had not tracked the infusion time and had to estimate. Adam returned to the living room, awaiting the introduction.

"Henry?" Lindsay called, as she tapped on the door and entered.

"Hey Lindsay. I hope you don't mind, but my cousin dropped by."

"Of course not," she replied, before closing the door. Adam's curiosity brought him to the hall. He forced his mind off of her breasts as he watched Lindsay remove her shoes. When she looked up there was an instant, but unspecified, recognition between the two of them. The familiarity was stronger for Adam but a hint was all that Lindsay needed. Her mind worked through possible scenarios of damage control as she walked toward him.

"Have we met before?" Adam asked.

"Possibly."

She stopped in front of him, her hand extended. "I'm Lindsay."

"Adam."

He managed heroically solid eye contact during their handshake, after which Lindsay continued into the living room and he slipped into the kitchen. Henry was rummaging through one of the cupboards when Adam entered. Henry stopped his search for the biscuits and looked at his cousin.

"Okay," Adam whispered. "Two things. I'm pretty sure I know her, but not by the name Lindsay."

"And two?" Henry asked.

"I don't know about the rest of her, but those cans of hers are definitely way older than five and definitely way younger than a thousand."

PAIRS

"I knew you'd be like this. I suppose you just stared all slack-jawed."

"No. I was unshakable. She probably thinks I play for the other team."

"Yes, that is the very first thing a woman thinks when a guy doesn't ogle her breasts."

In the corner of his eye, Henry finally caught sight of the biscuits that he'd been searching for, retrieved the box, and gestured for Adam to take it.

"Go out there with these," Henry said. "Otherwise, she'll start to think that we are talking about her."

"We are."

"Go already."

Adam stared down at the box in his hand and somehow, in the tenuous associations of his mind, the word Arrowroot prodded his memory. Unfortunately the name he'd been searching for arrived prior to the setting in which he had first heard it. He went out into the hall, and his certainty built.

"Alex," he said to Lindsay. "We have met and your name was Alex."

She was sitting on the couch leafing through a magazine, which she placed on the table before acknowledging him. She leaned back against the armrest. Without realizing it Lindsay assumed her stage persona, a confident, seductive mask from behind which she would tantalize men while making out her grocery list.

"So you've seen my act," she said.

The memory of their initial meeting had been distant for Adam, a tiny spec of light deep within the black well of a tunnel. However, with Lindsay's reminder, it all came rushing forward.

"You've got an act?" Henry asked, as he brought the teapot to the coffee table.

Adam remained silent, his thoughts not readily ladled out as he watched events unfold. The tiny spec, he realized, was the headlight of a locomotive, a momentous juggernaut that was about to rail into the room.

"Had," she said. "I was stripper."

Henry was at once amazed, surprised, and, to his embarrassment, a little aroused. All of which he had hoped to conceal by his chipper tone.

"I did not know that," he said, sounding as if he had just been pleasantly stumped by a particularly obscure piece of trivia.

"Strictly above board stuff," Lindsay clarified, unsure why she felt the need to make certain he understood that she was never a hooker.

"Arrowroot?" Adam asked the room.

Chapter 10

"Adam's home," Terra called out, louder than was necessary to alert her mother.

Kayley was in her bedroom, working on the final crucial touches of her casual, laissez-faire ensemble. She had been in front of the dresser mirror deciding between pulling her hair back or wearing her BHD baseball cap. Kayley had just decided on the cap when she heard the knock at the front door and the second call from her daughter, who was wailing her reproof up from the main floor.

"Mommy!"

"I'm coming, Mouse."

Kayley gave what she had hoped to be her departing check in the mirror but found herself transfixed by her own image. There was something a little too dowdy about the way her coils of hair seemed to squeeze out from under the rim. She removed the cap, gathered her hair into a single billowing mass and fed it through the opening at the back of the hat, which she placed *just so* onto her head. With a final lipstick check, Kayley felt confident.

She had achieved the perfect laid-back, no-fuss semblance for which she had been striving for all morning. Sweatshirt, with just enough plunge to the V of the collar, jeans, with just enough give in the butt, and deck shoes, worn-in just the right amount. It was the ideal outfit for a non-date excursion to pick out the finishing touches for her basement.

PAIRS

"Mommy!"

After leaving her room, Kayley found Terra standing at the base of the stairs, peering back over her shoulder toward the front door. When Kayley started to descend the stairs, Terra turned to face her. At four years of age, her daughter had managed to accumulate a very extensive repertoire of subtle, and for the most part communicative, expressions. Kayley was most definitely being admonished for her tardiness.

"Sorry, Mouse," Kayley said.

Terra plunked herself down on the first stair as her mother slipped past her to unlock the bolt. Kayley recalled the peculiarity of her daughter's comment, Adam's *home,* as she was opening the door. Her attention became divided between Terra and Adam, who was standing on the other side of the screen door with two Tim Hortons coffees. Behind him, framed within the opposing fence posts of the open gate, Kayley could see the passenger-side door of his white pickup. The soft, idle rumble of its diesel engine wove with belonging into the sounds of the neighbourhood beyond the front yard. Both Kayley and Terra had come to associate that contented mammoth purr with the arrival of Adam.

When she opened the screen door, her attention was mainly on her daughter. Though Kayley was primarily concerned with addressing Terra's remark, some other mom part of her did an inventory of her mouse's appearance, and noticed that her shoes were on the wrong feet.

"You've got duck feet, Mouse," she said. It was mother-daughter shorthand that had, in its origins, been specific to footwear but, over time, had come to be a general reference for getting anything backwards.

Terra assessed the situation and, in agreement, pulled loose the Velcro straps of her sneakers. Kayley and Adam waited patiently for Terra to complete her reshuffling.

"Terra, did you say that Adam is home?" Kayley asked.

"Yes."

"You know he doesn't live here?"

"It probably feels that way lately," Adam said.

"I know," Terra said. "He lives in the house."

"Actually," Adam said, as he handed a coffee to Kayley. "I live in an apartment."

Terra stood up and held out her hand for Kayley. She seemed to neither accept nor dismiss their input and, in so doing, relayed an air of agreeing to disagree. Adam was amused by the shrug that was not gestured but yet very clearly communicated.

"Heigh-ho, heigh-ho," he said. "Off to Home Depot we go."

Chapter 11

The small park across the street from Henry's apartment building was a community hub during the summer. It was a wonderful place to hide from algebra for a while, and to people-watch.

"Algebra can be such a pain in the ass," Lindsay said.

"If algebra is hurting your ass, then you are using the text book in an entirely inappropriate manner," Henry replied.

They were under the shade of a large oak, sitting beside each other on the bench of a weathered picnic table, using the top as their backrest. Lindsay smiled and briefly glanced in his direction. Henry could sense her fleeting attention on him, and he grinned.

"You're not trying to fix me up with your cousin are you?" she asked, while casually surveying the park.

The young men playing a game of pickup basketball provided Lindsay with some pleasant optics, as did the children playing on swings nearby: from provocative to maternal in the sweeping pass of her gaze.

She found herself becoming fixated on a child playing in the park's wading pool, a little red-haired girl who kept glancing at her with friendly curiosity. Sunlight bounced in the ripples all around her. She was a shimmering naiad. When Lindsay smiled, the girl waved in response, but became shy and wandered closer to a blond woman who was standing in the water with her jeans gathered up just below her knees.

"No. I'd never be so presumptuous," Henry replied. "Anyway, he's in the process of attempting to date someone. He was off to see her when he left."

"Attempting to date?"

"He's doing some renovation work at her house," Henry said.

"And he's kind of got a little crush on her?"

"Kind of. He doesn't give it much chance though. Not sure why."

"Sometimes a crush can be enough," she said. "Sometimes that's all it can be. A happy secret."

"Sometimes," Henry agreed.

Lindsay turned around to face the bench's tabletop. She traced her finger through some of the carved initials as she thought about her relationship with Henry. It was becoming important to her.

"Henry? What did you think when you heard that I was once a stripper?"

He was not one to be a patron of strip clubs, but he had sense of the atmosphere. A flash of Lindsay strutting down a runway in nothing but a G-string and stiletto heels played out inside his mind. It was the very same image that had been jumping into his thoughts, without warning, ever since he had heard the news.

"Surprised mostly. Not in a bad way, just surprised. So how did you come up with Alex?"

"Alexandra. It's my name."

"Then who is Lindsay?"

She couldn't really answer. She could describe who she *was*, a beautiful and frail young woman who needed to get stoned to perform, but couldn't really define who she was currently.

"A set of ID I carry," Lindsay said.

"Should I ask?"

"Not yet."

"Should I call you Alex?"

"Not yet."

There was such honesty to the moment that Henry felt overwhelmed. He didn't sense that she was avoiding him, but rather dealing with something complex and painful that needed time to work through. He felt close to her and didn't like the idea of deceiving her any longer, even if it was an unintended misunderstanding.

"I'm not gay," he said. His voice was low and emotionless, almost sleepy.

Lindsay's gut reaction was to feel manipulated. He had devised some twisted ploy to get into her pants and was now confessing. But she reminded herself that Henry wasn't like that. He wasn't from her nightclub world of date-rape drugs and hurled obscenities.

"Are you sure? You seem a little gay."

"I bet Adam would second your motion, but really, I'm not."

"Really?" Lindsay asked.

"Positive."

The news floated happily inside of Lindsay, but jarred up against the memory of Henry's date.

"What was the Michael episode about, then?" she asked.

"I want to be gay."

"I've never heard a guy say that before," she said. "I thought about going lesbian for a while. But it seems that kissing women is about as far as it goes. So why do you want to be gay?"

"Kissing women?"

"I like kissing," she explained. "Sometimes backstage I'd have a little make-out session with one of the other performers. Nothing outside of the clubs though—just something about the setting."

"The general air of sexuality?"

"I suppose it was something like that," she replied. "Anyway, don't change the subject. Back to your date and wanting to be gay."

PAIRS

Henry wanted her to know, to know everything about his experiences. He'd never before had anyone to share his frustration with. Knowing that she had also been pushed and driven into such a depressed low that she too considered homosexuality, that she was kindred in a sense, removed any hesitation he might have otherwise felt.

"Have you read *Self-Made Man* by Norah Vincent?" Henry asked.

"Nope."

"Too bad, that would've been a good jumping-off point."

Lindsay's attention moved briefly to events by the park gate. The little red-haired girl was standing with her mother by the Goldenrain tree. They were examining its wisteria-like trains of bright yellow flowers as the blond woman was explaining something. The little girl glanced over to Lindsay and waved goodbye when her mother took her hand.

"In a nutshell," Henry said, "I've never been able to successfully roll a friendship into a relationship. I'm not sure where the issues are, but I kind of think it's with women. I stay the same but they want something different. Suddenly the games begin. Suddenly we are on opposite sides of the fence. Suddenly I'm guilty until proven innocent. Suddenly they want all these attributes that I never had in the first place."

"And that's it?"

"No. That's just a symptom of bigger problem."

"Problem?"

"With women."

"That *you* have with women?"

"No, with women. Others guys see it too. Oh, and they complain. But it doesn't really seem to bother them as much. I'm not sure why."

Had it been any other man than Henry, her back would have been up immediately. She likely would've stormed out. Instead, she anchored herself in place by the memories of her own despair with dating, reasoning that if she could hit bottom then so could he.

"So what is the problem with women?" Lindsay asked.

"They're nuts. To date, I mean, at least for me. Great friends, great co-workers but lousy dating material. Such a frustrating sense of entitlement. Valentine's Day goes both ways, you know what I mean?"

"You are sort of babbling a tiny bit, Henry. Reel it in for me. What is so nutty?"

"Okay, an example of nutty: my favourite gal non sequitur. The one that finally got me to throw in the towel."

"Non sequitur?"

"A statement that doesn't logically flow from what preceded it."

"Ah."

"The same woman who wants to compete with me on equal footing for a job can also manage to hold the opinion that if we were to go out on date, I should pay. I don't know how a woman can hold both those diametrically opposite beliefs in her head without her brain exploding. I know it makes my brain want to explode."

"So the issue is that you're cheap?"

"No."

"Alright. I can see how that might appear a little *cake and eat it too*. But still. Driven to guys because of it?"

"There's more. Lots more. Another personal favourite of mine is the time it takes the average woman to ask me what I do for a living. You know how long? Within 15 minutes after introductions. You know how many times a gay man who I've just met has asked me what I do? Zero. Zero times."

"Maybe the women are just making conversation. And, for the record, men are a lot faster to peer down my top."

"Maybe. Or maybe I'm being appraised. Maybe women are just constantly checking out *my* cleavage and I'm really starting to resent it. Equality, my ass! Studies show that high-status women date higher-status men. Women complain about being objectified. Well, assessing is pretty much the same thing."

Lindsay mulled over Henry's issues. He didn't seem to her to have any anger or resentment. The nearest she could come to understanding the gist of his explanation was that he had been annoyed into homosexuality, so completely irked that he didn't want to face another date with a woman. Lindsay held her smile back. She didn't find humour in Henry's troubles, but rather in how well his explanation fit his left-brained personality. She understood that he simply wanted consistency and equity and it was driving him crazy that he couldn't find his version of it.

"Lindsay, there is no one thing. It is not like my feelings can be traced back to a scarred childhood. It is just a ton of little things that add up. And what it adds up to is that women really aren't very good dating material for me. They all seem to have the same simplistic, sexist opinion of what a man should be and I'm just not that. I always feel like I'm walking on glass."

"I know a lot of women that want a sensitive man," Lindsay said.

"In theory," Henry replied. "In practice they want everything in a man that they complain about. At least the ones I've dated do. They all had a much narrower definition of what it is to be a man then men have of what it is to be a woman. Clothes, types of cars, types of occupations—it's all so very sexist. And strangely, the more feminist a woman appears to be, the more sexist she is. I've fallen into that trap one too many times."

Lindsay couldn't quite place the reason for her attraction to Henry. She found him a little trying, yet couldn't deny that she enjoyed his company. She wondered how a right-brained woman, such as herself, could date a man like him. As he spoke, it occurred to her that she would think of him as her girlfriend. The relationship would have equity and consistency, she reasoned, without any expectations of machismo.

"I don't want to sit here and shit on women," Henry continued. "I like women. Just not to date."

"So you don't have issues with women, you just think they blow chunks when it comes to dating and you don't want to deal with the bullshit anymore?"

"Well, not blow chunks per se."

"I know all about not wanting to deal with the bullshit," Lindsay said. "Maybe it's kismet that a wannabe lesbian and wannabe gay found each other."

"Still friends?" Henry asked, concerned that he may have overstated his case.

They had never previously acknowledged that they were anything more than teacher and student. Although the understanding had been there, they were both happy to have it spoken.

"Can't deny fate. Two future crazy cat people," she said. "So, no women, no men, you must be jerking off something fierce these days."

Henry was caught completely off guard by the forwardness of her statement. His expression, one of both surprise and declaration of guilt, caused Lindsay to smile. His reaction, the shock and confession, was far too precious for her to let the moment pass easily.

"I could flash you my boobs," she said. "It may help."

"No. I'm good, thanks," Henry said. The image of her strutting down the runway exploded into his mind.

"Are you sure? A daily dose of boobs can prolong a man's life."

Lindsay watched Henry tense up and become progressively more fidgety. He couldn't find a comfortable resting spot for a single part of his body. Flustered and clearly unable to focus, he stuttered the opening of his response.

"We-we are just friends, a couple of homosexual want-to-be's. Remember?"

"We-we certainly are. But where is it written that one friend can't show another her boobs? I could look the other way while flashing you if that'll help."

"No thank you."

Henry's endearing, stymied shyness was far too adorable for Lindsay to continue tormenting him. He was like no man she had ever met, the shy girlfriend with the male body that Lindsay realized she had been searching for.

"I'm just messing with you, Henry," she said. "You're too easy."

Henry smiled meekly, attempting to convey that he had known all along that Lindsay was just making a joke.

"Unless of course you actually do want to see them," she said.

The even delivery of Lindsay's offer left Henry once again wondering about her sincerity. His imagination stepped in before he could gather his composure and he became briefly lost to the runway. Lindsay grinned, her lips slowly opened into a smile, revealing the slightly out-of-line incisor. The runway strut fell away in his mind, replaced by Lindsay's charming smirk. Henry laughed at himself. He shook his head and looked out into the park. He became filled with questions about Lindsay's past.

"So why did you consider becoming a lesbian?" he asked.

"Not yet," Lindsay said. "Soon. I promise. I haven't really thought about it all. I've just been reacting. I like that you analyse the crap out of things. I could do with a little of that myself."

"Could I ask why you stopped being a stripper?"

She thought about the young girl, Lindsay, before answering. Her mind's eye filled with the lights of the ambulance that, ironically, could have had a place within the club.

"I've discovered that I'm a romantic, Henry," she said. "And stripping is not romantic."

They both rested back against the tabletop, sat quietly, comfortable in each other's company, and watched those around them revel in summer.

"Your letter is never coming, Henry," she said in a soft voice.

"Letter?"

"The one signed by all women everywhere apologizing for being such a bunch of schmucks."

Henry shifted his position on the bench, turning toward Lindsay, and rested his head on the palm of his hand. She noticed his focused interest through the corner of her eye, but continued to watch events in the park.

"If it's any consolation, mine is never coming either."

Chapter 12

Curious, Kayley gazed at Terra through the rear view mirror. "Mouse, did you know the woman in the park?"

Terra knew of her, but sometimes recalling was a jumble that would lead to duck-feet memories.

"Yes," she said. "From next door."

"Visiting Gina or Sal?"

"No."

Terra was aware of who lived next door to them, Gina with the cat on one side, and Sal who would fix things on the other. But the woman in the park also lived beside them. Or was it that she lived with them? Terra had trouble making sense of it. She felt that she might be remembering backwards and decided to stop talking.

Kayley didn't want to keep glancing into the back seat while driving, so she let the topic die. With one last quizzical peek at her puzzling little nymph, Kayley brought her complete focus to the road.

"Adam should be there when we get home," Kayley said, without taking her eyes off of the traffic. "What do you think? Should we ask him to stay for dinner? We could barbecue."

Kayley turned onto Moncton Drive, an older, house-proud street with mature trees, well-established flowerbeds, and homes that through years of personalized touches, had lost most of their inaugural cookie-cutter homogeny. It was also the street where Kayley's townhouse complex resided. When she rounded the bend onto the long stretch of road she could see two pickup trucks in front of her place. Adam's, and another jet-black king-cab, parked directly behind him.

"And the woman, too?" Terra asked.

"Woman? From the park?"

A woman in scruffy jeans and a formerly white T-shirt stepped down from the driver's seat. The aviator glasses that rested within the tuft of her silver-white hair flashed in the sun. A cigarette nub smouldered in the corner of her mouth. Her sleeves were rolled up to the crest of her shoulders, revealing a large tattoo on one arm. Before heading into

Kayley's yard, she dropped the cigarette butt onto the road and crushed it under the sole of her work boot. To Kayley, even at a distance, the woman looked rough but attractive.

Rivalry instincts pushed Kayley to go directly to her townhouse, but she managed enough restraint to pull into the drive leading to the communal parking of her complex. By the time she had found her spot, helped Terra out the car seat, and retrieved the knapsack that she had taken to the park, she had forgotten about her daughter's question. Kayley walked quickly, trying to convince herself that her speed had nothing to do with jealousy. She reasoned that she had a right to know who was in her home.

Adam, as always, was considerate of the fact that he was working in Kayley's yard. He tried to keep loose cuttings and the miniature dunes of sawdust to a minimum. However, in spite of his best efforts, the front yard in its role as the temporary home for his table saw, workbench, and sundry power tools, was clearly the beachhead for a major renovation offensive.

Courteously, when he had begun the project, he had cordoned off the vegetable patch with a low makeshift fence. Kayley had assumed that Adam's intent was to give the garden some minimal protection from any accidental mishaps. However, to her, it seemed to give the depressed plot a Sleepy Hollow graveyard effect. She sighed with disappointment and apologized to the fallen as she passed on her way into the townhouse.

When Kayley opened the front door she could hear voices coming from the basement. She picked up Terra and moved to the top of the stairs to eavesdrop.

"Adam, I don't get what's taking so damn long," the woman said. Though not upset, her solid tone of voice carried a definite expectation of getting answers.

"You said I could have the time it takes."

"I didn't expect you to move in with her."

"This is the time it is taking."

"Does she keep change'n things on you? What's the deal?"

"Tess, I'm almost done. I promise. I will be back full-time. Soon."

"Soon has to be real soon, Adam. I can't have my best guy and foreman working for me half-time during the height of framing season."

"Soon will be soon."

"I don't want to bust your nuts here. It's real admirable that you're help'n this woman out. But your charity work doesn't do shit for my bottom line. I have a business to run. You know?"

"Sure, Tess."

"That's a bad word," Terra called out. "Hi Adam."

Adam and Tess fell silent listening to Kayley as she slowly descended the newly enclosed staircase. Kayley wasn't sure about the specifics behind the *charity work* that was being performed but the very phrase upset her.

When she reached the basement, Adam and Tess where already facing the bottom of the stairs, waiting on her arrival. The moment Tess saw Kayley she knew the cause of the delay. Beyond their working relationship, Tess and Adam had developed a close bond. They shared a great deal in common outside of carpentry, which included a similar taste in women. It occurred to her that Adam had been stretching the work, and all for the cookie. If Tess hadn't found humour in his little crush she would have been livid. Although prepared to let his little indulgence slide, she still planned on embarrassing him in front of the crew.

Kayley could tell that they regretted her overhearing them, but it was the pity that she read in their eyes that flooded her thoughts. She didn't want pity. It was apparent to Adam and Tess that Kayley was on the verge of tears when she finally spoke.

"What did she mean by charity?" Kayley asked. She forced herself to be angry in order to keep from crying.

"I'll call you later," Tess said to Adam.

While her back was to Kayley, Tess winked to Adam. He understood the meaning. She had figured out the cause of the delay. And while seeming alright with it, he knew that Tess was still going to exact some form of restitution. On her way out of the basement Tess turned to face Kayley and gave a quick, tight-lipped smile to her.

"Nice meeting you," she said to Kayley in passing. "He's a good guy. Does great work."

Kayley acknowledged the greeting with an impatient short-lived smile. She waited for Tess to leave the basement before speaking. Her eyes bored into Adam the moment she heard Tess reach the main floor.

"What did she mean by charity work?" Kayley demanded.

"Not charity exactly. At cost."

"At cost?"

"I am charging you what it costs me to do the job."

"And is your labour included in that cost?"

It was one of the few times in Adam's life that he wished that he was a better liar. Even in silence he told the truth and it made Kayley feel like she was sinking in ice water, a slow drowning numbness.

Kayley put Terra down and patted her on the back as a means of directing her to her play area. But Terra remained standing between her mother and Adam, her gaze alternated between the two of them. They were upset and she didn't know why.

"How come?" Kayley asked.

"Helen asked me."

"So if Helen asks you to work for free, you just run off and do it?"

"She told me a little bit about you."

"What bit exactly?"

It was obvious to Adam that the news was somehow crushing her. The emotions went far deeper than anger. She appeared defeated, yet trying to rally.

"Kayley, it's not charity," he said, trying to second-guess her thoughts. "It's just levelling the playing field."

"What bit exactly?" she asked again. The insistence in her tone was escalating.

"The bit about your husband leaving you with nothing. About you having to start over from ground zero with a newborn that he wasn't man enough to be a father for."

The departing shots of Kayley's husband swarmed her mind and she fought becoming lost to them. Yet Kayley could not shake her self-doubt, because he was right, someone else had always cared for her. If he was right about that, she thought, maybe he really was right about everything. She was pathetic and destined to leech off those around her.

"So what are you suppose to be? My knight in shining armour?"

"Haven't you ever helped out someone just because they deserved it?" Adam asked.

It was obvious to him that something in her was trying to hold on, a bravado that held back his cynicism of having *no good deed going unpunished*.

"Like I said to Tess," he said. "I'm finishing up soon."

"Perfect," Kayley said. "And I won't be paying you the charity rate."

Adam couldn't end it without her knowing the entire truth, of what had happened and why. When he began to explain, he wasn't exactly sure how he would proceed, or how it would end.

"Kayley, Tess would never have come here if I hadn't been dragging it."

It was not so much his words that captured Kayley's attention, but rather it was the earnestness with which they were spoken that caused her to pause and rethink.

"Dragging it? Why?" she asked.

"Because," he said, with a boyishly nervous plunge, "I like being around the two of you. I wanted to ask you out. But I was afraid you'd say no, so I just kept hanging around hoping for a clear signal."

Emotions had never changed so quickly for her, a dizzying spin from despair to happiness. Her ex-husband's voice dissolved back into the shadows from which they had crawled out. Kayley saw it all so very differently. Adam had lent a hand, sight unseen, with no expectations. He had held no agenda except to help, but somewhere along the way he had become interested in her, child and all. Kayley made a mental note for herself. She would have to thank Helen, right after she tore a strip off her.

"So?" Kayley asked, after a brief smile. "In terms of clear signal, what would work for you?"

"You're staying for din-oh," Terra said to Adam, glad to be relaying the news.

Kayley and Adam smiled at each other. They were relieved that their relationship had transitioned. Both were also amused that a four-year-old had been the closer.

"Not sure exactly," Adam replied to Kayley. "I'm pretty dense, so it would need to be real obvious."

Chapter 13

"You are not going to believe this," Henry said, as he juggled to keep the cellphone by his ear while slipping on his shirt. He needed to hear a familiar voice. Someone that could help bring order to the crackling discharges of emotion and thought. He needed to get focused.

"Henry?" Adam asked.

"No. Genghis Khan, warrior chieftain. Of course it's me."

Henry sat down on the edge of his bed and cradled the phone between his shoulder and ear while he pulled on his jeans. The small lamp on his bedside table provided the only light, painting his room with odd, stretched shadows while leaving the open doorway a pristine blackboard.

"Take a couple of breaths, Genghis," Adam said.

"Lindsay's at the police station," Henry blurted, his own words sounding strange to him. They reminded him that while he felt very familiar with her, she was still a complete enigma. His cautious and planned life had been invaded by anarchy. It bothered him yet somehow he welcomed the intrusion, a storm of living. He felt at once rather perturbed and extremely energized.

"She's been arrested?"

"No," Henry replied as he stood to zip up his pants. "She was caught up in some raid on her housemates."

"Raid? Holy crap! Like a drug raid?"

"Exactly like a drug raid," Henry said as he stepped, barefoot, toward the doorway. From the hall he did a tight U-turn toward the adjacent entry of the apartment's foyer.

"No shit!"

"That's not the half of it," Henry said as he reached inside the room and fished along the wall for the switch. "Her ID says that she is seventeen."

"Ooh, my cuz has got himself some jailbait."

Henry grimaced at the idea. Against his better judgement she was becoming part of his life, and as much as he wanted to be cautious about a relationship with a teenage girl named Lindsay, his need for her to be a woman named Alexandra was overwhelming him.

"Well, here's something for the mix," Henry said. "She told me this afternoon that her name is actually Alexandra and that Lindsay was just some ID she carries."

With the pass of Henry's hand, the overhead fixture came to light, revealing a room that was a hybrid of foyer and office.

"What?" Adam asked. "Why is she calling herself Lindsay then?"

"She didn't want to talk about it," Henry said, as he opened the centre drawer of the desk to retrieve his keys. "I get the feeling she wants to though. Anyway, she had her Lindsay ID on her when the cops came a-call'n."

The foyer, for all its size, lacked a closet. An armoire against the wall across from the apartment's entry door was used to hang seasonal outerwear and store the overflow of shoes that could not find a place in his bedroom. Under the coat hooks, opposite the desk, was a boot tray, on which Henry would only ever keep two pairs of shoes. During the summer his sandals would join the tidy arrangement.

"When she phoned me to see if I'd give her a ride she warned me that the police where a little funny about a *friend* taking her home," Henry said. "Imagine when they discover that the friend turns out to be a thirty-three-year-old man. They should find it fucking hilarious."

"There's no law against a seventeen-year-old girl having a thirty-three-year-old man as a friend," Adams said.

"Do you actually think before you speak?"

A brief interlude in the conversation allowed the balance of Adam's sensibilities to catch up to his mouth, during which he thought about how he would react to a thirty-three-year-old man dating his hypothetical seventeen-year-old daughter. His fingers curled into a tightly clenched fist.

"No," Adam conceded, "apparently not."

Henry picked up his sandals and leaned against the door as he slipped them on, moving the cellphone from ear to ear as balance and positioning demanded.

"I'm a little concerned that I'm getting in over my head in crazy," he said. "Women! They do this, you know."

"Do what?"

"Mayhem! Intrusive mayhem!"

"But you're still going." Adam confirmed.

"Yeah."

"Calling for advice?" Adam asked. Henry could hear the sound of a passing car in the background.

"Where are you?" Henry asked.

"Kayley's yard. Sipping beer and getting strafed by mosquitoes."

"At this hour? Sorry, Adam. Am I interrupting something?"

"Not at the moment. She's gone inside to check on her kid and get a couple more beer. I'm going to be dead tomorrow."

"Things are going well, then?"

"They're going. Not that I mind you calling, but I'm not really sure what you're looking for from me."

"I might just be venting. Or maybe I just need to say it all out loud so that I know this isn't simply a really lucid dream," Henry said, as he left his apartment. "Or maybe it is just a precaution in case I go missing."

Chapter 14

"Did I hear your cell?" Kayley asked, as she stepped out into the yard of her townhouse.

Adam was sitting in the folding lawn chair. His features, though diffused into the night, where not entirely lost. There was a bright crescent moon directly overhead and a streetlight that shone through gaps among the leaves of a street-side linden tree that perfumed the air with its adornment of flowers. Flames from a pair of citronella torches cast a radiant orange and yellow glow which flickered against the fence.

"It was my cousin." Adam replied. He slipped his cellphone back into the front pocket of his pants.

"Anything urgent?" she asked. Kayley handed off the bottle of beer and then sat in the chair across from him.

"Nah. Just a frost alert."

The night, while not stifling, was definitely warm and stirred with the subtle living resonance of summer. The faintly medicinal scent of DEET filled the air around them. It was a setting in which Kayley could not imagine the intrusion of anything remotely related to the arrival of winter.

"What? Tonight?"

"No, no. Not weather wise," Adam said. "It appears that hell just might be slowly freezing over."

"Your cousin just called to tell you that hell is freezing over?"

"Pretty much."

Kayley found Adam's amusement to be contagious. "Are you going to let me in on it?" she finally asked, unable to wait any longer. "Or would you have to kill me if you told me?"

"Not that I am superstitious, but I don't want to jinx it."

"You brat!" she said, before leaning forward and slapping his knee.

Adam was at first startled but soon began to laugh. Kayley glanced down at the bottle, which rested in the burrow of her crossed legs, and her thoughts stepped aside from their conversation. She saw herself having a wonderful time. When Kayley lifted her head once again she found Adam watching her. Words would have fallen short of the compliments in his eyes.

"Adam. What exactly did Helen tell you about me? I mean, what was it that brought you out here in the first place?"

"That your ex left you high and dry with a newborn four years ago. That you've been making it work, but it's been rough. If anyone has earned a little hand up, it is you."

"Derek and I met in university," Kayley said, recalling his powerful physique and thick, shoulder-length red hair with little effort.

"I had just been through an odd relationship," she continued. "It had been very vague and complicated. I couldn't really put a label on it. And it just finally unravelled. After that relationship I was in the market for something very simple and straightforward. And that was Derek through and through: simple and straightforward. He was a stoic and emotionally repressed man with poster boy good looks. Exactly what I thought I had wanted. He was also a man-child. He had no sense of responsibility, and while loving to sow his oats, he really didn't want to waste any time reaping. My pregnancy was a sign for him that his work was done. So he left. The moral? Careful what you wish for."

Adam took a long sip of beer and then grinned when he lowered the bottle. "Okay," he said, in a tone she found comforting. "I'll be careful."

Chapter 15

"It wasn't that bad," Lindsay said.

She was standing in the entry of the kitchen, watching Henry prepare camomile tea. He had barely glanced at her after leaving the police station and ever since returning to his apartment had stuck primarily to monosyllabic statements.

"I'm the one that had the front door of her place rammed in," she said.

"Right."

"I was this close to being put up on charges," she said, pinching her index finger and thumb together to paper width.

Henry did not notice the gesture. He remained with his back to her, focused on the brooding kettle.

"You're right, Lindsay. Everything is just peachy."

"It speaks."

"Lindsay," he said, facing her in frustration, "you're seventeen. I'm a teaching professional. I can't have the police department even remotely suspecting that you're my girlfriend."

She felt her patience with Henry slipping away. She had been making allowances for his mood but was starting to resent his self-absorbed concerns and the assumption of her guilt she felt they implied.

"Or my pimp," Lindsay needled and then watched with satisfaction as a rigid spike shot up through Henry's spine.

"Oh God," he moaned.

"Henry, I'm twenty-four."

"Twenty-four? Sure. And your name is Alexandra. And you're a former stripper. Got it."

"Don't be such an ass," she said, her voice strained.

The emotional charge of Lindsay's tone washed through Henry, subsided his anger, and pulled him away from his own tiny world. He gazed upon her with a newfound sympathy, and something more.

A realization of how important she had become to him. He didn't like to think that he was upsetting her.

"I'm sorry," he whispered.

"I didn't do anything wrong here," she said, if only to hear it aloud. "I can't get my stuff, I have no place to stay, I missed my shift, and I had to lie to my boss."

"You can stay here."

There was gentleness in his manner, a genuine concern and caring that lured her into the kitchen. The attraction she felt was confident, peaceful, and resolute.

"I promise," he said. His words were unsteady. The intent and tenderness in her eyes made him wonderfully nervous, "no funny business. All legit."

She reached to Henry's face, her hand caressing along the stubble of his unshaven cheek while she moved closer. Her gesture and the longing he felt for it surprised Henry. He remained perfectly still against the counter when she kissed him. His tenderness gave her new confidence. She might be able to be Alexandra once again.

"You and I are like simultaneous equations," she said, in amusement. "You need to have both expressions to find the solution."

"An algebra metaphor," he said. "Impressive."

"An algebra *simile*," she replied, feeling a small ego boost from finally being the one to do the correcting.

She took hold of his hand and stepped back, to a less intimate distance. She was finally prepared to let Henry into her world. Although desiring to reveal her past to him, she nevertheless felt anxious.

"I go by many names," she said, in a quiet voice. "Babe, chick, slut, whore, dyke, and bitch to name a few, I think there are a thousand. But I prefer Alexandra. I'm twenty-four."

"I believe you," he said.

"Lindsay was a girl I knew, another stripper. She was sixteen when she died."

Chapter 16

In darkness Kayley lay on her bed, thinking about her evening with Adam. She had yet to close the drapes. Through the open window she could hear the pale, murmuring rasp of small life sounding large against the stillness. The moon cast a frosted band of neatly hemmed light along the wall directly across from her.

She was happy about their evening together, but it also served to remind her of the long absence of companionship. Restless and wide-awake, she remembered a fitting verse from Sappho.

The moon has set

and the Pleiades. Middle of the

night! Time passes,

and I lie here alone

In the context of elevated words, the melancholy she felt led her to memories of Gavin and the poem that they had written together. Back and forth it had passed in cooperative competition. She had been unable to throw out the copy of their unfinished work. Kayley pushed off her covers, turned on the reading lamp overhead, and retrieved the poem from the dresser drawer closest to the bedside. She had kept it safe in a manila envelope amongst her other important papers. With the headboard as her backrest, Kayley recited it in a soft voice suited to the late hour. Poetry should be heard. Gavin had not taught her that, but through his narrations had proven it.

Memories of the poem's birth during their outing to the Public Gardens and the game that she and Gavin had made of unsuspected hand-offs, were at once joyous and sorrowful. Vividly she recalled her laughter in the stall of a dorm washroom when she discovered that the toilet paper had been repurposed as a tissue scroll for his calligraphy. Tag, she was it.

Kayley viewed the poem as unfinished. Although flawed and suffering from the intentions of youth, she felt that it was still a piece of art and deserved closure, the final stanza that she had thought Gavin would provide yet had not.

Staring at the page, she wondered if they had a shared inspiration. As she reread the poem in silence, searching for different interpretations, it occurred to her that she would never know. And, in that condemned understanding, found the catalyst that had been evading her. A cathartic sorrow overwhelmed Kayley, and she wept quietly.

Chapter 17

Henry and Alexandra were standing together in front of the couch, both having lost track of time. Their only light came from a small grouping of white, mug-sized candles that flickered by the hearth of the electric fireplace of Henry's apartment.

They had decided to forgo the camomile tea in favour of wine. On a dark tray atop the coffee table was a sweating bottle of Pinot Grigio resting in its coaster, two stemmed glasses, and a white plate of sliced sections from a Golden Delicious apple and a Bosc pear. All were untouched.

"Okay, I really mean it this time," Alexandra said, speaking between her repeated return to Henry's lips. "I'd like to talk."

"This is nearly narcotic," Henry said. He was surprised by the easy surge of emotion and by his lack of desire for anything else than to prolong their endless kiss. "I feel like a teenager."

After she stepped back far enough to rest her forehead on his mouth, she replied. "I know."

In Henry she had found her girlfriend. With a gentle touch from the side of his index finger under her chin, Henry gestured for her to look up. His contentment was apparent and shared.

"You want to talk to me about Lindsay?" He asked.

"Yes."

Alexandra took Henry by the hand and guided him down to join her as she moved to sit on the couch. Had it not been for her seriousness, he would have reached out to continue, but instead he poured the wine and handed her a glass.

"It's probably not as chilled as it should be," he said.

"I'm sure it's fine."

"The fruit makes for a great pairing," he added, "if you're hungry."

Alexandra's smile was a melody of gratitude for the offer, the humour she found in the gracious antithesis to the pretzels and beer to which she was more accustomed, and the nervousness she felt anticipating Henry's reaction.

"So what's with all the candles ready to go?" she asked, biding her time as she built her courage. "Are you some kind of player?"

"I just like candles."

"Are you sure you're not gay?"

"From what I've seen, I don't think candles are a gay thing. Cherubs maybe."

"They're a girl thing."

"I guess that makes me a lesbian."

Alexandra delighted in the quick badinage of his response and thought about how lucky she was to find her wonderful *lesbian* girlfriend. She tapped her glass against Henry's and took a long sip before speaking.

"When I was working as a stripper I kind of had a little circuit of clubs," she said when she returned the glass to the table. "Lindsay worked at one of them. I knew her by the name Candy."

Alexandra was making a concerted effort not to talk quickly or jump the conversation in tangent directions, both of which she was in the habit of doing when she became nervous.

"Candy, or Lindsay rather, never really seemed comfortable with it. She always had to get high before going on."

To pace herself, Alexandra sampled a section of pear and took a slow sip of wine. She paid attention to the blend of flavours and nodded to

Henry with approval. Had it not been for her obvious apprehension, Alexandra's action might have been mistaken by Henry as nonchalance, instead of the delay that it actually was.

"For some reason I became like her mentor," Alexandra said, and then laughed self-consciously at the thought of it before continuing, "or confidant or…"

"Friend?" Henry offered.

"Maybe. Sometimes I felt sort of like her mom."

The precise nature of her relationship with that young woman was elusive for Alexandra, and yet had enough substance to it to make her feel blameworthy. Not quite guilty, but not innocent.

"One night when she was stoned," Alexandra said. "She told me that Lindsay was her real name. She showed me her ID."

Henry felt that there was so much more to her tone than a mere recount of sad events. Shuffled in with her sorrow was a bystander's remorse.

"Christ, Henry! She was sixteen."

Alexandra finished her wine in a quick series of gulps and then informally grabbed the bottle, by the neck. She led it through a mid-air dance. Every motion with the bottle was redirected before completed.

"Candy was the name on her fake ID. Not that anyone checked too close," she said, as she brought the mouth of the bottle up to her lips. Remembering Henry's civility, she caught herself and veered in a singularly fluid motion to fill her own glass.

"She just up and OD'd backstage. I found her. She was so pale. Fragile. I'd seen overdoses before. I knew that she wasn't coming back."

Before pouring the wine, Alexandra corrected herself and topped up Henry's glass first. He noticed the slight tremor in her hand and gazed into her eyes. The candlelight reflected in lenses of water.

"I had a real crappy childhood, Henry," she said, attempting to provide a framework for Henry and herself that would give some level of rationale for her actions.

"It doesn't matter what you've done," Henry shared during her hesitation. Sensing her regrets, he wanted to assure her that he wouldn't judge. He could only think to squeeze Alexandra's hand.

"I took her ID, Henry, her *real* ID. She was too young. It was so wrong. She should've had a better life."

Memories of the lifeless body that was draped into the chair melded with images of the flashing ambulance lights. The shimmer in Alexandra's eyes finally collapsed into tears as she recalled the overwhelming bereavement that had led to her vow: through her Lindsay would be born anew.

"Lindsay couldn't die. I wouldn't let it happen. I kind of snapped. I decided to live her life for her. A *way* better life. I know it makes no sense. I couldn't better myself for me, but I could for her. I had to live her better life. The life that should've happened."

"So you quit stripping," Henry said. He slid across the couch toward Alexandra.

"I had to," she said, reaching her arm across his back and drawing him closer, to rest against her body. "I tweaked Lindsay's ID a little and became her."

"And you went back to school," he added, as he nestled his head against her shoulder. Henry had never before felt so completely immersed in another person.

"When I ran away from home I was Lindsay's age."

A cathartic sorrow overwhelmed Alexandra, and she wept softly.

Part III

These stepping-stones,
Moments,
Living glimpses

Chapter 18

The last what of your poem? Stanza? Sorry dear, that doesn't make the least bit of sense to me. Now Kayley, why on earth would Gavin have the last stanza of your poem? And why would he wait until he's dead before getting it to you?

Kay, now I don't want you think I'm belittling you here, and I'm sure as stanzas go that it's a fine one, and perhaps I'm missing something, but it's not like it's precious. Just write it again. You were always good at writing and a bit of a logophile to boot. I bet you didn't think I had a word like logophile in me. Been doing word of the day. Only I've been doing it once a week. Hey, as such, do you find it ironic that the word onomatopoeia *has zero onomatopoeia?* Ironic *has got a good dose of it though. I guess that makes me a bit of an opsimath. Zero onomatopoeia there, too.*

Yep. I have the nose, your mother had the gift, and you could always write. Omne trium perfectum—everything that comes in threes is perfect.

My father, your great grandfather, he could write. Not like you though. He was a speech man. Being a lawyer and all. Good thing they were only for him though, because he couldn't spell to save his life. Except in Latin. It was the oddest thing.

Not as odd as the way that good-for-nothing Hair Farmer you married kept stalking you after he walked out. Nut. To quote Heinrich Heine, "Ordinarily he was insane, but he had lucid moments when he was merely stupid."

Chapter 19

A fine rain fell upon the city. Through the bank of windows along the balcony wall of Adam's apartment it had the appearance of drifting fog. The weather had not changed his plans, merely the venue.

"Terra is officially dead to the world," Kayley said in a low voice as she came into the room from the hall. Adam was sitting on the picnic blanket they had laid overtop the parquet floor. All of the furniture had been set aside against the walls of the L-shaped living and dining area, creating the open space in which Terra and Adam had pretended to fly a kite.

"I'm glad we decided to go ahead with this," she said, after sitting down across from him. Kayley enjoyed that Adam had planned such a wonderfully simple and romantic way to spend time together, inclusive of her daughter. The fact that the setting was not the textbook norm made it more special, more memorable and perfect.

"Me too," Adam agreed. He enjoyed his role in the ease that seemed to have washed over Kayley the moment they had laid out the blanket. It was in her mannerisms, and had become even more apparent when she had returned from putting Terra down for a nap. With her return, Adam sensed that there was something more, something amorous in her mood. He stirred at the possibility.

Tranquil sounds of a phantom meadow wove through their conversation, an auditory mirage courtesy of the CD playing in his stereo. The falsetto pitch of a lone cicada, the warble of distant birds, and the serrated chirp of crickets testified to summer's fair weather within the apartment. After they touched glasses, Kayley grinned playfully and glanced down at the blanket while she brushed her hand across its soft fibres.

"Have many women seen this blanket?" she asked, with her eyebrow arched.

"Today is the debut. And if we don't spill anything on it I can take it back to the store tomorrow," Adam replied.

Otherwise nondescript, there was the boyish glint that Kayley always noticed when he was teasing her. Without a word, he could at times make her laugh with just the cast of his eyes. Noticing that she was once again enjoying Adam's company, Kayley felt a playful ease to her mood, a feeling that had been restrained while she had been continually refocusing her attention on Terra. Inspiration was carried in on the crest of her release. She took a quick sip to moisten her lips and briefly closed her eyes to focus her thoughts before giving her minute recital.

How beautiful is the rain!
After the dust and heat,
In the broad and fiery street,
In the narrow lane,
How beautiful is the rain!

Adam sat in silent wonder. The spontaneity had caught him off guard and the life she had imbued into the words had captivated him. He was at a loss about how to respond. But he knew that the onus was on him to comment.

"That's nice," he said, during his brief, padded applause. "Yours?"

"Those are the words of Henry Wadsworth Longfellow, a nineteenth-century American poet."

"The nineteenth you say? Good century, that one."

Kayley knew that Adam's literary world consisted of graphic novels and comic books. Yet she had confidence that he had an innate appreciation for the spoken word. His burden was reading, not language. Not expression.

She believed his praise to be genuine. There was nothing about him that seemed to her to be contrived. Honesty was his blessing and, if it were possible, his curse. It was contagious, early symptoms manifesting in Kayley as guilt.

"Have you had regrets over how you handled a relationship?" she asked.

"Nothing leaps to mind."

"Or some date where you could have treated someone a little better?"

Adam retrieved the carton of wine from the insulated pouch of his backpack and topped up their glasses while he thought. He conceded to himself that adult relationships were woefully absent in his life, which, in turn, inspired thoughts about the allure of Kayley.

"Well, I was once in bed with a woman," he said, "both of us buck naked and rarin' to go and then I had to stop."

He placed the carton inside the backpack, took a considered taste from his glass and thought about his night of callous chivalry.

"Stop? Why?"

"We had just met," he prefaced, feeling a slight twinge of embarrassment over his behaviour that night. "My buddies and I had gone into the chalet bar to have a little après-ski drink, and there she was, lust at first sight. One thing led to another, and before you know it we end up in the sack together."

Adam paused his recounting and he tried to gauge Kayley. She was pleasant, but frustratingly withholding. In addition to being amused by his growing discomfort, Kayley was also fascinated by the keyhole peek she was getting into the workings of a young man's mind.

"Go on," she said.

"There we were, buck naked, in missionary, and rarin' to go."

"You mentioned that bit."

"And then I saw it, a tiny scroll of jet-black hair between her breasts. If it had been red, or even blond, I would have chalked it up to being one of mine. But it wasn't. It was jet black. She had a chest hair. Game over."

"Over?" Kayley asked.

"Over."

"Oh my God! What did you do? What did you say?"

"I played the sensitive card. I said something like it being too fast for me. I was a little more traditional. That I would like to get to know her better."

"You played the sensitive card?" Kayley giggled and gently shoved the palm of her hand against his shoulder. "You're terrible! What did she say?"

"She called me refreshing. But I sort of got the feeling that *refreshing* wasn't exactly what she was hoping for. I never called her. I just kept thinking pubee-boobies."

"You're awful," she said, feeling mortified on the woman's behalf and yet finding the entire scenario hilarious.

For all their effort, neither Kayley nor Adam could repress their smiles as they thought about the woman and the rogue chest hair that had swapped out her night of non-committal sex for an exchange of fraudulent explanations and insincere sentiment.

"And you?" Adam asked. "Do you have skeletons?"

Skeletons—Kayley stuck on the word. She had never really labelled her feelings about her time with Gavin. What word fit? *Love? Admire? Regret? Guilt?* Kayley agreed with her grandmother's thoughts: he was the great *poser* of her life, perplexing in himself and also someone who set tests for her.

"Yes," she said.

After a taste of wine she sat in silence, formulating her thoughts about where exactly to begin. Gavin had been part of her life for such a long time. It was difficult for her to say when he had stepped out of the background. Adam saw the distance in her eyes as she wandered the cheerless residence of her skeleton.

"I grew up in a small town," she began. "Everyone knew everyone. If not well, at least to say hello. So when I went off to university I was a little overwhelmed. By chance I met up with a familiar face from back home. Gavin McKay. He was a couple of years older than me, and growing up we didn't really hang with the same crowd. I actually only knew him by his nickname, Spaz. As a matter of fact, that is all I ever knew him as for the longest time."

Although rummaging through the knapsack, Adam's attention remained primarily on Kayley. It was clear from the effort she was making to provide context that more than a mere anecdote was being shared. She was revealing an important life event. Through touch alone, he managed to locate one of the items that he was in search of, the pill bottle of toothpicks.

"I was sure glad to see him, though," she said. "We were both English majors and he even ended up as a TA in one of my courses. Over time, we became close friends."

As a result of a second blind hunt, Adam retrieved the rubber container that held bite-sized cubes of assorted cheeses. As with the picnic and the selection of wine, the cheese had been Henry's suggestion.

"The friendship evolved over time," she said. "Finally leading to that fork in the relationship road where you either remain friends or it becomes something more."

Listening intently, Adam dumped the container of cheese onto a white plastic serving plate and proceeded to skewer each cube as Kayley spoke.

"One night," she continued, "after a little drinking, the two of us ended up back at his dorm room. And I made a move on him. He seemed surprised. It became obvious to me over the years, as I have thought about that night, that he was put off."

Kayley paused, sighed, and glanced down at her crossed legs. She wanted Adam to know about Gavin, but she didn't want him to view her as a complete rube, or worse, a total bitch. She felt a need to prelude her recounting with a clarification of her inexperience with men at the time. Kayley wanted Adam to understand the extenuating circumstance that downgraded the unkindness to plain stupidity.

"I thought that guys always wanted sex," she explained. "No other possibility ever occurred to me. It never occurred to me that a guy might not be in the mood, for whatever reason."

Kayley watched a small grin appear on Adam's face as she attempted to justify herself, or at the very least, impart that her actions with Gavin had been free of malice. She assumed that Adam's smile was not because of her preconceptions about men, but rather the sexism at its foundation. But he was merely taking pleasure in the naivety that was part of her charm.

"With my persistence he finally made some reciprocal effort," she said, "but it became clear that he really was not feeling comfortable. So we just stopped. It was horribly awkward. I didn't know what to think. The first thing that leapt to mind was that he was gay. I had just hit on my gay friend. What else could it be? Right? Guys want sex all the time, regardless."

Through her own words, Kayley once again began to relive a condensed consequence. Her demeanour and voice radiated her emotional state. The regretful depth did not escape Adam.

"Later on, he attempted to rekindle our closeness, but I didn't really see the point," Kayley said, followed by a short laugh that was bitter and self-mocking. "He was gay and therefore nothing romantic could come of it. And why would a man and woman become emotionally close if not for romantic reasons?"

Kayley laughed again, defensively, lost for anything else to do. Adam reached to her. She wanted the contact but, strangely, wanted to suffer almost as much. The internal quarrel caused a hesitation that Adam viewed as reluctance. His confusion subsided when she finally took his hand.

"I didn't want to risk my heart, so I just kept it as a casual friendship. He slowly distanced himself. It really didn't register until he was all but out of my life. For the longest time I never understood what happened. Or why. I just knew that I felt hurt and upset."

Kayley squeezed Adam's hand and he reciprocated. He knew she needed to finish. Kayley sat quietly while her angst subsided, leaving her with nothing to feel at all.

"He wasn't gay," she said, in a low, sterile tone. Kayley paused for a long time and stared out the window, watching the rain. Adam waited patiently. Kayley remained looking away from him when she at last found her words.

"He eventually married and had two children. I learned several years later that he had been molested as a child. Jumping him was likely the very worst thing I could have possibly done."

A weak grin slid onto Kayley's face and led into a quiet pop of breath that Adam interpreted to be a distant and shattered cousin of laughter.

"No," she said aloud, but exclusively to herself. "The very worse thing possible was treating him like my *gay* friend. And you know, I felt very cosmopolitan having a gay friend. Très *Sex and the City*."

"You weren't a horrible person, Kayley," Adam said, "Just small-town naive."

"I feel like a horrible person. He passed away recently. I've been thinking about him, about everything."

"Sorry to hear that," Adam replied. "The *passed away* bit, I mean."

He moved closer and gently cupped her jaw in the palm of his hands. When Kayley finally met his gaze, she couldn't stop herself from relinquishing to his warmth and forgiveness. Nor did she want to. When her mood had lightened, Adam leaned forward and kissed her. Kayley was not expecting the softness and wasn't prepared for the tenderness.

"You weren't," Adam reiterated when he sat back. "A bad person I mean. And if it makes you feel any better I can be the one in charge of the bones-jump'n when it comes to us."

The wonderful glint that Kayley had come to watch for made a brief, welcome appearance. She responded with a short, quiet giggle.

In the bedroom, Terra remained sleeping. Images of a broad green space filled her mind. It was a wide river of grass that meandered calmly between the backyard fences of the homes along its banks. Just ahead of Terra were her mother and Adam. He was happily whispering secrets to Kayley's round belly. Close behind, Terra could hear the voices of a man and woman talking in gentle infant words. A baby laughed in response. She felt as if she knew them.

Chapter 20

"Really, you don't have to do this," Henry said. Although committed to his sentiment he was hoping for some opposition from Alexandra.

"I know I don't *have* to," she replied. "I want to."

The mist that had been flurrying throughout the afternoon had glazed the city and fashioned streets into burnished veins of onyx. They strolled together from Henry's car to the bank, hand-in-hand under the shelter of his Berber umbrella.

"I do believe you," he said.

"I get that," she said, while holding open the door into the enclosed foyer of cash machines. "But I want you to *know*. You've been really great. We've turned the girlfriend corner, Henry, and before we get too far underway, I'd like to share a couple of things with you. This is one of them."

Henry found something peculiar in her phrasing. Or perhaps, he speculated, it was more her tone which suggested that Alexandra viewed girlfriend as being the singular descriptive which fully encompassed the nature of their relationship.

"As in, you are *my* girlfriend?" Henry clarified, before he stepped inside. He closed the umbrella and tapped it against the tiled floor to shake the excess drops free.

"That works," she said.

The interior of the bank, while attempting grandeur with height, was actually a pen the size of a two-bay garage fenced in by the glass wall of the entry and a horseshoe of wickets. Alexandra took Henry's hand once again and walked with him toward an unattended section of counter that resided directly under a signboard of uninspired lettering that dryly proclaimed *Customer Service,* as if that was the only spot in the entire establishment where any was to be had.

Unsatisfied with Alexandra's vague response, Henry sought to corral her, ever so gently, into labelling the variables. He didn't like the matter being unsettled or ill-defined. He needed to know if she viewed him as her boyfriend or her girlfriend. Henry recognized that it was peculiar inner dialogue for a man to be having. Yet, he had to admit, not all that atypical for himself.

"I am a guy, you know," he said, hoping to find clues in her response.

"Henry, you are most definitely male, and a snacky one at that, but you are most definitely not a *guy*. I've dated guys. Not a fan. If you were a *guy,* we wouldn't be having this conversation."

"You think I'm snacky?"

A woman working at a desk behind the counter noticed their arrival and stood to greet them. It appeared to Henry, even before she spoke, that Alexandra was a familiar and welcome face.

"Lindsay," the woman said. "Nice to see you again."

Without letting go of Henry's hand, Alexandra locked forearms and pulled him closer before whispering.

"That's who my paycheques are made out to."

"Are you here to see Vic?" The woman asked.

"Actually, Barbra," Alexandra said, "I am here to see my safety deposit box."

"I'll just get the keys and take you in," Barbra replied before leaving.

"Who's Vic?" Henry whispered to Alexandra.

"My financial advisor. He helps me with my portfolio."

Henry did a double take, first quickly acknowledging her response, then taking a second, transfixed pass to relay his astonishment.

"You have a portfolio?"

"Don't look so surprised. Being an exotic dancer can pay very well."

"How well?"

"*Real* well."

Alexandra enjoyed her effect on Henry. She relished his amazement and the resulting milling of his mind as he re-examined her once again. She was the equation that he couldn't quite solve, and she enjoyed that.

"Not pro-athlete ridiculous, but well," she said. "No medical benefits or pension though."

Barbra returned to the counter, unlatched the waist-height door next to the wicket, and led them into the vault. How strange it was for Henry, as he watched events from his removed, third-party state. The rapport between Alexandra and the staff at the bank, the regard with which she was obviously held, was so very foreign to him. Alexandra's *real well*, while lacking a specific, quantified earnings value, was becoming quite defined for Henry.

When they were at last in the confines of the small viewing room Alexandra lifted the lid of the safety deposit box and retrieved a plastic zip-lock bag. She poured the contents onto the table. It was the identification of a twenty-four-year-old woman named Alexandra, who could pass for her clone.

Henry was not one to seek fault. He didn't seek out all traces of inconsistency, they just leapt into his mind. All of Alexandra's identification, as with Lindsay's, was new—brand new. To Henry, it was as if both young women had recently become citizens, an observation which immediately bridged him to the awareness that neither of these individuals had a passport.

The freshly pressed appearance of Lindsay's identification had initially been understandable for Henry, given the explanation. However, within the new context, it was now part of a bigger puzzle. He wasn't entirely certain of who she was or how she could pull fully formed identities out the air.

"See," she said, like a gleeful child who had just won the largest stuffed animal at the carnival.

Henry looked at her. His speculations over the incongruities remained, but his concerns about them fell at her feet. She was so utterly beautiful—alluring. Completely different from any woman he had ever met. Whoever she was, he knew she cared for him, and he knew that he was in love with her. Nothing could matter more.

"Yes," Henry said. "I see."

Chapter 21

"I can't remember the last time I was in a make-out session like that," Adam said. "It was nice. Like being back in school again."

"I hope you don't think I'm easy," Kayley replied, with overacted demureness.

Amused, Adam suggestively raised an eyebrow and then stood up. He had no idea how long they had been kissing. Time with Kayley had no meaning for him. It at once whisked by and yet stood perfectly still. She had always been in his life and always would be.

When the albeit deflating yet still significant bulge in his jeans passed through Kayley's line of sight, her eyes widened briefly in surprise. During her struggle not to stare, she found a cuticle that desperately needed her immediate attention.

Without explanation he went to the entry closet. The suddenness of his actions and the absence of any reason made Kayley curious. She watched him as he opened the bifold door and rooted inside. When he turned to face her, Adam was holding his high school letterman jacket.

"Would you be my girl?" Adam asked, with exaggerated earnestness.

Kayley smiled and blushed more than she would have liked. Adam opened the jacket on his way back to the picnic blanket. He draped it over her shoulders and then bent down to bring his mouth by her ear. The subtle petal fragrance of her hair and skin briefly delayed him from speaking. She could feel his warm breath while he lingered.

"My crush," he whispered and then kissed her on the nape of her neck before standing.

She leaned to the side and found the glint awaiting her. Adam repositioned himself in front of her, at a more comfortable distance for eye contact.

"Well, I guess it's time to turn on the dishwasher," he said, and then gave his nipples a quick circular rub with his fingertips before starting to collect the plates from the blanket.

It took a moment for Kayley to work back from his peculiar actions to the double meaning in the phrase *turn on*. She laughed aloud as he disappeared into the kitchen.

"You are an odd man," she said.

Leaving his jacket across her shoulders, Kayley gathered the remaining containers, plates, and cutlery before joining Adam in the kitchen. The room was narrow and seconded as a hall between the apartment's entryway and the dining room. He was standing over the sink, in profile to her. For Kayley there was a relaxed, domestic instant that she extrapolated far into the future and she knew that she could easily fall in love with him—and then reconsidered that perhaps she already had.

"Did you get an invitation to Daleesha's cocktail party?" she asked.

"Henry is her aesthete. Daleesha's word by the way, not mine. Since she found out my relation to him, I've apparently been put on her A-list. Henry's account of it, not mine."

"Your cousin Henry?" she confirmed, while placing the dishes on the counter.

"Sorry, yes, one and the same. I keep forgetting that you've never met."

"I've heard more about him from you over the past weeks then I ever got from Helen," she said, grabbing the towel that hung over the handle of the oven door.

"He's a little," Adam began, but hesitated and glanced to the ceiling during his word search, "fussy."

"Were you planning on going?" Kayley asked, while moving toward the dish rack.

"It sounds dull. But Henry is bringing a date. And I have got to see the two of them in action together. You?"

"I think it might be interesting. How come you want to see the two of them *in action*?"

"I'm not really a cocktail party kind of guy and I think it might be a little egg-heady," Adam said. "She is the total opposite of who I ever thought Henry would've ended up with."

"Definitely a lot of potential for egg-heady, but I was hoping we could go together. Who did you think Henry would have ended up with?"

Adam chuckled, stopped washing the dishes, and looked at Kayley. From his reaction, she was expecting some form of tease, and waited.

"Are you asking me out, Kayley? For a while there I thought he would end up with a guy, a reserved guy, an accountant maybe, or a professor of some sort."

"Yes, Adam, I'm asking you out. So I take it, then, that in addition to the gender surprise, his date is nothing like what you expected?"

"I'd be honoured. *Nothing* is an understatement. I couldn't describe her to you if I tried. I like her though. I think she's good for him."

"Does she have a name?" Kayley asked.

"Actually," Adam replied, "*that* little ditty might be a great indicator of what I'm talking about."

Chapter 22

The third floor of Daleesha's house served as her personal residence. While the apartment conversion was not exactly true to the original architecture of the home's construction, it did manage to maintain the essence: a vague historic period of dark wood panels, satin drapery, regal ceiling medallions, and artistically patterned parquet flooring. The eclectic furnishings shared a common theme of great taste and little else, yet worked well as a whole. One was as likely to be sitting in a Frank Lloyd Wright barrel chair as a bergère. The cohesive genius of the menagerie was all in the placement. Oscar Wilde could have written magnificently self-indulgent passages about the foyer alone.

Henry had helped translate the feeling Daleesha had been hoping to capture into a tangible design. The William IV writing desk that sat in his foyer had been a token of her appreciation for the extensive contribution he made in helping to plan the renovation.

He and Alexandra had arrived at the cocktail party early to provide Daleesha with moral support and to allow Henry time to review the efforts of the caterer. Over the course of their long friendship he had slowly eased into the role of Daleesha's societal counsel.

"You've never met Kayley?" Daleesha asked, after a sip of wine. "I find that so odd. She is Helen's best friend."

Daleesha was standing by the entry to the kitchen, watching Henry wander along the length of her dining room table as he inspected the presentation and quality of the hors d'oeuvres. The caterer had removed the chairs to allow for ease of traffic flow, and Henry had placed them throughout Daleesha's apartment to provide additional seating. In keeping with the casual, self-service mood, the top of the sideboard had been converted into a very extensive bar.

"Helen has had boyfriends come and go before I ever got to meet them," Henry replied while selecting a canapé to sample. "It's not so odd if you think about it. We have little in common and really have no reason to be around each other, except for the marriage between our parents, of course."

"Odd," Daleesha replied.

A young woman peered at Henry from within the kitchen. She was standing to the side of Daleesha, dressed in her white kitchen uniform with her dark hair tucked under a checked beanie.

"Ginger crepes with roasted vegetables and piquant orange sauce," she said in reference to the appetizer that Henry was holding.

He took a bite and nodded with approval. Gratified, the woman disappeared back into the kitchen. Unconvinced, Daleesha waited for the real review.

"A tad too much cayenne," he whispered, "but very passable."

He stepped back from the table. He squinted as if searching for dark spots on a Christmas tree, and circled the table in one final lap before stopping at the makeshift bar and pouring himself a glass of Beaujolais.

"You're going be okay tonight?" Daleesha asked.

"Of course. Why wouldn't I be?"

"Because it's an entire evening dealing with your two hot button issues."

Henry felt slighted by Daleesha's remark and made no attempt to conceal his feelings. He would agree that he could be impassioned, but found her allusion that it was anything more than enthusiasm to be preposterous.

"Anyway," Henry deflected, "Adam seems to like this Kayley woman. A lot. I'm really happy for him."

"Funny," Daleesha said. "At first glance I never would have put the two of them together. Yet they make sense. Like you and Alexandra, only not quite as dramatically so."

"In what way are Alexandra and I dramatically so? The *never have put us together* part or the *make sense* part?"

"Both."

"I admit, not so long ago, if anyone would have told me I'd be as happy as I am with a woman like Alexandra, I would have called them nuts. But here I am."

"I'm glad, Henry," Daleesha replied.

With a loud, sharp whistle Alexandra announced her arrival into the apartment. Henry was amused by the startling affect it had on Daleesha. She was vigilantly disoriented. He was getting used to his live-in guest and had become immune to *some* of her antics.

Alexandra bounced into the room. He could tell that the five-year-old was definitely running the show, with the thousand-year-old nowhere to be seen. Henry cherished the company of the five-year-old. He found her joy to be contagious, as if she was teaching him how to be happy.

"Holy fuck," Alexandra exclaimed. "This place is huge! Like a fuck'n museum!"

She watched Henry's face drop into the familiar denial-of-association, snobbish grimace it would take on whenever she did something that ruffled his sensibilities. Alexandra liked that he was a bit of a princess. She felt that they balanced each other.

"I said *fuck*, didn't I?" Alexandra asked. "I meant *frig*."

"*Fuck* is a perfectly good word," Daleesha said. "I've been known to use it myself from time to time. The museum bit bothered me a little though."

"I only meant in size," Alexandra said. "Not boringness."

"Good. I would fuck'n hate it if my guests thought my place was boring."

Alexandra found the juxtaposition of Daleesha's comment against her own to be weirdly humourous. The word *fuck* had rolled out easily enough, and in no way sounded new or foreign, but it had somehow managed to be cleaned of all its grit, as if decreed by the Queen of England. She suspected that had been Daleesha's intent, and was fairly certain that it was meant as a bit of a chide. Alexandra respected her instantly.

"No home that comes with an indoor sandbox and a play structure in the backyard could possibly be boring," Alexandra replied, while removing her cotton sweater. In the motion, the white T-shirt underneath was drawn up to the cusp of her bosom.

While her hands were in the air and her head was buried inside the bundle of cable-knit, both Henry and Daleesha took a moment to reflect on Alexandra's breasts. Henry's reasons were twofold. Although they had agreed that she would wear a bra for the evening, he was certain that she would renege. This led neatly into the second reason, the one that he would never admit to. He was glad he was right.

Daleesha's reasons were also twofold. For many years she had been of the opinion that Henry was gay. Alexandra's bust, strangely more than the woman herself, was a very cogent indicator that he was not. Her second reason lay somewhere between a critique and awe. She felt that she had just discovered the model for Kayley's comic book heroine, the one with the showgirl legs, wasp-like waist, and the impossibly gravity-defying shelf of cleavage.

"It's decorated like a gentlemen's club up here," Alexandra said, while taking in her surroundings and slipping her arms out of the sweater.

Both Henry and Daleesha were snapped out of their enchantment and became cognizant that they had been gawking.

"Yes, I suppose it is." Daleesha said.

"A really nice one, though," Alexandra said, after tossing her sweater onto a nearby chair. "And, believe me, I've seen my share."

PAIRS

Daleesha made a point to catch Henry's eye and relay her amusement before leaving to the kitchen. Normally the impropriety implied by Alexandra's numerous visits to gentlemen's clubs would have mortified him. Yet it did not. He found only humour in the exchange between her and Daleesha.

"Forget something?" Henry asked Alexandra.

"Your words said bra but your eyes said boobs. You practically begged me not to."

"I begged you not to wear a bra?" he asked.

"Yep," Alexandra said, as she sauntered toward him.

"So it's my fault?" Henry asked, while pouring her a tumbler of Scotch.

"No one's fault," she replied, as he passed the glass to her. "You asked and I agreed. It's the kind of thing couples do."

Henry was becoming flustered by images of her G-string strut that had begun to flash in his mind. Alexandra remained cool. She liked revving him up, keeping his interest, priming the pump before moving their relationship forward.

"I'm not fixated on your breasts, you know," Henry said, with an overtone of guilt, which had surprisingly welled up from a source that he couldn't quite identify.

Alexandra placed her glass on the sideboard, took the hem of her T-shirt in both hands and flashed Henry. His mouth went agape as his eyes popped and he spilled his drink. Daleesha, who had been in the kitchen doorway at the time, retreated without comment. Alexandra lowered her T-shirt and picked up her glass. Henry was staring into space, befuddled, unsure about the reasons behind the efforts of his rapid blinking. He didn't know if he was trying to clear the afterimage or focus it.

"Practically begged," she said.

Chapter 23

Helen stood with Terra in the doorway of her Tudor-style townhouse. They were waving back to Kayley and Adam who were sitting in his idling pickup truck.

"Now?" he asked, through his frozen smile while continuing to exuberantly bid farewell.

"Yes," Kayley said, feeling very unsure about her decision.

When he took hold of the shift arm of the steering wheel, Kayley's apprehension immediately crested. She placed her hand over his, and gestured with a slight upward pressure for him to keep it in park. Adam sighed. Kayley acquiesced, released her grip, and sunk despondently into the seat. She did so speculating that Terra likely had far less separation anxiety than her mother.

"She'll be fine," Adam said, as they drove off.

"It's her first sleepover."

"That's not written in stone. If you change your mind we can always come get Terra. I've even brought cab money if we drink too much at the after-party. And Helen said you could call any time. I've got my cell."

"Helen is so sweet to do this for me," Kayley said. "She would've had fun tonight."

Adam doubted very much that Helen would've had fun. He doubted very much that he was going to have fun. He suspected that Helen had leapt at the opportunity to get out of going to what she had labelled the Lost Boys conference. An evening of educators discussing what Henry referred to as *the crisis of the ever-declining academic performance of boys and the long-term repercussions resulting in their dwindling enrolment in post-secondary institutions* sounded like a yawnfest to Adam. Daleesha's shorter *taking a child's gender into account* didn't help jazz it up for him. Dull was dull.

He really didn't understand the fuss. As a future general contractor, he had no issues with bright, well-educated women working for him as his accountant, his lawyer, his architect, or his structural engineer.

"Yeah," he said. "Helen is a really good friend."

Chapter 24

Prior to the arrival of Daleesha's other guests, Henry had thoroughly nagged Alexandra into putting her sweater back on. She knew he would, and didn't mind. She had achieved the desired outcome.

As the evening progressed, it became ever more apparent to her that the prerequisite for getting an invitation was that the person must be stodgy. She felt herself quickly caked in a mind-numbing, chalky, moth-eaten blanket of dull.

She had slipped away from Henry under the guise of refreshing their drinks when he had begun a discussion concerning a more holistic approach to gender roles. On her way to the bar she passed by shifting pockets of dry academic chatter. To Alexandra, boringness had become as tangible as cobwebs. Phrases such as "gender schematicity is much higher in boys" and "rigid parameter of acceptable characteristics," while being made up of English, and English-sounding, words, were strung together in an intellectual meander to form something quite foreign to her. She was becoming desperate for the arrival of Adam and the chance for a normal conversation. Henry had been too involved in presenting his views to notice Alexandra pacing like a dog needing to be let out.

After refilling Henry's wine glass and pouring herself a shot of Scotch, neat, she focused once again on developments at the party and, to her relief, saw that Adam had arrived with his date, a very beautiful plump woman with curly blond hair. The woman was familiar to Alexandra but she couldn't remember where they had met. Alexandra smiled and, after sip of Scotch, gestured for them to join her.

Kayley recognized Alexandra immediately as being the woman from the park. Accepting the invitation to the bar, Kayley and Adam passed by Henry and the small group to which he was speaking. Adam gave a brief wave.

"That's Henry," Adam explained to Kayley.

Adam noticed that Kayley was fixated on his cousin. He watched her stare for a moment before gently prodding her with his finger.

"I can get you his autograph if you'd like," Adam said.

"Oh, sorry," Kayley replied. "He just looks a lot like someone I knew."

Without interrupting his conversation, Henry winked his acknowledgement as they passed. It was a greeting that reminded Kayley of Gavin, and she found herself entranced by the uncanny resemblance. Henry became ever more distracted by Kayley's interest in him. In short spurts, his gaze shifted to her. She looked away when their eyes finally met.

"Seriously," Adam whispered. "I can give you his number if you'd like."

Kayley glanced at Adam and blushed. She smiled apologetically, shook her head, and slipped her hand into his. Reassured, he brought their clasped hands to his mouth to kiss her fingers.

"That's so sweet," Alexandra said.

"Alexandra, this is Kayley. And Kayley, this is Alexandra. She is Henry's date. They live together."

Both women noticed Adam's tone change from cordial to serious when he clarified Alexandra's status, which left them feeling awkward in each other's company. In prelude to her escape, Alexandra brought the glass of wine she had poured up to eye level.

"I should get this to Henry," she said. "I'll be right back."

Alexandra moved backwards through the crowd, continuing to face them as she departed. A question had popped into her head and she wanted to be sure it was asked before she forgot.

"If either one of you know what *didactic* means," she said, "let me know when I get back. I heard Daleesha mumble the word to herself when she was eavesdropping on Henry's little talk over there."

Alexandra turned around but, in order to finish her conversation, peered back over her shoulder while continuing to walk away.

"The *ass* part I get," she said. "It's just the particular specialization that I've never heard of."

Kayley laughed and watched her weave around people until discreetly merging into the group that Henry was talking to. She found Alexandra to be a captivating person, sexy, fun, and maybe a little dangerous.

"Men must just fall at her feet," Kayley said.

"She has definitely piqued Henry's interest," Adam said, unsure if she had expected his reply.

Henry appreciatively took the glass of wine offered by Alexandra and stood aside to welcome her back into the group. She immediately felt the scratchy tedium, but held a brave front.

"We, as a society," Henry said to the group, "need to deal with human rights and move away from the silos of special interests such as gay rights, minority rights, and feminism."

Alexandra couldn't even force herself to be interested, so her mind roamed. Panning the room, she noticed Daleesha slowly working her way closer. Daleesha had overheard Henry's trigger word, feminism, and had become concerned that he was about to step up onto his soapbox.

"Relevant to the situation at hand," Henry said. "The myopia of feminism has had an odd yet, given human nature, predictable outcome. It has been my experience that women who by their career aspirations are feminists can be quite sexist when it comes to their opinions on men. One would expect that women who struggle against *type* would be more sensitive to gender pigeonholing. Yet they have quite simplistic views regarding men, granting a much narrower range of occupations, dress, and behaviour than they afford to women."

Daleesha wasn't catching every word but the little shrapnel snippets that did manage to fly her way alarmed her. Although she normally found Henry to be a very charming and eloquent individual, when it came to the topics of education and gender equality, all his pleasant objectivity seemed to go up in a flash fire. She had known from the start that mixing the two in one evening was risky.

"With men under-represented in the teaching profession," Henry said, "and with women holding such views, the impact on a young male cannot help but be less than positive. Suicide rates, alcoholism, and drug abuse are all much higher for boys relative to girls. Boys are not as happy in school as girls and are therefore less engaged."

"Henry is very passionate about his students," Daleesha said, as she joined in the conversation.

She was hoping to offset Henry's alarmist bent. With women in positions of power and influence on the school board and in the teachers' union, Daleesha didn't want to risk him alienating their potentially greatest supporters.

"For the most part, boys are doing fine," she said. "As a matter of fact, there is greater academic variance within the population of boys than there is between boys and girls. It just appears that when things go bad, they seem to go extremely bad for boys. Part of the problem facing young men, as Henry alluded to, is the lack of an older male presence in the form of a mentor. Many of these young men are growing up without the active presence of a father."

Alexandra's interest was reeled back into the circle of onlookers. Not because of the topic, but because of the arrival of Daleesha. Henry's manner changed instantly in the tiniest of details that would be overlooked by those that didn't know him. He wasn't quite as relaxed.

"Other boards have introduced a mentoring program," Daleesha said. "I think that would be good place for us to start."

Alexandra concluded that there was a silent war of wills going on between Daleesha and Henry. Although they agreed on the surface, they were arguing in the undercurrent. Daleesha's coolness was not intended to be complementary to his passion, but rather an opposition to it. She was the water on his flame, and steam was everywhere. Alexandra found it fascinating to watch. A *girl*-fight at a calibre she had never before been privileged to witness. She was surprised by just how feisty he was. Alexandra felt a sense of pride.

"Please understand," Henry said. "I am not holding feminism to task for what is happening in our schools, but there is partial cause here. Twenty years ago it was the girls that were underperforming. Then accommodations were made—without considering the impact on the boys. The great social experiment that held gender to be learned has failed. Boys and girls are inherently different and they need to be treated as such."

"Ultimately," Daleesha amended, "we need to understand that the genders are different and that different approaches are required in their education. Both would benefit."

"Exactly," Henry slipped in. "The best possible situation would be to segregate them. Not necessarily by schools, but certainly by classroom. They have different requirements that can only be fully addressed in segregated classes."

"You have got a long road ahead of you, Henry, on that one," a portly man said.

His blue twill suit hugged him like a sausage casing. For reasons not clear to Alexandra, he reminded her of a penguin, a navy blue penguin with shiny black Cole Haan feet.

"Think of the cost of having separate classrooms for boys and girls," he added.

Henry's brow knitted. He was noticeably irritated, which resulted in Daleesha becoming visibly concerned. Alexandra, while not knowing exactly what was to come, sensed that she should intervene. She looped arms with Henry's as she addressed the group.

"If I could just pull Henry away for a second," Alexandra said. "I promise I'll set him free shortly."

She guided him in the direction of Adam and Kayley, who stood, drinks in hand, beside the bar. Although Henry was perplexed by Alexandra's actions, he did not protest, and followed along with catatonic interest. His thoughts were still focused on his conversation, and in particular, on the money-centric man that he deemed to be an atavistic cretin.

"I thought you might want to meet Kayley," Alexandra said.

"Kayley?" he asked.

"Adam's girlfriend."

Before Henry fully appreciated the close proximity of his cousin and his date, the need for a final parting volley to the cretin became too much for him. He absolutely needed to vent.

"Cost!" Henry rasped, in a low voice to Alexandra. "I know. Let's continue to alternate in the bias of our teaching methods. We've ruined a generation of men, so I guess the women are up again."

Alexandra cleared her throat in an effort to draw Henry's attention to the presence of Adam and Kayley. He greeted them with a hastily slapped-together cordial deportment. Adam had no clue about the reason behind the ranting and he had even less interest. He wanted to sort out Kayley's fascination with his cousin.

"Henry," Adam said, "this is Kayley. Apparently you remind her of someone."

"Really?" Henry asked her. "Anyone special?"

"Just an old boyfriend."

Three out of the four regretted her candour instantly. Adam just stared.

Chapter 25

Kayley didn't find Adam's jealousy threatening, and in the absence of concern, was open to accepting the flattery of it.

"It was years ago," she said, with a casual, defusing indifference. "I broke it off."

Henry's initial silent rebuttal to his cousin's adolescent snit was a patronizing eye roll. Meeting Adam's stare, Henry gave a lustreless smile as he put his arm across Alexandra's shoulders. She, in response, gave an appearance of deep contentment and put her arm across Henry's back. Their staged choreography melted into a natural fit, and neither wanted to move away.

"We've met before?" Alexandra asked Kayley.

"In the park."

Kayley discreetly scrutinized Alexandra's beauty, searching for flaws and hoping to find none. She had never before been so close to such a remarkably attractive woman and she wanted it to be real. No tricks, nothing fake or manufactured—a living, breathing poem celebrating the power, the grace, and the aesthetic of the female form.

"Of course, you and that little redheaded girl," Alexandra replied, oblivious to Kayley's focused but surreptitious interest. "She's adorable. Your daughter?"

The amorous affects of the Scotch got the better of Alexandra and she moved her hand down past Henry's waist and into his back pocket while she spoke. He was very cognizant of the position change and offered no protest.

"Yes, she is," Kayley said. "Her name is Terra. She's just turned four."

"You're so lucky."

Henry felt himself being gently cupped by Alexandra's hand. As nice as he found the flirtatious overtones, he enjoyed the playfulness more. Everything that had been so cumbersome and complicated with other women was effortless with Alexandra. Yet he was hesitant to move forward, toward the nearly inescapable, looming romance.

"I feel lucky," Kayley said. "Terra seemed to know you. But I couldn't figure out from where."

"That was the first time I'd seen either of you."

Adam noticed Kayley's sudden pining. He pulled his cellphone out of his pocket and held it out for her to take. At first she was surprised by the offer but quickly grasped that her parental sentiment was readily apparent. She mouthed *thank you* as she took the phone from his hand.

"Do you have any children?" Kayley asked Alexandra.

The question stung Alexandra. The feelings surprised her. She had thought she had come to terms with the practical reality. Alexandra rationalized the melancholy as being the result of the amplifying effects of alcohol.

"No," she said. "That's not really an option for me."

"Sorry," Kayley said.

"Don't be. There is always adoption."

Alexandra's comments left Henry curious and the life-weariness concerned him. Her flame burned a little lower. Henry sensed that the thousand-year-old had decided to make an appearance at the party after all. Although he cherished the woman's insights and strength, he wanted the return of the five-year-old. The other guests would soon be leaving and then it would be about just enjoying the company of new and close friends. The party to come was about having fun. With his arm still outstretched across the top of her back, Henry squeezed the ball of her shoulder to get her attention.

"You can always help me raise Adam," he said. She looked at him, appreciative of his comforting.

"So, Alexandra, what's Aunt Henry like to live with, anyway?" Adam asked.

She laughed at the remark. She had believed her assessment of Henry had been a private matter, and uniquely her own. The astonishment of finding out that it was a shared and likely common opinion magnified the humour of the question. After a contagious series of staccato snorts that chimed out a wonderful melody for Henry, she managed to compose herself and respond.

"Wonderful," Alexandra said, in a stiff robotic voice while staring blankly. "Just wonderful. Absolutely wonderful. So very, very wonderful."

Henry was happy to see her laugh, even if he had to bear a little teasing to draw her out. He found himself observing the moment. He took pleasure in being around her, in watching her.

"Well," he said. "Thanks to my house guest here, I don't have to worry about cleaning the bedroom floor anymore since she has graciously covered it with her clothing."

Within Henry's back pocket Alexandra fingers clamped down as her reprisal. His only acknowledgement was a brief glance in her direction and a barely detectable smile that drew her in completely. She swung around to face him, and they kissed. She stepped back to rediscover Adam and Kayley. Both were grinning. One of Adam's eyebrows was arched.

"The bedroom is our shared change room," Alexandra explained. "I'm on the couch."

"Uh-huh," Adam replied.

Chapter 26

Adam and Alexandra had relegated themselves to the sidelines of the cocktail party. They were sitting at either end of a tufted, black leather couch watching others mingle, with particular interest on Kayley and Henry, who both appeared to be entirely in their element.

The thinning group of guests had broken off into small pockets of conversation. The evening's topic had given way to current events and subjects of personal interest. Kayley and Henry stood together discussing literature with a high school principal. She was a thin, silver-haired woman that Adam thought looked rather bookish. Earlier in the evening she had been introduced to them as Ms. Lacelle.

Alexandra's feet were perched on the edge of her seat cushion with her legs pulled up against her chest. She was using a knee as the coaster for her nearly empty highball of Scotch. Adam was slouched against the armrest, with his feet on the floor and his legs apart. He had plugged his index finger into his beer bottle and was spiralling it like a gentle centrifuge. Onlookers would be tempted to conclude that both were in detention. Unbearable ennui had anesthetised them.

They watched Kayley wet her lips and heard as she cleared her throat. Before speaking, she drew in a long, relaxed breath through her nose and held up her glass in salutation.

"To quote William Wordsworth," she said.

"With many a fond embrace, while joy runs high,
And goblets crown the proud festivity,
Instil thy subtle poison, and inspire,
At every touch, an unsuspected fire."

"Does she do that a lot?" Alexandra asked Adam, while watching Kayley.

"Burst into spontaneous poetry? I'm starting to think so, after a couple of drinks anyway. I think it's cute."

"It is kind of cute. Is she tanked?"

"Nah. Just artsy."

Alexandra brought her curled legs to rest sideways on the seat cushion when she turned to face Adam. In response, he pivoted his head on the back of the couch in her direction. While she took a sip from her glass he waited on the question that the position change suggested was coming.

"Do you think she is smarter than you?" Alexandra asked, after lowering her drink and resting it on top of her outer thigh.

"In a lot of things, none of them practical. Like, I think she has memorized every poem ever written. Published or not. Do you think Henry is smarter than you?"

"Same thing as you," she said before lowering her feet to the floor. Alexandra stood and then explained during her departure, "I need a top up."

PAIRS

She finished her drink as she walked in the direction of Henry. Her initial intent had been a short visit but as she drew closer the conversation became more audible to her and was a motivation to veer away. *The elegant economy of Jane Austen's plot* diverted Alexandra straight toward the bar. Before passing by Henry's little discussion group, she got his attention with an animated wave and then extended an offer to refill his glass by a mimed sipping gesture. Without breaking stride she took hold of his extended glass and made her escape as *the limited scope of Jane Austen's works* nipped at her heels.

Henry found the pace of Alexandra's exodus rather entertaining. He had a sense for the reason, having previously noticed that both she and Adam, giving the impression of sulking children in the back seat of the family car, had taken refuge on a distant couch.

Upon remembering their brooding, he turned to his cousin and was met with an inert stare. Henry found it almost as entertaining as Alexandra's recent harrowing escape. He excused himself from the conversation and headed toward Adam.

"You two look like you're having a blast," Henry said as he approached.

"We decided that we are double-dating at the very next monster truck rally that rolls into town," Adam replied. "You guys owe us. Big time."

"Fair enough," Henry replied.

Adam popped his finger in and out of the beer bottle as he watched Henry park himself at the opposite end of the couch. They both sat quietly, listening to the one-note pan pipe of Adam's lager and watched the respective women in each other's life.

"I like Alexandra," Adam said. "The two of you seem good together."

"Thanks. I like Kayley. She's very smart and very well spoken."

"She's great. Any further than first base?"

"Second," Henry said, "...*ish*"

"Second-*ish*?"

"To be honest, I'm really hesitant about moving in that direction."

"Why?" Adam asked.

"Sex has a habit of turning great friends into girlfriends," Henry said. "And I don't want to lose what I've got going with Alexandra."

Adam's puzzlement was obvious but Henry was not in the mood to elaborate. He felt it was neither the time nor the place to share his theories on dating.

"You?" Henry asked. "Have you kissed her yet?"

"We had a grand session which featured a little groping but nothing more. I like the way things are going. It seems adult to just date for a bit."

When Alexandra was finished at the bar she was surprised to find Henry sitting on the couch and talking to Adam. She became a little concerned that she was about to lose her party buddy to the creeping dull of *Jane's scoping plots* and felt a compelling need to rescue him. Not wanting to offend Henry, she decided that the easiest way to liberate Adam was to ask him to participate in something she knew Henry would not be interested in. While returning to the couch she was trying to recall if she had spotted a pool table during her tour of the mansion.

"There is a play structure outside," she said to Adam, while handing Henry his glass of wine. "Want to join me?"

"A play structure?"

"There's a tire swing," she said, as she extended her hand to him.

Adam's focus alternated between Alexandra and Henry. She sensed his hesitation and tried to win her cause with a light-hearted but pleading smile. Henry loved watching her weave her charm. He gave his consent to Adam with a casual shrug of his shoulders.

"We can spin each other," she said. Her eyes widened at the thought of such a magical possibility.

Chapter 27

It was an overcast and starless evening. If not for the light glowing through the windows of the house, Adam and Alexandra would have been in total darkness when they walked out onto the flagstone patio on their way to the fenced-in park of the backyard. In the diffused light, the distant play structure looked like the remnant framework of an abandoned beach shanty.

"Oh neat," she said, after they descended the steps to the lawn. "There's a pole. I didn't see it from the house."

Alexandra's glee in her discovery reminded Adam of the boys' night out when he first saw her. Her act had fascinated him. Graceful and powerful, she had been part exotic dancer, part erotic gymnast, and part seductive force of nature. The cauldron of ferment coursing through his bloodstream had brought a quaint succinctness to his praise that evening. *Fuck'n* a*wesome!*

"If I recall, you're an amazing pole dancer," Adam said. "Holding yourself upside-down with your legs like that. It was cool! I'm not really into the naked dancer scene, but that was definitely worth the price of admission."

"*Was* an amazing pole dancer," she said, and then tapped the inside of her leg with the palm of her hand. "Lots of inner-thigh strength. Why aren't you into exotic dancers?"

"I bet you have a ton of inner thigh strength. No disrespect, it's just that I don't know what watching a woman dance naked on stage has to do with me actually getting laid."

"I can crack a walnut between my knees," she said, as they manoeuvred through a large swing set. "Getting laid? Valid. I guess if you dance naked at any place that offers a businessman's lunch you can't call it art."

"A walnut? Get out!"

"It's true," Alexandra confirmed proudly. "I put a walnut between two blocks of wood and squeeze."

"That's freakish!" he responded. "You should've put that in your act."

"I did once, but it wasn't quite the hit I thought it would be. Apparently men don't get horned up by a woman crushing nuts between her legs."

Adam visualized the exploding walnut and the rifled discharge of shell fragments blown in all manner of trajectory. It was an image that held a surprisingly visceral association to his anatomy. He flinched.

"Yeah," he acknowledged. "I could see that."

Liquor logic seeped into Alexandra as she stared at the pole. She took hold, tested its stability and recalled her nights on stage. For all that had been bad about that world, the one thing she felt had been very good was her performance. Her arm coiled around the pole and she slid her hand along the cool, damp metal. Alexandra knew, was positively certain, that she could swing herself upside-down right then and there.

"Want to see me upside-down?" she asked.

"Not naked. But yeah, it's so cool."

"I wasn't planning on naked," she said, as she began to remove her shoes.

Adam took her at her word until she unfastened the clasp on her jeans, and dropped them to her ankles. She stepped out of the denim bundle and, with ballerina poise, lifted it out of the way by the tip of her toe.

"Skin has a better grip than cloth," she explained.

Alexandra turned from the pole to find Adam bent over and taking an up-close gander at her butt. She was about to smack him when she recalled that tomorrow was her laundry day.

"You know you want it," she said.

"No I don't!" he protested, as he snapped upright. "I'm nuts about Kayley. And you're with my cousin. I was just trying to read your underwear."

PAIRS

They blinked at each other. Alexandra allowed for his initial defensiveness to subside and then gave him a moment to connect the dots.

"And your underwear says: *You know you want it*. I'm up to speed now."

Neither had noticed the silhouette of a woman in the third-storey window of the dining room. They could not have guessed that she had been witness to Alexandra removing her pants and casting them aside. Adam's sudden fixated interest had not escaped her either. She watched Alexandra take hold of the pole before her legs sprung into a scissor kick that spun her upside-down as her feet went into the air. Her top slid down her torso during the motion until finally draping over her head and exposing her inverted breasts, which sent stupefying rays directly in Adam's brain, rendering him useless.

What was not evident from the dining room window was the reason for the misfired execution. The metal was greased with dew and Alexandra's hands slipped down in their positioning, which threw off her aim. Her leg smacked into the pole. Adam jolted from his captivation and moved to catch the ricocheting limbs but found his head engulfed between her thighs. They twisted sideways and hit the ground. Dazed, Adam had landed between Alexandra's straddled legs, face down in her panties.

"I know both of them very well," Henry said, as he moved beside Kayley for a clearer view of the events in the yard. "And in spite of the overwhelming circumstantial evidence, I can assure you that what you have witnessed is nothing more than the outcome of some kind of childish bet."

Kayley waited until she saw evidence that Adam and Alexandra were not hurt before slowly stepping back from the window to respond to Henry.

"She's quite nimble."

Chapter 28

When Henry opened the French doors leading out to the backyard patio, he heard Alexandra and Adam before he saw them. They were both in comical hysterics. He strolled onto the lawn in the direction of their laughter. At the play structure Henry found them sitting in the sand. Adam's legs were crossed and Alexandra's legs were stretched out in front of her. She had yet to put her pants back on.

He shared vicariously in the levity, while he waited for them to realize that they had an audience. After becoming aware of his presence, Alexandra looked up and rallied her composure. She stood and brushed the sand off. With the conclusion of her snorts, Adam also became aware of Henry and he, too, rose to his feet.

"It's not what it appears to be, Henry," she said.

"I believe you," Henry replied.

"I swear," Adam said.

"I believe you," Henry repeated. "But the two of you may want to smooth things over with Kayley, and maybe Daleesha."

"You are the best girlfriend ever," Alexandra said, as she slipped into her jeans. "I'm serious. Ever."

"Kayley?" Adam asked, feeling apprehensive. "Why do I need to smooth things over?"

"She saw everything," Henry said, while pointing up to the dining room window.

"Well, nothing happened," Adam responded, defensively. "Right, Alexandra?"

"Right," she agreed, as she put on her shoes. "Except that I did take off my pants, and you did stare at my butt, and I did expose my breasts, and then you did do a face plant into my crotch."

Adam was motionless while he tried to fully digest events from an onlooker's perspective. Alexandra walked over to Henry and, with great exuberance, hung her arms off his shoulders.

"I am a man, you know," Henry said. He knew she wasn't calling him her girlfriend out of malice, but the mislabelling perturbed him.

"I know," Alexandra said. "But you're also a girl."

"Why do you keep saying that?"

"Because it's true," she said before kissing him.

"What do you mean it's true?"

The pieces came together for Adam in a painful leap of maturity. His head dropped, his eyes closed, and he let out a long exhale that fell, in pitch and agony, between a sigh and a groan. Adam understood that it really didn't matter that nothing had happened. He was alone with a former stripper, watching her pole dance, while his likely soon to be ex-girlfriend was at the same party. He groaned a second time.

"Okay, Henry," Alexandra said. "Name three things that a woman would do for you on a perfect date."

The question struck Henry as peculiar, but he was willing to indulge Alexandra. He thought about the dates he had in his life. He sifted out the best and wove together a theme of consideration that he refined before answering.

"That's easy," Henry replied. "She'd wear a summer dress—nothing fussy or overdone, but nice. She'd make dinner—again, nothing too fancy but something obviously thought out. And she wouldn't ask me to help clean up afterwards. That's just uncouth."

Alexandra had suspected that the focus of Henry's answer would be on the romance and not the sex. However, she had not been prepared for the degree of her accuracy. And it concerned her. Alexandra's thrill became tempered with scepticism. There was a small voice inside her wondering if he was intentionally saying the things he suspected she wanted to hear. She remained staring at Henry with wonder and suspicion. It was his growing confusion over her long stare that finally gave Alexandra confidence in his sincerity, and her attention switched happily to Adam.

"And Adam, could you please name three things that would make a perfect date for you."

He raised his head and looked at Alexandra. His concerns were not completely off of Kayley but he found the question intriguing, so his thoughts blended. The fantasy date that he imagined for himself had a face. A beautiful, blue-eyed, and pale-skinned face framed in blond curls. And, of course, there was that incredibly voluptuous figure to go with it.

"Okay," Adam said. "But what is said at the stripper pole stays at the stripper pole. She shows up naked. She brings beer. She initiates sex."

Alexandra looked back at Henry and after shrugging her shoulders, sauntered back toward the house.

"I'll talk to Kayley," she said.

Henry watched her walk away. He was reminded of his high school debating coach who had continually drilled into the team the importance of proof. *He who asserts must prove.* Or in the case at hand, *she* who asserts must prove. Henry finally managed his reply when she had reached the steps up to the patio.

"That has nothing to do with me being a girl," he called out to her. "It has to do with maturity."

"Dude," Adam said.

"Not a word," Henry replied, as he spun to face his cousin.

"Dude!"

"Nada!"

"You are such a girl!"

"Not you, too."

Adam walked over to Henry, put his arm across his shoulders and turned with him toward the house in time to see Alexandra disappear through the doors.

"Look cuz," Adam said. "She is good for you. She's what you need and she is sane in all the important ways. And I will deny ever saying this, but she has a body that should be insured by Lloyd's of London. If she wants to think of you as a cocker spaniel to help frame you in her head, I'd run with it if I were you. Focus on the important things. She is crazy about you."

PAIRS

Henry thought fondly about Alexandra, appreciating that she was not calling his orientation or his gender into question. She was simply packaging him in terms that helped her to understand who he was. No woman had ever before cared enough, or respected him enough as a person, to make the effort. Any misgivings about a future with her, all second-guessing, vanished.

He looked at Adam and nodded. Henry knew his cousin was right and decided that he was not going to let himself get caught up in semantics when the bigger picture brought him such happiness.

"Adam," Henry opened.

"Yeah?"

"I am in love with her."

"I know," Adam replied, happy to have his suspicions confirmed.

"So when I point something out, it's not that I'm speaking badly of her."

"What?"

"She means well."

"Heart of gold."

"But she can be very matter-of-fact," Henry explained. "Not one to buffer things. Pretty much direct thought-to-speech."

"And?"

"And you may want to find Kayley and explain things *before* Alexandra does."

Henry fell into a sympathetic silence, biding his time until the significance of his advice fully registered with Adam. Henry's wait wasn't long.

"Oh shit."

For Adam, there was something inherently unsettling about two women having a conversation involving him. From his personal experience, one way or the other, whether friends or foes, they end up sharing everything, absolutely *everything*.

He was fairly certain that Alexandra would eventually get around to telling Kayley about knowing him from the strip club and how much he liked her act. In response, Kayley would inform Alexandra that while her head had been buried inside her top, he had taken total advantage of the opportunity and just stared like a drooling pubescent. As an aside to his concerns, this struck him as a form of entrapment. His defence: there is much that is autopilot about being a man.

"I'm sure nothing will be said that you can't grovel out of," Henry teased.

Chapter 29

"Are you awake?" Alexandra whispered.

"Yes," Kayley said.

They lay on their respective sides of the king-sized bed in Daleesha's guest room. Both were staring up into the blackness. Although Alexandra's thoughts were on Henry, she was enjoying Kayley's company in the bed. As a young girl, she had never been to a slumber party. Alexandra breathed in Kayley's delicate floral scent. Even though the fragrance reminded her of baby powder, Alexandra found it pleasantly alluring. It was pleasurable having a quiet feminine presence beside her, and she wondered what it would be like if they were to kiss. She rolled on her side, toward Kayley.

"You and I are good about Adam, eh?" Alexandra asked.

"Very much so."

Kayley was too charmed by Alexandra to be upset with her. She thought Alexandra's sincere recounting adorable in its innocence. She wanted to share with Alexandra the gratitude she felt, but believed it could be misconstrued as a dig. She wondered how she could possibly relay the amount of confidence she felt in her relationship with Adam as a result of the events at the play structure. Kayley marvelled that Adam had declared that he was nuts for her. What was even more incredible to her was that he had done so in the presence of Alexandra's perfect, half-naked body. She was the most charismatic and stunning woman Kayley had ever been around. Alexandra was her first female crush.

"Have you slept with Adam yet?"

"No. You and Henry?"

"Nope. It's strange. We share his apartment and I was fine with me just sleeping on the couch. But now that I'm here and kind of separated from him, I really miss him."

"It's not so odd."

"Would you be insulted if I left?"

"Not at all."

"I'd like it to just be Henry and me. Would you mind if Adam came in here?"

Kayley thought about Adam lying next to her in the darkness. She wanted to be in his arms and work her fingers through his chest hair. She knew if he joined her they would very likely move beyond the caresses they had been sharing. If that was ever to happen, she wanted him to take the first steps. Kayley wanted to be absolutely assured of his desire for her.

"No, I don't mind. But you can't send him in. He has to want to come in."

"So if he wants to come in, you'd let him?"

"Yes, but he has to want to."

"Like, if he sees his opportunity and comes to you?"

"Exactly."

"I'm sure he will."

Alexandra was elated and slipped out from under the covers. She sat on the edge of the bed, but hesitated. Kayley felt a sudden movement on the mattress as Alexandra repositioned herself onto her hands and knees, then prowled lasciviously toward her like a stalking panther. She found the motion seductive and erotic. Kayley was certain that she knew the reason for Alexandra's approach and lay in anticipation. The sensual embrace of another woman was something that Kayley felt she should have crossed off her to-do list long ago.

Alexandra was completely unprepared for Kayley's eager reception. She felt fingers weave through her hair and draw her closer. Alexandra let herself be guided down to the mattress, where she was laid on her back as Kayley leaned over her and caressed her face while moving closer. Their lips touched and then kneaded passionately together into a churning conduit for exploring tongues. Kayley was surprised how swiftly her arousal grew. In hungry breaths their nostrils filled with the other's scent. Fingers traced gently along whiskerless skin and through soft, thick hair. Alexandra's wanted to consume Kayley and be consumed by her. Neither had any sense of the length of time that had passed when Kayley moved aside.

"Holy crap," Alexandra exclaimed, as she sat up. "You are one hot and steamy French-necking momma! I didn't see that one coming."

"Shh," whispered Kayley, as she rolled onto her back. "Me neither."

"You, like, hopped right into the driver's seat."

"I know," Kayley boasted.

Alexandra took hold of Kayley's hand. Sensual without being sexual, an intimate and intensely profound moment had come and gone between them and they both felt fortunate for the bond it had created.

"I'll be going now," Alexandra whispered.

"Okay," Kayley replied. "But remember, Adam has to come in by his own accord."

"You seduce me like wanton dominatrix and now you're all girly?"

"Who says that I won't seduce him like a wanton dominatrix? He just has to come to me."

"Ah. You like to draw your lovers in with your feminine wiles. I'm going to have get me some of those."

They laughed.

Chapter 30

A small Tiffany-inspired lamp provided the only light in the living room, where Henry and Adam had settled in for the night. Adam was asleep on an air mattress at the foot the extended Hide-A-Bed where Henry lay watching Alexandra, curious but without comment, as she quietly exited the bedroom.

She walked resolutely over to Adam and nudged him with her foot. When he failed to respond, she tapped against his ankle with her toes. It was an action that she repeated, with escalating force, until the desired effect was achieved.

"What?" Adam grumbled.

"Kayley and I were having a real great make out session, and it was hot and all, but I think I can speak for the both us when I say that we are so way more into men. So I hope you don't mind if I lie down with Henry."

Groggy, but rocketing awake, Adam sat up and blinked at Alexandra. He wasn't exactly sure what to make of the news, but managed a quick fantasy involving Kayley's breasts.

"I guess what I'm getting at is that I wouldn't want you to feel like a third wheel out here with Henry and me sleeping together."

Henry had taken an interest in the events unfolding at the foot of his bed and he propped himself up on his pillows to get a better view. He watched Adam's attention swoop away from Alexandra toward the guest room door. He was a five-year-old on Christmas morning.

He stared at Alexandra, seeking confirmation. She saw his confusion and yearning. Her eyes slyly directed Adam to the bedroom, and then returned with calculated indifference.

"Totally up to you, my friend," she said.

Adam threw the blankets off and stood. From his angle on the bed Henry had a full appreciation for the rigid measure of his cousin's anticipation, since it was on the verge of breaching his boxer shorts. With singular purpose, Adam passed by Alexandra as if she was a piece of furniture.

"Hey, mister happy pants," she whispered.

Adam stopped to reply. "If you think I am the least bit embarrassed by my erection, I am not."

"All I was going to say was don't charge in there. Knock. Of course you may have to stand sideways to the door to reach it."

"I wasn't going to charge in there."

"Yes you were."

"Okay. Yes I was. Thanks."

After Adam disappeared into the bedroom, Alexandra was surprised to find Henry wide awake and smiling. It wasn't a welcoming smile. It was the practiced communication of a teacher's disapproval. She made her way to the edge of the mattress, then crawled up, unsure of what was bothering him.

"You're making the rounds tonight," he said, with intentional traces of jealousy in his tone. Henry wanted to ensure that his displeasure was unmistakable. As wonderful as Alexandra was, he would not be on any sort of roster.

She grinned sheepishly. When Alexandra reached the top of the bed, she sat beside Henry, slouched against the backrest of the couch, and put her arm across his shoulders.

"She was the appetizer, you're the meal."

"Smooth."

His coolness troubled her. She had thought that her encounter with Kayley would be erotic news. But Alexandra reminded herself that she was with Henry because he was not a typical man. He was the girlfriend with the male body. Then she understood her transgression. She had cheated on him. A fact was a fact.

"I'm sorry, Henry. It won't ever happen again."

"Is she good at kissing?" he asked.

"Henry, I was foolish. Lying there with Kayley felt like my first slumber party. It was kind of fun. Female fun. I just got caught up. We both did."

PAIRS

They heard Kayley giggle and looked in the direction of bedroom. Its implication was not lost on Alexandra. At first she smiled and then thought of the discussion that still had to happen with Henry, the one that she had been putting off. Her avoidance had been made easier by sleeping on the couch at his apartment. However, as a result of lying with him, she no longer wanted to continue that arrangement. Although Alexandra knew her request would be strange, she was not anxious. Perhaps for the first time in her life, Alexandra was emotionally safe.

"Henry, I'd like to talk about something. It's a little awkward, because I know it's weird."

"You can talk to me about anything," he consoled, while cuddling up against her body.

"I was molested as a child," she explained. "One of the consequences is that I never want to be penetrated. Anywhere. Ever. Well, except tongue-in-mouth. But otherwise, no penetration of any sort."

Henry glanced up at her as he thought about her willingness to make herself vulnerable and about her honesty. Neither surprised him, yet he was still amazed by the offhand bravery. From their short history together, Henry recognized that she needed to share at her own pace, so questions about her childhood remained respectfully unasked.

Alexandra became a little disconcerted when Henry, lost in his admiration, didn't immediately respond. She felt a need to elaborate. "Don't get me wrong, I like sex. Actually, I really like sex. Just without penetration."

"That doesn't bother me at all," Henry responded, as he moved himself up to eye level and kissed her. At the best of times, intercourse was the least of Henry's concerns for a healthy relationship. And in the context of being with the woman he thought he'd never find, it meant even less. "I don't ever want to make you feel uncomfortable."

She was without pretence or judgement. Her candour made it easy for Henry to open himself up to Alexandra and share his own needs, which he privately conceded might also be viewed as peculiar.

"I also have a request of you," he said.

"Name it."

"I think I know what you mean when you call me your girlfriend. However, I also have a definition of girlfriend and it is slightly different. Girlfriends don't date. They get dated. They see themselves as the date-*ees* and boyfriends as the date-*ors* who do the dat*ing*. I want someone who is fully participating in the process. I want a boyfriend."

"With boobs," Alexandra amended.

"You get the picture."

"I'm living the picture."

Daleesha had been lying awake listening to the shuffling of bedmates and was feeling very self-congratulatory. She had been aware that neither couple had made that final step toward being partners. Assuming the role of matchmaker, she had reasoned that the fastest way to get them to come together was to separate them and add a touch of the forbidden. However, she had also needed to go to the washroom for nearly twenty minutes and was happy to hear the activity settle down. When she opened her door Daleesha heard both couples talking. She stopped in the hall to eavesdrop. Through the door of the guest room she could hear Adam's voice. Most of his words were indiscernible, but a few that were more energetic and jocular came through with great clarity.

"These seem real fun. What do they do? Never mind. I'm sure I'll figure it out."

Kayley's laughter faded into a giggle and then a soft, welcoming moan. Pleased with herself, Daleesha was about to enter the bathroom when she overheard the tail end of the conversation in the living room.

"So if you will be my boyfriend, I will be your girlfriend," Henry said.

There was nothing to think about for Alexandra. As far as she was concerned, he was merely verifying the obvious.

"Deal," she replied. Her initial thought was to shake hands, but decided that a kiss was a more appropriate way to *seal the deal*.

Quietly, Daleesha had begun to close the door, feeling very philosophic about the many forms that love could take. She was certain that the discussion was over, but she waited when she heard Henry speak again.

"You know the saying that there is more than one lid to every pot?"

"Yeah. Kind of like there are plenty of fish in the sea."

"Exactly. Well, I don't think that applies to us," he said. "I think you and I only have one shot, and this is it."

"I think you're right, Henry. Oh, and that penetration thing. It only applies to me. If you'd like me to penetrate you, I've no issues."

And with that, Daleesha slowly closed the door.

Part IV

Riddles that I marvel
Impossible with detail
Change should I hesitate

Chapter 31

Kay, I had the biggest laugh yesterday at Carver's. Biting-cold walk over, let me tell you, quite the peregrination indeed. Where did the summer go? Seems like I just get the screens back on the windows and poof, autumn.

Where was I again? Oh yeah, my big laugh. Mary and Joseph aren't I prone to divagation. Last week's word, divagation. Good one. Fitting. And there I go again. I'm sorry, dear, back to it.

As I was starting to say, Carver's cousin, Pete, cousin on his mother's side I believe, was over. He'd come from the mainland for a visit. For a week I think he said. Good Lord, Kay, he's a funny man. And can he spin a yarn. The things that have happened to him, well, I just hope he's keeping a diary for posterity's sake.

When I arrived he was just starting to talk about a recent trip to PEI. Good people on the island. Never been myself. The way Pete tells it, he found himself on a long flat stretch of road with nothing but fields and scattered houses on either side. It was a particularly clear day. Off in the distance he could see an approaching car, nothing more than a dot really when he first laid eyes on it. He said they must've been headed toward each other for close to twenty minutes. The dot, he said, slowly grew into an old pickup truck.

As they were about to pass each other, the truck swerved right in front of him. Out of nowhere, the other fellow just up and turned into Pete's lane. Needless to say that Pete was not expecting it, so he crashed right into him. No one was hurt, but the vehicles had seen better days. While the two of them were walking around the wreckage, Pete said he asked the man why he did it. Why on earth would he cut in front of him like that?

The man looks at Pete, all flustered-like, and says to him, "you should'a know'd I'd be turn'n into my own driveway."

Well, at that point, Carver and I were already busting a gut. Pete looks at the two of us, took a swig of beer, and then he says, in that droll Torontonian accent, "obviously."

The story reminded me of your mother, Kay. Bless her soul. The time Carl Fitzer was in line behind us at the cash at Woolworths and asked your mother how she knew that his wife would have a boy on March third. Like your mother's gift was suddenly a surprise to him. She smartened him up though.

"I had a dream," she says, "of a little blond boy. Sometimes there was one boy but sometimes there were two. So I knew that he'd be born under the sign of Pisces. He was playing with bloodstone agates, so I was certain it was March."

"But how did you get the date?" Carl had asked. "How did you know it would be the third?"

"Oh that," she says. "That was just obvious."

She took her change from cashier, smiled at Carl, and we walked away.

Chapter 32

"She is still a little off when it's foggy," Kayley said. She retrieved a serving tray from her kitchen cabinet and placed it on the counter. "But thanks to Adam, she is a lot better. As long as I'm with her and remind her that the clouds have landed she's not afraid."

"That's great news," Helen replied, while laying out assorted cookies and biscotti.

When Helen had finished, Kayley gathered the coffee mugs and carafe before heading to the living room. They navigated around Terra, who was sitting on the floor with her colouring book at the foot of Alexandra's chair.

"You have an admirer," Kayley said to Alexandra.

"I think so," Alexandra agreed.

PAIRS

Terra looked up from her colouring book and tried, again, to work through the before and after of remembering. She thought about the townhouse and the rooms, making an effort to place Alexandra in any of them. She couldn't. Yet, Terra was certain that wasn't correct.

Even though she knew that her mother never remembered backwards, Terra couldn't understand why she wasn't able to help her with duck-feet memories. Just as with her shoes, she sometimes needed things pointed out before it became clear.

"What's your baby's name?" Terra asked Alexandra. An island of trees had little meaning for her, and she curiously sought the answer.

The question, its unexpectedness, and the innocence of the one asking, had caught Alexandra completely unguarded. With Henry in her life her excuse was gone. She was no longer able to hide from her own crippling fears. Alexandra was overtaken by a profound sadness and struggled to maintain her composure. The effort was not lost on Kayley.

"Mouse, Alexandra doesn't have a baby," she explained.

Helen also sensed Alexandra's mood and she sought to quickly change the topic.

"So, Kayley how is Adam?" she asked, after placing the tray on the coffee table and taking a seat on the couch.

"Wonderful. I'm happy. I'm really happy. He makes me laugh."

"No, dear. I mean, how *is* Adam?"

Their knowing glances were the result of shorthand they had honed over years of friendship. The topic of sex was never too far below the surface with Helen.

"Three words," Kayley said, as she poured the coffee, "endurance, enthusiasm, and endowed."

"Envious." Helen replied.

Alexandra watched the two women, enjoying their openness and her inclusion. It was another keepsake playlet of her new, quaint, pedestrian life.

"Adam wants to meet with Henry and me," she said. "What's that about?"

"He's not telling me either," Kayley replied, while offering her coffee. "It's all a big mystery. He seems pretty excited though."

"Sorry to interrupt," Helen said. "But since these days I have to live vicariously through you both, and the curiosity is killing me, I have to ask. Alexandra, how are things going between you and Henry?"

Alexandra grinned and her eyes narrowed contentedly when she turned toward Helen. Echoes of sensations replayed faintly in Alexandra's mind while she thought about her response. They built quickly in magnitude until finally releasing in a shiver that shot up her spine.

"Really," Helen purred.

Chapter 33

When Henry was boy, his family had owned a golden retriever named TJ. TJ was a bundle of peculiar habits, sashaying when she trotted, eating the side of the house, and sleeping sprawled on her back, limbs drooping at her sides. She wallowed in sleep. It was a simple delight for her. In the act, or inaction, of sleeping, Alexandra reminded Henry of TJ. After returning from washing the dishes he stood watching her.

Their evening together had been Alexandra's best attempt at Henry's perfect date. She had struggled with her dress from the very start. Whenever she changed position it was as if she was sorting out twisted bed linens in an attempt to get comfortable. Even in her entanglement, Alexandra's beauty had held Henry captive. He had smiled when noticing her bare feet, recalling that he had not specified shoes during their discussion at the play structure. He had complimented her choice.

PAIRS

The food, bar none, was the worst Henry had ever tasted. However, the meal was, singularly, the best he had ever experienced. From the centrepiece of flowers and pretty weeds, which she had plucked from the apartment building's garden, to the absence of a request to assist with cleaning the dishes, the evening had demonstrated her care and consideration. The fact that Henry had to sneak out of bed and rewash everything was of no consequence to him. Alexandra had made her very best attempt to date him.

During his absence she had kicked the covers off. Naked, she was a collapsed marionette lying on her back, limbs askew. Her head was flopped sideways, mouth slightly open. Alexandra smacked her lips while Henry was standing over her.

She had been happy to spoil him, but the entire affair of delivering a multi-course meal in a dress, which Kayley had helped her pick out, left Alexandra in need of a few shots of Scotch and soothing hot shower at the evening's conclusion. She had promptly drifted off to sleep when they had gone to bed.

The absolute surrender to contentment of TJ had a magnetic quality that had drawn in passersby. As a boy, Henry had felt compelled to rub her belly whenever he saw her flopped on the floor in a deep, somnolent stupor. Alexandra had a similar effect on him.

Initially he traced the nail of his thumb along the pads of her feet, watching her twitch in response. The endless foreplay of their sex life was an arrangement that Henry had found to be extremely fulfilling. Alexandra's body was a smorgasbord.

When it was apparent that the sensations were not a dream, Alexandra's eyes fluttered opened. She peered at her feet to find Henry's tongue weaving between her toes. She laid back and closed her eyes, enjoying the many textures of pleasure being woven by his hands, tongue and teeth. With her growing arousal, Alexandra's hand slid down her stomach toward her pelvis. She was savouring his amazing abilities to bring her to shattering orgasms.

Chapter 34

"So you can cook, too?" Alexandra asked Adam. She had been fine with Henry dominating the domestic skills of their relationship. It was part of the give and take trade-off between the two of them.

But then she started to suspect that such skills were not merely common, they were a prerequisite for fitting into her new, suburban life. People actually lived infomercials, sharing cooking tips and cleaning-product finds and cherishing words like "brocade."

Alexandra was sitting in a tub chair that cornered the sofa where Adam had stretched out. Not wanting his surprise spoiled, he watched with veiled interest as her fingertips absentmindedly leafed across the clutter of the magazine rack that was nestled against the armrest.

They had been relegated to the role of passive spectators while Henry and Kayley prepared dinner. Snippets of poetry floated out from Adam's kitchen alongside the marvellous cooking odours.

"Yep," Adam replied.

"Well? You know, fancy?"

"Not like Henry or Kayley, but pretty good."

"I'm such a loser," Alexandra sighed.

Their conversation was interrupted by Kayley's squeal. When the oven door was opened the searing juices from the roast filled the apartment with a succulent aroma and the crinkling sound of a downpour that was soon accompanied by the hood fan. Henry popped his head out to provide a progress report to Adam and Kayley.

"We had a little spillover onto the element," he explained.

From within the kitchen Kayley's voice rose in lyric oratory.

We rode—the white mare failed—her trot a staggering stumble grew,—
The cooking-smoke of even rose and weltered and hung low;
And still we heard the Populzai and still we strained anew,
And Delhi town was very near, but nearer was the foe.

PAIRS

While Adam and Alexandra silently shared in their enjoyment of the recital with each other, Henry looked back through the doorway and saw Kayley fanning the smoke aside with a cooking mitt.

"The wine is flowing in the galley," Adam said.

"She is so cute," Alexandra commented.

"Kipling," Kayley announced.

"What's kipling?" Alexandra called back.

"Not what," Kayley replied, as she joined Henry at the doorway. "Who. Rudyard Kipling."

When Henry and Kayley disappeared into the kitchen Alexandra looked at Adam in a request for enlightenment. She couldn't link the name to food, but thought that Rudyard Kipling sounded like a variety of smelt. She'd never eaten smelt, but she thought it sounded awful.

"The guy who wrote about the cooking smoke," Adam explained. "She does that. Recites and credits. I think she can search her brain by title, topic, or author."

In the kitchen, calmness had returned. Henry and Kayley were leaning back against opposite sections of counter, sipping wine.

"If it's not too personal," Kayley began. "Have you and Alexandra talked about children?"

"It's not too personal. We haven't. I'd like to have children someday. If we do, it will likely be through adoption. I'd like to get married first though. Why do you ask?"

Kayley turned to the stove and made a perusal of dinner's progress. She lifted pot lids, releasing small billows of steam, and nursed her wine while estimating the time remaining. When Henry started to refill her glass she moved back to the counter and watched him, imagining his future with Alexandra and their unnamed children.

"Call it woman's intuition," she said. "You may want to talk to her."

"It is very difficult for me to explain things to you without going into way too much information. You'll just have to trust me that it would be a very touchy subject for her. When she is ready she can bring it up."

From the living room they heard Alexandra talking in gentle infant-friendly words and Terra's quiet responses. With the proximity of their voices drawing closer, Kayley placed her glass on the counter.

"Guess who woke up for dinner," Alexandra said.

She was standing in the entryway to the kitchen, holding Terra in her arms. Alexandra's attention remained on her when she spoke. She was infatuated, engrossed by clumsy waking movements.

"We heard her get up and Adam said it would be alright if I got her," Alexandra said, still facing Terra.

Kayley moved from the counter and tapped Henry's foot. When she had his attention she nodded toward Alexandra. Henry was watching Alexandra and Terra when Kayley passed by him, whispering.

"I think she's bringing it up."

Chapter 35

"Henry, why do you always have to use the most obscure word to describe the simplest thing?" Alexandra asked.

"You noticed that too, eh?" Adam said.

After dinner, Henry had a suggested a game of cards, one that he felt Alexandra wouldn't find too complicated and therefore too boring. Once he had laid out the deck, face down, on the living room floor, Kayley left her daughter to sleep on the couch, picked up her wine glass, and joined in. She sat across from Adam, reminiscent of their picnic.

"Pelmanism is not obscure," Henry said. "It just so happens to be what this game is called."

"The object is to find matching *pairs*. Not matching *pelmanisms*," Alexandra retorted. "That is why the game is called Pairs. If you had said Pairs I would have known, right off the top, what you were talking about."

PAIRS

"The game is named after Christopher Louis *Pelman*, the British psychologist, and not Christopher Louis *Pairs*."

"Mind if I go first?" Kayley asked cheerfully.

Adam watched Alexandra's eyes for the tell that Henry had mentioned. On cue, they narrowed as she took aim on Henry. When she had him alone, he would be groaning the word *pairs* repeatedly. Satisfied, Henry winked at his cousin.

"I hope you don't mind, Adam," Henry said, "but we won't be staying too late. Go right ahead Kayley."

"More than understandable, cuz," Adam replied. Then, seeing his opening, retrieved a file folder from the magazine rack.

He remained enigmatic about the night's agenda while they dined and had been equally unforthcoming as the table was cleared. Adam had put off the discussion until he was sure he could have their undivided attention.

"We should probably get down to business then. I have a proposition." Adam said.

Immediately Kayley jumped to the humourous speculation that the proposition was for group sex. In spite of her best efforts, she snickered. Adam waited on Kayley to elaborate but she simply grinned, shook her head, and, in an unspoken defence, blamed the tangent of her thoughts on the wine. Though curious, Adam let Kayley's interruption pass. He opened the folder to reveal a photo, which he passed to Henry.

Henry was at complete loss as to the possible tie-in between Adam's proposition and the abandoned, ramshackle squatter-magnet that the nineteenth-century, single-family home in the picture had become.

"We can get it for a song," Adam enthusiastically explained to Henry.

"That song being *Be Kind to My Mistakes* by Kate Bush?" he offered.

"Tess," Adam continued, unaffected, "my boss, has told me about a great opportunity. She knows of a handyman special that has come on the market. Even if fixed up it would be, price-wise, at the lower end of a great up-and-coming inner-city neighbourhood. It is prime for flipping.

We can easily make a twenty to twenty-five per cent return in six to eight months. Maybe even more."

"Handyman special," Henry said after he gave the picture to Alexandra. "That's a bit of an understatement."

"It looks way worse than it is," Adam replied. "Great bones."

"Every time I see a house like this in the movies," Alexandra commented, "I know that it is not going to end well for the people who enter."

She held the photograph for Kayley, who was in the midst of deciding on her next card. Kayley squinted at the picture and, although seeing something special about the house, looked questioningly to Adam.

"If it's such a good deal, then why isn't Tess jumping on it?" Alexandra questioned, as she passed the picture back to Adam.

"Her money is locked up in other things right now," he explained. "*And*, she likes me."

Kayley's ongoing intuitive success was a minor distraction for everyone. Her carefree manner was suggestive of someone joyfully picking flowers from the garden. As she whittled away at the tiling of cards, she thought about the four of them, coupling people in her mind, and cheerfully concluded that each pairing was, on some level, a match.

"We need to come up with the down payment," Adam elaborated. "And at first glance at the place, I think we might need fifty to seventy-five thousand to bring it up to snuff."

"Seventy-five thousand dollars," Henry exclaimed. "Seventy-five thousand dollars? And that's in addition to the down payment? Apparently you haven't heard. I'm a school teacher."

"We're smart people," Adam said. "We should be able to come up with some way to do this."

"I can help," Alexandra said.

"There is a lot of potential in this place," Adam said. "We could flip it. Heck, we have the zoning to convert it into an apartment if we wanted to."

"What about getting Daleesha and Helen involved?" Kayley suggested.

"Really," Alexandra reiterated. The irritation of being previously ignored increased the force of her voice. "I can help."

"Help?" Adam asked her.

"Help."

"How much help are we talking?" he asked.

"Fifty to seventy-five thousand dollars worth of help," she replied. "Plus the down payment."

Her response, not easily finding a place to land, circled in everyone's mind. In a quest for elaboration, both Adam and Kayley looked to Henry, who was stunned by the news.

"Being a waitress at a diner pays surprisingly well," she explained facetiously. "Lots of tips."

Chapter 36

"Well, hello," Alexandra said, after opening the apartment door.

"Terra's at the daycare," Kayley explained, in response to Alexandra downward inquiring glances. "With Daleesha."

Alexandra smiled and ambushed Kayley with a passionate kiss. She cradled the back of Kayley's neck in her hand and drew her in before she had time to react. When Kayley realized what was happening she placed her hand gently against Alexandra's cheek and kissed her back.

"Damn," Alexandra sighed disappointedly, and then stepped aside to allow Kayley into the apartment.

"You were going for shock value weren't you?" Kayley confirmed, while she bent over to remove her shoes.

"Yep. Kind of backfired though. Pardon me while I uncurl my toes."

Kayley stood up and smiled playfully. She reached out to Alexandra and touched her cheek with her fingertips before giving her recitation.

Never to let this lose me grace
But rather bring you back to me:
Amongst all mortal women the one
I most wish to see

Alexandra's softest side welled as Kayley's words and caress gently guided her to embrace the femininity within. For the first time in her life, Alexandra blushed. Kayley's astonishment was relayed in her eyes.

"Sappho," Kayley whispered. "Circa 600-something BC."

Alexandra finally grinned. "Have you been drinking?"

"A couple glasses of wine," Kayley confessed, as she removed her jacket and placed it on an available hook. "With Adam. We were pre-emptively celebrating the house. And thank you again, by the way—from all of us. Why do you ask? I took a cab."

"I could taste it on your lips," Alexandra lied, while deftly managing to conceal her amusement. She wasn't sure how conscious Kayley was of her two drink recitals and didn't want to burst the bubble.

Kayley looked around the foyer. It was her first visit to Alexandra and Henry's apartment. She had envisioned their place many times from Adam's descriptions and took pleasure in the neat organization of the room. However, her enjoyment was tempered by memories of Gavin and his orderly eccentricity. Alexandra watched Kayley assess the surroundings.

"I bet you love this," Alexandra said, recalling her visit to Kayley's tidy home.

"He is definitely a kindred spirit."

After ensuring that she complied with the order of the shoe mat Kayley followed behind Alexandra into the hall. While Alexandra's back was to her, Kayley licked her lips, tasting for wine. When Alexandra stopped to explain the apartment's layout she found Kayley checking her breath.

"Just so you don't get confused, like my first time. Although that is the bathroom," Alexandra said, directing her attention to the opened entry, "the can is actually in here."

Alexandra opened an adjacent door, which Kayley had assumed was to the linen closet. Spotless white subway tiles covered the walls and floor. There was enough space to comfortably fit the toilet and chrome toilet paper stand, but little else.

"Henry calls it a true water closet. Apparently that is they way they did it back in the day." Alexandra said. "It's kind of cool. Henry could be shaving while I'm taking a dump, or visa-versa."

She closed the door and led Kayley across the hall to the kitchen entry. It was obvious to Kayley from the trays of food, the neatly stacked plates, and the arranged glasses and cutlery that a great deal of effort had gone into preparation. When they entered, Kayley noticed a single piece of binder paper stuck to the fridge. It was the evening's serving instructions from Henry.

"Henry helped out a lot," Alexandra explained, when she noticed Kayley's interest. "I've never hosted a girls' night. Well, a non-professional girls' night anyway. It's nice to have you here before Helen and Daleesha show up, you know, to make sure I've got everything."

"Do you have wine?"

"Yep."

"Then you've got everything. And don't be nervous. Don't let Helen's businesswoman facade fool you. The first time I met her was at a house party. I wandered into the den and there she was the only woman at a table of four playing strip poker. Not much has changed."

"I'm not nervous, I just don't want to come off as a goomer."

"Just be yourself and they'll love you. Trust me. We're a sisterhood of goomers. We fear the normal."

Alexandra was surprised by the affect of Kayley's reassurance. She felt a release of tension she hadn't been consciously aware of carrying.

"My kind of people," she said, before retrieving a bottle of wine from the fridge.

While watching Alexandra, Kayley thought about how she would approach the topic of childbirth. Henry's comment had made her curious and concerned. Although Adam had advised her to leave well enough alone, she felt a strong compassion for Alexandra that made it impossible for her to assume the role of bystander. The interactions between Alexandra and Terra were too compelling for Kayley to turn a blind eye.

Alexandra uncorked the bottle and filled a glass, which she handed to Kayley, before pouring herself a shot of Scotch. Following Alexandra's lead, Kayley raised her glass and they tapped rims.

"To good friends," Alexandra said.

"And family."

Alexandra's Scotch went down in a single gulp but her attention stayed with Kayley. She found the addendum to her toast, while not unwelcome, to be a little bit off on a tangent.

"Family?" Alexandra asked. "Do you consider us family?"

"That's not what I was referring to, but now that you mention it, yes I do."

"What were you referring to then?"

"Nuclear family. You know, *and baby makes three*."

"Well, that doesn't apply here. I thought I mentioned that at Daleesha's party. It's just Henry and me. As long as he'll have me."

As if feeling a weather front moving in, Kayley could sense Alexandra's cool detachment. For the first time she could see something very ancient about Alexandra, a veteran survivor who had hardened with age. Kayley realized that it wasn't new. It had been there all along. She had simply not understood.

Kayley recalled how her grandmother had once explained that, when faced with the task of trying to enter an impenetrable fortress, it is sometimes best to simply knock. She took Alexandra by the hand. Alexandra was surprised by the gesture but allowed it to happen. Her eyes reddened and she squeezed Kayley's hand.

"I have phobia about being penetrated. I lock up," Alexandra explained, in a quiet voice.

She misinterpreted Kayley's expression as one of confusion about the nature of the penetration she was referring to, and shyly made a quick pointing gesture in the direction of her vagina. However, the prompting was not required. Kayley had understood. It had been concern that played out on her face as she speculated on the tragic events leading to Alexandra's emotional scarring.

"When I was a teenager my father died," Alexandra continued. She wasn't sure why she felt compelled to discuss her past with Kayley. "My mother wasn't a strong woman and latched onto the first man that promised to take care of her. He was a psychologist or psychoanalyst or something like that."

Fear, contempt, and rage began to roll silently down Alexandra's cheeks and she fought to remain calm. The effort didn't escape Kayley. She was engulfed by the emotions and sympathetic tears filled her eyes.

"Not long after they were married he started to molest me," Alexandra said. "He raped me. Repeatedly. No one believed me. He had everyone convinced that I was making it up. And my mother, my mother…"

They shared glances, but Alexandra had to look away when she found herself overcome by the memories and unable to stop herself from crying through the initial onslaught. When she had gathered the deadness that had been her shield during those years, she was able to continue.

"And my mother pretended it all away." Alexandra's words were even and detached. "One day I just lost it. He came to my room and my entire body just locked up. And my legs stayed clamped. He beat the shit out me, but they stayed clamped."

Alexandra poured herself a shot and avoided eye contact until she emptied the glass and whispered, "I ran away before sunrise."

She faced the cabinets but was watching the clipped images of her nightmare slowly fade, until nothing but the present surroundings remained.

"And baby makes three," Alexandra said to herself, before speaking to Kayley. "You can't laugh."

"I won't."

"Not even smile."

"I won't."

"Even if I was drugged to get knocked up, I'm afraid that if I ever got pregnant I'd clamp shut at the birth. There I'd be, in the middle of nowhere, couldn't get a C-section, and closed for business."

Kayley despised a man that she had only just heard of and knew little about. She had no difficulty understanding why Alexandra had never sought professional psychiatric help.

"I don't pretend to be to be an expert, but I think what you're talking about is called vaginismus. Have you talked to Henry about it?"

"I know. I've Googled the bejesus out of it. I kind of had to lay the ground rules for sex. As long as I stay on the outside, everything is fine. I can have great orgasms. He was very understanding."

"Because he loves you. I'm sure it's curable."

"I know it is. I can still have the big O so I never really cared. I never thought I'd need to care—until Henry."

From the hall, they could hear the static doorbell buzz from the apartment's intercom. Alexandra and Kayley unclasped hands and left the kitchen together. Before Alexandra could reply the intercom sounded again.

"Hello," Alexandra said, after opening the channel.

"Mommy?"

Terra's question crackled into the apartment. Alexandra's eyes squeezed shut and she rested her forehead against the wall. Her throat tightened and she swallowed so that she could speak.

"No, honey," she breathed, to the unseen child that was haunting the apartment.

It was obvious to Kayley that Alexandra had suddenly become too distraught to continue, so she moved into position at the intercom.

"Mommy?"

"I'm here, Mouse," Kayley said, in chipper welcome as she whipped the tears from her eyes.

"Okay. Are you going to let us in?" Helen interrupted. "Or is there some speakeasy password we need to know?"

Chapter 37

"*Decorate*," Henry and Adam proclaimed in unison.

Adam poured the tequila into their plastic shot glasses, which they tapped together before emptying in one swig.

"*Drama*," Henry said, pointing to the square on Adam's bingo card.

"What?"

"She described the colour as adding *drama*."

"I missed that."

"You were still recovering from *decorate*. And that is the last time I'm going to help you."

Adam lifted the shot glass from the square marked *drama*, drank the tequila, and set it to the side.

"I'm just a *whimsy* away from Bullshit," he noted.

Henry's version of Bullshit Bingo honed in on interior decorators. The rules followed the general premise of the classic Bingo game, except with a few minor variations. The alphanumeric squares had been replaced with a five-by-five grid of words that Henry believed common to all decorating shows. *Palette, tension, classic,* and *design* were scattered amongst words and phrases of similar utility to the interchangeable hosts and their guests. Victory was declared by announcing Bullshit. As an aside to the central game, *decorate*, or any of its derivatives, required all the players to shoot back a single ounce, *fabulous* meant an obligatory two ounces.

In spite of their differences, Henry and Adam viewed each other more as brother than cousin. Beyond their astonishing alcohol capacity, they also shared a very strong sense of family.

In the secret portrait Adam always envisioned, the wife and mother now had a face, fitting so comfortably it was impossible for him to imagine a time when it wasn't there.

"I'm thinking of introducing Kayley to Mom."

"Big step. She should find her a refreshing change from the plethora of bimbos, tramps, and barflies that you seem to constantly date."

Adam would have felt a deeper level of insult had he not acknowledged to himself that Henry's summary, while brutal, was fairly accurate. Henry smiled and patted him on the back.

"Your mom's observation, not mine."

"I've never dated a barfly," Adam corrected, in a matter-of-fact tone.

"Susan?"

"Bimbo."

"Tanya?"

"Bimbo."

"Chelsea?"

"Tramp."

Henry scooped a handful of peanuts from the opened can and sat back to reflect on his cousin's dating history. For his age, Adam had a rather extensive list of women who had passed through his life. Be that as it may, after his review Henry had to admit that Adam was spot-on, not a single barfly.

"You're right," he conceded, after sitting up. "Your mother and I stand corrected."

Adam smiled, took a peanut out the can and flicked it at Henry's forehead. Before Henry could protest, the host on the current show proclaimed something to be *fabulous*. After swallowing the second shot Adam nudged Henry to get his attention. The tequila was slowly broadening their range of thoughts and their definition of reasonable behaviour.

"So, are things with you and Alexandra still good? Kayley and I were just talking about her the other day. She blows us both away. I mean wow, a seventy-five K investment and willing to share the profit."

"The, *after a reasonable return to Alexandra*, profit," Henry corrected. "She shouldn't lose out because of the deal."

"Goes without saying."

Henry, as he was prone to do, had given a great deal of thought to his relationship with Alexandra. In search of the reason behind his happiness, he had analyzed her traits and made comparisons with the dissatisfaction he had felt with others in his past.

After a few derivatives of *decorate*, a couple of notably *fabulous* makeovers, and a trouncing declaration of Bullshit earlier that evening—sharing his thoughts, at length, was the natural thing to do.

"She blows me away as well," he said. "And not just because of that. For you to fully appreciate it, to really see how it's going, I'd like to tell you the story of Leonard."

At the news of the impending analogy, *didactic* leapt immediately to Adam's mind. And with it, the memory of the Daleesha's party where he had first heard what he had come to regard as the perfect adjective to describe his cousin.

"When I was going to university," Henry said. "I went out for a short stint with a woman named Alice. Alice had a best friend Susan. Susan's boyfriend was Leonard. One day Alice and Susan decided that it would be nice for the four of us to go on a double date. Leonard, as I came to find out, was a charming, clean cut, black freshman who happened to really love heavy metal music. Love is an understatement. He knew all the bands, all the members, and all the songs."

Adam's thoughts of Daleesha's party wandered to images of Alexandra's upside down breasts and finally to memories of his first night with Kayley. And there he remained, while Henry continued to speak.

"All evening Leonard would ask me questions on various heavy metal topics, to which I kept responding that I really didn't follow that type of music. It wasn't as if he was restricted to that one subject matter. He was smart, articulate, up on current events, and kind of a trivia buff. Yet we kept returning to heavy metal."

Through the din of Henry and the amorous memories, an important word floated into Adam's consciousness—*whimsy*. He looked down at his card, smiled, and shot back the tequila.

"Bullshit," he proclaimed, after setting the glass onto the table.

"At the time I really didn't understand why," Henry continued, initially unfazed by the proclamation of victory. "It just didn't register with Leonard that I knew nothing about heavy metal. Oh right. Bullshit. Congratulations."

Adam removed the remaining glasses, dealt two new cards and set them up for the next game while Henry spoke.

"Later," Henry said. "I caught on to the fact that I had been dealing with a stereotype. Leonard must have held the view that all young white guys were into heavy metal. Period. No exceptions. So imbedded was this opinion that any information to the contrary just didn't process."

When Adam had finished he noticed the rolling credits and retrieved the program schedule from the side table. Early in the evolution of the game, Adam had suggested that they keep step with the new millennium and simply record the shows, but Henry wouldn't have it. *Where was the sport in that?* Adam checked his watch, and after referencing the time to the listing, left the channel unchanged for the next round.

"My dating experiences were a lot like that," Henry explained. "Women have very imbedded opinions about male traits, and nothing to the contrary seems to get through. Think about it, Adam: women have been talking about themselves in every form of media, for over forty years. And to be fair, men really haven't been. Not even close. As a result, I believe we are at a time in human history, at least in G8 type nations, where men have a far more realistic and informed opinion about what it is to be a woman than women have about what it is to be a man. Men really only have themselves to blame, I suppose."

The title of the upcoming show included the word decorate, which Adam figured qualified. He poured the tequila and then pointed to the television for Henry's benefit, who, after a shrug of agreement, stopped talking long enough to toss back the shot.

"I had all but given up on dating," Henry said. "Then, out of nowhere, came this woman who had been right there all the time. Alexandra sees *me*, not just my gender. It's an exceptional and wondrous experience."

"So," Adam bottom-lined. "Things are good, then?"

"Yes. Things are good."

However, Kayley's opinion regarding children nagged at Henry, both on Alexandra's behalf and, he admitted to himself, his own. The Christmas trees to come would be so much more complete with siblings verifying the equity of the present count. Yet, in order to have a family, they needed to address one linchpin issue.

"The sex is a little," Henry began, "unique."

"Unique?"

"No penetration."

"None?"

"Ever. Not that I mind. She has a lot of interesting workarounds. But Kayley has got me thinking that Alexandra may want children."

Adam was not surprised to find out that Kayley had been talking to Henry and Alexandra. Helen had alluded to her quiet, blinders-on determination. He was seeing signs of it. Recalling Kayley's discussion with him on the matter of becoming involved, Adam reasoned that her question—S*hould I?*—had actually been a declaration of intent: *I should*. And he had merely been a sounding board. Although potentially frustrating, there was something Adam thought charming about Kayley's stubbornness. When he finally connected back to his conversation with Henry, there was a bright-and-shiny word distractingly glimmering.

"*Workarounds?*" He inquired, for the sole purpose of inviting elaboration.

"Focus, Adam. The topic is children."

"Well, I need to understand the workarounds to appreciate the big picture."

Henry wasn't completely sold by Adam's reasoning, but he didn't mind sharing. He found himself welcoming the opportunity. There were numerous examples, but it was Alexandra's surprise attacks that stuck out in his mind. At the most unpredictable times she would jump him, sometimes doing little more than tracing her exposed nipples along the skin of his back. But there were also the onslaughts, when she would wrap her naked body around his.

"Like once, stark naked, she surprised me in the hall," he said. "I was coming out of the shower and she did some twisty wrestler move. Before I knew what was going on she had me pinned to the floor and was giving this incredible hand job. It was so intense. I thought the top of my skull was going to blow off."

The premise, and a general flood of thoughts about naked female wrestlers, overwhelmed Adam's ability to trace back to the original reason for the discussion. He stared without comment.

"So what do you think?" Henry asked.

"I think I'd like Kayley to learn how wrestle."

Chapter 38

From her seat beside the fireplace Kayley had a clear view down the hall to watch Alexandra exit the kitchen with a freshly opened bottle of wine and veer in the direction of the bedroom. The door had been left slightly ajar so Kayley could keep tabs on the progress of her daughter's sleep. Alexandra peeked into the room and watched Terra for several minutes before realizing she herself had become the object of Kayley's pleased interest. Witnessing yet again Alexandra's tender admiration inspired a conviction. Kayley was going to help her friend have a child.

When Alexandra rejoined the three women, she was in time to catch the tail end of a conversation. In adhering to Henry's general guidelines of being a good host, she topped up Kayley's wine without impeding the conversation, and then moved toward the couch.

"That's sounds very exciting," Daleesha said, as Alexandra motioned to refill her.

"Kay," Helen said, while scooping salsa with a tortilla. "I never thought you'd be the type."

"What type is that?" Kayley asked.

"A risk-taker. I mean, flipping a home. I just never saw it."

"There is a lot more to her than you think," Alexandra volunteered.

She loved being *just one of the girls* and chatting about normal things. At times, Alexandra would step outside herself and watch the magnificent ordinariness. Women, she would always conclude, are so cool.

"Oh Kay," Helen clarified, apologetically. "I don't think you're dull."

"Well, what do you think?" Kayley asked.

"Suburban."

"Suburban? 'Suburban' sounds like spin-doctor for 'dull.'"

Alexandra stood in front of Daleesha and was at last about to pour when she stopped to glimpse back over shoulder at Kayley. Their eyes met only for a moment, but it was enough for a mutual recollection of their shared intimacy. An amused, tacit agreement was reached and Alexandra looked at Helen.

"The suburbanite and I had a hot and heavy make-out session. At Daleesha's party," Alexandra commented, nonchalantly. "Have you ever made out with a woman?"

The image gave Daleesha pause. She examined Alexandra's natural pout while her glass was being filled, and felt that the slight arch of her upper lip was the seductive allure. Reaching up, Daleesha gently caressed the corner of that beautiful mouth with her thumb.

"You had a bit of something there," she said.

"Oh," Alexandra replied, not completely buying into the courteous gesture. "Thanks."

"No," Helen replied, hoping not to sound defensive. "I haven't."

"I had always wondered what it would be like," Kayley explained.

"Not all that suburban, is it?" Alexandra noted.

"I could," Helen declared.

"No, you couldn't," Kayley retorted. "You're way too WASP."

It was obvious that Kayley and Alexandra were merely having fun. Yet the implication of their teasing bothered Helen.

"Just because I haven't, doesn't mean I couldn't," Helen said.

"And way too straitlaced," Kayley added.

"Are you a tight-ass?" Alexandra contributed.

"I am not straitlaced. And I'm certainly not a tight-ass."

"Tattoo?" Alexandra inquired. "Interesting piercing? Threesome? Anything funky?"

Helen had long ago convinced herself that her professional facade was simply that —window dressing she could slip on and off at will. Underneath was her true self. The fun, impassioned libertine she knew she was. Yet, with little effort, Alexandra and Kayley were quickly proving her self-image to be nothing but a wishful fantasy. With that realization, Helen made her stand. It was time to summon her inner profligate. She refused to be staid, she refused to be closed-minded, and, most importantly, she refused to be her mother.

"Alright. Fine," Helen demanded of Alexandra. "Kiss me."

"Well, barking at me isn't going to get me the mood."

"Sorry. Kiss me."

"Not even a please?" Alexandra asked, when she stepped in front of Helen's chair.

"Please."

"You're really not making this sexy," Alexandra said. "Without sexy, it's really just a pity kiss on my part. It wouldn't be my best work and I hate doing things half-assed."

Frustrated, Helen stood up. She cupped Alexandra's face in her hands and closed her eyes as she leaned forward. Alexandra moved her arms to her sides, but was otherwise motionless when their lips touched. From Daleesha's position on the couch, the uninspired effort could pass as a mock resuscitation. Helen stepped back and crossed her arms while she apprehensively waited on her grade.

"It felt a little staged," Alexandra commented.

"To hell with it!"

"You're fiery," Alexandra proclaimed buoyantly, before giving a playful and rolling growl.

Kayley managed to hold her laughter to a broad, toothy smile. Daleesha, reluctant to impede Alexandra's torment of Helen, remained a respectful and appreciative member of the audience.

"Now you're just making fun of me," Helen said.

"Don't focus on the gender," Kayley encouraged. "Just the sensation."

Helen took a cleansing breath and projected herself into Alexandra. She was determined to give herself the kiss of her dreams. Alexandra found it much softer than Kayley's. She quickly became drawn in by the consuming passion and was temporarily lost to it. This time, when Helen stepped back, both women dreamily opened their eyes. Helen waited without concern on her evaluation. She knew that Alexandra had been swept up.

"Hot," Alexandra acknowledged.

"Yes," Helen agreed, as she leaned to the side to have a clear view of Kayley, "I was."

Before sitting, Helen raised her glass and tipped it to Kayley who, in a jesting act of derision, stuck out her tongue in response. Alexandra stepped clear of the chair to stand in front of the fireplace. Her attention was on Daleesha, as she continued to work the room.

"You ever kissed a woman?"

Kayley and Helen glanced at each other, not knowing whether to feel awkward, sympathetically embarrassed for Alexandra, or simply focus on the humourous irony. Daleesha finished sipping her drink and placed it on a side table coaster before speaking.

"I'm a lesbian," she said.

"You're a lesbian?"

"Yes."

"Why didn't anyone tell me?" Alexandra asked, while looking back and forth between Kayley and Helen.

"What difference does it make?" Daleesha questioned.

"We didn't *not* tell you," Kayley explained. "We just didn't tell you. Helen and I don't even think about it."

"Obviously," Alexandra exclaimed, raising her hands above her head for emphasis. "I feel like such a dolt."

She sighed, crossed her arms, and focused apologetically on Daleesha.

"I hope I didn't offend you with this," Alexandra said.

"Are you kidding?" Daleesha replied. "I'm single, I haven't had action in months, and I've got a really great wine buzz on. I feel like I'm living in the opening scenes of a very promising pay-per-view."

She smiled when the other women began to laugh, and raised her glass to lead a shared toast. Alexandra drank directly from the bottle, which she felt to be okay since there was only a glass's worth left. And, more to the reason, Henry wasn't around. Thoughts of him led to a sudden spark of concern in Alexandra.

"Oh," she said, after lowering the bottle to her side. "We can't tell Henry about the kissing. He'll get jealous."

"Henry is the only man I know that would frown on his girlfriend necking with another woman," Helen said.

"Boyfriend," Alexandra said reflexively, and then immediately regretted her candour.

PAIRS

"Boyfriend?" Helen asked.

Alexandra took a swig from the bottle before responding to Helen. She knew that the labels in her relationship with Henry did not follow the convention and, although proud of what they had achieved together, was a little unsure of how to explain, if at all, publicly.

"Uh, yeah. I'm Henry's boyfriend."

"You don't say?" Helen pondered.

"Um," Alexandra began, diffidently. "It's like this. At Daleesha's party I proved to Henry that he was more like my girlfriend than my boyfriend."

"How?" Daleesha interrupted.

"Pretty simple, really. I asked Henry and Adam to describe their idea of a perfect date."

"What's Adam's idea of a perfect date?" Kayley sidetracked.

"I can't tell you," Alexandra replied. "Anyway, after comparing the two it was obvious that Henry was a girl. To everyone."

"Why can't you tell me?" Kayley asked.

"What is said at the stripper pole stays at the stripper pole," Alexandra elaborated. "Later that night, when Henry and I were in bed together—"

"Huh?" Kayley mulled.

"What stripper pole?" Helen asked.

"She defiled my play structure," Daleesha explained, while spreading brie onto a section of baguette.

Helen was taken aback by the laissez-faire enlightenment and stared questioningly at Daleesha, who answered with a reiterating nod.

"Do you want to know why I'm the boyfriend or not?"

"Oh, that's self-evident," Kayley interrupted. "I want to hear about Adam's perfect date."

"I can't tell you. I promised."

"Alexandra, it's not like it is a deeply personal secret. If you tell me and I don't mind doing whatever it is, I'm positive he'll forgive you."

"He'd probably be grateful that you mentioned it," Helen added.

"And if I don't want to do whatever it is then he'll never know that you said anything."

"The woman has a right to know," Helen said.

Alexandra looked at Kayley and took a long, contemplative drink.

Part V

Bridged, one to the other,
Revealed and relinquished

Through turnstiles

Chapter 39

That does sound like a puzzle, Kay. This Alexandra woman seems to be in quite the pickle. Poor girl. Maybe the upcoming New Year will hold promise for her. Sorry for my mood, with the anniversary of your mother's passing coming up I'm feeling a little low. As if winter alone wasn't bad enough. I wish you had gotten to know her, Kay. I really do.

She had left me with a bit of a puzzle herself. It took forever and a day to figure it out. I've never told you about it. Partially because there was no real reason to—she was gone and nothing would bring her back. And partially because it will only ever be just a theory, I can't prove what was going through her mind when she stepped onto that bus. But Kay, I know. I swear I know.

Your mother had the gift, I've told you that many times. But what I never told you was that it came at a price. To see meant to see everything. Everything.

After her death I couldn't figure out why she got on the bus. For a while I thought that maybe it was too close. She'd blocked it out. I held onto that for a few years, until I was reminded that she knew about the mines the morning your father went off to work. He was a good man, always did fine by your mother, but he never gave much heed to her visions.

So I was left with the puzzle again, quite the conundrum indeed. For a moment, and only a moment, I wondered if her intention was to kill herself. She was some torn up from your father's death, but she'd just had you. You were her world, Kay. You made suicide impossible.

She didn't kill herself—but she did let herself die, and left you behind to boot. There you have it, Kay: the ornery knot I spent years trying to untie. I won't tell you about the dead ends, Kay, there were many, but it's fair to say that I was like a dog with a bone. As I know you'll be for this Alexandra woman. You're like me in that way, pertinacious.

The answer finally struck me something like this. If she didn't kill herself, then why did she get on the bus? To fill a seat, I reasoned. And that was the key: to fill a seat. Why? So that someone else couldn't sit in it. The bus out of Halifax was always full that time of year, a lot of university students headed home to visit. They'd always have a few on the go.

Kay, she got on the bus to save a life. She took a seat so that someone would have to take the next bus out. But then whose life would be so important? Who? Who would she be willing leave her newborn for?

It was a few years and quite a bit of money on investigators, but I finally built up the passenger list of the next bus out. I didn't get all the names. I didn't need to. When I saw the name of the Hair Farmer's mother I knew the life she saved. It was Terra's. Think about it Kay—he's a year younger than you. If she'd gotten on the bus, there'd be no Hair Farmer. And Terra would have never been born.

Chapter 40

The main floor of Helen's townhouse was open concept, divided by purpose rather than walls. It offered ease of flow for people and chatting, which Helen loved. However, it also meant that there was no place to hide from having to respond to awkward questions.

"So?" Kayley asked. "What do you think?"

Neither Daleesha nor Helen was quick to reply. They were both very familiar with the stories about the psychic abilities of Kayley's mother. And, perhaps because Kayley herself always seemed a little sceptical, they were hesitant to accept them at face value.

The pop of the cork from the Beaujolais drew attention on Helen. It was an auditory short straw electing her to speak first. She looked up from the bottle and saw that Kayley and Daleesha were patiently awaiting her response. Her forehead knitted thoughtfully as she placed the corkscrew on the counter of the kitchen island, which suddenly felt like her podium. Helen waited until she returned to the living area and had started to refill Daleesha's glass before answering.

"I think it's possible, certainly not *im*possible. I could see a woman making that kind of sacrifice for her grandchild."

"According to the fundamental laws of physics we should have the same epistemic access to the future as we do the past," Daleesha contributed.

"As in predict the future?" Helen asked.

"More along the lines of remembering it. We should also be able to influence the past as we do the future."

"Do you ever make yourself dizzy?" Helen teased.

"I make a point of never talking to myself."

"Wise."

"Anyway," Kayley interrupted. "It gave me a chill. I had such a rough pregnancy. Grandma used to call Terra a miracle child, and now I really get what she meant. It's like she *had* to be born, no matter what."

"Ever hear of indigo children?" Helen asked, after topping up her own glass.

"Yes," Daleesha replied, "but really, it's kind of nonsense to me."

"I don't know much about it," Helen said. She placed the bottle on the pewter wine coaster atop the coffee table and sat on the couch.

"Indigo children?" Kayley asked.

"Children born to improve the world," Daleesha explained, with clinical dryness.

"You're kind of a spiritual person, Daleesha," Helen remarked. "I'm surprised you're not more open to the idea."

"I am spiritual, but I am not a fool. It seems a little over-the-top to me."

"Kayley? Have you inherited any of your mother's abilities?" Helen asked.

Their conversation was interrupted by a rhythmic knocking on the door, which all three women assumed to be Alexandra tapping out a song that was playing inside her head.

"Why doesn't she just come in?" Helen wondered aloud, on her way to the entry hall.

Daleesha listened to the polite but energetic two-handed drum riff reach its crescendo. She thought about Alexandra as a performer, and regretted never having had the opportunity to see her show.

Helen descended the two stairs from the hall to the ceramic floor of the foyer. She opened the door to the damp cold of the winter day and squinted as she followed the grand sweep of Alexandra's arm in the direction of a snowman. From the substantial cleavage, Helen assumed it to be a woman. The snow in the small front yard, which was shared with the adjoining townhouse, had been completely trampled into ruts and billows, like the quilt on a bed that has just been used as a trampoline.

"Presenting the beautiful and stupendous Mrs. Snow," Alexandra trumpeted.

Terra was beside Alexandra, looking up to Helen and praising with mitten- softened applause. Buried deep within the bundled confines of her snowsuit, Terra's legs were straddled like a gingerbread man. She was speaking unintelligible words into her scarf. Failing to get any sort of acknowledgement, she pulled the scarf down to her chin.

"Look!"

"I see," Helen replied.

"We made a lady."

"Yes," Helen acknowledged, after a darting glance to Alexandra, "you did."

Alexandra stuck her head into the foyer and called into the townhouse, "I think Mommy should come and see."

Kayley and Daleesha shared amused glances before heading toward the door. Daleesha remained at the top of the steps to the foyer, peering over everyone's head out into the yard, while Kayley continued down toward the entry to stand beside Helen.

"Look, Mommy," Terra exclaimed.

"Yes, Mouse. I see."

"A snow lady," Helen teased.

"Yes, Helen. I see," Kayley said, in a subtext acknowledgement of the snow-boobs.

"She's like you, Mommy."

Helen quickly brought her hand to her mouth in an effort to suppress her urge to laugh. She succeeded only partially, but did manage to roll her giggle into a cough when Kayley nudged her.

"We definitely share the same waistline."

"She has a little girl, too," Alexandra whispered. "She's sneaking up behind her."

"To say 'Boo,'" Terra explained.

"Okay," Helen said. "I have to close the door. If you're coming in, then come on in."

Terra looked up to Alexandra and then steadied herself against the doorframe before stepping up into the foyer. Kayley crouched down to meet her, while Alexandra slipped past Helen on her way toward the stairs.

"Did you have to give the snow lady breasts?" Helen whispered.

"We didn't give her breasts," Alexandra replied, in a perturbed but hushed tone. She glanced back to the yard. "She's crossing her arms. Geez, it's true what they say about these little suburban cul-de-sacs and the repressed women."

"Yes, Helen," Kayley tormented, while helping Terra remove her snowsuit, "how *does* your mind work?"

Feeling cornered, Helen decided that silence was the best course of action. She pursed her lips and closed the door. Alexandra smiled at her and moved to the stairs where she sat down and unlaced her boots. Terra was a passenger of her mother's efforts and was passively undressed while watching the interaction of the women.

"Did I miss anything?" Alexandra asked Helen.

"We were discussing indigo children," Daleesha said, from behind Alexandra.

"Oh, I've heard of them."

"What do you think?"

Alexandra replied, as she slipped off a boot. "Lee Carroll has gotten quite rich spreading the news he has supposedly received through channelling the spirit Kryon. We live in an age of prophets for profit."

None would admit to it, but neither succinct nor astute were attributes that Alexandra's friends would normally associate with her. Kayley stopped undressing her daughter and gawked. Helen froze in place on the step and Daleesha made a surprised but approving hiccup-squeak noise. Alexandra, sensing that she had suddenly become the central focus, stared in annoyance at each of them, before responding to their collective astonishment.

"I do know stuff!"

***

Kayley, Helen, and Daleesha watched from the living room as Alexandra carried Terra upstairs to bed. The drooling, red-headed cherub had everyone charmed.

"She is dead to the world," Daleesha said after Terra and Alexandra disappeared from sight.

"If you ever see Alexandra in action, you'll know why." Kayley responded.

"They make quite the dynamic duo," Helen noted, and then looked to Kayley. "Has she ever mentioned anything about having her own?"

Helen and Daleesha watched Kayley's mood change from maternal contentment to empathetic sadness. Kayley sensed the concern she had aroused.

"I don't even know where to begin," she finally said.

Chapter 41

It was an unusually mild winter morning when they all piled into Henry's car to meet the real estate agent at the house. Alexandra sat on the passenger side while Adam, who was giving directions to Henry, was in the back seat with Terra and Kayley.

"Once we get there," Adam said, "pull up so that Bill can park behind you."

When they arrived, Henry lined up his car with the tracks grooved into the snow of the uncleared driveway and drove toward the single-car garage near the back of the property. Alexandra was the first to step out, followed by Henry and Adam. Off in the remote distance, they could hear the disjointed caws from a murder of ravens. Alexandra looked across the roof of the car toward the side of the house and gathered her first impression while they waited on Kayley and Terra.

A handful of adjectives, none kind, applied: drooping, sagging, collapsing, chipped, and broken. If the house hadn't been so pathetic, it would have seemed scary. A minor thaw resulted in a profuse sweat of water dripping from the eaves, trickling down the aged brick and boarded-over windows. When Kayley emerged with Terra she took a long assessing inventory of the house and concluded that it seemed terribly winded, as if it had run to meet them.

"Fugly," Alexandra critiqued.

Kayley glared disapprovingly at Alexandra and angled her head in the direction of Terra. Confused, Alexandra mulled over the possible reason behind the unspoken chastisement as they all walked toward the street. Terra clarified the matter when they gathered on the sidewalk in front of the house.

"What's fugly?" Terra asked her mother.

Alexandra straight away understood her transgression. Strict attention needs to be paid around the sponge minds of the preschool set. Her unspoken request for forgiveness was presented to Kayley in the form of an *I'm an idiot* grin. The apology and the sentiment were both accepted with a stern glance. Although Alexandra's ever-absent sense of discretion generally amused Kayley. In her role as mother, she did not want to concede to the humour.

Yet it still rekindled her admiration. Such moments had caused Kayley to reinterpret the laissez-faire boldness she had witnessed at their first meeting. She had initially believed that Alexandra's apparent rebellion against convention was rooted in defiance but, over time, had come to see it as the outcome of childlike candour. Kayley marvelled that something so pristine could have survived.

"I think Alexandra said *funny,* Mouse."

"Don't you think the house is funny?" Alexandra asked Terra.

"No," Terra replied suspiciously, while scrutinizing Alexandra. She was not convinced that she had heard things incorrectly.

Alexandra smiled at Terra and then the two slowly, almost cautiously, turned away from each other. Henry was alerted by the tug on his jacket sleeve that Alexandra wanted to speak to him in confidence. She leaned in close and spoke in a very quiet voice.

"Well?"

"Well, what?" Henry whispered.

"What do *you* think?"

"Fugly."

Alexandra kissed him on the cheek, wove her arm into his, and rested her head against shoulder. Kayley, having a sense for what just transpired, laughed to herself as she placed Terra into Adam's waiting arms. He felt on the verge of a major step forward in his life and was overcome by a deep sense of family. His excitement was not universally shared. Mere photographs had not fully captured the desperate impact of reality.

"What do you think?" Kayley asked Terra.

"It's sad," she said. The depth of compassion in her voice evoked amused sympathy in Adam and Alexandra.

"Yes it is," Kayley agreed.

"Very," Henry concurred. However, where Kayley and her daughter had felt sorrow, he had meant deplorable. Alexandra picked up on his tone and poked him.

Altered by the sound of tire spray, they moved, as a group, to watch Bill's arrival. For Terra alone, there was a phantom procession of vehicles, varied and numerous, melded one into the next, which stretched out in a blur from behind Bill's car as he pulled into the driveway. When he stepped onto the ground, decades of arrivals collapsed, like a folding accordion, and disappeared into nothingness.

He was a tall, broad man with thinning salt-and-pepper hair. In spite of his age, his face had boyish charm, particularly when he smiled. His attention was on Adam as he strolled leisurely toward them.

"I bet you're raring to give the tour," Bill said.

"You have no idea," Adam replied. "So you still think we should stay single family?"

"In this neighbourhood? Definitely."

Before making the introductions, Adam moved to stand beside Bill. From her seat in Adam's arms, Terra was eye level to Bill's sternum. When she panned up the rock face of his chest, her view was primarily of the underside of his chin, the looming overhang of a great big head that was so very far away.

"This lovely young girl is Terra, our house sympathiser. That's her mom, and my better half, Kayley. She's part of the design team."

"Really?" Kayley asked Adam, as she reached out to Bill in greeting.

"The man beside her is Henry, my cousin," Adam said, which prompted Henry to offer his hand, "and the other half of the design team."

"And beside him, is his far-better half, our financer and my apprentice, Alexandra."

"Your apprentice? As in power tools?" Alexandra clarified in wonderment. She presented the loose coil of her gloved fist to Bill for a knuckle-tap. "Too cool!"

PAIRS

"Everyone this is Bill, close friend of Tess and real estate guru."

"I'm glad we could all finally meet," he said.

Bill spoke about proximity of schools, parks, and all other particulars that could potentially be of interest to a future buyer, while leading them up the side of the driveway toward the uneven steps of the front porch.

Heighten Park, in the midst of its renaissance, was an inner-city neighbourhood of residents who adored their address. Renovated homes, each boasting personalized takes on "chef's kitchen" and "en suite spa" and all nested in splendid landscaping, lined the streets. The cars were generally European and expensive, but otherwise sensible. It was a community situated close to everything that it should be close to, and far from everything it should be far from.

Adam saw only potential. Henry saw only problems. Kayley thought about the loving family to which they would eventually sell the house. Alexandra thought about power tools. Terra sensed the past, a reservoir filled with happening and occasion.

After Bill retrieved the key from the lockbox suspended on the doorknob, he knocked the snow from his galoshes and ushered everyone into the foyer. Once inside they fanned out into the living area, stirring up the dust on the floor planks. The house was completely empty. Daylight leaked in around the edges of the plywood that boarded the windows shut. For reasons Alexandra couldn't quite put her finger on, she was reminded of an abandoned saloon.

"Giddy-up," she whispered.

Adam lowered Terra and guided her toward Kayley before directing everyone's attention to the narrow galley kitchen and the family room beyond.

"You need to see the size of the backyard. It's huge," he said enthusiastically, before leading the way.

"If we do buy this place we should throw a block party," Kayley thought aloud.

"It smells funny," Terra complained.

"A block party?" Alexandra squawked. "Why?"

"Musty," Kayley explained to Terra, before responding to Alexandra. "To meet our neighbours."

"Why? We're not moving in. This is a flip."

They followed Adam out what had formerly been the back door and into a collapsing extension. When the women entered, he was fighting with a set of patio doors darkly tinted by dirt. Terra remained close to her mother. The room was dim and the floor creaked. Although she was not afraid, she felt uncertain.

"I think it would be a nice thing to do," Kayley explained. "We are going to throw the street into a little bit of disarray."

"You're right, Kayley," Henry acknowledged. "Excellent idea."

"What?" Alexandra questioned in protest.

"Well, it is," he retorted.

"I think the idea of an extension is good," Adam said, undeterred. "But this has all got to go."

After a minor struggle, he was able to slide the door open. The back of the house was a couple of steps above grade, which, in the absence of a staircase, forced him to hop down. From the tracks in the snow, it was apparent that there had been several other visitors. Henry followed his cousin. They assisted Kayley, who then helped Terra down. Adam headed in the direction of the side door of the garage.

"I think I can set up a workshop in there," he said, not knowing it was only to himself.

Henry and Kayley wandered out into the yard together to get a view of the back of the house. Alexandra noticed them talking and was certain that they were planning the party. She vaulted to the ground and briskly passed them on her way to catch up with Adam.

"So what do you think about this party thing?" she asked him in a low voice.

"A silly waste of time and money," he said, as he opened the door and peered inside. It was in need of a little structural attention, but was otherwise suitable.

The velocity of Alexandra's departure had surprised Bill, but he said nothing of it when he joined Henry and Kayley. Alexandra glanced over to the trio while Adam was busy perusing the garage. Their scheming bothered her.

"Waste of time is right," Alexandra agreed. "If we do this thing, I'd like to get right at it."

Adam's quick evaluation of the space reminded him about the troublesome detail he had yet to break to Alexandra. In good conscience he knew he had to clarify how the renovation would actually get done. He closed the door and faced her. It was apparent to Alexandra that he wanted to say something, but was having difficulty putting the words together. The longer he waited, the more annoyed she got.

"What?" She demanded.

"Alexandra, I know you'll be supplying the money and all, but you are aware that it's really just the two of us that will be doing the work."

"What about Henry?"

"Um, no. Maybe painting."

"Why no?"

"He helped me once. I had to ask him to stop. Actually, I *told* him to stop."

"How come?"

"He is so damn finicky and slow. Power tools fluster him. And he is just an all around construction spastic."

"That's not nice."

"I love him like a brother. But as God is my witness, it's true."

"Can he help tear stuff down?"

"Um, no."

"Oh come on. How complicated can that be?"

"Alright. But nothing that needs to be rushed."

Alexandra glanced back at Henry and Kayley, trying to imagine either one of them using a power saw. She envisioned Henry painstakingly creeping along the cut line that he had taken the better part of the day to ensure was exact. Kayley would likely freak out, and the saw would yank her along wherever it wanted to go. Alexandra nodded in sober agreement with Adam's assessment. It would only be the two of them. Joined by their shared fate, they stood or fell together, brothers-in-arms.

Adam angled his head in the direction of the house as a suggestion to return. During their walk, Alexandra remembered why she had rushed to catch up in the first place.

"So you're against the party, too?" she confirmed.

"No. I just think it's silly."

"You're not against the party?"

"You'd best come to terms with it now," Adam recommended. "We're having the party."

"You're pussy whipped."

"My father has a saying: *If the wife is happy, the whole house is happy.*"

"What? Screw that noise! I'm going to talk to Kayley."

"All righty."

In front of them, Bill and Henry were still focusing on the house, but Terra and her mother had moved off to play in the snow. Alexandra parted company with Adam, and veered in the direction of Kayley.

"Kay," Alexandra began, in a gentle voice. "About the party, a house flip is supposed to be a quick in-and-out thing. I think we should just focus on that."

"I know," Kayley said, while she and Terra rolled the base of their snowman. "But I think it would be good for the house. Good Karma."

"Good for the house? I thought you wanted to have the party for the neighbours."

"Same thing really. We need to bring the house back into the fold of the neighbourhood. Reintroduce an old friend."

"Huh?"

"Think about all the negative energy this house has endured for years."

"Negative energy?"

"From all those who were wishing that the old eyesore would just go away. A once Grand Dame, who, after sheltering generations of families, was abandoned to squalor."

Kayley stopped rolling the snow as she thought about the history of the home. The speculation gave her a romantic rush. Terra, confused by her mother's shift in interest, pulled on Kayley's jacket to get her attention.

"Mommy is talking to Alexandra, Mouse," Kayley said.

"Mommy?" Terra complained.

Kayley ignored Terra's persistent tugging and continued to explain the importance of the party to Alexandra.

"Or maybe," she said, "generations of the same family lived here. This house was a silent witness to all their birthdays and anniversaries, and a quiet refuge for them in times of tragedy. Think about the history resonating in those walls, the highs and lows of that family—of this nation."

"Mommy," Terra demanded, loud enough to draw the attention of the three men.

"How did it come to this?" Kayley asked, stretching her arms out as if to embrace the house. "Was this great lady the last companion of the final patriarch? Was this home a helpless bystander to his death? Or did she watch him become progressively feebler with age? Did she know on that final day, when he left for the last time, that he would never be coming back? Back to the home he had been born in. The home he had brought his wife to. The home he had raised his children in. Wouldn't you be depressed if, after all that, no one wanted you around?"

"Yes, I suppose. But I'm a person and this is a house."

"No Alexandra, this is a *home*. A *home*."

"Mommy!" Terra screamed.

Kayley looked down at her agitated daughter. She tried to be firm, but found Terra's flustered pout far too humorous. Kayley picked her up and did a spinning waltz into the yard. Alexandra's attention remained with them while they bobbed and weaved. Mother making silly faces, daughter delighted and giggling. She became preoccupied with thoughts of children, home, and life with Henry. She had not noticed the approach of Adam.

"So?" he asked. "Are we having the party?"

The question was simple, but the meaning woven between the words affected Alexandra. Adam might as well have questioned the sanctity of family, love, and her future happiness. Red eyed and sniffling, she spun and stared at him in disbelief.

"Damn straight! We're buying this place and having the best damn blowout this neighbourhood has ever seen!"

"You don't say."

"Men," she snapped. "They can be so insensitive."

"Yeah. Men."

Chapter 42

Alexandra had retrieved Kayley's Volkswagen from the back of the complex and parked across the street from the townhouse. Before getting out, she watched the wind gust through the neighbourhood, whipping the snow into sporadic tidal sprays of white powder. She imagined Kayley out in the freezing weather and took guilty pleasure in the hilarity of it.

She left the car running, locked the door with the spare set of keys, and then ran to the protection of the fenced yard. Alexandra quickly entered the townhouse to escape the giant veils of snow being whisked off the roof.

PAIRS

"I just finished my shower," Kayley called down, after hearing the jingle of keys when they were tossed onto the stairs.

"Wow! It's cold out there," Alexandra called up to the second floor, while removing her winter clothes.

In the spirit of the day's agenda she thought about Henry as she ascended the stairs. After reaching the landing she peeked in on Terra. Seeing that she was happily engaged in her little world, Alexandra positioned herself in front of the bathroom, sat on the floor, and listened to the activity behind the closed door. She stopped counting the number of times the wine glass clinked against the ceramic ledge of the sink when Kayley spoke her.

"Alexandra, are you there?"

"Yep."

"Have you heard of Elizabeth Barrett Browning?"

"Nope," Alexandra replied, which launched Kayley into a mini-recital.

How do I love thee? Let me count the ways.
I love thee to the depth and breadth and height
My soul can reach, when feeling out of sight
For the ends of Being and ideal Grace.

"Actually, I think I've heard that first bit before."

"Beautiful, isn't it."

"Yeah, it is."

The poetry rekindled Alexandra's thoughts about Henry and the plan she had made after their first visit to the house. She reclined against her outstretched arms and pondered the door, as if it could somehow give a reading on Kayley.

"I want to run something by you," Alexandra said.

"What?"

"I'm thinking of proposing to Henry."

Alexandra was startled by the speed at which the door swung open. A billow of warm humidity exhaled from the bathroom. Kayley was standing in her terry robe in front of the medicine cabinet staring at Alexandra.

"I know it may seem a little soon," she acknowledged, in the vacuum of Kayley's response. "But, as Henry puts it, we're pretty much each others only kick at the can. So I figured, why wait? Let's do this thing."

"Wow!" Kayley managed.

"Wow? That's all you've got? How about congratulations?"

"Sorry," Kayley apologized. "Of course congratulations! I'm just a little preoccupied right now. Not really processing things properly."

"I bet! Listen, I've done this type of thing countless times. You'll be fine."

Kayley motioned for a hug and squealed while they held each other. "Have you talked to Henry about," she asked, after Alexandra stepped back into the hall, "*everything?*"

"No. I was figuring I'd just bundle it all together."

From their tone, Terra sensed that something exciting and fun was happening. She was curious and wanted to take part. Her colouring seemed boring by comparison. It wasn't until Terra had reached the hall that Alexandra had noticed her approaching.

"Hey, Mouse."

Realizing that her daughter was approaching, Kayley stepped out of the bathroom. She watched Terra mischievously charge Alexandra. Terra had become swept up in the happiness and was sharing in it the only way she knew how—through playing. As she ran, she heard the giggles of another little girl. Terra wrapped herself around Alexandra's leg and the laughter faded into the distance, as if continuing on without her.

"Bye," Terra breathed. Although she was so curious about that island of trees, Terra didn't want to ask the little girl's name again, because it would make Alexandra sad.

"Well, at least you won't have trouble finding each other," Kayley said. She stepped around the pair on her way toward the master bedroom.

Alexandra enjoyed the feel of the tiny grip and the warmth of Terra's body. She glanced down to her smiling face before taking a step. When Terra felt Alexandra begin to move she held tighter and began to laugh.

"Do you want my help?" Alexandra asked Kayley.

"To pick out my clothes?"

"You have a point."

Kayley entered her bedroom and closed the door. She stood in front of the dresser mirror, removed her robe and tossed it onto the bed. With a critical eye, she took inventory of the naked reflection.

"Want to hear something odd?" Kayley asked.

"Sure."

"Adam wanted to know if I would take up wrestling."

"Wrestling? As in self-defence? I can teach you some stuff."

"No I don't think he meant it in a self-defence way. He had that look he gets when we pass lingerie stores. You wrestle? Actually, I'm not that surprised."

It occurred to Alexandra that Henry had been talking with Adam about their sex life. She knew Henry liked the surprise attacks, she just hadn't known how much, until that moment. If he sold Adam on the idea then, she reasoned, Henry probably liked them a lot. Alexandra made a mental note to read up on knots and then responded to Kayley with her best attempt to sound perplexed.

"Really? Hmm?"

The creak of the floor followed Kayley, as she stepped forward and back, peered over her shoulder at herself and bounced in place at various angles.

"Are you ballroom dancing?" Alexandra asked.

"Yes. It relaxes me," Kayley replied, while slowly flapping her arms.

"You're checking for jiggles aren't you?"

"No."

"Yes you are."

"You're right. I am."

"I'm pretty sure that Adam sees jiggles as a good thing."

"I'm okay with a little jiggling, but I don't want to be doughy. Do you know what I mean by doughy? Am I doughy?"

"I don't know. Want me to feel you up?"

Kayley glared through the door before she retrieved her robe and attended to her hair. In long, loose, spirals she twirled locks of damp hair around her index finger so that her curls would dry in ringlets.

"Now what?" Alexandra asked.

"I'm doing my hair."

"You're not putting it into a bun or anything like that?"

"Two buns to be exact," Kayley bantered. "One over each ear."

"Who's a sexy girl? With a mop like that, you're obviously going to be a while, so Terra and I are off to colour."

"Walk," Terra giddily requested, and held tighter in anticipation.

Kayley enjoyed the comic drag and stomp of their departure. Her thoughts remained with them while she continued to style her hair. It was very apparent that Alexandra and Terra shared a mutual admiration for each other. However, Kayley was certain that Alexandra's affection, although very genuine toward her daughter, was rooted in a desire to have her own children. All the pieces were there for Alexandra to have the family she wanted to build. Yet they would not fall into place. She was trapped as an eternal maiden. When Kayley was finished with her hair, she refocused on the day's agenda and became nervous. She began to recite random stanzas of poetry while applying her makeup.

Alexandra stopped her clownish lumbering in Terra's room when she heard Kayley's faint voice. Although the words were indiscernible, the lyric flux was unmistakable. She grinned and wondered about the amount of wine that had been consumed prior to her arrival.

"Walk," Terra said, while looking up and poking Alexandra in the thigh.

Alexandra whinnied and made her way out into the hall, where she found Kayley waiting for a final pep talk. Black-framed sunglass rested atop waves of blond hair. She was bundled in a cream coloured wool jacket, which would have left her legs exposed below the knee had it not been for the white tube socks. From her shoulder, a small patent leather purse that coordinated with her gloves, hung by its strap.

"I'm with you right up to the gym socks," Alexandra said.

"They'll be hidden in my sexy new boots," Kayley replied, after glancing down to her feet and wiggling her toes.

"Then you're good to go."

"So you're sure you're okay with watching Terra?" Kayley asked, as she moved to the staircase.

"Positive."

"Terra, no games on the stairs," Kayley instructed when she was halfway down to the first floor.

Her mom's eye, the one in the back of her head, had caught the pair very close to the landing. Terra dismounted, took hold of the railing, and followed her mother. Alexandra remained close behind, anxiously assessing the stability of each step Terra made during her cautious, but determined, descent.

Kayley wasn't sure why she felt a need to rush, but there seemed to be some kind of momentum carrying her along that she didn't want to tamper with, for fear of stalling out completely. When she reached the foyer she immediately retrieved her boots from the closet and held them up for Alexandra, who growled seductively in response.

"You're sure you're okay with this?" Kayley asked.

"Yes. I am absolutely, totally, one-hundred per cent positive."

Terra stopped beside her mother, who had taken a seat on the staircase while putting on her boots. Kayley turned to her daughter and paused. They hugged and kissed before Kayley resumed her preparations to leave.

"You have Adam's phone number," Kayley said to Alexandra after grabbing her car keys and standing.

"I have everybody's number," Alexandra replied. She took Terra by the hand and walked with her down to the foyer.

The two women stood across from each other in a brief silence before Kayley leaned forward and kissed Alexandra on the cheek, talking to her when she moved back.

"So you're sure you'll be fine?"

"I'm positive."

"Good. Because children can smell it, you know."

"Smell it? Smell what?"

"Fear."

From the matter-of-fact delivery, Alexandra wasn't sure if Kayley was teasing. She didn't have a chance to confirm before mother and daughter were once again hugging. After Kayley stood up she smiled and then, with bracing trepidation, stepped out into the blustering cold.

"Bye, Mommy."

"Bye, Mouse. Bye, Alexandra, and thank you."

"Bye," Alexandra replied. Still analyzing the factualness of Kayley's warning, she was only partially engaged in the farewell.

Behind the protection of glass of the storm door, Alexandra and Terra watched Kayley tread carefully down the path. A gust of wind blew snow up inside Kayley's jacket when she reached the gate. She yelped and rose up on the balls of her feet. Terra giggled. Once the initial shock subsided, Kayley waved, opened the gate, then closed it after she had left the yard.

Alexandra slowly shut the door. She looked at Terra and, upon meeting her angelic face and cinnamon eyes, felt suddenly overwhelmed.

Chapter 43

After Alexandria was one of Henry's favourite bookstores. It was small and chockablock with books, which were as likely to be piled vertically up from the floor as they were to be stacked horizontally along a shelf. The ambiance was that of a disorganized study rather than a place of business. A crotchety, eccentric, and rumpled elderly man, prone to conspiracy theories, ran the store. He had left Montreal during the 1960s, when the United States was destabilizing Canada in preparation for invasion through the use of the CIA-funded FLQ: Operation Manifest Destiny. The regular patrons knew him simply as Tennyson. Faced with customer complaints, he was just the manager. Otherwise, he was the owner. No one knew the truth.

When Henry and Adam entered the store and shook off the cold, Tennyson was behind the counter, in Ebenezer repose, engrossed in the store's ledgers.

"I'm going to have to cut out shortly," Adam said. "Kayley's coming over to my place. We're bonding over some chick flick."

Overhead, on the wall behind Tennyson, were an old pendulum clock and the shop's single policy, stated in homey needlepoint.

"In God we trust. All others pay cash."

—Jean Shepherd

Tennyson greeted them with a fleeting glance above the rim of his bifocals as they opened their jackets. The look struck Adam as overtly snobbish and judgemental. It served as poignant reminder.

"Mom is supposed to swing by, too," Adam said. "I totally forgot. She's bringing a housewarming gift for the new place. Even though I told her that it was an investment."

"Introduction time?"

"I was kind of hoping for something a little less off-the-cuff."

Henry knew that what Adam had truly wanted was more time, a longer lead-up in which he could prepare Kayley and soften his mother.

Without that preparation, the outcome of that first meeting was anyone's guess. However, the amusement Henry felt at Adam's expense quickly circled back through the housewarming gift to the house itself and came to rest on Alexandra's apologetic news. Henry's smile disappeared.

"Alexandra told me that you don't want my help," he said.

"I want your help, just not building anything."

"Why?"

"Because you're too slow and it is obvious that it doesn't interest you."

"It interests me."

"Uh-huh."

For Henry, entering After Alexandria was like walking into a lush garden of books. He cherished the rich and musky fragrance of the written word. For Adam, even the dust in the air seemed held in suspension by the gummy intellectual miasma of printer's ink and parchment.

"After Alexandria," Adam whispered to Henry, as they walked toward the shelves. "Where do people come up with this stuff?"

"Tennyson claims that if the book wasn't lost in the destruction of the Library of Alexandria then he can get hold of it. And usually he can."

"The what?" Adam asked.

"Library of Alexandria. Hence, *after* Alexandria."

Henry assessed Adam's blank stare. As a teacher, he was familiar with subtle nuances of vacancy. *I have no idea what you are talking about. I don't care what you are talking about. I'm actually stoned right now—call back later.* Henry decided that the issue was an absence of knowledge.

"You're kidding, right?" Henry asked.

"What's a sister joist?" With satisfaction Adam watched his cousin blink without comment.

"Point taken," Henry conceded. "The Egyptians built the Library of Alexandria back in the times of the pharaohs. It was said to hold the culmination of all human knowledge up to that time. It was destroyed late BC, early AD. No one really knows exactly when or how, hence *after* Alexandria."

"Now that I know, I think it's kind of a cool and cocky name—in a really, really nerdy way. Thanks. Want to know what a sister joist is?"

"No."

"This is why I don't want you to help."

"Okay. What is a sister joist?"

"You don't sound like you genuinely care."

Henry's response was checked into the boards when an attractive, dark-haired man appeared from the alley between a pair of shelves referenced as "False Gods." The big chains would label a similar grouping of books as "Business." Before Henry could manage an evasive manoeuvre, he was noticed.

"Henry?" Michael asked.

"Michael. How have you been?"

"Good. It's been a while."

"Yes it has. I'm sorry I didn't return your call."

"Calls," Michael corrected. The pluralizing stretched out into a slow hissing air leak. "Don't worry about it. What brings you here?"

Henry didn't want to expose his compartmentalized life. Preparing to guard it was all he seemed able to manage. Since he was in a small panic, he managed it poorly. Adam studied his cousin and relished his obvious discomfort. Through his dealings, Adam had become very adept at picking up on the cues of body language and intonation. Although his sympathies went to Henry, Adam felt the pleasure of finally having his suspicions validated.

"I'm in search of a book on tantric sex," Henry explained, regretting his frankness immediately.

"Really," Michael said, as he appraised Adam before sauntering away. "You'll have to let me know how that works out for you two."

Adam wanted to come across as ultra-sexy, but wasn't exactly sure what that entailed to a gay man and could only come up with pouting his lips. When Michael was out of earshot, Adam quickly turned to Henry.

"My boy's a player!"

"Don't be foolish," Henry replied.

"*That* had one-night stand written all over it. Only he wanted more. I can tell these things. You callous bastard. Or should I say bitch?"

"Must you be like this?"

"I must. And he thinks I'm your boyfriend, like you'd have a chance in hell. Maybe if you were paying. But if he's seen your place he'd know that's improbable."

Henry didn't know if he should feel mortified, agitated, or relieved. Choosing to ignore Adam he continued on toward the fitness section. Adam followed closely behind, a little brother tagging along for the sole purpose of being an annoyance.

"Henry, you cannot possibly imagine how many times I've had that exact same conversation, only with women. Does Alexandra know? Are you bi?"

It was the combination of Adam's incessant pestering and non-judgemental acceptance that finally broke Henry. He felt safe to confide in him. He stopped walking and faced his cousin.

"Yes," Henry said, in a library hush. "Alexandra knows. And no, I'm not bi. It was a one-time thing and it really didn't work for me. I was at a point in my life where I wanted companionship but hated the idea of going on one more date. Then it occurred to me, that I did have an option. Can we talk about this later?"

"I'll buy the first round. So what's this about tantric sex?"

Merely thinking about Alexandra in a sexual context was often all it took to arouse Henry. He thought about the new wondrous possibilities promised in yoga, sighed contentedly, and then refocused on Adam.

"You know," Henry began. "When you take penetration out of the equation it is like the mind seeks out all kinds of incredible alternatives.

I remembered Daleesha mentioning her tantra experiences and I thought *what the hell*."

"Funny, eh?"

"What's funny?" Henry asked.

"Being at After Alexandria because you're *after* Alexandra. Get it?"

"Sometimes talking to you causes me physical pain."

Chapter 44

Kayley didn't remember that she had left the six-pack on the kitchen counter until the Beer Store came into view. Sitting at the stoplight, she had time to debate the importance of the beer relative to the convenience of purchasing it. There was one important caveat weighing heavily on her decision: she would actually have to go into the store.

She reviewed a series of worst-case scenarios, such as a strong upward gust of wind or slipping with her feet flying overhead, and assigned odds of accruing to each. She concluded that she had a fifty-fifty chance of getting into the store and back without incident. She and sexy should never attempt to travel together. Kayley was certain that the universe would surely make her pay.

When the light changed to green, she was positive that the beer didn't matter at all. Adam didn't know that she was bringing beer. *How could he miss what he didn't know about?* But she would know. *Damn it.*

Perhaps if the entry into the parking lot had been on the other side of the road or even if there were a need for an awkward lane change, Kayley would have driven past. Instead, she watched herself pull into the parking lot. A busy parking lot filled with people, mostly men.

Kayley sat in her car, gazing warily out the rear window toward the store. The snow between her and the entrance was a mix of all-purpose flour and a pulverized, slippery paste, the consistency of apple filling. It was teeming with disaster. Predatory splits, spills and total wipeouts were waiting for her under every footstep.

Resolute, Kayley picked her purse up from the passenger seat and left for the store. The car chirped its bolstering farewell as she cautiously made her way. Kayley buried her hands deep inside her pockets and drew them together across her waist in an effort to wrap inside the coat and thwart updrafts.

The motor of the automatic door gave a coarse yawn as a line of customers entered, Kayley among them. She stepped out from the flow of pedestrian traffic, lifted her sunglass to orient herself and became suddenly very cognizant of her circumstances. She was unsure if she was embarrassed, secretly enjoying it, or embarrassed because of secretly enjoying it. She decided to let herself take pleasure in the moment and lowered the zipper of her coat to expose the top of her cleavage. Men noticed.

Kayley strolled toward the counter and, as she thought about Alexandra's comment regarding repressed women from the suburbs, found her stride becoming a strut. In line at the cash, Kayley made note of the details of her surroundings, questioning, in jest, if this was to be the birthplace of a fetish. First the Beer Store, then grocery stores, entire malls, and finally, airports—flying into Pearson just to amble around in a cream-coloured wool coat.

Kayley felt empowered by the experience. Her buoyant jaunt back to the car was defiant of winter. The wind was a suitor hoping to get closer. Once inside, she stowed the case on the passenger-side floor and then admired herself in the rear-view mirror. Adam wanted her. She could've hooked up in the Beer Store had she been so inclined. Even Alexandra, the sexiest woman alive, had made a move on her. Kayley seductively flirted with her reflection, winked, and then started the car.

During the short drive to Adam's apartment, her confidence built into anticipation. By the time she had found an available space in the building's guest parking, Kayley was unable to stop smiling. She stepped out of the car, closed the door and walked around to retrieve the six-pack. There was a rattle from the bottles when she lifted the case, which prompted her to giggle. The beer was important. It made everything perfect.

She playfully sashayed toward the portico and on to the door of the main entrance. Kayley managed to work her smile down to a vague, same-as-always countenance of nonchalance before facing the camera inside the vestibule. She removed her gloves, tucked them into the pockets of her jacket, dialled Adam's call number and looked into the camera. She was let in without a word being spoken.

Securely alone in the elevator, Kayley placed the beer on the floor and unzipped her coat—making sure that it didn't fall open in the process. After picking up the case she stared up to display as it counted off her ascent. When she exited the elevator, Kayley envisioned herself in Alexandra's world. The hall was a catwalk.

Adam was already opening the door when Kayely knocked. She pushed the case into his stomach and he reflexively cradled it in his arm. Kayley kissed him passionately and they retreated into the apartment. She closed the door with a gentle sidekick, stepped back, extended her arms straight down behind herself, and let the coat fall to the floor. Adam's jaw dropped. His eyes trailed up and down her naked body. She watched him, revelling in his desire for her. After closing his mouth and blinking, he slowly turned his head toward the living room.

"Mom, this is the woman I was telling you about."

Chapter 45

"I thought I'd just bring the bottle," Adam said, as he exited the kitchen.

In addition to the Sauvignon Blanc, he was also holding a wine glass and his can of beer. Kayley was sitting on the couch, waiting for his return. Had it not been for the intensity in her eyes, an outside observer might be inclined to assume that she was in a trance.

She was dressed in the baggy flannel shirt and rugby shorts that Adam had hurriedly provided her. He was fully aware of the fact that they would never be returned, and he would never ask. His rush to find her clothing had been bogged down by self-serving indecision. He had found a pair of long track pants prior to the shorts, but he enjoyed the shape of Kayley's legs so he had kept digging.

With uncharacteristic gallantry, Adam forced the image of her standing naked in the doorway out of his mind—each and every time it reappeared. He made a monumental effort to remove from his awareness the fact that she was without underwear. Regrettably, the cognitive resources available to Adam that were not related to sex were sparse.

"So I guess a romp is out the question?" he asked, as he sat down beside her.

It was not difficult for Adam to see where Terra had gotten her expressive face. The message Kayley relayed, while not precisely clear, was understood. Many interpretations could be made of the fixed, stone-set stare that he found himself suddenly contending with. The kindest of which would be along the lines of *Just how much an idiot are you?* He poured her wine.

"It was joke," he lied. "To lighten things up."

"That was a lasting first impression." She took the offered glass, and stewed over being blind-sided. "You could have told me she was here."

"I didn't know you'd be throwing yourself at me. Very sexy by the way."

"Still, you might have mentioned something when I was in the entry. Sexy? Really?"

"Secretly inform you that my mother is in the apartment—while she was right there? I know her. She would have thought something was up."

"Something *was* up."

"I didn't know that."

Adam put his arm around Kayley and gently pulled her closer. Initially resistant, she allowed herself to find comfort and rested against his shoulder. He kissed the top of her head and then tiny spurts of laughter started to escape. Hearing him, as well as feeling the unmistakable reverberations in his body, perked up Kayley, in spite of herself.

"Your mother thinks I'm an airheaded bimbo," she said.

"No she doesn't. Trust me, she has seen her share. And lady—I think it's an incredible statement about your strength of character that you didn't bolt."

"I was a deer in the headlights."

For emphasis, Kayley did her best saucer-eyed impression of blank shock. Adam's laughter at the mimed trauma channelled into a sympathetic pout that melted her frozen stare. Their eyes met, she smiled meekly, and he kissed her.

What had actually kept her at the apartment was her belief that they were building a life together. Had their relationship been anything less, she would have run from the building, packed everything she could into a suitcase, and left no forwarding address.

"I take it Alexandra told you about the perfect date discussion."

"Yeah, she did. But don't be upset with her. And don't tell Henry, but she's giving the perfect date another try."

Kayley had intentionally omitted that Alexandra would be proposing during the perfect date. She was struggling with the possibility of Adam's mother being an in-law. Forever. Complete denial offered her a temporary reprieve.

"Alexandra is making dinner? Poor Henry. Having to eat her cooking. Wow. The things guys do for the women we love."

Kayley was flabbergasted. "Hello!"

She sat up and drew attention to her current attire with an emphatic pass of her hand and then slapped him on the shoulder. Adam sheepishly acknowledged the obvious and kowtowed into a gentle kiss on her assailing palm.

"I might be ticked at Alexandra," he said, "if that wasn't the hottest thing that has ever happened to me."

"Hottest? Really? No."

"Really. Yes. You have a wicked body."

Although still working through personal mortification and his unspecified culpability in the matter, Kayley found herself charmed by Adam's flattery and captivated by the sincerity.

"You did seem really turned on," she said.

"Turned on doesn't even come close. I was having a horny meltdown."

"I felt pretty sexy."

"I could have objectified your brains out right there on the entry mat."

Adam's words, while lacking poetic grace, held an unornamented, mannish appeal for her. Visions of him being overcome by desire filled Kayley's imagination. She curled up against his body suggestively.

"How about we start this again," she proposed, "right at my arrival, and see how things should have gone?"

Chapter 46

Red wine exploded from Alexandra's mouth and a vast, ruddy constellation sprayed across the kitchen cupboards. She propped her arms against the countertop for support, as her initial hysterical scream of laughter quickly subsided into a staccato barrage of deep snorts. When Alexandra finally caught her breath, she managed a raspy apology that amounted to the word sorry looping mirthfully around inside a wheeze.

Kayley grew tired of waiting on Alexandra to gain her composure and smacked her butt with a large wooden ladle. Alexandra snapped upright and peered over her shoulder. Staring at Alexandra's flushed complexion, puddled eyes, and running nose, Kayley was unable to remain stern.

"Done?" she asked.

"His mom was there?"

"On the couch drinking tea. She actually took a sip before speaking. The bitch."

"I am so sorry. I should never have told you about his perfect date."

Alexandra wiped her tears and then padded her fingertips against her dress. She sniffled, tore off a section of paper towel, and while blowing her nose, examined the mess that she had made of the cabinets. Kayley interpreted Alexandra's resulting widened eyes and approving nod as a combination of amazement and pride.

"I'm an adult," Kayley said. "I make my own choices. However, I would like to point out that if Adam's idea of a perfect date was Henry's idea of perfect, there wouldn't be an issue."

"So you blame Adam?"

"Not really. But I'm thinking of working it."

Alexandra tossed the paper towel into the wastebasket under the sink and then moistened the dishcloth before returning to the cabinets. Kayley placed rolls into the oven, set the timer, and then did a quick review of the list she had placed on the fridge. She wanted to ensure that all possible contingencies were completely covered. The entire evening had been reduced to a timed agenda. She knew that Alexandra would be anxiously fixated on her watch until the meal was over. Kayley also knew that Henry would understand. She was confident that he would avoid any distractions, like asking about her day, and restrict his minimal conversation to sentences that started with *please pass me the*. Kayley watched Alexandra wipe the cabinets and thought about her and the odd, but very loving, relationship she shared with Henry. While thinking about the future they would share, the solution to Alexandra's pregnancy issue became suddenly blatantly obvious. It had been right there the entire time, just a matter of thinking a little outside of the box, or rather, the womb. Kayley revelled in her own genius.

To reach a particularly elusive droplet Alexandra raised a leg flush against her shoulder, causing the lace hem of her cotton dress to slide down from her mid-calf into the tuck between her pelvis and upper thigh, and took hold of the dishcloth in her toes. She arched forward during an amazingly elongated stretch that extended way up to the farthest, most northern, snow capped reaches and wiped it away. Satisfied with her facile victory, one that had astonished Kayley, Alexandra dropped the cloth into her hand, tossed it into the sink, lowered her leg and attempted to straighten out the dress. She did a few exasperated tugs against the fabric and then shared her frustration with Kayley.

"Frig! Why does Henry like dresses and complicated dinners and shit? Naked and beer looks real good from where I'm standing."

It took a moment for Kayley to fully digest the casually executed impossibility that had just taken place right before her eyes. Alexandra's complaint waited in the queue of Kayley's consciousness, while all the *agog* was being whisked away.

"Because he wouldn't be your girlfriend if he didn't. Ready for the walk-through?"

"You're right," Alexandra agreed. "Walk me through."

"The timing of everything, down to the smallest detail, is in the instructions."

"What if there is a snag and I get delayed on something?"

"Just stick to the agenda."

"Stick to the agenda," Alexandra reinforced to herself.

"Think of the agenda as the evening's choreography. You're a dancer, you get choreography."

"Let's be blunt here. Sure you can call me an exotic *dancer*, but really—I'm a stripper. All that matters is that I'm naked. After that I could sit on a bar stool and read a magazine for all anyone would care."

"You are a dancer, an exotic, erotic, mind-blowing, top-billing dancer. And you know it. Don't psyche yourself out. When entertaining, it's all about going with the flow. I've done this kind of thing numerous times. Nothing goes wrong, there is merely a change in plans."

"What if I ruin dinner?"

"Then serve it naked," Kayley joked. She walked to Alexandra and gave her a hug.

PAIRS

Kayley reviewed the itinerary, item by item. For Alexandra's sake the meal had been laid out in a step-by-step fashion. Cooking temperatures and approximate durations were clearly specified. Kayley avoided terms like pinch or dash in situations where ingredients needed to be added. Not wanting to panic Alexandra, Kayley bypassed any mention that not all stoves were equal. She simply provided her with a cooking thermometer.

Once the kitchen overview was completed, Kayley led Alexandra out into the living room. Alexandra wished desperately that she could make crib notes on her hand, but Kayley wouldn't let her. The evening needed to be perfect.

White cylindrical candles, each the thickness of a newel post but varying in height, were arranged in small groupings waiting to be lit. On top of the coffee table was an opened bottle of Merlot, flanked by a pair of wine glasses. Kayley walked Alexandra through the evening, ending at the couch where they rehearsed the proposal.

"Are you nervous?" Kayley asked.

"Very. I'd much rather wander around naked at a frat house than this."

"Which you've done?"

"I wear shoes though. God only knows what gets on those floors," Alexandra replied, before surprisingly fishing her hand around her cleavage. "You really do need to wear a bra with a dress like this. No pockets."

"Pockets?"

"For the ring," she answered, while reconfirming its snug position.

"You do know that guys don't get engagement rings? They just get wedding rings."

"Kind of a rip, eh? I know. It just seemed stupid to propose and not slip a ring on his finger."

"So what are you going to use for a wedding ring?"

"Same ring. I'll just re-slip it on."

***

The apartment had begun to fill with the aroma of cooking bread by the time Kayley left. It comforted Alexandra, and gave her confidence. Feeling a little more at ease, she took the long-neck butane lighter from the desk in the foyer and returned to the living room.

Set into the corner, between the window and fireplace, was a cluster of three white pillar candles—the tallest rising up from the floor to knee height. Alexandra tapped the flame against the wicks, as if the lighter were her magic wand.

With the ding of the timer she spun around in the direction of the kitchen. The lace of her dress passed over the flame of the candles, becoming alight. She could feel the heat against the back of her legs and looked down over her shoulder to find that a smouldering fire was slowly eating the dress. Alexandra shrieked and fished between her shoulder blades to unfasten her dress. Panicking, she felt for an opening in between the seams, dug her fingers in and tore the dress open. The buttons fell like hail. Alexandra quickly pulled off the straps, dropped the dress to the floor and jumped back. She landed on the hem of the curtain, which lay in a puddle of fabric on the floor behind her, and promptly started to lose her balance as the fabric slid along the hardwood. Her arms thrashed in the air until one managed to wrap in the curtain. Under the force of her erratic tugging the metal rod was pulled out from the wall and knocked her on the head before hitting the floor. Alexandra stepped forward, slipped off of the drape and reeled a few gangling steps, then tripped and smashed the bridge of her noise against the edge of the coffee table. She rolled onto the floor with a thud and stared blankly at the ceiling, which shimmered in double vision. The wine bottle, peeked down, spat on her face, then tumbled onto her forehead and trundled aloofly away while burbling incomprehensible criticisms. The odour of smouldering cotton wafted in the air.

"I fucking hate, hate, hate! Fucking dresses!"

The smoke detector screamed to life.

Chapter 47

When Henry arrived home, a fire truck was pulling away. The last of the tenants, some with their coats over pyjamas, were heading back inside. He walked with the procession into the lobby and climbed the stairs to his apartment. The door was slightly ajar. Alexandra's winter jacket was flopped across the desk in an uncomfortable contortion.

"Hello?" he called, while cautiously stepping down the hall. "Alexandra?"

"I'm in the living room," Alexandra mumbled, sounding very defeated. Her congested words tumbled out in a Rocky Balboa accent.

When he passed the kitchen he looked in, with forensic interest, at the cookie sheet on top of the stove. The batch of charred biscuits sitting in a skim of water served as a telling indicator of what awaited him. Once at the living room, Henry's pace slowed considerably as he attempted to fully digest the scene before him. Alexandra was sitting on the floor underneath the window, holding a small bag of ice to her nose. Her knees where up by her chest supporting an arm. She was barefoot and dressed in a bra and track pants. Henry's track pants.

On the floor, beside a singed dress, was a partially emptied bottle that lay in a pool of its own red wine. A large chunk of plaster was missing where the bracket of the curtain rod had once been. Alexandra looked at him. There were dark crescent bruises under her eyes.

"Oh my God," Henry exclaimed as he rushed to kneel in front of her. "What the hell happened?"

"A change in the stupid plans happened." Alexandra replied, sarcastically.

"What?"

"Nothing. Sorry. I was just remembering something Kayley had said to me."

"Are you okay?"

"I never, ever, want to wear a dress again."

"Sure. Whatever you want. But are you alright?"

"Yes, I'm fine. Just disappointed. I wanted this to be special."

Alexandra reached under her bra and pulled out the ring, a single gold band. "I want to explain to you why I don't want to be penetrated and why I'm afraid of getting pregnant. Then you can decide if you'll marry me."

"Of course I'll marry you." Henry was amazed that she could think otherwise. And he was equally astonished when he realized that she was proposing. "I love you like oxygen."

It physically hurt to cry and even more so to smile, but she did both anyway. Henry kissed her. Alexandra flinched when he brushed against her nose.

"Sorry."

"Sshh."

Although enjoying the moment, Alexandra wanted to share her story before she lost her courage. It had been relatively easy informing Henry that she didn't want to be penetrated, but it was very different and difficult for her to now share the reasons why. Not only was there the pain of the memories, but also the fear that he might see her as someone to pity. Alexandra didn't want to be pitied. She only wanted to be understood.

With the gentle pressure of her hand against his shoulder, she guided him back and then pointed to the couch. Henry followed her and they sat facing each other. She placed the bag of ice on the side table before speaking.

Alexandra had difficulty with eye contact as she recounted her past. After she was done, Henry moved with uncustomary speed. He cradled the back of her head and drew her into his chest.

"My *nothe*!" she protested, before pushing herself free.

"Sorry," Henry replied, as he watched Alexandra softly clasp the bridge of her nose.

She studied him, and to her relief found only sympathy and understanding. "What was your childhood like?"

"Typical WASP," he said. "Nothing remotely approaching what you went through. It seems almost petty talking about it."

"I'm interested. I shared, now you share. It's a couple's thing. Geez, and I thought I was bad at this."

"Alright, but if I get the least bit self-indulgent or maudlin, you have to intervene."

"Can't promise anything, mostly because I don't know what maudlin means. But if you start to annoy me I'll cut you off. How's that?"

Henry leaned forward and kissed her on the forehead. "Fair."

"My mother and I were very close," he began. "She was a gentle, understated, and cultured woman. I loved her dearly. She passed away from cancer when I was twenty-two. My father and I are not close. Never were actually. I don't think I was the son he had been hoping for. I wasn't a jock. Actually, I think the existence of professional sports is clear indicator that humanity is not going to make it. And he wanted me to follow in his footsteps to become a lawyer. I am an all around disappointment for him. He remarried a few years back to Helen's mom. I hardly ever hear from him. All rather 'Cat's in the Cradle.'"

"As in the song by Guns N' Roses?" she asked.

"I was thinking Harry Chapin, but yes."

Noticing that Henry was seeking to cuddle, Alexandra lifted her arm to allow him to slide under. He lay back against her torso, and rested his head on the front of her shoulder. She lowered her arm, kissed the top of his head and breathed in his scent.

"One thing is for certain," he said.

"What's that?"

"I'm sure not marrying my mother."

"No shit! You might actually *be* your mother."

Chapter 48

"Kayley, I'm telling you, she looked like she went for a tumble inside a cement mixer," Adam said, while drying his hair with a towel.

"I haven't seen her yet," Kayley replied. "But she tells me she looks pretty roughed up."

He draped the towel across the back of his neck and chuckled. "When I first saw her, I thought she'd been mugged. I have to give her credit though. She put in a hard day's work at the house. Afterward, she asked me to take her on full-time. You know, teach her the trade."

"Alexandra wants to be a carpenter?" Kayley asked.

"She's got a knack."

Adam hung the towel on the doorknob and then slipped under the covers beside Kayley. He lay on his back and she cosied up against his body. She rested her head on his shoulder, warmed her bare feet against his, and traced her fingers through his chest hair.

"I don't know what Helen sees in smooth men," Kayley mused.

"I always figured that any woman who wants a smooth man secretly wants another woman."

Kayley gave a front of coming to her friend's defence by tugging on the chin whiskers of his beard. "Is that what you figure?"

"Yep."

The two lay in silence thinking about Alexandra. Kayley was filled with wonder about a woman who seemed to tirelessly reinvent herself, and always for the better. It gave Kayley hope that perhaps she could do the same. Much like Alexandra and even the Grand Dame, it would just require a little help from loving friends.

Adam replayed her arrival at the site that morning wearing brand new work boots and an empty tool belt. He had been on the porch when Henry had dropped her off. In spite of the numerous bruises and scrapes on her face Alexandra had been grinning from ear to ear. With her index finger and thumb in her mouth she gave a piercing whistle to announce her arrival on the outside chance that Adam had somehow failed to notice her explosion from the car. As she charged toward him, Alexandra had raised a cardboard carrying tray in which two cups of Tim Horton's coffee rested snugly.

He had led the way into the house. For the official start of the demolition Adam had thrown a claw hammer, like a hatchet, across the expanse of the addition and into the far wall. It was trick he did to impress the newbie. She nodded and, without speaking, pulled the hammer out, drew a hand-sized circle on the wall with a piece of gypsum, came back to stand beside him, and then threw a bull's eye. He gave her the hammer to keep.

"What do you think about their engagement?" Kayley asked. She propped herself up on her elbow in time to watch the colour drain from Adam's face.

"I'm happy for them," he replied, cautiously.

"Don't worry, Adam. This isn't a devious ploy to trick you into proposing."

"Worried? Why would I be worried?"

Kayley's plan had been so very clear to her, but on the cusp of saying it aloud for the first time, she began to have doubts. She lay back down and rested her head on his chest.

"Adam."

"Yes."

"I've been thinking," she said, in gingerly spoken words. "About Alexandra."

"Her getting married?"

"Um. No."

"About what then?" He asked.

"About her vaginism. And children."

"Yeah. Henry seems perfectly fine with things, but I guess that really does impact them having kids."

"Interestingly enough, I have a solution."

"That being?" Adam inquired.

"I could be their gestational surrogate."

"As in carry their child?" He confirmed, while peering down at the top of her head.

"Exactly, her egg and my womb," she clarified. And then after a brief forgetful pause finalized her explanation of the arrangement. "And, of course, Henry's sperm."

Had Kayley been watching Adam, she would have seen his agitated disbelief take hold. He felt possessive and encroached upon. His resentment came out reasonably sterilized when he put into words.

"How long have you been thinking that?"

"Funny you should ask. I believe for a while now."

"Believe?"

"Subconsciously."

"Ah."

Adam's carefully metered reply concerned Kayley. It reminded her of the night at Daleesha's party when she had first met Henry. Where previously she had been flattered, she now found herself worried about Adam. Although his role, for the most part, would be physically uninvolved, it could be emotionally tumultuous.

Adam's cool reception, although not entirely unforeseeable, had surprised her. During the uncomfortable silence that followed, Kayley considered his reaction and came to a sympathetic understanding. In many ways, she had been alone during her first pregnancy. And it was in that mindset that she had become determined to carry Alexandra's child. She had not given his feelings much consideration during a decision process that had revolved around Terra, Alexandra, and herself.

"What are you thinking?" she finally asked.

"Thinking? I'm not really thinking about anything, nothing rational anyway."

"What do you mean?"

"It's wonderful that you want to help. Henry is like a brother and I think Alexandra is great."

"But?"

Sometimes the most basic thoughts and emotions are the hardest to express, at least in a manner that doesn't expose the tantrum of an inner child. This was the issue that Adam was contending with as he assembled the wording of his response.

He wanted Kayley for himself. Terra was a wonderful part of the package but the idea of her carrying another man's child, now that they were together, bothered him. Even if that other man was Henry.

"But it bugs the shit out of me that you'll carry their child before you'd have ours."

Kayley sat up, crossed her legs, and stared at Adam. She was flabbergasted, more by what was implied than what was said. He wanted a family with her. He wanted a life together.

"You want to have children with me?"

"Yes, but I'd like to be married first."

"Are you proposing?"

It was Adam's turn to sit up. He rested against the headboard, took hold of Kayley's hand and smiled. Outmanoeuvred and outgunned, there was nothing left to do but concede.

"So this *was* a devious ploy to get me to propose—spooky. Alexandra was right. You do have feminine wiles. This is so not the way it should go. I'm ringless. Can this be a proposal to propose?"

Kayley squeezed his hand. Neither the artist nor the romantic in her wanted to let the moment slip away unfulfilled. When she started to slowly shake her head, Adam was initially concerned that she wasn't accepting.

"No," she said, her grin blossoming. "You're a resourceful man. Fashion something."

"You want me to fashion a ring? Now?"

"Yes."

Adam swung his legs around to sit on the edge of the bed. He glanced back at Kayley and then leaned sideways to retrieve his jeans, which were draped over the footboard. He dug inside a front pocket and pulled out the pair of keys for the new padlock he had just purchased. A thin ring of open-ended wire joined the keys. He freed the band and sized it to fit Kayley's finger. Satisfied, he stepped onto the floor and knelt before the bed, in the nude. Kayley extended her hand from underneath her bedsheet toga. Before Adam's proposal was underway, there was light knock.

"Mommy. My bed is wet."

"I promise. I'll do a better job of this later," Adam whispered, after he and Kayley had glanced at the door.

"It will never be more perfect then it is right now."

"Mommy?"

"In a minute, Mouse."

"I'm wet!"

"Soon baby."

"I. Am. Wet!"

Frustrated, Terra grunted, slumped into a seat on the floor and proceeded to rap the back of her head against the door. Neither Kayley nor Adam was overly sympathetic to Terra's plight. Bubbles of suppressed laughter ran amok throughout his proposal and during her acceptance. The rhythmic thud of Terra's head gave their exchange a medieval chantefable quality. It couldn't have been more perfect.

Chapter 49

"This was a great idea," Alexandra said while peering over her shoulder as she backed the car into the parking space. "I've never been to a spa."

"So you've said." Kayley was still astonished by the possibility.

PAIRS

For her, it was like meeting a woman that didn't like chocolate—you hear about them but you never expect that you are actually going to meet one. She sat, guilt-ridden, watching as Alexandra put the car into park before turning off the ignition. Kayley was tweaked by concern that she had somehow forced her own version of a perfect girls outing onto Alexandra.

"Would you rather be doing a pub-crawl?" she asked.

"With Henry and Adam?" Alexandra responded, as she prepared to step out into the cold.

"No, no. Our own pub-crawl."

"Don't be silly. I know Henry is really the bride in all this, but I still want to girly up for the wedding. Pedicure, manicure, facial, get the pubes done—shit like that." Alexandra gave a friendly pat on Kayley's knee and then stepped out of the car. She walked around the front and opened the passenger side door. Kayley looked up.

"And I still feel funny about you paying," she said, as she stood. "I'm supposed to be taking you out."

"First, you are not taking me out," Alexandra replied. "We are going out together. And second, stop being so silly. I want to be here. I want to pay."

Kayley knew that it was a matter of economics. Alexandra had much deeper pockets. A great body earns more than great greeting cards. Being the benefactor of a friend's generosity was not a new experience for Kayley. Both Helen and Daleesha had paid her way before. Extravagant expenses such as cruises, resorts, and spas were simply not in her budget, and they had known and accepted that reality. Kayley was always grateful. However, with Alexandra, she felt more than gratitude, Kayley was also very flattered.

"This is so awesome!" Alexandra said.

She was staring up to the main lodge at the top of the steep, snow-covered hill. The building exuded calm. It was a peaceful temple of wood and glass nestled amongst regal evergreens and tall, slumbering hardwoods.

"It's sort of romantic," Alexandra said.

"Yes," Kaley agreed contentedly, while weaving her arm into Alexandra's. "It is."

***

"So?" Alexandra asked, with childlike enthusiasm.

The two women, clad in plush, white terry robes, were standing across from each other in the middle of the change room. Kayley debated with herself whether she would prefer to step into one of the privacy stalls. Alexandra sensed her hesitation and playfully rolled her eyes.

"Just a quick flash," she said.

"Alright then," Kayley replied.

Wine had made her a little daring. She scanned the change room for onlookers and then slowly parted her robe just below the tied belt.

"A Brazilian," Alexandra cried out in surprise.

"Yes. Lower your voice."

"Won't Adam be surprised?" Alexandra commented gleefully.

Kayley relished the thought as she let her robe fall closed. Alexandra waited until she had Kayley's full attention before untying her belt, taking the side hems in each hand and, in theatrical grandeur, performed the unveiling.

"An exclamation point?" Kayley verified.

"Yep."

Kayley saw the choice as perfect. It was a fitting crest for a woman who lived life in exclamation. Caught up in the energy and charm of the moment, Kayley stepped forward, placed her hand behind Alexandra's neck and kissed her. Alexandra, while surprised, had come to the conclusion that such passionate sessions were merely part of how their relationship worked. As their lips continued to roll one into the other, she recalled her former life and how she would sometimes make out with other performers backstage or in the washroom. It was releasing and yet focused her to the role. It was raw, sexual, and tied to the circumstance.

However, with Kayley, it was tender and tied to the person.

"Sorry to gawk," a woman said.

Kayley and Alexandra untwined and looked in the direction of the voice. A middle-aged woman was standing just inside the doorway, watching dreamily.

"It was just so romantic," she continued. "How long have you two been together? I wish I could inspire that kind of passion in Harold."

"Well," Alexandra responded proudly, as she stepped aside to allow the woman a full view. "I inspired it by getting my pubes done."

***

Alexandra slipped her robe on over her bikini, then sauntered over to the privacy stall were Kayley was changing and knocked on the door. Their earlier encounter, especially with it having taken place in front of a witness, had stirred Alexandra to sensual thoughts.

"Kay, have you ever wanted to use a strap-on?"

"A strap-on? A strap-on what?"

"A strap-on dildo. I'd like to do Henry."

"With a strap-on?" Kayley exclaimed in surprise, and then repeated the question softly, as if to counteract her previous volume. "With a strap-on?"

"Yeah."

"Like, up his butt?" Kayley whispered. The image of Alexandra wearing a strap-on dildo cleared all other thoughts out of her head.

"Just like," Alexandra replied, in a quiet yet exuberant tone. "Henry may be prissy in some ways, but in the sack, he is up for anything. Oh, and I'd nail him good! First I'd start off doggy. Give little nips on his back with my teeth. Then I'd weave my fingers through his hair and pull him back for a long, hot, kiss."

It was such a strange visual for Kayley. She stopped putting on her bathing suit and remained seated on the bench half-naked, imagining.

"Kissing like we did at Daleesha's?" She asked.

Alexandra found the association to their night together to be a curious choice on Kayley's part. Her interest was further piqued by the enticed quality of Kayley's voice.

"Exactly like that." She purred into the stall door, fishing for revealing intonation. "Maybe I'd give a smack on the ass, and all the while I'd just be pump'n away."

"And missionary?"

Alexandra misinterpreted the reason behind the continued suggestive questions. She thought that it was a game of arousal. Up for the challenge, she was determined to win.

"Definitely," Alexandra replied.

"And nibble on toes?"

"A little."

"And body kisses?

Alexandra had to concede that Kayley was a better player then she had anticipated and cursed herself as she glanced around the change room for curious eyes when her fingers, veiled within the robe, seemed to take on a life of their own under the bikini briefs of her swim suit.

"All over," she whispered into the gap by the door's hinge.

"And suckling?"

"Oh yeah."

"And kissing around the neck?"

"And all the while I'd just be pump'n away."

"Just pumping and pumping."

"Yes." Alexandra's agreement trailed off in a long seductive hiss, as she became lost to the fantasy.

"And ears?"

"For sure."

"And you would just keep on pumping?" Kayley confirmed, sounding to Alexandra was if she was a little breathless. "Pumping hard?"

Alexandra's legs were giving way underneath her. With her knees buckling together, she stood pigeon toed and grasped the top of the stall's door to keep her balance.

"Like a piston," she grunted.

The stall had rattled with the impact of Alexandra's hand. Kayley's attention was immediately drawn up to the powerful grip that held on like the paw of a great panther that was threatening to rip the door from its hinges to ravage her.

"Oh Gawd!" Kayley blurted.

Alexandra's response was interrupted by Kayley's moan, which quivered into dead silence. During the afterglow, Kayley's unfocused stare remained on the door. It took her a moment for Alexandra's questions to register.

"Kay? Hello Kay? Are you in there? Earth to Kay."

"Here," Kayley managed, as she finished putting on her swimsuit. "Sorry, I just had a cramp."

"Was it in your clit?" Alexandra teased.

Kayley composed herself, gathered up her belongings, put on her robe, and opened the door. Alexandra, who seemed rather mischievously satisfied with the outcome, was standing right outside.

"Did your mind wander off to Adam land?"

Slightly flustered, Kayley eyelids fluttered before she nodded. Alexandra stepped aside as Kayley strolled lazily past, distracted in thought. Her motions seemed slow and unfocused as she fumbled around inside her locker. Alexandra was overcome by a childish desire to revisit their word of the day.

"Pump!"

Kayley instantly drew a deep breath and shivered.

***

Alexandra was sprawled in her chair like a large pampered cat, passively letting attendants work on her hands and feet. Her eyes and mouth were the only parts of her face not concealed under a cleansing mask, and both displayed gratification. Kayley sat in the chair beside her, equally spoiled and every bit as content.

"Well?" Kayley prompted.

"Not to upset anyone here, but I think I'm getting a little frisked up. I can't imagine what the full body massage is going to do."

"It's not upsetting," said the woman who was kneading pleasure into the pads of Alexandra's feet.

"Not all-out horny, but definitely on the runway. If you know what I'm say'n."

Drawn by the ensuing quiet titters, Alexandra tilted her head sideways toward Kayley and, after making eye contact, winked. There was something Kayley found flirtatious in the gesture. She winked back.

After a fleeting smile of ease, Alexandra slowly rolled her head to watch the primping of her fingers and toes, and, in so doing, was reminded of the reason for their visit to the spa.

"Henry keeps fighting me on the whole wedding thing," she said.

"What do you mean?"

"He keeps telling me that he just wants it to be the four of us. But I know he's lying."

"What makes you think that?"

"Kayley, all brides-to-be want a big wedding. But even if you ignore that, we're talking about Henry and his chance to throw the event of the year."

"You have a point I suppose."

"I can't figure it out. And every time I push for an answer he goes bridezilla on my ass."

***

The two women sat across from each other, picking at the final course of their meal. A candle flickered on the table. Kayley sipped her wine and absently watched the light catch in Alexandra's eyes and radiate softly against her flawless skin.

"Do you get tired of people calling you beautiful?" she inquired, after lowering her glass.

"No," Alexandra replied, with matter-of-fact candour. "But it really only holds meaning when said by a few people."

"Like Henry?"

"And you," Alexandra said, briefly holding Kayley's gaze. "But for different reasons. It is nice hearing it from a woman."

"You are beautiful, you know."

Kayley took another sip of wine and compared herself to Alexandra. In contrast to the reserved modesty with which she hid her body, Alexandra's robe was draped on her with casual allure; seductively open, so as to tease passersby with the possibility of it falling off entirely.

"I should be jealous, but I'm not. Do you want to know why?"

"Why?" Alexandra asked.

"Because your beauty wells up from inside you. Unaffected. How can I be jealous of something so wonderful?"

Alexandra had not expected Kayley's reason or the sincerity and smiled shyly. She felt her cheeks begin to blush and she glanced down to take a brief respite from the honesty.

"*When she lowers her eyes, she seems to hold all the beauty in the world between her eyelids,*" Kayley said, in a soft voice. "*When she raises them I see only...*"

Alexandra looked up and Kayley fell silent, she was captivated. Alexandra knew the day's wine would, sooner or later, lead to the wonderful, pearl-sized recitals. She remained appreciatively quiet while Kayley recalled her intended words.

"*I see only,*" Kayley whispered, as she regained focus, "*I see only myself in her gaze.*"

"That was beautiful."

"You can thank Natalie Clifford Barney."

"And you. Thank you."

***

"That was Alexandra, they're nearly here," Adam said, as he placed his cellphone back into his pocket. "Kayley sounds a little tipsy. I could hear her performance in the background. And something about a Highlander."

Adam and Henry quickly finished their drinks and were making their way to the door when a large, sweaty man stepped out of the backroom. He recognized Adam's red hair immediately and yelled at him.

"You're that little shit that had me barred from the Elm Street job site."

Adam and Henry faced the man as he marched toward them. A hush fell and the bartender reached for his baseball bat. In the excitement no one noticed the arrival of a beautiful woman with short dark hair. She strolled up behind Adam and Henry and began to carefully remove her shoes, so as not to chip a nail.

"Listen you drunken, fat turd," Adam shouted. "*You* got you barred."

"Perhaps we could settle this over a drink," Henry offered.

"Stay out of this Henry," Adam said.

"Yeah Henry," the man barked, as he raised his fist, and then suddenly dropped from sight.

In the blink of an eye, a man's ugly head had changed into a very recognizable foot that remained in front of Henry's face while the pretty toes wiggled. He knew that Alexandra was attempting to draw attention to her freshly painted nails. It was as if showing off her pedicure had been Alexandra's sole intention, and it was haste that had caused her to accidentally, and quite unwittingly, punch a man's skeleton out of his body.

"What do you think babe? Isn't it just so girly?"

Chapter 50

Silence comes in many forms. It can be serene and thought-filled or, as was the case while Kayley waited on Helen's reaction, it can be a lit match floating down to a puddle of gasoline.

"What?!" Helen's voice shrilled up an octave.

"Lower your voice. The idea was really brought home to me after our time at the spa. I could carry her child. It is as simple as that. Voilà, baby makes three."

Kayley became briefly lost to the image of Alexandra sitting across from her in a veil of candlelight, and she recalled the wonderfully fitting words of Natalie Clifford Barney. *I see only myself in her gaze.*

"Voilà! For God's sake, Kay, give your head a shake."

Helen hung the bra and matching panties over the door of the change room, which was Kayley's signal to promptly whisk them away. There were two events in Helen's life that led her to splurging on insanely expensive undergarments—when she felt she'd gone without sex for far too long and when she was having an overabundance of it. Regrettably, the current foray was the result of the former, which thereby had set a less than jovial mood for the sharing of Kayley's news.

"Could you imagine shopping here with Alexandra?" Helen commented offhandedly. "I'd be depressed for weeks."

"I think it would be a hoot. She'd be just as likely to try things on right in the middle of the store as to bother going into a change room."

"Okay, that would be funny. But still depressing. And don't change the subject."

"You brought it up."

In hurried frustration, Helen put on her skirt and blouse. Kayley could hear the annoyance in Helen's breathing and was prepared for the lecture when the door swung open.

"Kay, you can't have this woman's child. You barely had your own."

"And I learned from that experience. I learned about my body and how to manage myself better."

"It is not as if this woman is barren, she actually can reproduce. Can't she?"

"Outside of that one tiny hurdle of nothing goes in and nothing comes out. Yes, I imagine she can."

"Look Kay, honestly, I'd be a little more sympathetic if there was no other way. But the issue really is a psychological one. She just needs to attend to that."

"Psychological is every bit as real as physiological. Helen, she deserves a child."

"Then she can adopt."

"There is nothing wrong with adoption. But I think my solution is better. Alexandra would be part of the miracle of birth. It may inspire her."

"You are too much of a romantic," Helen said as she closed the change room door. "And as stubborn as they come."

Kayley remained staring at the door. She thought about Alexandra and the words of Sappho that at once warmed her and strengthened her resolve. *Amongst all mortal women the one I most wish to see.* Kayley felt a need for the last word, if only as a symbolic blow to any challenge.

"It's only being stubborn if I'm wrong," she finally replied. "And I'm not."

There was a long, heavy sigh from the other side of the door.

Chapter 51

The wedding ceremony had been an uncomplicated event. As the honorary bride, Henry had made demands for simplicity. At his insistence, the entire affair had been contained to themselves, two witnesses, Kayley and Adam, and a pretty little red-headed flower girl.

Terra might have been more impatient but she had been distracted by contradicting memories and conflicting emotions. Terra recalled the baby with greater clarity then ever before. The memories brought a deep sadness but it was soon forgotten in a rush of incredible joy. And there was still the puzzle of the island of trees. She had glanced down at her shoes, to help solve the maze of duck-feet remembering.

Kayley was the only one who knew the reason behind Henry's persistence to keep the wedding ceremony scaled down. It had occurred to her during the vows, when she had thought, briefly, of her own wedding. As she began the list of those she would invite, Kayley also drew a parallel list of those Alexandra could have invited. And then she knew the protective care Henry had taken.

Who would sit on Alexandra's side? The answer had already registered with Kayley before she finished asking herself the question—very few. Alexandra was a runaway who had become a stripper to survive and then gave it all up to become a waitress. Kayley's attention had changed to Henry. She watched him, the bitchy bride who had stubbornly held steadfast to his decision. Brushing aside her tears, Kayley was uncontrollably happy.

Most of the guests at the reception didn't know that they were at a reception. All, except Helen, Daleesha, and Tess, thought that they were at a housewarming being thrown by a very peculiar group of investors. When the bridal party arrived the atmosphere was that of a country fair. Hot dogs, sausages, hamburgers, fries, and poutine were being served to order by the caterer. Pop, beer, and bottles of uncorked wine were on ice in large metal basins scattered about the main floor. Bales of hay were strewn around the front yard and provided extra seating inside the house. Out back a miniature pony was giving rides to neighbourhood children. Circulating among the guests were a clown and a magician. Alexandra had been in charge of the reception. This had been the trade-off Henry had agreed to so that he could have the wedding ceremony his way.

Adam looked over to Kayley, as he parked the car alongside the curb. She saw the teasing commentary coursing to the surface. Her eyebrows crimped and she gave a subtle disapproving shake of her head. His amusement was in response to the bunting around the porch and eaves and the balloons that covered the facade like hives. Through the living room windows they could see the magician, who appeared to be wondrously removing a coin out of an elderly woman's ear.

From the elevation of the car seat, Terra had a clear view of the house. It wasn't sad anymore. She wondered whose birthday it was and began to think about cake. The only person in the car more excited than her was Alexandra.

Alexandra could barely contain herself. When Adam had stopped the car, she squeezed Henry in a tight hug, then shot out toward the house. She bounded through the snow in her high heels and stopped midway to the porch to admire how well her plan had come together. When Alexandra looked back at Henry she was beaming.

"So?" Adam whispered.

"Anything less and it wouldn't be Alexandra," Henry replied, as he smiled and waved to her. "Besides—it is kind of barn-like in there right now. I think she did well."

"But this is not what you would've done."

"Not in a million years."

"Do I hear music?" Kayley asked.

"John Denver, I believe," Henry said. "*Take Me Home*. And I think it's coming from the backyard."

"Whose birthday is it, Mommy?"

Daleesha opened the front door, a simply adorned Nubian princess, beautiful and regal in spite of the beer bottle in her hand and the short length of straw that hung from the corner of her mouth. Her arms opened flamboyantly to greet Alexandra.

"It's not a birthday party, honey," Kayley said. "This is for Alexandra and Henry because they got married."

"Look!" Terra shouted. "A clown."

Alexandra galloped through the snow to the porch, kicking up a cold, white wake. Daleesha moved forward to meet her. Tess stepped into the doorway. She glanced at the two women hugging, then looked over to the car when Adam stepped out. She nodded her greeting and, for his benefit, visually surveyed the surfeit of festival adornment.

"And the party is a little bit for the house, too," Henry explained to Terra.

His comment redirected Terra away from the unfolding events of the present and back to her home. She recalled the time she had been sitting on the floor colouring and had been trying to figure out where Alexandra's room was. In an instant, Terra knew she had remembered the place wrong. It was clear to her that it had always been the birthday house. She was certain.

Inside, Alexandra's magnetism had several husbands in trouble before she had her first drink in her hand. Adam's entrance had quelled the wives. Turnabout was fair play. The residents on the street had been debating the nature of their relationship for several weeks. Although the interaction between the two of them suggested friendship, it was too tragic to image that the gorgeous pair were anything but passionate lovers.

It wasn't until Helen announced a toast to the bride and groom that the neighbourhood began to piece together the relationships. While everyone was outwardly happy for the newlyweds, they all felt a profound letdown when their collectively crafted story of steaming, torrid beauty was lost forever. All the evening's unguided tours to rooms that could have served as carnal dens were for naught. Adam and Alexandra were merely buddies.

During the course of the evening, Kayley found herself alone with Henry in the newly reconstructed addition at the back of the house. The room was a much brighter incarnation of the original, due to the large windows. When he entered, Kayley was standing at the patio doors, watching Helen walk beside the pony while Terra was having her ride. He was curious about the temporary bedroom that had been framed within the addition.

"She's a beautiful little girl," he said. "You're very lucky."

"Yes she is. And yes I am." Kayley said, while turning toward him.

Henry was standing where the former entry had been. In the redesign the kitchen space simply flowed seamlessly into the room, as if it had always been that way.

"Congratulations," she said.

"Thank you. Have you and Adam given any thought to a date?"

"After the house is done," Kayley replied. She glanced down to the ring that had replaced the original wire band when it had been retired to her jewellery box. Both would become heirlooms.

Henry directed her attention to the bedroom with his thumb. He was obviously perplexed and Kayley reasoned that he was hoping she could provide an explanation.

"In case of working late," she said. "But primarily for conjugal visits. Alexandra stumbled across us once."

"She mentioned that. Adam has a nice ass I've been told. Apparently not as nice as mine though. Why not upstairs?"

"That's because of me. I go to the bathroom at least twice a night, and with no running water upstairs, I got tired of coming down here in the dark. Adam said it was easier to build a bedroom than to quickly fix the plumbing."

Kayley became aware of Terra's cranky tone and looked out into the yard. She found her daughter refusing to let go of the reins. Helen was attempting to reason with her, but to no avail. A young male attendant was waiting patiently. Kayley opened the door and called out to her daughter.

"You have to share."

"No."

"Terra!"

"I want to go again."

"Terra."

"It's my house."

"Don't make me come out there, young lady."

There was a brief staring contest before Terra released her grip. As Helen lifted her from the horse she mouthed *thank you* to Kayley, who similarly replied *sorry* before closing the door.

"Still think I'm lucky?" she asked Henry. He had moved beside her to watch.

"Yep."

"You're right."

Beyond wanting to extend the offer of bearing Alexandra's child, Kayley really had not planned out the timing or place where she would talk to them. She had imagined tiny parcels of the conversation, during which they were all together, as two couples. Yet, for whatever reason, as she and Henry stood observing the pouting exploits of her little red-headed Veruca Salt, it felt like the moment had presented itself.

Henry wasn't sure how long he had been the focus of Kayley's benevolent attention. She was obviously very happy for him, which he found confusing. He thought it similar to the inebriated affection that frequently accompanied the announcement of a heartfelt *no really, I mean it* affection. Yet the poetry hadn't started.

"His own parents," she said.

"Whose parents?" he asked, which launched her into a recital.

His own parents,
He that had father'd him, and she that had conceiv'd him in her womb,
and birth'd him,
They gave this child more of themselves than that;
they gave him afterward every day—they became part of him.

"Oh," Henry said. "Those parents."

Kayley giggled before offering her succinct explanation. "Walt Whitman."

She clasped his hand inside of hers and her eyes joyfully welled up. Not understanding the nature of her tears, Henry was surprised by the sudden surge of emotion and became concerned that something was horribly wrong.

"Henry."

"What is it, Kayley?"

"I'd like to propose something."

Chapter 52

As tends to happen at receptions, the new bride and groom spent a significant portion of time apart. Many of the neighbours had a genuine interest in the plans for the house, and found Henry's use of layman's terms and his vivid imagery far more accessible then Adam's dry contractor-speak. Throughout the evening he found himself heading up various small clusters of people, mostly women, who were eager to hear about the design. During each of these tours Henry was inevitably questioned on what he thought about the name of the neighbourhood. The general consensus, he discovered, was that Heighten Park was felt to be too short for an area of such growing calibre. *Estates at Heighten Park Reserve* seemed to be the crowd favourite. While holding some minimal appeal, it struck Henry as trying too hard in a new money, tract housing sort of way. His response was a polite, noncommittal smile that skimmed ever so close to being patronizing.

Alexandra, on the other hand, found herself continually engaged in conversations with men from the neighbourhood. She did not talk about design. She could have recited the alphabet or counted to one-hundred, and that would have been perfectly fine.

In the living room Tess had joined Adam and Kayley by the fireplace. Over the course of the evening the more Tess drank, the less she spoke to Adam and the more attention she lavished on Kayley. Adam's close proximity by no means left him anything more than a sidelined spectator. He felt almost intrusive, but was finding the flirtation too funny to walk away from. Through the long gaps of his exclusion, Adam would periodically take curious visual passes of the room.

It was during one these sweeps that he noticed Henry taking Alexandra aside. He sat with her on a nearby bale of hay and took her hands. Adam could see that Henry was explaining something, but he couldn't make out the words. After Henry stopped talking, he waited. There was an initial delay and then the burst of life. Alexandra squealed aloud and wrapped her arms around him, appearing to squeeze out his breath during the embrace.

PAIRS

For her part Kayley behaved with Tess, right up until the moment she excused herself to go to the washroom and brushed her cleavage across Tess's arm. Adam studied the affect. Tess's eye's widened and then nearly rolled up out sight when Kayley had left the room.

"Have a boner?" Adam asked Tess.

"Pretty obvious eh? Sorry for cruising your girlfriend."

"Fiancée actually—and no you're not. Go right ahead. She laps that stuff up. And I'm going to reap the benefits tonight."

"You're right. I'm not. Fiancée? Congratulations! God, I love her tits."

"Me too. Then Alexandra must float your boat, too."

"Great bod for sure—but you know I like'm real femme. No doubt about it, Adam, we share the same taste in women."

"Alexandra is kind of guy, eh?"

"With great tits."

Daleesha, upon hearing Alexandra's name, wandered into the conversation. She put her arm across Adam's shoulder and smiled at Tess, before raising her empty beer bottle for a toast.

"To Alexandra's great tits."

Not all of the onlookers close by were sure they had heard correctly. Of those who were, the reactions varied. But none were spoken. Some were offended, others amused, one or two were sympathetically embarrassed, but several raised a glass—if only in their mind.

Adam was a little hesitant to join in. It seemed odd to objectify his friend. Alexandra was close enough to overhear Daleesha, and witness Adam's discomfort. Without Henry's awareness, she caught Adam's eye and winked her approval.

For a brief moment, after Adam and Tess had lowered their drinks, Daleesha remained with the bottle to her lips, as if waiting on the remnants of a slushy to slide down. She finally gave up and quizzically peered inside, becoming too preoccupied to notice that Alexandra was coming over to join them. Daleesha concluded that the bottle was empty, lifted her head, and was happily surprised.

"You know," she said to Alexandra. "I really regret never seeing your act."

"Stripping? I've stripped for a bunch of lesbians before. It was fun. Women are a lot more vocal and encouraging. Men tend to quietly gawk."

Alexandra peered around Daleesha and giddily waved to Henry, who was on a search for Kayley.

"Hey," Tess offered. "A couple friends of mine are getting married. Maybe you can give us a show. I'd pay."

"Oh hell, I'd do it for free," Alexandra said. "I sort of miss it. I'm pretty damn good."

Adam, both amused and amazed, stared at Alexandra. Initially she didn't understand the reason behind his shock, but after spotting Henry bringing a glass of wine to Kayley she remember her nuptials and his fussiness.

"Actually, I should probably run it by Henry first."

"He's a man," Tess noted. "Wouldn't he get off on you stripping for a bunch of horny lesbians?"

An emphatic response simultaneously leapt from Adam, Daleesha, and Alexandra.

"No."

Chapter 53

The wedding reception, housewarming, and county fair ended in the early evening. The streetlights had yet to reach a unanimous decision that the sun was setting.

By all accounts the celebration, in its many facets, had been a resounding success. A Grand Dame had been returned to the fold of her neighbourhood. Alexandra and Henry had celebrated their union with those they loved and those they had just met. Daleesha had gotten pie-eyed for the first time in her life, and Terra had calmly understood that even though Barley the horse had had fun, he wanted to go back home to be with his family.

It wasn't long after the horsey had left that Terra went down for the night, but only after being assured that the balloons on the front of the house would still be there in the morning. She had kept a suspicious eye on Alexandra, searching for crossed fingers.

When the door closed on the last of the departing guests, namely Daleesha and her designated driver, Helen, Alexandra turned slowly toward Kayley—who, upon seeing her friend's uncoiling excitement, braced for impact. Under the influence of liquor-fuelled elation, Alexandra's sudden embrace of Kayley shared the qualities of a hug and a tackle. With one arm still wrapped around Kayley, Alexandra reached her hand behind Adam's neck and pulled him close for a long, full-lip kiss. His mind leapt away in startled bewilderment.

"You guys are awesome," she declared, as she moved to stand beside Henry.

"I think there is a lot to this," he said to Alexandra. "Maybe we should all have a little sit-down to make sure we are all on the same page?"

"Are you kidding? I want to do cartwheels."

"We need to give some thought as to how this would all transpire."

"Duh! You boink her," Alexandra replied, and then stopped to think about the arrangement. "Actually, no. That doesn't work."

Her outburst gave Adam his bearings and he finally understood all that must have been discussed earlier that evening without his involvement. Alexandra had also affected Kayley, leaving her with emotional afterimages. There were selfish elements to her offer, an infatuation she was unable to completely ignore.

"If this is some ploy for a swap," Adam said jokingly, to mask his annoyance at Kayley, "what the hell. But I will be thinking about my girl the entire time."

Henry and Kayley gave the barest acknowledgement to Adam's comment. Alexandra, however, found it hysterical. Initially, Adam had assumed that her laughter was the result of his joke, but as they waited and waited on Alexandra to catch her breath he began to wonder if the humour she found was at the thought of the two of them together. In principle alone, he was slightly offended.

"To the living room?" Henry suggested.

"I don't think we can hammer this out now," Adam replied.

"Well, I'd like to hear Kayley's thoughts. And yours as well."

"Me too," Alexandra said. She walked toward a small cluster of bales.

Henry followed her into the room and helped to arrange a loose circle of hay benches. Kayley was unsure about Adam's mood. With his arms crossed, he was watching Henry and Alexandra. He smiled when he noticed Kayley attempting to read him. Her reciprocation was hedged.

"I'm okay," he said. "I was just caught off guard."

"Are you sure? I'm sorry. There was just a perfect moment."

"Yes. My inner Neanderthal is just whispering stupid stuff."

"Your inner Neanderthal?"

"Henry used to say that to me whenever I did anything he thought was particularly macho-stupid or testosterone-laced. He is also the inventor of 'testosterone-laced.'"

"I love you," she said. "You know that."

Once the bales were positioned, Alexandra took Adam and Kayley by the hand and led them to their seats. Henry felt a growing sense of pride as Alexandra filled a glass of wine for Kayley and brought a bottle of beer to Adam, opening it for him. She was attempting to be gracious.

After refreshing Henry's drink she sat down, wove her legs together, brought her hand by her ear and aimed at a can on the mantle.

PAIRS

She snapped her fingers and the bottle cap shot from her hand. Accompanying a dull metallic ping, her target popped into the air then hit the floor with a hollow rattle before cadaverously reeling into the wall.

"Five-by-five," Adam said, as he leaned forward to smack hands with Alexandra. After sitting back, she opened the group discussion. "Let's chat."

"So close," Henry mumbled.

"What are you talking about? I nailed it!"

Kayley enjoyed the unforeseeable, unpredictable, and quirky coupling of Henry and Alexandra. She patiently watched their silent repartee of annotated postures, his disappointment and her confusion, play out.

Adam became mildly amused when he noticed Alexandra's eyes narrow slightly as she stared at Henry. There were times when his persnickety behaviour had a rather unusual affect on her. He could irritate her into wanting to rip his cloths off and drive him insane with desire—oddly, as a means of teaching him a lesson.

"A few things leap to mind," Kayley said, once the couple had settled. "From least important to most important. First, I don't know a lot about the process but my understanding is that there is heavy medical intervention both before and after. Hormone injections and such. And that is going to cost money—pretty big money. Also, this could be a long process. I think it's fair to say that transplanting an inseminated egg into me is not a guarantee of success. There could be a few attempts."

"I've got pretty big money," Alexandra said.

"Does stripping really pay *that* well?" Adam asked.

"It pays well. If you're in demand."

"Adam!" Kayley berated.

"Sorry."

"No, it's fine," Alexandra replied. "But the big coin came from my dad. When he died his life insurance money went into a trust for me. My mother went ballistic. And it all became mine at eighteen."

"What else have you been thinking about?" Henry asked Kayley.

"That egg would be my egg right?" Alexandra verified. Her question coincided with her realization and ensuing apprehension. A simple, yet unsettling, biological reality took centre stage in her mind.

"I know we are all close," Kayley said, favouring Adam as she spoke. "But this will either make us closer or put a huge strain on things. I'd like everyone to be involved. And finally, and most importantly, I have to think of a way of explaining things to Terra."

"Of course your egg," Henry said, after taking Alexandra's hand. "And my sperm. Kayley would be our gestational surrogate."

"Your sperm! Big deal. Like getting that will be a real complicated procedure. How exactly do they get my egg?"

"Actually," Kayley corrected, "eggs. Plural."

"Guzz! Eg-guzz! How do they get them?"

Alexandra sat upright. Her eyes darted between the consoling faces. Sympathetic, but telling, smiles confirmed her worst fear. Her head dropped briefly to stare down at the only possible entry point and then, aghast, she looked at Kayley.

"I'm not a chicken coop," she proclaimed. "I mean, it's not like you can just pluck them from the nest."

"Not the best analogy," Kayley said, softly. "But that is pretty much the process."

Initially, as Alexandra's head fell back and her eyes furled into their sockets, Henry thought that she was building up to one of her all too familiar total-body sneezes. However, when her colour began to drain away and her hand became limp, it occurred to him that she was fainting. Henry rallied to catch her fall. Kayley and Adam rushed to help.

"In hindsight I probably should have mentioned early on that she'd be asleep," Kayley surmised, which earned the understated ire of Henry's rebuttal.

"Yes," he agreed, dryly. "In *hindsight*."

Chapter 54

Adam fell into an introspective mood after they had left the house. He wasn't sulking, but he was definitely elsewhere. Kayley had become aware of his distraction the moment they had entered his truck. She didn't regret her actions, the universe had presented the moment, but she did wish that her offer to Alexandra had hatched with more tact and less *dropping of bomb*.

She used the excuse of attending to Terra, who was asleep in the car seat between them, to spend time gauging Adam. His reflexes managed the driving while he sifted through the events of the evening in an attempt to isolate what was truly bothering him.

The full moon, high overhead, shone through the windshield and flooded the cab in soft alabaster. Within the veil of powdery light, Adam appeared to her to be made of Carrara marble. Only the occasional eye movement and steering adjustment told otherwise.

Adam went back and forth in his mind between the idea of Kayley carrying another man's child and the feeling that he had been relegated to the role of spectator. He supported the right of a woman to control the fate of her own body, yet his internal debate concerning freedom of choice continued to chase its tail around searching for consistency. If he believed that a woman had the moral right to have an abortion without her partner's agreement, did he also believe that a woman had the moral right to have a child under the same conditions? Was it the same thing?

"What are you thinking about?" Kayley asked.

"Not much. Just tired I guess."

Adam wanted to ask Kayley about her opinion of his role. He wanted an understanding of just how far removed she thought him to be, but he feared the answer. "Are you staying over?" Kayley asked.

"Not tonight. I have to get an early start tomorrow."

"Terra and I don't mind."

"Well, there is stuff back at my place that I'll need. It's just less of a hassle if I sleep at my place."

They rounded a corner and Adam fell into darkness as the moon swung to the passenger side of truck. Kayley looked out her window and up toward the universe she had trusted earlier that evening. It offered no counsel.

"This is important to you," Adam said, without taking his eyes off the road.

"Yes," she said, facing him. "But so are you."

"Kayley, I want to be in your corner. I just need a little time to digest everything."

"We did talk about it beforehand."

"Not really. It was more like you informed me. And then you just sprung it on them without giving me any advance warning. Until Alexandra said that Henry should boink you I had no idea what she was going on about."

It was an unpleasant enlightenment for Kayley to discover her lack of empathy for the man she loved. She had gotten swept up ahead of herself. She hadn't appreciated Adam's perspective. Upon further reflection, Kayley conceded that she hadn't really given it much consideration at all.

She knew he was right: inclusion did not equate to involvement. Telling him of her plans was not enough. He needed to feel that they, as a couple, would be helping Alexandra.

"I'm sorry," she acknowledged. "I just got this idea in my head and ran with it. Or rather, it ran with me. This could have been done a lot better."

Adam drove onto Kayley's street, thinking about her apology as he followed the bend down the short hill. When they arrived at the townhouse he parked the truck across from the gate and left it to idle. Before preparing herself for the cold night, Kayley reached over the car seat and took Adam by the hand.

"We are in a partnership. Really," she said. "I'm just not used to being in one."

"Me neither."

"This is a good thing we are doing."

"I know. Rationally, I know. And now that the offer is out there—it's real. Just give me a night. I have a Neanderthal to talk down."

"Okay," she whispered.

They remained looking at each other as Kayley retracted her hand. Adam, unfastened his seatbelt, leaned over Terra, and with a long and tender kiss reassured Kayley that he was truly asking for only the one night to let everything settle in his mind. Terra's only protest to the intimate scrunch was a soft gust of air from her nose.

Chapter 55

"Adam?" Henry asked.

"No. I just killed him and took a break from disposing of the body to answer his phone."

"You're in a mood."

"No mood. What's up?"

"You seemed a little out of sorts when you left."

"I *was* a little out of sorts when I left. I'll be fine. I just need some adjustment time."

"Kayley's offer?"

"You picked up on that, eh?"

"Look, Adam, if this is going to cause grief between the two of you—let's just forget anything was ever mentioned. We never want this be a source of tension."

"Henry, there's a couple of layers to this."

"Which are?"

"You cannot make fun of me, or pull any sort of big brother bullshit if I tell you."

"I won't."

"The offer itself bugged me a little. She will be carrying your kid before she carries mine. She is my fiancée. It is her body and all that, but still—she's with me. I'm working through that. I'll be fine. I get that it is a good thing. And I'd do anything for you."

"I can understand that."

"But the part that really pissed me off was that Kayley didn't include me. She told me. But she didn't include me."

"I don't get the distinction."

"She didn't talk to me about it. Never asked my feelings. At no point in her thought process was the impact on my life, my plans, my hopes for us, factored in. She just kind of dumped it on me."

"Ugh! Adam, I didn't know. Honestly, I didn't know. Have you talked her about that?"

"Yeah, on the way home. She apologized."

"So what now?"

"I brood for a night. Then suck it up. And we all move forward."

"Adam, I can never repay you."

"We're family—no repayment required."

"Adam."

"Oh shit. Don't."

"I love you."

"Aw fuck. I love you too, Henry. Good night."

Adam hung up, placed the phone on the coffee table beside his laptop and returned his attention to the screen. He had been researching vaginismus since his return to the apartment. With minimal effort he discovered that, while severity and manifestation varied, vaginismus was considered the most successfully treatable female sexual disorder. His findings supported his initial thoughts about Kayley's offer and prompted a call to her. The phone rang once before being answered.

"How are you doing?" She asked, after noting the name on the call display.

"Kay, I have a question."

"Okay."

"I've been doing a little digging and it seems to me that vaginismus is pretty curable. I mean there are even self-help kits. I guess my question is why doesn't Alexandra get cured and then have her kid."

"She has to want to first. She can't be forced."

"And you can't bear all her children. What if she wants a second?"

"One step at a time."

"Step? This isn't a step, Kay, this is BASE jumping!"

"Adam, a very wise and charitable man once asked me if I've ever helped out anyone just because they deserved it. For the first time, I can now confidently answer yes." As Kayley waited on his response, she deliberated on her philanthropy. She was unsure if she would do the same for anyone other than Alexandra.

Adam stared at the receiver and then rested it against his forehead. She had convinced him, with his own words. For all that didn't rest well with Adam, he had no counter-argument to offer. He took a deep breath before replying.

"Kay?"

"Yes."

"I'm not going to win too many with you, eh?"

She smiled broadly from within the cocoon of her blankets and then rolled onto her side to nuzzle affectionately against the handset of her phone. Kayley was relieved that their first disagreement had past.

"I love you," she whispered intimately, before teasing him. "And no, not likely. But never let the odds stop you from trying."

"I love you, too. And I won't."

Chapter 56

Autumn had left barren the linden tree outside Kayley's townhouse. She was transfixed by the image. It was larger than she remembered and closer to her bedroom window than she recalled.

A vast crown of branches married into the surrounding darkness, inseparable from the night, frenetic desperation frozen into the ground.

Blackened limbs,

Reaching,

Grasping

Petrified
Death-throw

Horror

The horror.

Kayley awoke in fear. Instinctively she reached to Adam's side of the bed. But he wasn't there. She sat up and switched on her reading light to find herself alone. A gust of wind rattled the panes of her window, reminding her that it was still winter. She recalled that Adam had gone to his apartment.

Though her initial panic had receded, she still was not at ease. The experience couldn't be dismissed as a nightmare. It was too vivid, and left her feeling compelled to check on Terra.

Kayley got out of bed and went out into the hall, with only the light from her bedroom to guide her. She found her daughter, in the barest silhouette, sitting up in her bed and looking out the window. She glanced briefly at her mother.

"Did you have a nightmare, Mouse?"

"No." Terra faced Kayley once again.

"Are you okay?"

"Can I sleep with you?"

"Of course," Kayley said, extending her hand.

Terra slid herself toward the edge of the bed, hopped down and joined her mother in the hall. Holding hands, they walked back to Kayley's room and climbed into bed together. Terra snuggled up against her mother. Kayley switched off the light, put her arm around Terra, and stroked her fingers through her hair.

"Mouse, Alexandra and Henry want to have a baby. And while the baby is waiting to be born he, or she, is going to be staying with Mommy in my tummy."

Terra glanced up at her mother. Kayley didn't know how to interpret her daughter's minimal response. She had expected questions, but Terra didn't seem the least bit curious.

"Do you understand, Terra?"

"Yes," she said, and then buried her head into the safe comfort of her mother's shoulder like she used to do to escape the fog.

Chapter 57

"Kay, please tell me you're joking," Helen said, after taking a sip of coffee. The mug nested in her hands, close to her torso. She was hoping to hold onto some of the radiant warmth.

Kayley and Helen were the lone patrons in Decadence. The shop offered a splendid array of desserts but was, unfortunately, located in a converted warehouse on the ground floor of a drafty old building. In the depths of winter, chills wandered through like miserable ghosts.

The sole employee was a gothic, flaxen-haired, young woman. Friendly on approach—but otherwise stoically fixed behind the long bank of display cases, where she was putting in a marginal effort to ensure the cash register wasn't stolen. This was the usual state of affairs during the mid-afternoons of the workweek.

"If I told you that, then I'd be lying," Kayley replied. Without stretching her arm, she lowered her fork across the small café table into Helen's marble cake and scooped a little piece for herself.

"You're actually going through with it?" Helen confirmed, before sampling Kayley's slice of caramel pie.

"Yes."

"What are you thinking? What does Adam think?"

"I'm thinking I'd like to help Alexandra. Adam? Well, he was a little put off at first. But he's come around. I think this has actually made us closer. Made us appreciate what it means to be a couple."

"Put off? He's probably worried sick."

"Worried? No, he's not worried."

"Not worried? Why not?"

Helen took a very modest piece of cake onto her fork. Her theory, which she knew to be silly and therefore never shared, was that if fat was eaten in tiny morsels it would just pass through the body undetected and exit without leaving a trace. She had been judging the size of the speck when Kayley had responded. The marginal confession of her tone had not immediately registered with Helen. Her eyes widened when the implication finally dawned on her.

"Oh God, Kay! You haven't told him. You have got to tell him!"

"Then he'll worry. And if nothing happens he'll have worried for nothing."

"Do Alexandra and Henry know?"

Kayley peered, childlike, over the brim of her mug as she took an evasive sip of coffee. Helen stared flatly back and placed her fork firmly onto to the table, as if dropping a gavel.

"Oh my God! You have got to tell them. They need to know what they are asking of you."

"They didn't ask me, I offered. And if I did tell them they may not take me up on it. Then what?"

"Then you don't have a stroke and die!"

"Don't be so melodramatic. They would need to find another surrogate. Do you have any idea what an ordeal that can be? Or how long it can take?"

"Now that you put it that way, endangering your life seems like the only rational course of action. Unless of course you factor in *adopting*. Then you come off as a complete flake."

The showdown was brief. Had there not been a long, shared history together, Helen might have spent a little more time trying to persuade Kayley. But she knew her friend too well. Kayley's mind was made up. *Damn all reason—full-speed ahead*. Helen shook her head and, before taking a sip of coffee, lobbed her closing remark on the subject.

"Your doctor is going to have a cow. An absolute cow."

Chapter 58

"There she is," Alexandra said.

Helen and Daleesha twisted around in their chairs. Kayley was unzipping her coat while entering the restaurant. Alexandra recognized the creamy colour from the fateful perfect date. She had been under the impression that it had been permanently retired, but began to speculate that Kayley might have simply stopped wearing it around *her*, likely because of the teasing.

Kayley scanned the surroundings and slipped the strap of her purse off her shoulder. She had never before been inside a Hooters restaurant, with all its orange and white and its cloned beauty. During her panning sweep she spotted the women and waved. Alexandra was smiling very broadly. Kayley realized the error of her hasty choice earlier that morning, yet managed to conceal her mortification.

Alexandra stood, and reached for a hug. However, with her hands starting just below her sternum and the right-angle bend at the elbows one might be more inclined to believe that she was simply mimicking a flasher. They embraced nevertheless.

"I hate you," Kayley whispered into Alexandra's ear, before stepping back and quizzically taking in their surroundings.

"Alexandra's pick," Daleesha explained.

"Isn't your birthday coming up?" Alexandra asked, as a prompting reminder to the *obvious* motivation behind her choice.

"So this is for my benefit?" Daleesha questioned.

Alexandra cupped her hands under her breasts, bounced in place, winked, and returned to the table. Daleesha, at once flattered and embarrassed, felt obliged to express gratitude for the consideration. She winked back. Helen and Kayley froze, marrying their efforts not to laugh. Alexandra looked up toward Kayley and patted the seat of the adjacent chair. Helen waited until Kayley had settled in before starting her well-mannered cross-examination.

"So?"

"My doctor said that we are a go. Suggested that I lose a few pounds before starting anything," Kayley replied.

"Really?" Helen asked. "Is that all she said?"

"More or less. I'll just have to watch things." Kayley pulled a business card out of her purse. "Even gave me a referral."

"More or less?"

"Isn't that a little personal?" Alexandra asked Helen, while plucking the business card from Kayley.

Helen raged a non-verbal siege against the stubborn bastion of Kayley's stoic resolve. The battle was held to a draw when Daleesha intervened.

"That's good news then."

An impossibly cute cheerleader in a shrink-wrapped T-shirt and shorts found her way to the table. She had perky blond hair, perky French manicured nails (which Helen and Kayley assumed were fake), a perky body, and a light, airy, blue-eyed gaze that attempted friendly interest. Alexandra did a quick up-and-down inventory and was satisfied on

Daleesha's behalf. Helen made a bet with herself that the first words out of the young woman's mouth would be *hey guys*. She was not disappointed. While the drink orders were taken, Alexandra examined the business card.

"Doctor Hugh Jass?" she questioned, after the waitress had left the table. "That's a joke, right?"

"What size do you think she is?" Kayley wondered aloud.

"Which parts?" Helen replied.

"Hugh-jass," Alexandra reiterated, melding the doctor's first name into his last. From the general apathy at the table, it was obvious to Alexandra that she was alone in her observation. She was annoyed that no one else could see the humour.

"Hughjass!"

Kayley recognized that Alexandra was attempting to make some sort of point about the doctor, but the gist entirely escaped her. She was trying to connect the name to an event in the news or to a literary character, but finally accepted her own ignorance and slowly shook her head.

"Huge! Ass! You've been referred to Doctor Huge Ass."

"Bummer," Daleesha noted.

After an audible *tsk*, Kayley snatched the card and returned it to her purse. Alexandra was surprised and confused by the terseness. For Helen, the overreaction was the first visible sign that her romantic friend might not be immune to concern.

"I'm not taking this as a joke, Kayley," Alexandra assured her.

"Oh really? Doctor Huge Ass?"

"I was just goof'n around. That doesn't mean I'm not taking this seriously. It's exciting for me. I'm happy, so I make jokes. Sorry if I upset you."

Helen and Daleesha waited on Kayley to complete her scrutiny. She was pushing time forward, envisioning what Alexandra, the earnest child maiden and life's veteran, might be like as a parent. Although she knew the nature of the relationship between Alexandra and Henry, Kayley could not envision her in the role of father. She saw her as a wonderfully playful mother. It was not an entirely clinical exercise, for Kayley was also admiring Alexandra's pleasing beauty and melting to her charm.

"Huge ass is pretty funny," Kayley finally agreed. "Of course, now I'm going have it on the brain when I go to meet him. Thanks."

"I want to do something mommy-ish now. Like bake cookies," Alexandra announced, and then quickly deflated. "Only I can't bake."

"Use the premixed stuff," Helen said. "Couldn't be easier."

"Yeah?"

"A tube of dough. Preheat the oven, cut up the tube into medallions, and bake. Voilà—cookies. All the instructions are right on the package."

"Wouldn't Henry be surprised?"

Part VI

Chapter 59

Kay, you remember Andy Garrison's girl, Tanya? Well she's in university now. Can you believe it? He was over the other day, re-shingling the shed for me. He's good with the odd jobs. I always used to hire him to do something or other for me. He needed the cash back then, but was too proud to take charity. Hard-working man. Of course, now that he's been doing those stints out in Fort McMurray, he wants for nothing. Did the shed for free. Said my money was no good.

Why do you let me ramble dear? Anyway, Carver and I were out on the deck, giving ol' Andy moral support and shooting the breeze over some lemonade. If that's not one of the best things of summer, I don't know what is. He is some proud of that girl of his. She's the first in his family to make it past high school. She may not find work from it, at least not out here, he says, but she'll sound real smart when she's complaining about the lack of jobs.

She's helping to foot the bill, too. Just like her father, not the kind for a free ride. Didn't a grand story come out of that? Andy says that Tanya tells it best, but he gave it a shot.

Seems last summer Tanya ended up working at some posh restaurant in Moncton. Tourists mostly. On one particular shift Tanya was stuck serving a table-load, and they were giving her the gears, a real demanding lot. When it was time to clear the table, apparently Tanya wasn't doing it fast enough for one particularly supercilious—love that word—mare. There was poor Tanya, loaded with plates, and this woman pipes something about hers being left. The woman stands up and dumps everything on top of the stack that Tanya was carrying. And then it all came crashing down. The woman shrieked and tore a strip off poor Tanya, up one side and down the other. "Stupid, incompetent, lazy, good-for-nothing French tart." Tanya, head high, holds the woman's gaze, musters all her courage and dignity and replies, "I am not French." I thought Andy was going to fall off the roof, he was laughing so hard. I bet Tanya will relive that one for a while. All the things she could have said, and then saying the most foolish thing possible. At least she can laugh at it now.

Reminded me of me, Kay. I'd like to apologize. I just want you to know I said what I said out of love. For you and that girl of yours. I didn't mean to obtrude my opinion upon you. Obtrude seems like an appropriate description for my actions.

I just want you to know that I worry. Your pregnancy was such a hard one and then you go off and volunteer to help that poor couple. You can see how I might be thrown. It is commendable, dear, very heroic—it shows the strength of your mother. I'm proud of you. And I'm glad that things have worked out. I'm so happy it is going well. You know that my prayers have always been with you and Terra. Well, I just want you to know that my prayers are with the little one, too.

Chapter 60

<u>Beep-beep</u>

Spring crawled from the ditch,

Soggy and beleaguered,

Lay on the roadside gravel

Panting in shallow breaths

Run over by Summer

Reckless and wild-eyed

Kayley was sitting at the picnic table they had built inside the back addition of the Grand Dame. She giggled softly at her tiny poem and then returned the notepad and pen into the side pocket of her robe and resumed nursing her daily mug of mildly sweet tea made from the flowers of the linden tree in front of her townhouse. Under advisement, it was habit she had taken up during her pregnancy with Terra. She was certain its benefits had made all the difference and abated her hypertension.

Before her rush of inspiration, Kayley had been admiring her garden. The dew sparkled in the morning sun on the leaves, which had taken on the rich colour of jade in the yellow light. All of her plantings were doing well—but the sheer bounty of tomatoes, above all else, gave her the greatest sense of pride. After picking her very first tomato Kayley had held it in her open palm with enamoured disbelief. Later she had done a sketch, which now hung in the kitchen. Her quiet mornings alone, gazing out into the backyard and musing, had become the contemplative ritual she reserved for her visits to the house. The impending arrival of Adam's mother was the current morning's topic for rumination.

Without conscious effort on anyone's part, the Grand Dame had become a cottage where the two couples would lodge together, in their collective getaway, for extended periods. Exposed joists, drapes of vapour barrier, partially completed sections of drywall and visible pipes and wiring all contributed to the pseudo-rustic ambiance that gave a feeling of being at camp.

Kayley had taken the role of preparing all the meals and the unfinished kitchen was her cookhouse. It was not that she lacked faith in Henry's epicurean skills. It was merely that roughing it dictated comfort food and *vittles*. He couldn't seem to fathom the concept.

After finishing her tea, Kayley went to the kitchen and quietly began preparing breakfast. She was careful not to disturb Alexandra and Henry, who had claimed the temporary bedroom in the addition as their own. Thinking about the unborn child she shared with Alexandra, and the bond it made, brought a wonderful sense of contentment. The journey had been physically difficult for Kayley, and there were many disappointments. They had all but given up when the miracle had taken hold in late spring. Kayley was not aware that she had begun to hum.

***

Alexandra lay beside Henry, who was still sleeping. She raised her hands into the radiant yellow-gold sunlight that shone between the curtain panels of the tall window, causing a momentary tussle in the lazy school of dust that was basking in the warmth. After noticing the shadows on the wall she attempted hand puppets. To her frustration, everything ended up as two encephalitic, large-billed ducks. While the ducks mimed an argument, Alexandra listened to Kayley and tried to guess the tune. She raised her leg into the band of light and it reminded her of the Loch Ness monster. With both hands she took hold of her toes and the image played out as Nessie being kissed by the ducks. When Alexandra decided that the ducks were actually Nessie's children it occurred to her that Kayley's song was "Hush, Little Baby." She thought about her child, wondering how the lullaby would sound from within Kayley's womb.

Henry had been watching Alexandra out of the corner of his eye. He hadn't made the association between her movements and the unfolding melodrama on the wall. He thought that she was stretching. Speculating that she might be performing yoga, he was reminded of his purchase at After Alexandria.

"Have you ever practiced tantra?" Henry asked. His voice startled Alexandra and her limbs quickly withdrew to the mattress.

"Tantra?"

"Weren't you just doing yoga?"

"No." Alexandra sat up and re-enacted the duck argument for Henry's benefit. "Shadow puppets."

"Oh."

"What's tantra, anyway?"

"I'm not sure. But I bought a book. I wanted to read up on tantric sex."

"Why?"

"I thought we could try something new. For fun."

"That is so bizarre," she proclaimed. "I bought a book, too—on knots. We are so in sync!"

Kayley wasn't sure that she had heard Alexandra correctly, but gave odds that she likely had. Either way, it was obvious to her that they were awake, so she was no longer concerned about muffling her activity. From the bedroom Alexandra and Henry could hear the unguarded clatter of dishes and pots.

"You should make breakfast this morning," Alexandra said. "Really."

"She doesn't want me to. Besides, I have a hankering for toast with a heaping smatter of tomato preserves, or eggs Benedict avec tomato, or—dare to dream—a great scoff of tomato flapjacks served with a choice of tomato tea or tomato coffee.

Alexandra smiled and slapped him on the chest. "You're terrible."

"Yes I am. Anyway, I've got lunch duty today."

"That's right! The monster-in-law is coming."

"I told Kayley that it would free her up so that the three of them could spend some quality time together."

"But?" Alexandra asked, sensing from his tone that there was a hidden agenda.

"But the real reason is to save Kayley from a subtle barrage of culinary critiques."

"You're a martyr, Henry. And a true friend."

"Martyr? No. Adam's mother loves me. *I'm* gainfully employed in a real job and not a Mrs. Robinson sort."

"Henry, seriously, you've got to stop with all these weird references. What is a Mrs. Robinson sort?"

"Does the term cougar mean anything to you?"

"Yeah. But you're older than I am."

"True. But that's socially acceptable and, more importantly, you're not her son."

"Socially acceptable? That's the stupidest thing I've ever heard."

"Really? Then the conversation at lunch will set a whole new standard for you."

Alexandra wasn't completely certain what she was to make of Henry's statement. However, she did extract from his tone that

High Noon was a fitting time for Kayley to re-acquaint herself with Adam's mother.

She began to wonder what Henry's parents would make of her. She decided they would not approve of her past and felt indignant at the imagined dismissive judgement.

"Am I ever going to meet your mother and father?"

"Mom is a little difficult to get ahold of, being dead. And dad is even worse."

"You know what I mean. Dad and stepmom, then."

"Did you notice them at the wedding?"

"No."

"I didn't tell you—but they were invited."

"Then where were they?"

"Tuscany. They sent their regards and well-wishes."

"Any money?"

"Nope."

"Nothing?"

"Zippo," he confirmed.

"They kind of suck."

"Kind of."

Chapter 61

As with a falling man and the ground, the reunion between Kayley and her prospective mother-in-law was both inevitable and doomed. In many respects, it was a seamless continuation of their initial meeting, beginning with an unexpected and jolting piece of news.

"Kay," Adam said, as he entered the en suite bathroom. He had a little boy manner that suggested a forthcoming apology. "I need to tell you something."

Kayley was standing in front of the large, maple-framed mirror. She was nervously putting the final touches on her old-fashioned, girl-next-door, *honest I'm not a tramp* look. The timbre of Adam's voice gave her pause. It was too soothing. Her attention moved between his reflection and her own.

"What is it?" she asked, with wary optimism.

"I probably should have mentioned this sooner."

It was Adam's mannerisms, as much as his choice of words, which snuffed out Kayley's glimmer of hope that the news might have actually been good. She did a slow about-face, dread and anger jostling for position. Her eyes narrowed slightly as she stared at his sheepish grin.

"I never actually got around to telling Mom about your pregnancy—or the arrangement."

The sound of Alexandra's entry into the house sailed energetically up to the second floor and cheerily into the dead calm of the bathroom. Kayley had never noticed the quiet grace and speed of Alexandra's movements, which was why she was surprised to see her when she peeked into the bathroom.

"Monster-in-law is pulling into the driveway."

"You are talking about my mother," Adam reminded her. "And I am in the room. If you could refer to her as Deirdre instead of monster-in-law, I'd appreciate it."

"Deirdre's here," she reiterated, her tone was flat and unapologetic.

"Thanks," he replied.

It occurred to Alexandra after reading the body language and noting their physical distance from each other that Kayley and Adam had not been talking when she had arrived.

"Am I interrupting something?" She asked.

"That depends," Kayley vented. "If the fact that Adam has been too embarrassed or ashamed to tell his mother that I am carrying your child is *something*, then yes, you are interrupting something."

PAIRS

After a darting glance at Adam, Kayley stared directly ahead and marched toward the door. Alexandra looked disapprovingly at Adam. Her chastising critique was relayed in one evenly delivered word.

"Wow."

"It's not like that," he replied, and then looked out into the bedroom and repeated his reassurance to Kayley's departing back. "Aw, Kay. Really. It's not like that."

She stopped in the doorway and spoke out into the hall. "Oh really? Well, what's it like then?"

"I just wanted to avoid the grief," Adam said, as he approached her. "She just wouldn't understand."

He felt more than mere uncertainty in his ability to present a strong case against his mother's objections. Adam feared that she would validate his own unsettled misgivings.

Kayley accepted his hands on her shoulders and she let herself be brought around to face him. Her mood softened. Adam comforted her with his smile and they kissed. Smitten and shored with confidence, Kayley stepped out into the hall and walked toward the staircase. Hearing Alexandra's lyrical playground taunt behind her, she grinned.

"Adam is afraid of his mommy, his mommy, his mommy."

"No, I'm not."

Alexandra's voice dropped to a deep, dim-witted, mock-male voice as she ridiculed Adam's justification. "*I just wanted to avoid the grief. She just wouldn't understand.*"

"It's true! And I don't sound like that."

"Pussy."

At the base of stairs Kayley listened to Alexandra's mimicked chicken clucking as she put on her sandals. Although Kayley had accepted Adam's reasons and had forgiven him, Alexandra's pummelling torment gave her an otherwise missing sense of satisfying requital. She felt protected.

Outside on the porch looking out to the lawn where Henry and Terra stood with Adam's mother, matters were very much the opposite. Kayley felt exposed, emotionally and physically. Deirdre's eyes moved from the architectural feature, at which Henry was pointing, to Kayely and then to Kayley's belly, a suddenly protruding colossus. It was at that moment when Adam stepped onto the porch, followed by Alexandra.

Adam noticed his mother's sifting assessment of Kayley's weight gain. Spurred on by the recent prodding, he knew that he should come to her defence and clarify that Kayley was not merely getting dowdy.

"Kayley is pregnant, Mom."

"I can see that, Adam," she gushed. "I'm going to be a grandmother. I was getting worried that this day would never come."

"Uh, Mom."

Deirdre, lost in her fantasy, was deaf to her son's interruptions. "I would love a granddaughter. But a grandson would be nice, too."

"Mom."

"I assume that you two will be getting married."

Kayley, Henry, and Alexandra watched with growing sympathy has Adam dug himself deeper. Deirdre remained oblivious. Her enthusiasm temporarily gave way to a tangent of social propriety.

"Soon," Adam replied.

"Soon? Very soon I hope."

"After we are done the house."

"You may not have that long. You don't want your child being born to unwed parents."

"Mom, this is different."

"Different? Don't be ludicrous. How could it possibly be different? I wish your father was here."

Alexandra, remembering Henry's comment about the afternoon's discussions, stepped to the side and judged the level of stupidity. Disappointed but patient, she held onto high hopes. There was a great deal of potential in the air.

PAIRS

Deirdre's badgering of Adam upset Kayley. She couldn't continue to watch him squirm and, without thinking of the fallout, jumped to his defence. "It's not his."

"Bingo," Alexandra whispered, in appreciation of Henry's unfolding prediction. Adam overheard the comment, but didn't react as he was too wrapped up in desperate thoughts of damage control.

"Oh?" Deirdre inquired, hesitantly.

"The child is Alexandra and Henry's," Kayley explained, sounding at once defiant, brave, unsure, and guilty.

Stunned, Deirdre was still in the process of digesting the news when she looked first at Henry, who smiled pleasantly, and then to Alexandra, who winked and gave two thumbs up.

"My God, Adam," his mother exclaimed. "Is this a commune?"

"No," Terra piped. "It's a house."

Henry patted Terra gently on the back, sending her in Kayley's direction.

Deirdre fell silent. Her glassy eyes stared far away to a safer place and a simpler time. Her unnerving calm was the result of war of attrition being fought between her need to faint and a desire to scream. Henry, sensitive to the shock, which he had foreseen at the onset of the conversation, looped his arm around Deirdre's elbow. He stroked the top of her hand reassuringly and proceeded behind Terra, in small steps, toward the house.

Seeking to assist Henry, Alexandra moved to the top of the stairs, meeting Terra who led the way up to the porch before strolling towards Kayley. With her pregnancy, Kayley was having bouts of exhaustion and light-headedness and at that moment didn't feel confident enough to take her daughter into her arms, so she guided her toward Adam. Terra was disappointed but became sidetracked by the odd lady and the strange procession. Henry walked backwards through the door and Alexandra rubbed Deirdre's back as she followed them into the house.

"If it means anything," Alexandra consoled, softly. "Henry and I are married."

As the triage conga line disappeared, Adam put his arm around Kayley's waist. They both remained fixated on the afterimage of his traumatised mother being led to the comfort of a very dry gin martini.

"Maybe the *third time* will be the charm," he speculated, unconvincingly.

Chapter 62

Alexandra was wearing a white tank top that had matted to her body as a result of the sweat that oiled her tanned skin. It was becoming translucent at the points where it met her skin. She had decided to take the opportunity of Adam's decreed beer break to start on a batch of cookies. The plastic-wrapped tube of dough was retrieved from the fridge, peeled open, and then carefully sliced into uniform discs that were spaced evenly on the buttered cooking sheet—as per the package's instructions. Lovingly she slid them into the preheated oven—as per the package's instructions. However the package, as it always did, let her down in the end. It never actually mentioned the use of a timer. It never did. Happy with her efforts, Alexandra returned to the fridge, grabbed a can of beer, and then joined Adam on the front step. She promptly forgot her baking.

"So," she said. "Lunch with your mom went well."

Adam's eyes narrowed to a razor's edge as he glanced acidly at Alexandra. He was shirtless. His defined stomach fit into his jeans like a smooth, firm pin. They were watching Kayley hand out small baskets of tomatoes to the entire neighbourhood. Her visits were in short bursts, with long rests in between. Everyone was conveniently puttering in the yard, having all emerged from their homes with a timing *coincidental* to the arrival of Adam and Alexandra on the porch.

Kayley had brought her daughter along, as a means of spending more time with her. She was feeling guilty about her lack of energy and her reduced ability to give Terra all the attention she deserved.

"That is just freaky," Adam said, after taking a sip of beer. "Preternatural."

"I used to like tomatoes," Alexandra complained. "I think what pushed me over the edge was when she started decorating with them. It's kind of getting bizzaro-spooky. She's named the one in the kitchen. Preternatural?"

Following her mother from yard to yard, Terra would periodically crane her neck back, in order to see past the large floppy brim of her hat, to eavesdrop on adult conversations. But, for the most part, she was drawn to events at ground level—like the gooey chew toys that a family pet had left on the lawn.

"Preternatural means abnormal, but not supernatural. Named?"

"Are you making that up? Yep. Named. *She* is called Lalita."

"Nope. I'm not making it up," Adam replied. "It's a real word. The tomato fountain out back is definitely preternatural. She's artsy. Naming tomatoes is the sort of thing artsy people do."

Kayley was speaking with the man across the street. They were standing on his driveway where he had been methodically washing his car (much to the suspicion of his wife). While talking, Kayley selected a single tomato, polished it against her dress and took a bite. There was an amiable yet focused passion to her sales pitch.

"It is so weird the way she eats them like apples," Adam commented.

"So—preternatural? Is that like sacred-burial-ground stuff?"

"No. That is supernatural."

"Atomic waste?"

"No. Maybe. I'm not sure. The atomic waste wouldn't be preternatural, but the resulting mutant tomato plants might qualify. I'm not sure about aliens, either. I'll run it by Kayley."

"Nice *use it in a sentence* by the way," Alexandra congratulated.

"Thanks."

The endless tomato bounty had started off innocently. Kayley had been amazed when the plants grew. During late spring she had sat and read, sometimes aloud, amongst the vines. By early summer when the weather permitted she had set up a makeshift office in the backyard to work alongside the budding garden.

She had made chow chow from the very first yield of green tomatoes. It reminded her of her grandmother. No one in the house particularly liked chow chow, but Kayley had been smitten, so it went unmentioned. Had they known that chow chow was merely the foreshadowing of the much greater invasion to come, things might have gone differently. But all were caught sleeping as Kayley slowly integrated tomatoes into every meal.

Tomato jams, jellies, and marmalades at breakfast. Tomato relishes, both green and red, for lunches. Fried tomato fritter, bolognese sauces, and Creole gumbos and jambalayas were served at supper. Pesto, salsas, chutneys, soups, and homemade catsup were part of various meals throughout the day. And, of course, there was the infamous East Texan Piccalilli. Kayley had explained that Piccalilli was usually made with cucumbers, but that East Texans were adaptive. Henry, Adam, and Alexandra had planned a trip to East Texas that very night. The agreed vendetta went unspoken. Everything was laid out in sidelong glances.

"Did you know that tomatoes are a member of the nightshade family?" Henry asked.

He was standing behind the screen door and holding a box of dryer sheets. He stepped out onto the porch. Alexandra and Adam looked back, waiting for him to elaborate on the relevance of his comment. He continued, but remained fixated on Kayley.

"A plant with leaves and berries that are highly toxic," he explained, and then glanced at the pair. "That's it. Nothing else. I just feel a need to trash-talk tomatoes."

Satisfied by the response, Alexandra and Adam turned back to find Terra staring in the direction of the house and waving. Reflexively they all smiled and waved back. Terra was drawn to look up by the group gesture that was barely visible in the upper periphery of her brim. She tilted her head back and smiled at them. The little girl sitting on the lawn, close to Alexandra, disappeared. Terra returned to examining the activity of the ants on the driveway.

"So how did the doctor's visit go?" Henry asked Adam.

"She'll give us the update over dinner."

"Very exciting," Alexandra said.

In the corner of her eye, Kayley noticed Terra poking the ants with her index finger as they emerged onto the driveway. Kayley excused herself from the conversation with the neighbour, handed him her final basket and tugged on the back of her daughter's sundress. The signal was ignored. Terra wet her finger, dabbed up an ant, and brought it toward her open mouth.

"Terra!"

"I'm an ant *eat-tore*."

"Terra! Don't put that in your mouth. It's filthy."

The ant was swallowed whole. Kayley grabbed her daughter by the hand and marched across the street toward the house. Prior to her mother's insistence, Terra had wanted to return home. But now that she was being forced, she wanted to stay with the ants. She protested until reaching the front lawn. Terra fell silent and concentrated on Alexandra. Kayley was too preoccupied to notice her daughter's sudden, intense interest. After they disappeared inside the house, Alexandra became the centre of attention.

"Don't look at me," she protested. "I didn't have anything to do with that. Terra is just trying to deflect blame."

"She's four years old," Henry countered.

"Almost five," Alexandra offered.

"That explains it then. She's going through the *evil mastermind* fives."

Alexandra mouthed an unflattering parody of Henry's response and then stuck her tongue out at him. He attempted to grab it, but she blocked his hand and stepped forward into a kiss—which ended when she tucked the cold can of beer under his shirt and placed it against the small of his back.

Adam laughed as Henry struggled to break Alexandra's viselike hug. As he watched them, it occurred to Adam how much he enjoyed such moments. Knowing that the house would soon be completed, he had felt an ill-defined sense of twilight, like the end of summer camp or closing the cabin for the season. The new beginning that he planned to spring on Kayley after dinner took on a different meaning for Adam—it was an underscore to the closing chapter in his life.

Alexandra caught a vaguely familiar scent on the breeze. Puzzled, she stepped back and searched her memory. Henry was surprised by his sudden release, but quickly gathered that she was attempting to source out the strengthening odour of burning dough.

"Your cookies," he said.

"Fuck," she yelped, as she charged into the house. "I mean frig!"

"Has she ever *not* burned them?" Adam asked.

"Nope."

Chapter 63

Kayley wanted to capture the moment. She closed her eyes, quieted her thoughts, and listened. Summer was in the eddies on the breeze. It sizzled on the grill, hummed in a distant lawn mower, spoke of domestic issues in the surrounding yards, and periodically let out the joyful scream of a child. It was in the idle chatter between Henry and Alexandra, in the laughter from her daughter, and the horse brays of Adam.

"Time for a rest, little lady," he sighed. "Horsey needs a beer."

"All them-thar good hops and barley," Henry collaborated.

"Exactly."

"At the house," Terra suggested, requested, demanded, commanded.

With the sound of Adam's voice, Kayley remembered the phone call from Daleesha and the message that she was supposed to have relayed. Keeping her eyes shut, she chose to pass on the request in the form of an omnidirectional public address.

"Hon, Daleesha was hoping you could swing by after dinner to take a look at the play structure. She told me to remind you that it was the one that you helped to defile. In case you had forgotten."

"Okay, sweetie," Alexandra teased. Stretched out on a section of the bench that had been built along the perimeter of the deck, she needed to peer over her shoulder in order to see Kayley. "But I think Adam would be more qualified."

"What's wrong with it?" he asked.

"She's worried that it might not be secure. Or safe. Or something. Anyway, there's a bolty-thingy involved."

"And if she would have recited a poem, you'd have gotten every single word in one shot."

"Poems are important."

"And bolty-things?"

Henry stepped back from the barbecue, reached for his glass of wine and looked across the yard to Kayley. She remained silent. Reclined in a chaise that faced the sun, her eyes were closed and she was smiling broadly.

"Soaking it in?" Alexandra asked.

"Recording."

"Recording?"

"Recording," Kayley confirmed.

"Poem-worthy?"

Kayley thought about her little "Beep Beep" ditty, but she wasn't sure if it was fully formed and, additionally, feared that the humour might be lost on her current audience.

"Definitely." Kayley tilted her head in the direction of Alexandra's voice, used her hand as a brim on the side of her face and then opened her eyes. "I just can't come up with one that covers motherhood, love, friendship, summer, and a craving for sauerkraut and chutney on my burger."

"That is a tall order for one poem," Henry acknowledged.

"I guess there are things that even art can't capture," Alexandra said, after she stood.

The offhand delivery of her summation gave it a quality of pristine innocence. Henry and Kayley silently traded their mutual surprise and approval while Alexandra filled her tumbler with ice from the cooler.

Adam galloped toward Henry. His little red-haired knapsack clung tightly and laughed contagiously. When he was close enough, Adam positioned his back toward the deck in a gesture for assistance with the dismount. Alexandra passed her glass of Scotch to Henry and then reached across the railing for Terra.

Kayley was the audience and the deck was the stage. The vignette before her was another memory she wanted to hold. She watched contentedly when Adam asked Alexandra to pass him a beer. Obliging, Alexandra pulled a can from the cooler, but shook it vigorously before handing it to Terra for delivery. Adam accepted his beer genially from his young server and then charged onto the deck with his finger on the tab and the business end of the can pointed at Alexandra. Laughing in snorts, she ran toward the railing, which she effortlessly hurtled, before disappearing up the side yard. Adam did a one-hand vault off the deck in pursuit. During the chase Henry had picked Terra up. Together they tracked the antics.

The episode, though brief, left Kayley with a sense of family. Unconsciously, Kayley rubbed her stomach as she thought about how she would deliver her news.

"Any bets on the outcome?" Henry called to her.

"She is fast."

"And freakishly strong."

"I still think Alexandra is in for a beer shower," Kayley said.

"Adam is my cousin, but I can't bet against Alexandra."

"Looks like we've got the makings of a wager."

"You're on."

"What's the stake?" she asked.

"A candlelit dinner."

"Together?"

"No. No. If I win you prepare and serve a romantic candlelit dinner for Alexandra and me. And I'll do the same for you and Adam, if you win."

"Perfect."

Adam and Alexandra strolled side by side into the backyard. They were both still catching their breath, but managed small bursts of laughter. All of the exposed skin above the collar of Alexandra's tank top was glazed with beer. Her jet-black hair glistened. Adam was definitely the day's champion. However, from the grass stains and their generally dishevelled appearance, it was apparent that victory was hard won.

"I'm thinking pork tenderloin," Kayley said. "Barbecued."

Chapter 64

The hamburgers were served on the picnic table inside the house—primarily to escape the bugs. Atop the red checkerboard tablecloth were the condiments, place settings of plastic dishes, and a single tray of burnt chocolate chip cookies wrapped in foil, which shared the role of centrepiece with a vase of garden flowers.

"Really, babe? You bet that I would win? That's so sweet. Well, I would have out run him if…"

Alexandra glanced down to the end of table where Terra was sitting in her high chair, preoccupied by the crumbled bits of meat that she was attempting to stab with her fork. Alexandra didn't want to have another *fugly* incident on her hands, so she thought about alternate words for breasts that everyone, except Terra, would understand. Quickly dropped from the running were *the girls* and *puppies*, because she feared innocent curiosity could result. Without much concentrated effort, she found herself flooded with alternate contenders. Cans, jugs, and melons led what amounted to a cascade. She became distracted by the count, lost track of her original purpose, and tried to think up as many breast synonyms as she could come up with.

Alexandra took great pleasure in the exercise, recalling Henry's explanation for the reason behind all the terminology surrounding wine tasting—*concern about a particular subject results in a proportionately detailed vocabulary for it*. Thus, the means of assessing the priorities of a society.

"If what?" Adam asked.

"If," she replied cautiously, "if my *cans* had of been strapped down."

Terra was the only one at the table unfazed by Alexandra's reason. She alone continued jabbing food with her fork and suckling from her juice cup.

"Your *cans* you say?" Henry asked. His hamburger was suspended in his hand mid-air. "So the cans you were carrying were unfettered?"

"If that means not strapped down—then yes. You know that."

"Yeah, your cans slowed you down." Adam replied, with taunting sarcasm.

"You try sprinting down the street with a set bouncing all helter-skelter."

"Attract any admirers?" Kayley asked mischievously, while wiping the corner of Terra's mouth.

"You should've seen it, Kay," Adam commented. "It was like running behind Medusa."

Henry closed his eyes briefly and after a deep breath resumed eating. Kayley managed to keep her composure. Alexandra took a moment to work through Adam's analogy. She had at first thought that he was calling her homely, but then it occurred to her that he was referring to all the slack-jawed faces that had lined the street. Alexandra snorted twice and nodded.

"So Kayley," Henry inquired, in an effort to change the topic. "How did it go at the doctor's?"

She angled her head toward Terra and widened her eyes for emphasis before responding. "Boring stuff. It can wait until after dinner."

The postponement surprised Henry. With a glance, Kayley once again reiterated the presence of Terra. It was a gesture that concerned both Alexandra and Adam. Kayley held a reassuring smile and Adam felt comforted.

"Well then, I have some news," he said. "Not news, more like a dream really. Kay, I was thinking that with our share of the profits from this place that we could build a house. I brought some plans home."

"I'll help," Alexandra offered.

"You'll be too busy building our house," Henry tormented.

Kayley was entirely unprepared. She had no visible reaction. She was working through a cognitive stasis that had resulted from numerous and divergent forces of excitement bottlenecking on the path to expression. Lodged in the doorway, limbs flailing, were images of their marriage together, their future home, siblings for Terra, and holidays with family. Unsatisfied with the inscrutable reception, Adam played trump.

"There's this one plan with a back office," he continued. "It would make a great studio for you."

Kayley's emotions finally broke free and she squealed with delight before focusing on her daughter. She stroked Terra's hair as she spoke to her.

"What do you think? Adam is going to build a house for us to live in."

"I did say I'd help," Alexandra reiterated. "I swear it's like I periodically go invisible around you people."

"You could never be invisible," Henry said. "Ever."

"Thanks, babe."

Terra looked up from her food. She watched her mother reach across the table and take Alexandra by the hand. Their fingers wove together. In spite of a couple of escaped tears, Terra knew her mother was happy. She could tell by the tone of Kayley's voice as she recited a wish list. The particulars made little sense to Terra, but she did understand that they were talking about a different house. Previously, she had always assumed that all of her memories of home, even those that were backwards, were of the townhouse. While her mother spoke, the overlapping images began to separate and the blur started to come into focus.

"And big windows," Terra exclaimed.

"Yes, Mouse," Adam replied. "Your mom would finally get those big windows. Did I mention that? They're in the office-slash-studio. It's practically an atrium."

"For drawing," Terra continued.

"You got it."

Henry became a spectator to the conversation at the table, retreating into his thoughts. He was proud of his cousin and happy for him. Yet there was a tinge of sadness to his quiet rejoicing. Although the same four people would continue to meet and cherish each other's company, it would never again be their first house together. A sunset, regardless of its splendour, was still an end.

After the dishes were gathered into the kitchen, Alexandra offered around her plate of cookies. Compassionately, Henry, Kayley, and Adam made their selection. Terra was too young to be gracious. She turned up her nose and asked for ice cream.

"She's the only honest one in the bunch," Alexandra moaned, and then lowered the plate onto the table.

"You have to learn to cook with love," Kayley noted, before excusing herself to the kitchen.

"With love?"

"Watch whatever it is you are preparing," Kayley explained, while pulling the carton of ice cream from the freezer. "No matter how simple. Cooking food does not tend to itself."

"Love?" Alexandra asked Henry.

"Stop wandering off," he summarized. "You have baking ADD."

"Are you saying that I wander off?" Alexandra called to the kitchen.

"That is exactly what I'm saying," Kayley said, while walking back toward the table. "Food preparation requires commitment."

Alexandra was going to make a defensive rebuttal but was stopped cold by Kayley's topic-is-closed mommy face. Instead, she took a cookie from the plate, and after a quick visual examination, knocked it on the table. It had the hard acoustics of a knuckle. In defeat, Alexandra nodded.

After dessert, Kayley brought Terra upstairs to get ready for bed. Henry served a round of drinks while they waited for her return. Their idle chatter made progressively tighter circles around the topic of Kayley's visit to the doctor. Alexandra was the first to break.

"Adam, fess up. You have to know something about her visit to the doctor."

"I don't."

"That is not possible. How could she not tell you?"

"Alexandra," Henry said. "You know I love you dearly, but not everyone speaks all the thoughts that pass through their head."

"Hey! Are you saying I do?"

"Don't you?"

"Alright, most. But not all. Man, tough room tonight. First I'm invisible, then I have ADD, and now I'm a blabbermouth. Who gets roasted tomorrow?"

"We may not be done with you," Adam joked, which earned him a cookie bullet to the chest.

He was reaching for ammunition when he heard Kayley filling a glass of water at the kitchen sink. He sat back when she entered the room and waited for her sit down.

"Okay. What's the big, not-for-little-ears secret?"

"It's nothing to worry about, but my blood pressure is up."

"How up?"

"The low end of up. Technically it's called gestational hypertension."

"Low end, but it's serious enough that you want to talk about it."

"It's a little serious."

"How serious?"

"Statistically, I am at greater risk for some complications."

"Technically. Statistically. Theoretically. Hypothetically. Kay, I need some straight answers. What kind of complications?"

"Pre-eclampsia, for one."

"Yeah. And?"

"Which could mean being hospitalized and in its most extreme is life threatening."

"Fuck!" Alexandra snapped. "And I sure as shit don't mean *frig*!"

"I had high blood pressure with Terra. It can be managed."

"You knew this would happen?!" Adam exclaimed.

"I knew it was a possibility."

"Why didn't you tell us?" Henry asked, calmly.

"Because if nothing happened, you'd all be worried for nothing."

"If Henry and I knew, we would never have asked." Alexandra berated.

"You didn't ask. I volunteered."

"Christ, Kay!" Adam said. "You know what she means."

"Could you settle down?" Kayley retorted. She was beginning to resent the inquisition. "Terra is trying to sleep."

Henry attempted to sooth the escalation. "Let's hear her out."

"Gavin, I appreciate your gallantry—but there is really nothing to hear out."

"Who's Gavin?" Alexandra asked.

"The old boyfriend," Adam reminded her.

"What the hell? Are you carrying some other guy's kid?"

"The dead ex-boyfriend," Adam elaborated.

"Deceased," Henry muttered to himself.

"Whatever."

"Huh? How does that work?" Alexandra panned the grim faces for an explanation.

"I meant Henry," Kayley said. "You've all got me so flustered. I am pregnant. That can't be undone. It's now about how we deal with it moving forward."

Abortion was the word that Adam bit down on furiously before it could escape his mouth. Alexandra was too upset to say anything more. Thoughts couldn't form. They were shred apart by the unrelenting guilt of her cowardice. The table fell silent.

In the maelstrom's hush they could hear the light stomp of small feet on the hardwood floor upstairs. The sound ricocheted off bare walls and through the empty rooms. Starting from the bedroom at the end of the hall, the slapping rhythm strolled toward the top of the stairs. Expectation made the intensity of their pause impossible to maintain.

"Alexandra?" Terra called down.

Alexandra's brow crimped with curiosity. Before responding, she gave a petitioning glance to each of her unhelpful advisors and then peered toward the front of the house.

"Yes?" She fished, cautiously.

"Why were you running with cans?"

With that single question, the strain passed into amusement. All focus was on Alexandra. Kayley took hold of her hand and smiled.

"You really do fascinate my little girl."

Chapter 65

The porch lights in the backyard of Daleesha's house were little more than beacons for insects. They did a poor job illuminating the patio where she stood watching the conic beam of Adam's flashlight dart and bend around the play structure with hummingbird dexterity until disappearing into blackness.

"Verdict?" She called out.

"It's safe," his disembodied voice replied. "Just a little wear. I can take a look at it tomorrow in the daylight."

Adam wasn't visible to Daleesha until he had reached the swing set, barely registering as perceptible movement when his shoulder brushed against one of the chains. The motion reminded her of a recent purchase.

"I bought a little swing set for Terra," she said.

"That's nice of you."

Adam's tone and manner reflected his sullen mood. He was a man going through the motions of interaction.

"Are you alright?" Daleesha asked.

Adam looked up at Daleesha. Raised by the massive stone pedestal of the patio and backlit into silhouette, she was a faceless apparition reaching to him by thought. Her empathy wicked Adam's concerns out of him.

"No," he said, as he ascended the steps. "I'm quite shitty actually."

They stood together for a moment, gauging the possible new direction their conversation could take. Daleesha extended her arm toward the house and Adam accepted the invitation.

"Want to talk about it?" she asked, as they made their way to the French doors.

"Can it remain between us?"

"Of course." She held open the door for Adam and then followed behind him.

Daleesha secured the key-locked deadbolts. Adam waited for her, assembling his grievance against Kayley.

"Kay's blood pressure is up," he said, as they made their way into the large expanse of the former living room.

Where there had once been Victorian furnishings, the great room of the daycare housed a sandbox; a wardrobe for costumes; child-height, built-in shelves filled with bins of toys; a long, squat, wall-anchored bookcase; and two crafts centres, which flanked a low vanity cabinet that held a deep basin sink. On the countertop sat a sizeable bowl of fruit.

"I didn't know. It's not the best news, but she's been through this before, Adam. She'll be fine."

"I know she's been through this before," he said, stopping beside a craft table. "She told me that *after* becoming pregnant and only then because she had to. From the start of this whole thing I've been pushed to the sidelines."

"Have you talked to her about it?" she asked, after resting back against the bookcase.

"Yes. When she first decided to go through with it."

"How did that go?"

"I think she wants to involve me—but it doesn't seem to be exactly second nature to her."

"Talk to her again. Kayley's been alone for over four years. She's had to do everything herself."

"I know. That's not totally it. I'm also worried. I don't want to lose her."

"You're not going to lose her. She'll be fine."

All of his concerns boiled down to a single question, one that he had been hesitant to speak aloud. "Do you think she'd get an abortion if it came down to it? I mean—really came down to it."

While Adam's question was not entirely unwarranted, the bleakness gave Daleesha pause and she considered her reply for a moment before speaking.

"She loves you both so much. And she'd want to be there for you both."

"You're right."

"Of course I am. But Adam, keep in mind that Kayley is a spiritual person. She believes in a greater purpose. And what that means for you—is that your idea of *really coming down to it* and hers are likely very different."

"Right. The universe factor."

"I take it you're not a spiritual man."

"Not really. Not like Kayley."

In an effort to help Adam glimpse the majestic sweep of life through Kayley's eyes, Daleesha quickly constructed a Rosetta Stone in her mind, one that would translate religion into its most austere incarnation, science.

"Theoretically, do you think a being could exist that is more than three-dimensional?"

"Sci-fi, but possible," he acknowledged, surprised by the conversation's sudden change in tack.

"What about less than three-dimensional? What about a two-dimensional being?"

"Two-dimensional?"

"Like our own shadows." She grabbed an apple and strolled over to a craft centre.

"Sure. Why not?"

Daleesha retrieved one of the jars of finger paint from its carousel and a sheet of off-white construction paper, which she placed flat on top of the low table. She opened the jar to reveal a shiny blue paste. As a demonstration for Adam, Daleesha put a small dollop on the tip of her finger and then licked it off.

"Eatable. Not the best tasting. But eatable."

"I think your tongue is blue."

"How do you think our two-dimensional friends would perceive this Red Delicious apple?"

Daleesha touched the bottom of the apple against the paint and then pressed it onto the paper. The result was a gathered cluster of four blue dots. She repeated the process for the top of the apple and printed a fat O. The side of the apple created an egg-shaped blob.

"They would never know what an apple looks like," he volunteered.

"Well done! But more than that, Adam, the apple would seem to them to be separate entities."

"Okay," he said. "I'm following. Not sure where to, but I'm following."

"How do you think we would perceive our four dimensional friend? Hard to imagine? Let me tell you. It would be ever changing, appear as multiple entities, and if it spoke, its words would seem like they were coming from inside us."

"And this lesson is sponsored by who?" Adam asked.

Daleesha smiled, walked over to the sink and spoke while rinsing off the paint. "Do you think it's plausible?"

"Plausible."

"Good," Daleesha began, while drying the apple with a sheet of paper towel. "I just explained angels, devils, demonic possession, divine inspiration, and a god that we could never fathom. Only I spun it as science. Does that help you any?"

"So the Bible is an account of what a four-dimensional being has been up to?"

"Maybe the take-away from this could be that things exist that are beyond our perception and understanding. Throw into the mix that atoms, of which we are made, are not actually things but are more like tendencies, no more substantial than a thought. Well then, *then*, it starts to get a little awe-inspiring! And that is where faith comes in."

"There are more things in heaven and earth, et cetera. Got it."

"Shakespeare, Adam?" She was pleasantly surprised that he was quoting literature, even if it was to relay teasing belittlement. "Kayley's rubbing off on you."

While good-natured, it was apparent to both that they had reached an impasse. Daleesha's eyebrow arched playfully before she held out the apple as an offer. It was an act that relayed that she wasn't merely being polite. The Biblical reference, although merely inferred, was abundantly clear.

"No thank you," Adam said.

"Suit yourself."

After taking a crisp bite, she walked back toward the craft table to admire her creation. She lifted her painting to eye level and flipped it around toward Adam.

"It is the purpose of art to heighten the mystery," she said.

"You've missed your calling."

"Artisan?"

"High Priestess."

"Oh, and I forgot to mention," she noted, while gazing once again at her work. "The constituent parts of an atom pop in and out of existence. Existence, it would seem, is a tricky bit of business."

Daleesha looked at Adam, who was somewhere between completely blank and in utter process overload.

"The superpositioning principle tells us that there is no *out there* out there," she summarized, vaguely gesturing one hand to encompass their surroundings. "Reality, dear Adam, is a construct of the observer. And the observer is but a remembrance of a dreamt ghost."

"My brain is starting to hurt."

"Quantum physics can do that. Ugly math at times, but it can be great fun to watch it trying to walk."

Chapter 66

Kayley didn't have her usual stretch of solitude on the morning following her news. Disoriented when she awoke, Kayley had thought that she was in her bed at the townhouse. The new-home smells alerted her otherwise. She sat up and found herself alone. Adam was gone.

PAIRS

After slipping into her nightgown Kayley went out into the hall and descended the stairs. Henry was in the foyer below putting on his running shoes.

"Everyone is up early," Kayley remarked.

"Alexandra and I decided to go for a run."

"Do you know where Adam is?" she asked when she reached the main floor.

"The garage. I believe."

Kayley took her flip-flops from the shoe mat at the entry and carried them to the back of the house. She stopped at the patio door, looking at her garden and then to the garage while listening to Alexandra's movement inside the bedroom. Kayley stepped into her flip-flops and went out onto the deck. While sliding the door closed she heard Henry call impatiently to Alexandra.

Her feet became covered in dew as she strolled toward the back of the yard. Although headed for the garden, her attention was constantly pulled in the direction of the garage. She caught sight of Adam in the doorway. To her relief, he looked back and appeared happy.

Kayley left the flip-flops at the edge of the garden and stepped onto the cool, damp soil with her bare feet. She slowly wandered through the rows in search of the perfect breakfast addition. In the far corner, barely visible under the morning shade of a neighbour's elm, she saw a beautiful, plump tomato. She weaved through the plantings and plucked it from the vine.

Upon turning back toward the house, Kayley noticed that she could see into Alexandra's bedroom through a separation in the curtain panels. Alexandra was placing a chair alongside the window. She was wearing a red satin robe. It draped open across her naked body, revealing the profile of her breasts and her taut flat stomach. The robe's deep ruby colour enlivened her tanned skin and set off the rich inkwell of her jet-black hair, from which darkness itself was created. Her thighs, visible above the windowsill, would emerge and disappear from under the robe as the fabric flowed around her legs when she moved.

Kayley was transfixed. She could think of no words to express the pure radiance. It could only be captured as an image, an anima rendering of the goddess of bliss.

Within the room Alexandra turned toward the door, and then seductively presented her foot on the chair seat and pointed to it. She was wearing red stilettos. Henry rushed into view. They kissed passionately and then he dropped to his knees. His hands caressed her leg as his mouth moved up from her toes toward her thigh.

Kayley stepped cautiously forward. Her eyes widened when Alexandra guided Henry out of her way by using his hair as her reins. She sat down. Henry pulled his track pants down and began to grind against the leg she extended for him. His mouth traded between her breasts and lips, lusting for both. She remained unaffected, caressing his face and stroking his hair. Her fingers periodically disappeared inside his suckling mouth. In a sudden spasm he went rigid, shivered, and then melted against her leg. Kayley had never been so aroused in her life.

Alexandra pulled a hand towel off of the bed and gave it to Henry. He wiped Alexandra's leg first and then himself. They kissed and he left. She remained in the chair. Kayley had thought that the exhibition was over, until Alexandra buried her hand below her pelvis. Kayley stepped forward toward the house, watching Alexandra as she began to rock in the chair, her head changing direction in a loose swivel. The full body throb of Alexandra drew Kayley further into the yard. Alexandra's eyes opened wide, her mouth gaped and when her head rolled to the side the two women's eyes connected. Kayley was mesmerized as Alexandra's seizure took control and bucked her out of the chair. She disappeared from view below the horizon of the window ledge. Kayley was snapped from her trance when Alexandra's forearm rose up and flopped onto the seat of the chair. She wearily got up onto her knees, looked out the window and smiled deviously, before being overcome by a delicious twitch.

Adam was on a short stepladder, installing the garage door opener, when Kayley appeared at the side entry. He was uncertain how he should interpret the urgency in her emphatic gaze. This conundrum was quickly resolved when she unfastened his pants and pulled them, along with his underwear, down to his work boots.

Chapter C67

Alexandra was barefoot, sitting on the kitchen floor with her legs crossed. She was resting against a section of lower cabinets across from the stove. Track pants and one of Henry's T-shirts had replaced her satin robe. In a meditative calm, Alexandra was watching her cookies bake while processing Kayley's news from the previous night. Her guilt was giving rise to fortitude, which in turn was building into conviction.

"Where's my mommy?" Terra asked. She was standing in the hallway leading to the kitchen. Alexandra hadn't heard her come down the stairs.

"In the garage, Mouse. She's helping Adam. She'll be back soon."

"I smell cookies."

Alexandra reached toward Terra. It was an invitation that was happily accepted. They sat together and enjoyed, without interruption, the events that were taking place inside the oven. With Terra on her lap, Alexandra felt a stronger connection to Kayley's strength and her conviction became a plan. She decided on her course of action. She was buying a dildo that very day—and bottle of tequila, Añejo tequila. Helen was the first and only person that leapt to mind as a resource.

"I think they're done, Mouse," she said, while gesturing for Terra to stand.

"Can I have one?"

"After breakfast."

Alexandra rose to her feet, put on the oven mittens, removed the tray, and placed it on top of the stove. Terra, an experienced kitchen assistant, knew when to stay away from the action and knew when it was safe. The sound of the metal cooking sheet touching down on the ceramic burners was her *all clear* to approach.

Alexandra took off the oven mitts, looked down to the anticipating eyes, and then gently guided Terra in the direction of her high chair by the picnic table. They both caught sight of Kayley walking along the deck toward the patio doors. Terra quickened her pace to meet up with her mother as she entered the house.

"I smell cookies," Kayley said, after picking up her daughter.

"Alexandra made them," Terra replied.

"Did she now?"

"I can have one after breakfast."

Kayley settled her daughter into the high chair and indicated to Alexandra that they should meet in the kitchen, away from curious ears. Alexandra grinned.

"So what were you doing in the garage?" Alexandra asked, as she sauntered away. "You were in there an awfully long time."

Kayley blushed slightly, smirked, and followed behind. They stopped in front of the cabinets. They stood briefly, just facing each other. Laughter built until it burst free in unison.

"Oh my God," Kayley exclaimed in a coarse whisper. She reached into the overhead cabinet for a bowl. "I'm some type of voyeuristic pervo."

"I was definitely headed for the big O," Alexandra explained, while Kayley retrieved the cereal from the pantry. "But when I saw you standing there, watching—I think my circuitry was pushed into overload."

"That was the hottest thing I've ever seen. Am I a sicko?"

"No. You're not a sicko. I made the cookies as a thank you."

"Thank you? For what?"

"For the biggest big O of my life!"

When Adam entered the house he did not notice Terra. Nor was he aware that everyone else was awake. If he had known of either, he would not have announced his arrival with such a jubilant proclamation after he slid open the door.

"Jesus, Kay! What's your button? Do you have thing for stepladders? That was the most amazing, mind-blowing—"

"Little ears!" Kayley interjected.

Startled, his first thought was to look in the direction of the high chair. Without uttering a single word, Terra managed to successfully relay her opinion that he was acting very weird.

"The most mind blowing garage door opener installation I've ever experienced."

In strategic retreat, Adam sat down at the picnic table, facing toward the kitchen. He was surprised to see Alexandra as she gleefully strolled into the room. There was something about Alexandra's swagger that caused Kayley to wonder if the whole thing had been set up.

"A great installation?" Alexandra questioned. "Is that so?"

"Not great," Adam corrected. "Mind-blowing."

"Mind-blowing. Really?"

Kayley glanced toward Alexandra, eyebrow raised. "I'll bake some muffins for you later."

"That would be nice."

Chapter 68

Henry ended his jog exactly where it had begun—at the front porch. Although he would have welcomed Alexandra's company, he had enjoyed his time alone. Being able to go at his own pace permitted him to think. He had wanted to mull through his feelings about Kayley's announcement.

Running with Alexandra was not conducive to any sort of internalised musing. She tended to cruise along at much faster pace than Henry found comfortable and she would talk continuously while doing so. To add to the agony, she'd fully expect him to converse back. Inevitably, by the time they neared the end of the run, Henry would be reduced to huffing out monosyllabic responses: *yes, no, right, sure, cramp, pain, stop,* and *God*.

It had been a peculiar run and he was now the bearer of some not unforeseeable news. Henry sprung up the front steps, entered the house, and slipped off his running shoes before following the smell of fresh baking into the kitchen. A tray of muffins was cooling on top of the stove. On the counter was a plate of cookies.

Through the screen of the patio door he could see out into the backyard. Kayley and Terra were in the garden, wearing their flop-brimmed hats. Alexandra was standing by the side entry of the garage, talking. He stepped out onto the deck and removed his socks before crossing the lawn to join Alexandra.

"Hey babe," she greeted.

They kissed and then Henry stepped inside. He stopped to watch his cousin work on the garage door opener. At first Henry assumed that Adam was in the process of installing it but he soon realized that he had arrived in the midst of it being taken down.

"Not working?"

"It works just fine," Adam replied.

"Then why are you taking down?"

"To put it up again later."

"Do I want to know?"

"Not really."

Henry looked back toward Alexandra and then angled his head sideways in a request for her to move closer. She stepped into the doorway.

"When I was out on my jog," Henry said in a low voice, "a few of the neighbours stopped me. Actually more like a committee-mob of neighbours stopped me. They love Kayley and all…"

"But," Adam interjected, as he loosened the mounting bolts.

Henry had a flashback to earlier that morning when the neighbours, jogging along behind knobby-tired all-terrain baby strollers, spotted him and united into a posse that was somewhat reminiscent of a rickshaw cavalcade in reverse. The scene, if nothing else, was uniquely memorable.

"It's about the tomatoes, isn't it?" Alexandra confidently speculated.

"As a matter of fact, it is. They are hoping that we would talk to her. Apparently she has a cult zealot approach that people find a little off-putting."

Adam freed the garage door opener, climbed down the ladder, and placed it on the floor before responding. "You let me know how that goes."

"Why me? Why not you or Alexandra?"

"Not me because, as her boyfriend, things could go way worse for me than they would for you. And not Alexandra because Kayley has a way of talking her into things."

"What's that supposed to mean?" Alexandra countered defensively.

"The housewarming party mean anything?"

"Once! One time! She talked me into something once."

"Fine—go talk to her then."

Recognizing that she had lost track of the bigger picture to claim a small victory, she shook her head slowly while repeatedly mouthing the word *no*.

"Cowards," Henry said. "I figured as much. I have a plan, but I'll need your help."

"We can't gang up on her again," Alexandra replied.

Feeling guilty and protective, she peered back over her shoulder toward the garden. Terra noticed her watching, and waved. She was close to her mother, beside a large basket that was filled with the morning's harvest.

"Look, Alexandra," Terra called. "Lots and lots of tomatoes!"

She stretched her arms wide, closed her eyes, and tilted her smiling face to the sun, then twirled in place. Kayley looked up. Although her daughter's abilities had not yet consciously registered with Kayley, she saw poetry in the moment. The artist perceived the splendour of the feminine mystique, earth mother to goddess, with a beautiful sorceress dancing in between. For Alexandra's benefit, Kayley joyfully swept her arms open to present the recent bounty. Alexandra happily nodded and then rejoined the conspiracy.

"Let's do this thing," she hissed. "Today. She's got the next payload ready to drop."

"Good," Henry said. "I need you two to get the neighbours into their yards."

"How?" Adam asked.

"The way you two usually do."

"What?"

"On it, babe." Alexandra winked and then left.

With her departure, it was Henry's first time alone with his cousin since the prior night. He had been thinking about him during the jog. Although Adam had a temper, it tended to subside as quickly as it had risen and generally burned off all the emotional fuel. But Henry was unsure of his state of mind.

"How are you doing?" Henry asked.

"Buddy, the start to this day was fan-funk'n-tastic!"

"I was referring to last night. You seemed pretty upset."

"I was. But I'm not. I believe Kayley when she says that she can get it under control. If not for me, then certainly for Terra—there is no way she would put herself at risk. There was one thing that took a bit to work through."

"Which is?"

"Her calling you Gavin."

Henry had skipped over that curious titbit. He knew from their first meeting at Daleesha's party that she did see some similarities between Gavin and himself. However, he had heard nothing more about it since. It did seem peculiar that it should resurface so many months later.

"That was odd," Henry acknowledged.

"Well, here is what I came up with." Adam said, "If she had called me Gavin I'd be concerned. That would be along the same lines as moaning the wrong name in bed—if you know what I mean. But her calling you Gavin? I don't think much of it. It happens. You remind her of the guy. Period."

With nothing more to say on the matter, the discussion Adam had wanted to have with Henry took up residence in his mind. He wanted to share his amazing story about Alexandra.

"You know when I was chasing Alexandra," he said, his words conducted by the ratchet that nodded in his hand.

"Yeah?"

"We were running at full tilt and she managed to leap ahead, land sideways on one leg, and hold the other up at chest height. It all happened so fast and I was too close to stop or even change direction. She hooked me, used my own momentum and sent me flying onto some guy's lawn. I lost my footing and hit the ground. We're red-lining down the road and she lays a patch and pulls away. Anyhow, she felt bad and rushed over. I tripped her and sprayed her face. That, and not her cans, is how I got her. Funny thing is, I think I was only able to keep up as well as I did because of her *cans*—so that is how she remembers it. Bralessness cost her speed."

"She's pretty incredible," Henry proudly agreed.

"Incredible? She's like a fuck'n superhero," Adam exclaimed. He was filled with awe and possibility. "Ever notice how all the great icons of the comic book world—Superman, Batman, Wonder Woman—are brunettes?"

"Can't say as I have. I'm not really versed on the topic."

"I guess that makes you a Steve Trevor," Adam said.

"A Steve Trevor?"

"Wonder Woman's love interest. Or, in your case, probably more of a Lois Lane."

Alexandra's shadow stretched into the garage with her return to the doorway. She was wearing a snug, white T-shirt that was tied into a knot at her sternum and Henry's favourite pair of cut-off denim shorts. Adam had a saying that Henry never fully appreciated until he had met Alexandra. He was reminded of it again. *Her legs start at her ass and go all the way down to the ground.* Seeing her in the shorts outside the bedroom inspired a transient fantasy that put a new alfresco twist to the travelling salesman and the farmer's daughter role-play.

She held out a bucket. "Take your shirt off, Adam, we're washing the truck."

"What?"

"Catch up. This is an emergency."

He paused and tried to read Alexandra in an attempt to understand the reason behind her seemingly random insistence to clean his truck. He failed.

"Why are we washing my truck? And why am I taking my shirt off?"

"Oh my friend," she replied. "You can be so naive."

Chapter 69

Kayley was in the process of rinsing the soil off her daughter's feet when she noticed Henry walking toward the garden. She found it odd that someone as fussy as him wouldn't have promptly changed out of his sweaty clothes. He appeared to have something on his mind and she suspected she knew what it was.

"Kayley, do you have a sec?"

"Of course. Is this about me calling you Gavin last night?"

"Actually I wanted your opinion on something."

"My opinion? I'm not really a believer in random slips of the tongue. Gavin must be on my mind in some way. But I honestly don't recall thinking about him for quite awhile."

"A subconscious thing?" Henry speculated.

"Apparently. But what caused it? And why at that moment?"

Kayley noticed Terra's intense examination of one of the vines. She watched her daughter shift through various angles of approach. Upon closer inspection Kayley saw that the source of her daughter's interest was a ladybug.

"Terra, you can look, but you are not an anteater," she said, to a lukewarm reception.

"Could you be over-thinking this?" Henry asked.

"I don't like the idea of suppressed thoughts running amok."

"Calling me Gavin isn't exactly amok."

"Could be a small outward sign of a much bigger internal issue."

"Do you think that whatever it is will lead you to killing me in my sleep?"

"No." Kayley laughed. "Of course not."

"Could we maybe then set it aside for the time being?"

"Sure. Sorry. You wanted my opinion on something?"

"The landscaping in the front yard."

"A year ago I would have told you that you've got the wrong lady. But now..." Kayley summarized with a broad pass of her arm that encompassed the breadth of the garden.

She took her daughter by the hand and followed Henry's lead toward the side of the house. By the garage they could see down to the end of the driveway where Alexandra and Adam were washing the pickup truck. Kayley started with Adam, admiring the lean musculature of his body. Then she noticed Alexandra in her barely there cut-offs. She would bend at the waist on her return to the bucket of soapy water. The white tassel threads of the shorts' hem ebbed and flowed over her backside like the sea foam of a gentle wave. Her tanned legs glistened from the spillage that fell from the oversaturated sponge.

Kayley didn't know Alexandra's motive, but it was very apparent to her that the overt teasing was intentional. It was different than tantalizing a lover. The wonderful and unaffected charisma had been replaced by a distasteful, plastic sexuality. Complete nudity would have been better. Kayley became upset watching the exhibition.

Henry stood with her during the long pause, equally lost in thought—but for entirely different reasons. They were mannequins when Adam took notice. He coughed to get Alexandra's attention and then pointed them out with a directing shift in his eyes. She waved to them with the sponge. Henry's boyish solicitation was familiar to her. She entertained the offer in his eyes, but knew that she might have to take a rain check since Helen would soon be by to pick her up for their shopping date. Reading Kayley, on the other hand, presented a challenge. She appeared offended.

"This is stupid," Adam whispered across the hood. "Really stupid. I feel like I'm in the opening scene of a porno."

"Hopefully the neighbours feel that way, too," Alexandra replied. "And from the look of things—they seem to."

"I feel kind of cheap."

"And what exactly does that make me?"

"I didn't mean anything by it. Guys just don't do this."

"Do what?"

"Get checked out."

"Uh-huh."

"Well then, I don't get checked out."

"Again, uh-huh."

"Not like this anyway."

"Suck it up, princess. The other option is that you could be the one breaking it to Kayley."

"Princess?" He exclaimed.

Adam dropped from Alexandra's view. Suspicious, she cocked her arm—ready with the sponge for immediate retaliation. Adam braced one arm on the side of the truck bed and jumped in with the hose, the nozzle salivating with malicious intent. She turned in the direction of the thud from his landing. He saw the whites of her eyes and opened fire, sending a single spear of water to collapse into her face. Terra screamed with giddy excitement.

"Can I play, Mommy?"

"We can ask them, Mouse."

"Can I play, too?" Terra called out.

Adam looked to the top of the driveway. Alexandra, seeing her opportunity, whipped her sponge into the side of his head. It stuck for an instant. Adam wiped the suds off his face and pointed the spitting nozzle at Alexandra while he spoke to Terra.

"Sure, Mouse. But you'll need to get your swimsuit on."

"You don't have your swimsuit on."

"I made a mistake."

Through a reasonably judicious conference between mother and daughter it was agreed that, while getting wet in clothes may appear fun, in reality it was not. Assistance changing was offered and declined, with the understanding that Terra could, at her own discretion, call for aid if the straps proved to be too much of a bothersome entanglement. Henry and Kayley accompanied her as far as the front door. They remained on the porch after Terra had entered the house.

"I feel bad," Adam said. He picked up the sponge and tossed it back into the bucket before jumping down onto the driveway. "This seems a little excessive."

"It has to be like this, Adam. She's pretty far gone."

"She's not *that* out there."

"She's decorating with them."

"People decorate with flowers and fruit."

"Oh for Christ's sake. Wake up. She's starting to name her favourites. They're becoming frigg'n pets, Adam. Kayley has pet tomatoes!"

They stood waiting on Henry. He became very aware of their pressing anticipation. Their actions appeared ever more contrived to come across as natural. The result was a poorly choreographed tandem fidget that made Henry itchy if he watched them. It was his burden for working with the cripplingly honest and the childlike.

"Kayley," he said. "Everybody seems to be in their front yard. This can wait if you want to hand out your tomatoes. I noticed that you had a bunch ready to go."

"Do you mind?"

"Not at all."

Kayley smiled and took her leave. On her way toward the driveway she noticed the peculiar, *look busy, God is coming* mannerisms of Adam and Alexandra. She couldn't put a label to it, but she knew there was definitely something stirring. They were far less skilled than her four-year-old daughter at concealing the trail of a secret. Kayley was certain that she could sweat it out of them, given enough time. She decided that her efforts could wait until after she had visited the neighbours.

Alexandra wanted to leave nothing to chance. She felt that an ad lib was in order. When Kayley returned with two baskets, Alexandra called out to her at a volume she felt would give the neighbours fair warning.

"Hey Kay, what are you doing with those baskets of tomatoes?"

"I'm going to drop them off at the neighbours," Kayley replied. She was confused by Alexandra's bellowing and spoke cautiously in response, in case it was a trick question.

"Oh!" Alexandra hollered, after Kayley had passed by. "So you're going to drop off tomatoes at the neighbours!"

Kayley went from being perplexed to being annoyed. "Yes. That is correct." There was sarcastic edge to her retaliatory shouting. "I am going to drop tomatoes off at the neighbours."

"Thought so," Alexandra said, in a greatly reduced, and very pleasant, conversational tone.

Kayley continued toward the sidewalk, where she stopped to reconnoitre. During the survey she noticed that the neighbourhood had become eerily quiet. Evidence of bustling activity lay strewn across the yards. The scurried exodus had left garden tools and children's toys abandoned in its wake. A soft breeze blew grass clippings along the street. Suds from partially washed cars floated atop dirty water toward the storm drain. A house door slammed shut. Kayley was baffled—a lone villager who had somehow managed to sleep through the wailing of a civil defence siren. She only became aware of Henry when he put his arm around her shoulder.

"The neighbours were hoping that we could talk to you about the tomatoes," he said.

"My tomatoes?" she asked. Kayley first looked down to the baskets and then to Henry. "What about them?"

"They don't want any more."

"That's not possible. They're beautiful."

"You've gone a little over the deep end, sweetie," Alexandra said, as she strolled down the driveway.

Kayley looked back over her shoulder, tracking Alexandra's approach while questioning her. "Deep end?"

"Honey, you decorate with them," she explained, in her best *keep the crazy person calm* voice. She passed by Kayley and stood on the street in front of her. "You put tomatoes on the mantle."

"Tomatoes on the mantle are supposed to bring prosperity. It's quaint folklore."

"You name them."

"Are you talking about the one in the kitchen? Lalita? The Red Goddess."

"Are you telling me that you have a tomato shrine in the kitchen? Honey—it is just a tomato. You know that, right?"

For Kayley it was not a shrine but it had recently taken on the role of living keepsake. An ever-refreshed, delightfully secret reminder of the morning she had stood in the garden and watched her Red Goddess through the bedroom window. Her intuition had been right. It belonged. Now she knew why, but no one else ever would.

"Of course I know that. I just named the tomato *after* the Hindu goddess. I don't think the tomato *is* the Red Goddess. That's silly." Kayley sensed their gentle scrutiny but didn't know their reason. "You don't think that it is sacrilegious—do you? I didn't mean to offend anyone."

"Sacrilegious? No sweetie," Alexandra consoled, as if to a child. "It's just really, really nuts. That's all."

When the pieces finally dropped into place for Kayley she gasped aloud. It was unthinkable that her tomatoes were unwelcome. In a tangential thought she forgave Alexandra. Not for her participation, but because of the good intention. Kayley saw the shorts as a private costume, one that Henry was likely very familiar with, much the same as the red satin robe. She imagined Alexandra, in a noble act, leafing through her private tickle-trunk of intimate dress-up in search of the perfect draw that would help to save her supposedly loony friend— admirable. With her universe made right once again, Kayley promptly rebounded to her original issue.

"Oh my God!" she squawked and then shot a glare back toward Adam—the sheepish member of the jury. At first Kayley was completely flabbergasted, but rapidly became incensed. "You think I'm a crazy tomato lady. And this is your intervention."

"No," Henry comforted, resulting in Alexandra's nodding agreement with Kayley to change mid-stream to a slow headshake of supportive reassurance.

"But," he continued. "The entire neighbourhood *is* praying for an early frost." Terra stepped onto the porch. She was wearing her water shoes and a one-piece bathing suit—which she had on backwards. Her navel peered out where the small of her back would normally show.

"Well done, Mouse," Kayley said. She was both amused and proud. "The cross straps usually go in the back. Do you want me to help you fix it?"

"No," Terra replied, as she descended the steps leading down from the porch. It was not that she was being independent—it was simply a matter of being fine with the way things were. Her casual stroll to the driveway captivated everyone. It was Alexandra who broke the charm.

"Well, I should get changed before Helen gets here," she said.

"Helen?" Henry asked.

"She's taking me shopping."

"For?"

"Stuff."

Henry hooked his index finger through one of her belt loops. He reined her in and they stepped away from Kayley. Alexandra provocatively slid her leg between his thighs and they shifted into a flamenco inspired stance.

"Do you need to change right away?" he whispered.

Adam opened the hose on both of them.

Chapter 70

Clothes changed, Alexandra popped out of the house and launched into the front yard. In five bounding strides she arrived at Helen's parked car and pressed her hands against the window of the passenger side door to peer in. Helen and Kayley's presence on the porch had completely eluded her. They were ignored onlookers who had been amazed by the grace and power of her charge.

"That absolutely exhausted me," Helen commented.

"She's a woman on a mission for sure. Where are you two going?"

"I'm sworn to secrecy."

"Helen, we don't keep secrets."

"Really? How's your blood pressure?"

Over the course of their friendship Kayley had become very familiar with, but never quite used to, Helen's pointed questions. The two women butted wills and then acknowledged a draw.

"It's fine," Kayley said.

"Glad to hear."

Adam stopped washing the grill of the truck after noticing the confusion at the car. He covered Terra's ears, and fired off a piercing whistle. Alexandra swung to face him and then followed his signpost index finger around to the porch just as Henry was stepping out of the front door. She greeted him with an intentionally alluring fingertip wave and then, after noticing Helen, threw her arms up impatiently.

"I am being summoned," Helen said. She sauntered toward Henry. He knew he was in her crosshairs.

"Bonjour, Henri," Helen meowed softly.

He never understood what caused Helen to periodically slip into the use of French when she spoke to him. He theorized that it gave her a shared sense of family, tenuous as it may be. And because Henry welcomed the connection, he never questioned the behaviour.

"Bonjour, Hélène," he replied.

She glanced meaningfully in the direction of the car. Henry followed suit. Alexandra was playing bongos on the roof while her hips gyrated to the energetic rhythm.

"J'espère que vous prenez vos vitamines," she said, lightheartedly.

"Et ginseng," he added, as she passed by on her way to the stairs.

"Salut," she said from the lawn.

"Salut, Hélène."

Kayley knew that Helen was adept with languages but she was surprised by Henry's fluency and curious about what had just transpired.

"Well," she prodded, after the car pulled away. "Translate."

"She hopes I'm taking my vitamins," he explained as he moved beside her.

"Are you?"

"And ginseng." He leaned back on the railing.

"You know, you two should get to know each other better. Family is important. Even extended family."

Kayley's words had brushed against something deep inside Henry. Perhaps it was that Alexandra was in his life, or perhaps it was that he was going to be a father, but whatever the cause, he suddenly felt a strong need for the connection of family. In that moment he knew the nature of the bond that he needed to make with Helen.

"Get her more involved in your life with Alexandra," Kayley elaborated. "You know, dinners and family holidays. Stuff like that."

"You're right and very insightful. Thank you. I think I know just where to start."

"I can be sometimes."

"You can be sometimes?"

"*Sometimes* insightful," she said, before smiling. "*Always* right."

"Yes Adam has mentioned your stellar record." Henry met her gaze for a moment, sharing in the fleeting humour before changing the topic. "And speaking of you, how are you doing?"

Kayley sat alongside Henry and smiled optimistically. "Me? I'm fine. I was actually just thinking about landscaping. Besides, my tomatoes might be better served at the food bank. And hey, if they don't take fresh produce, we could always have our own little *La Tomatina*."

"La Tomatina?"

"It's a tomato festival in Spain. The highlight is a massive tomato food fight."

All concerns that Henry had about the vehemence of the intervention fell by the wayside. Beyond using the possessive tense to speak about vegetables, the woman knew way too much tomato-specific trivia. Pregnancy was indeed a mystical force. He tried to think of a response—but after failing to come up with anything relevant, stood and faced the yard.

"So what are your thoughts about landscaping?" he asked.

"I had a vision. I'd like to plant a birch tree."

"A vision? Just now?"

"Earlier. Before Helen arrived. Sometimes, you need to go quiet and listen to your soul."

Henry's cynicism and sarcasm were quickly outmanoeuvred by his civility. He focused, as if her vision was a silent but engaging movie that the audience was expected to talk through—respectfully.

"Not a vision really," she corrected, in response to his squinting out at the yard. "More along the lines of a very clear thought."

"My understanding is that birch trees don't handle transplanting well," Henry said, with his eyes fully opened.

"It will take," she replied.

He smiled. She recognized its likeness from the party when it was suggested that the neighbourhood would be better served with the name Estates at Heighten Park Reserve. Observing this dubious acceptance, she felt a need to justify her confidence.

"You know that Goldenrain tree that grows in the park across the street from your apartment?"

"Goldenrain tree?"

"The one that flowers in summer."

"Okay. Yes."

"Well, it shouldn't be there. There aren't any others anywhere around. And you know why? We are in the wrong zone. It is too cold for too many days for a Goldenrain tree to survive. Yet…"

"A birch it is."

"I'm glad you're with me. I like what it symbolizes."

"How so?"

"In the Wicca religion the birch is associated with protection, purification, new beginnings, and fertility. Babies' cradles were once made of birch wood as a kind of mystic protection. And the birch is also linked with spirits of the dead."

"Except for that last bit, I can see the fit."

"I think that part fits, too. I just haven't been able to piece it together. I wonder if it is related to Gavin?"

Kayley trusted her intuition. It was her guide and companion when she wrote. There had been many instances when she had read back what she had put on paper and discovered, as an outside observer, the meaning and significance in her own work. Yet she was struggling to tie it together, uncertain of whether she was even on the right path. The two sat pondering the possible connections between seemingly unrelated things when it occurred to Kayley that they had not entirely completed their conversation about Helen.

"So?" Kayley asked. "Where are you starting?"

"Starting?"

"With Helen."

Chapter 71

Alexandra was absolutely mesmerized by the plethora of dildos and vibrators. Some hung in suggestive packaging on the wall, while others were piled along several tiers of shelving. The display was overwhelming. It was one and a half storeys tall and the width of a double door. She stood in silence wondering if there were as many nicknames for the penis as there were varieties of sex toys that emulated it. Alexandra came up with a paltry few—which she couldn't help but compare to the innumerable synonyms for breast.

"Did you just say *boobs so rule*?" Helen asked.

She was standing beside Alexandra, mostly as moral support, but also searching for any interesting new arrivals. Alexandra hadn't realized she'd spoken aloud.

"Relative to penises," Alexandra explained. Helen's blank stare prompted further elaboration. "There are a lot more names for boobs than there are for penises. And, as Henry explained, the more words something has describing it, the more important that something is to a society."

"Henry said that about breasts?"

"*He* was talking about wine tasting. I just figured it applied to names for boobs, too."

"Ah."

Alexandra went back to the vast selection. She was at a loss. It wasn't like shopping for groceries—or even for clothes. The nearest relevant experience she could come up with was the time she had gone looking for a dependable cordless phone, one with nice ergonomic functionality. Feeling a need to make a decision, any decision, she moved cautiously forward, but stopped when Helen advised against the choice with a counselling headshake. Alexandra stepped back and crossed her arms.

"I wanted to talk to you about something," she said, without diverting her attention from the display.

"What?" Helen asked.

"Kayley."

"What about Kayley?"

"A couple of things, actually."

Helen watched Alexandra shuffle through hues of cautious beginnings before she spoke. "Her blood pressure. And calling Henry *Gavin*."

"Her blood pressure? It's up?"

"You knew?"

"No. She didn't tell me—*of course*. She had the exact same thing happen when she was carrying Terra. Damn it!"

"What happened?"

"It was hell. They did everything for her, but nothing seemed to work. Not well anyway. Finally a nurse at one of her checkups recommended a female physician that also practiced herbal and holistic medicine and that is what turned it around. Kayley's blood pressure was brought under control. Still a little up. But under control."

"It can be controlled, then?"

"Unless the first time around was just a fluke."

"Is that possible?"

Alexandra's concern was visible in her manner. There was apprehension in her wide eyes that Helen didn't want to trample. She changed her tack to a gentler approach. "I just worry a little," Helen explained. "But she'll be fine. I'm positive. My God, she's stubborn."

"I was pissed at first," Alexandra said. "That she didn't tell me, I mean. But now, I admire her."

Helen resumed browsing but soon became distracted by Alexandra. She was testing the weight of various dildos, balancing them, like a teeter-totter, across her index finger. After her assessment, Alexandra made a choice of three. She tossed them into the air and began to juggle. Three helmeted batons, two black and one pink, were flipped, end-over-end, in a Ferris wheel trajectory.

"Would you like me to set them on fire?" Helen asked.

Alexandra stopped and put them down. "Kayley called Henry *Gavin*? Odd, eh?"

"You mentioned that. When?"

"When she told us about her blood pressure. We went a little lynch mob on her, and when she snapped back, that slipped out."

"I guess he's on her mind."

"Why?"

Helen would be the first to admit that she never could define what Gavin represented to Kayley. Their relationship, if nothing else, was complex. It had ended with the emotional qualities of a breakup. Yet, like the poem Kayley thought she didn't know about, it remained unfinished.

"I really don't know what to make of it."

Alexandra was not one for wasting time pondering the imponderable. She didn't know why Kayley called Henry *Gavin* and neither did Helen. So be it. She returned to the monumental task of selecting her sex toy, deciding to give her search some criteria in order to narrow down the field.

"I should probably get something Henry sized," Alexandra concluded.

"Why would you say that out loud?" Helen reprimanded. "Now I'll be checking out your purchase. And that's not true, by the way. Is this your first time?"

"Yep. I'll just get a few different sizes to throw you off."

Alexandra had an epiphany as a result of her own response. It occurred to her that she didn't need to restrict herself to a single purchase. Her limits were set only by the available stock. Alexandra turned toward the woman at the cash register.

"Excuse me," Alexandra called to her, while pointing at the display. "Do you have a starter kit or sampler pack or assorted gift basket or something?"

"I'm sure we could put something together," the woman replied.

Helen was intrigued.

Chapter 72

Henry had lost track of time. It was the hunger pangs, not a clock, that told him he should take a break from painting the basement. He placed the brushes and roller onto the paint tray, then slid the lot into a large plastic garbage bag that he tied closed.

After climbing the stairs to the main floor he was surprised to hear Alexandra's muffled voice. Walking toward the kitchen it became apparent that she was muttering to herself from within their bedroom. Curiosity tugged at him as he quickly rinsed his hands in the kitchen sink. He kept glancing in the direction of the closed door while trying to make sense of the mumbled words.

The agitation in her tone prompted him to approach with caution. He placed his ear against the door but recoiled when a violently hurled projectile slammed against the other side.

"Fuck'n, fuck, fucker-up," Alexandra screamed.

PAIRS

Henry swung open the door into the room, knocking aside the assailing rubber mortar. Alexandra was sitting naked on the bed. Her legs were stretched out in an impossibly wide V and her head was slumped forward. Scattered about the hills and valleys of the blanket was a disorganized herd of dildos and vibrators, some purring with the soft hum of a cellphone determined to be answered. On the stool, which served as their bedside table, was an open bottle of tequila. He went unnoticed. She was preoccupied with the pep talk she was giving her vagina.

"I didn't mean to yell," she said, soothingly as she patted her pubic hair. "But if you could just take in one, even a really small one, part way, I'd be so proud of you."

"Alexandra." Henry said.

"Oh my God," she yelped, amazed that her vagina was responding—and in a man's voice. "You sound just like my wife!"

He walked over to the bed and sat down beside her. When the mattress took his weight she looked up, blinking deep brown puppy eyes as she processed his unexpected arrival. She nodded when she understood what had transpired.

"That was you."

"Honey, I don't understand."

"Babe—it's time I faced this thing."

"Your phobia?" Henry asked, as he attempted to track down and silence all the insistent droning.

"Exac-attack-ally."

"I don't think this is the healthiest approach."

"I'm not going to a psychiatrist!"

"A phobia is not something you try and bust through. It is something you must just release. Over time."

"Easy to say. You have an outty. Try managing an inny for a while and then talk to me."

"Well, this obviously isn't working or you. You want to try it my way?"

Alexandra sighed, nuzzled the top of her head into the nape of Henry's neck and nodded before adding her stipulation. "Today."

He stroked her hair as he spoke. "First, I'd like you to take nice long shower."

Alexandra found his request peculiar but followed his instructions without question. After she put on her robe and left the room Henry started to plan. The details were sketchy but the premise was simple. He wanted to get Alexandra into an extremely deep state of relaxation.

His first order of business was to collect the phallic menagerie and toss them under the bed. He removed the tequila, retrieved the massage oil, tidied the room, and remade the bed. Candles replaced lamplight.

Adam's *Sounds of a Meadow* CD was confiding to the room when Alexandra returned—a tad more sober. She saw the oil on the table and knew her role. The robe fell to the floor and she crawled into bed and lay on her back.

"Turn over," Henry said.

"To do my feet?"

"I'm going to do your body."

"And you want me on my stomach?"

"Correct."

"It is my *vagina* that you will be attempting to enter. Right?"

"I'm starting on your back. And, I'm not attempting anything—beyond a massage," Henry said, as he removed his shirt in preparation.

"Okee dokee," Alexandra replied, before repositioning herself.

Chapter 73

The house appeared empty when Kayley opened the door. She stepped into the foyer, switched on the hall light, and moved aside to provide room for Adam. Terra was asleep in his arms. Kayley gave her a peck on the cheek, then kissed Adam.

PAIRS

"I'll take her up," he whispered. "Then I'll unload the swing set."

"Thank you."

They kissed again and parted. In search of snack food, Kayley went to the kitchen and plugged in the kettle before perusing the disappointing contents of the fridge. She decided toast would be a good accompaniment to her ginger tea.

***

Alexandra was completely relaxed, lying on her back and sunk into the comfort of the mattress. Her body was heavy and distant. Tenderly kneading hands and a restful field were all that she was aware of.

An icy tingle travelled along her stomach to her breasts, as Henry lightly traced the tips of fingernails up her body. Her nipple was drawn between his warm lips and was caressed by his tongue. She moaned softly.

***

Kayley was sitting at the picnic table, resting and quietly reflecting on the birch when a sound registered somewhere in the outskirts of her subconscious. On a hunch, she looked toward the closed door of the bedroom. Uncertain if she had heard anything at all she returned to her thoughts. Kayley had confidence in her intuition about the tree, but was unsure if she had interpreted the link with spirits of the dead correctly. Gavin might not be the connection. Or, he might not be the *only* one. The noise happened again— pleasured, erotic, and a little louder than before.

"She's dead to the world," Adam said, as he wandered into the kitchen.

Kayley waved him to silence. Puzzled and a little miffed, he stopped talking and walked over to the picnic table. When she saw his mouth opening to speak, Kayley quickly stood and pressed her index finger against his lips. He was upset by her bizarre behaviour until he heard Alexandra's succulent groan.

"Jesus, Kay," he hissed. "We can't just eavesdrop on them having sex."

"I know, I know," Kayley replied. "It's perverse." She sat down and fixated intently on the door.

***

Henry was lying on his stomach with his shoulders between Alexandra's legs. She could feel his mouth tenderly moving down her pelvis toward her vagina. Alarm bells attempted to sound, but could only manage a remote echo that dissipated during a sudden rush of pleasure. It was all she knew. There was nothing else. She squealed and whimpered.

***

Adam unplugged the kettle, but on unspecified moral grounds, left the toast to get cold. His cousin and his best bud were doing the wild thing and his girlfriend was getting off listening. He was debating ethical issues and the creep-out factor while getting a can of beer from the fridge. The only acknowledgement Kayley would give him was a frustrated flailing of her hands if he made too much noise.

***

Pleased with his progress, Henry glanced up to gauge Alexandra's state. He interpreted the fact that she was chewing on her own lips to be a positive indicator. Henry's mouth and tongue continued to play, focusing exclusively on the exterior of her vagina. She groaned.

***

Adam had returned to the picnic table but had refused to sit. Kayley, irked by his distracting indignity, glared at him.

"You can leave, you know," she whispered.

"I know that."

Their erupting spat was nipped by Alexandra's sudden guttural howl and the subsequent crash against the door. Henry stumbled out of the room, cracking his jaw as if attempting to depressurize his eardrums. He had reached the fridge by the time Alexandra came charging out after him. She was completely naked, her skin oiled to a semigloss luminescence.

"Henry, I'm so sorry!"

"I'm fine," he said, while pulling out a bag of peas from the freezer.

"You're not fine."

Alexandra followed him to the sink. He wrapped the peas in a tea towel and held it against the back of his head. Before Henry could turn around to face her, Alexandra straddled her arms on either side of his waist, pressed her body against his and put her mouth by his ear.

"If you're fine, then I'd like to do that again."

"My jaw is out of commission."

"I was thinking you could rub against me," she said, while tracing her nipples along his back, "using something else."

"Something else?"

Alexandra didn't pick up on the coy nuances of his inquiry and, as a result, decided that a more blunt approach was required. "Henry, I'm talking about your dink."

Adam dropped his beer can. Henry and Alexandra were startled and turned, together, in the direction of the noise. Kayley was doing her best to appear very prim. Her belly wouldn't allow her to cross her legs comfortably, so she placed her hands, one over the other, atop her knee. Adam's mouth was still open when Henry bid his cordial greeting.

"Hello, Adam. Kayley. This is a bit of a surprise."

"Hello, Henry," Kayley responded. "Alexandra."

Alexandra nodded her reply, stared vacantly for a moment, then raised her arms as if to take flight, and looked down at herself with feigned astonishment.

"Oh my. I appear to be completely naked. And oiled. Henry and I should probably go take care of this."

Kayley stood up and reached for Adam's hand. "Yes. And we should probably go check on Terra. Together."

The draining can and resulting puddle of beer were forgotten in their divergent, but equally hasty, departures.

Chapter 74

When Alexandra awoke, still feeling a slight tequila buzz, she stared dreamily at the ceiling and grinned. The covers had been stripped from the bed and lay in a mound on the floor, along with the towels they had used after the shower Henry had insisted on. He was next to her and also quietly monitoring the non-activity overhead. He was reassuring himself that the timing, to share what he had been up to over the past week, would never be better than that moment.

"Alexandra?"

"Yes."

"I've been researching vaginismus on the Internet. There are self-help programs. You don't need to see a therapist."

"I know there are. And Henry, I think its time that I take back my vagina. I'll start by giving her a name."

"A name?"

"A name. What do you think of Kitten? That, or Love-heart."

"You're naming your vagina *Kitten*?" Henry clarified.

"Or Love-heart. Why not? It's mine." She felt a glorious new sense of empowerment. Something important had happened. "And today I'm ordering one of those self-help thingies."

Alexandra rolled on her side toward Henry. She was surprised by his joyless expression and lost a little confidence as a result. He could be so finicky about certain things. Alexandra wondered if she had committed a sexual faux pas. He noticed the interest and faced her.

"What's wrong?" She asked.

"Nothing's wrong."

"Yes there is."

Henry sighed. His words felt their way carefully into the room. "I was wondering, given recent events, and this wonderful and brave step that you're undertaking…"

"What are you wondering?" She asked anxiously.

"If we were going to continue to do the *other* stuff?"

Alexandra's apprehension was released in a joyous snort. Henry could be so peculiar. He was uncertain how to interpret the reaction.

"Definitely," she growled seductively—much to Henry's relief.

They moved toward each other but the small hand that slapped against the door forestalled their kiss. Sitting up in bed, Alexandra glanced at Henry, both knowing who had come to visit. Before either could respond there was another smack.

"Alexandra," Terra called. "Are you in there? Are you asleep? Come and see what Daleesha gave me."

"Henry and I are getting dressed, Mouse. We'll be out in a minute."

When they emerged from the room, Terra had already left to join her mother in the backyard where Adam was assembling the swing set. Alexandra followed Henry out onto the deck. Kayley glanced at them and shared a jovial remembrance of their kitchen meeting. She was sitting on the step. Terra was standing on the grass, between her mother's knees.

"Go for it, kiddo," Adam said to Terra, as he walked toward the group.

Kayley opened her legs slightly and Terra bolted out. Once at the swing she took hold of the chains, sat down and adjusted her position until her feet were off the ground. They all kept an eye on her spasmodic oarsman thrusts until she began to smoothly take flight. It was wonderful for Adam.

"Aren't we selling this place?" Henry asked.

"I'll take it down," Adam replied. Seeing his cousin standing next to Alexandra rekindled his curiosity. He wanted the details on Henry's accident. "What the hell happened to you?"

Henry knew exactly what he was referring to and replied coolly. "It's personal."

"Aw. Tell him, Henry," Alexandra cajoled. "It is kind of funny."

She elbowed his side, which only served to add fuel to his highbrow obstinance. Henry crossed his arms and took a stonewalling interest in the swing set.

"Alright then," she said. "I'll tell him."

Alexandra eagerly stepped out into the yard, a few paces away from the deck. From her enthusiasm, Henry knew that she would not only recount, but also re-enact. The woman was, by nature, a performer.

"In my defence," she began, "no one has ever gone down on me before—because I never let them. So when Henry did, it was all very new to me. Then add tequila into the mix."

Sensing that her play might last longer than the actual event, and fearing the level of detail, Henry waited for his opening. No matter how narrow it was, he would take it. She paused while straddling her legs well past shoulder width. After she goal-posted her groin between her hands, Henry forced himself past his mortification to interrupt.

"When Alexandra had her orgasm, her legs snapped closed across my shoulders. My head was clamped between her thighs."

"Sorry, babe." She brought her feet closer together.

"Leaving my face pressed into her…"

"Vagina," Alexandra contributed. "Which I've decided to name, by the way."

"I couldn't breathe," he interrupted. "I started to panic. So I pushed against the mattress to try and free myself."

"When I understood what was happening," Alexandra explained. "I opened my legs."

"And I flew backwards into the door."

The corners of Adam's mouth curled into a greasy smile and his eyes leisurely narrowed as he took aim at Henry. "So, then, you nearly mufficated?"

"Yes, Adam—I nearly mufficated."

Alexandra noticed the quiet inside herself while watching Kayley lean forward and playfully smack Adam on the leg. Lindsay had been released.

Chapter 75

Club 23 was the martini bar of choice for Helen. It was sleek, chic, offered impeccable service and had an extensive choice of variations on the shaken-not-stirred classic. As such, it would have been utterly common had it not been for the rumours.

The original owner, who also happened to be the designer, had a flare for style, a passion for the sophisticated elegance that a martini evoked, and, as the urban legend would have it, was a twenty-thirdian. He had left a smatter of two-three combinations subversively imbedded throughout all aspects of the club. Not surprisingly, there was a direct correlation between the patrons' alcohol consumption and their revelations. Why, even the address fed the lore. 1967 Fifth Avenue: $1+9+6+7 = 23$ and $2+3 = 5$. *Eerie*.

Helen had happily accepted Henry and Alexandra's invitation to meet, but from the onset had a hunch that there was something more than mere socializing on the agenda. When she arrived, they were already seated at a high table near the bar. It was the ideal perch from which to sip martinis and watch the door. Henry's demeanour was casual and unforthcoming but Alexandra had the semblance of a vigorously shaken bottle of pop. They both stood to greet Helen as she approached. After welcoming hugs and cordial pecks on the cheek, Helen draped the strap of her purse over her chair's backrest and sat across from the two of them—interview style.

"Nice day, huh," Alexandra said, then grinned broadly. She was leaning forward, resting her elbows against the tabletop and swivelling from side to side on the bar stool. As much as it was killing her, Alexandra accepted that it was Henry's show. Until, of course, her patience ran out. The clock was ticking, and it only possessed a second hand.

"Yes it is," Helen agreed, with light-hearted suspicion. "Is there a written agenda for this meeting or are we winging it?"

Alexandra was confused by the question and glanced quickly at Henry before replying. "Winging it, I guess."

Henry reciprocated Helen's smile before elaborating. "Alright, there is more to this than just catching up over drinks. But nothing subversive, I promise. No prelude to network marketing or joining a cult or anything."

"That's a relief," Helen said, while attempting to catch the eye of a server.

"Henry and I asked you here because we think family is important," Alexandra prompted impatiently, and then motioned for Henry to continue.

Helen's private enjoyment at watching the two interact was briefly interrupted by the arrival of the waiter. He was a handsome young man that she felt had some rather appealing qualities. She flirted her order for a Cosmopolitan and after he had left the table, discovered that her window-shopping had not gone unnoticed by Alexandra, who gave sisterly advice by gesturing for Helen to undo the next button down on her blouse.

"Helen," Henry began. "Although you and I were thrust together, so to speak, as stepsiblings. I think, and especially so lately…"

"He wants, well *we* want, to be more family-like." Alexandra explained.

"Is that true, Henry?" Helen asked.

"If I'm lying, I'm dying," Alexandra reassured.

"Yes it is, Helen," Henry said. "And in that vein, the reason we wanted to meet with you was to ask a huge favour."

"Listening," Helen replied cautiously.

"We'd be very appreciative. And honoured."

"Still listening."

"It is a lot to ask of someone. And you don't have to answer right away. And we will understand if you say no."

Alexandra began to focus intently on keeping her mouth closed. *Henry's show* became her desperate mantra to remain silent. The monumental effort had surpassed even the release that incessant fidgeting could provide. To the untrained eye she was sitting perfectly still with incredibly rigid posture. However, Henry sensed the ultrasonic micro tremor of a vibrating tuning fork that would escape casual observation. He could almost hear a power-line hum. Alexandra was on the verge of drawing the entire bar into their very private conversation. Henry spoke quickly.

"We were wondering if you would be our child's godmother."

"Finally," Alexandra exclaimed in a gust.

Helen was unable to provide an immediate response. The request was so completely unforeseeable that she was not sure if she had heard correctly. Alexandra's toothy, radiant smile was all that Helen seemed capable of processing as she reviewed the conversation.

"So?" Alexandra blurted, which rebooted Helen and popped a question from her.

"What about Kayley?"

"She thought it was a wonderful idea when I ran it past her," Henry replied.

Helen surprised herself with the depth of emotion she felt. Certainly there was flattery in their request, but there was also profound trust, binding and familial. Helen was overwhelmed.

"Of course," she gushed.

"I'm cancelling your order, Helen," Alexandra announced. "This calls for something special."

She smiled at Helen, pounced with a long passionate kiss, and then hopped to her feet. Standing beside the table, she pointed her finger gun at Helen and winked.

"Still hot," she said. Immediately after which she noticed Henry staring.

"That was a happy one. Not a sexy one." Alexandra explained to him while leaving for the bar. "No tongue."

"Next time." Helen teased.

Henry enjoyed the speed and bent of Helen's humour. For it was much like his own, refined. But where he was cultured she was cosmopolitan. They might not be related by blood, but they were kindred. How wonderful family occasions would be with Helen working her charm.

"*Still* hot?" he inquired. His intent was to playfully torment her with an awkward moment.

"Yes," she replied, reading his good-humoured needle. "Still."

"Oh?"

"Technically, that would have been our third kiss. But I don't count the first time."

"And why is that?"

"I wasn't *in* the moment."

"Ah."

"You're not jealous?" Helen confirmed, seeking to ensure that their conversation was all in jest.

Henry thought about Alexandra. Privately, so privately that his secret would accompany him to the grave, Henry had found that it helped to think of Alexandra's meandering anarchy in terms of a large, otherwise playful dog. If it tastes good, eat it. If it feels good, do it. If it smells good, roll in it. If it threatens loved ones, destroy it. He revisited his feelings at Daleesha's party, marvelling at how much everything had changed. Alexandra's love and attentiveness had given him confidence. He was no longer so intensely insecure.

"No. Not really. It is just part and parcel of who she is," he explained, but after Helen raised a curious eyebrow conceeded, "Okay, a teeny tiny bit."

"A teeny tiny bit is healthy. She worships you, you know."

"I know," he replied, in thoughtful appreciation.

Helen looked toward the bar, watching Alexandra's gesturing as she spoke to the bartender. Life sparkled in her. Helen was in awe at how a human being could blossom from such a dreadful past. She found herself comparing Alexandra's carnal extroversion to Gavin's cautious intimacy.

"I heard somewhere that sexual abuse can lead to hyper-sexuality," she said. In response to Henry's questioning glance, she reached across the table and placed her hand atop his before explaining, "Kayley told Daleesha and me. Enough to give us an understanding."

"Understanding?"

"In hindsight I believe that Kayley had been preparing us for her decision to be the surrogate."

"We love her for that."

Henry looked toward the bar, amused by Alexandra's gesticulation. She wouldn't be the woman he loved if she didn't make things a grand and wondrous production, which, he acknowledged, included kissing anyone and everyone who made her happy.

"You know, Henry, we really could be family," Helen conjectured, "We do share some similar interests.

"Do tell," he prompted.

"I, too, want a gorgeous younger boyfriend with boundless energy."

Henry was initially confused by the boyfriend reference until he made the link to Alexandra. He surmised that a great deal had been shared among the women in his life. He raised a toast to Helen's future success.

"What sort of martinis do you suppose she is ordering?" he wondered aloud.

"I don't know," Helen replied as she deliberated on Alexandra's animated movements. "But I'm getting the impression that flames will be involved."

Henry nodded. Helen remained distracted by Alexandra as her instructions to the bartender began to rise toward an excited and very audible crescendo.

"You know what I mean by *oomph*?" Alexandra's arms rose for emphasis.

After Helen's attention returned to Henry, they shared a brief smile over the antics.

"And," Helen speculated, with an intentional air of sophisticated detachment, "perhaps explosives."

Chapter 76

On the afternoon that the landscaper arrived with the birch tree, Alexandra was in the kitchen cutting up Lindsay's identification and letting the pieces fall onto a swatch of cheesecloth. Alerted by the warning beep of the truck as it reversed, she gathered the corners of the cloth, bound them with a piece of twine, and brought it with her when she left to join the others in the front yard.

From the doorway Alexandra could see the truck. The tall birch was reclined on the flatbed, its root ball hidden within the cone of the tree spade's large, triangular blades. She watched the flagman guide the driver into position at the large basin that had been dug in the yard. Once in place, outrigger stabilizers lowered to the ground.

Adam was standing on the street with Terra in his arms, talking to one of the workmen. He became aware of Alexandra and waved her over. Kayley and Henry watched from the far end of the porch as she walked sombrely from the house.

"Henry, did you mention anything about our discussion to Alexandra?" Kayley asked.

"No. Why?"

"Interesting. I still think Gavin is in there somewhere, but I think she is the main connection."

"Connection?"

"Spirits of the dead."

Alexandra approached the flagman. He had moved to the control panel that was mounted on the side of the flatbed. She tapped him on the back of the shoulder to get his attention. When he turned, he went from annoyed to awe. The transition was clearly visible from the porch. Both Henry and Kayley enjoyed witnessing Alexandra's impact.

"Yes, ma'am?"

"I have something I'd like to do before you drop the tree in. Mind?"

"Not at all."

Adam was curious to know the reason for delay. Alexandra, noticing his approach, held up the cheesecloth.

"A send-off for Lindsay," she said. He nodded sympathetically.

Henry and Kayley, sensitive to the observance, left the porch to stand beside Alexandra. She greeted them and reached for Henry. He took her hand and felt her grip squeeze lightly just before she tossed the tiny bundle into the mud.

"I don't know if there is such a thing as reincarnation, but if there is, I wish you a better go of it the next time around. *Way* better."

Reflecting on the life that a few pieces of plastic wrapped in cloth represented, Alexandra vowed to herself that if her child were a girl, she would name her Lindsay. Alexandra knew Henry would understand. Kayley put her arm around her and quietly recited a poem that she felt suited the moment.

Let me arise and open the gate,
to breathe the wild warm air of the heath,
And to let in Love, and to let out Hate,
And anger at living and scorn of Fate,
To let in Life, and to let out Death.

"Thank you," Alexandra said.

"And Violet Fane. Those are her words."

"Thank you Violet Fane."

"How did you come up with the idea?" Henry asked Alexandra.

"It was time," she replied. "I wanted some acknowledgement of Lindsay's life, but I didn't want it to be a funeral. It just occurred to me that a hole for the root ball isn't a grave. That hole is to *let in life*."

Cued by Alexandra's nod, they moved back and Adam gave a thumbs-up to the flagman. The tree was lifted, suspended in place, and then slowly lowered.

"A living thing ain't a tombstone," Adam contributed.

"Exactly."

Chapter 77

A once solid world had become the realm of spectres where parked cars were ghosts-ships on a lifeless black river, and phantom houses were epitaphs to the passage of families. Terra knew this place. She knew this fog, numinous and encompassing. She had been awaiting it her whole life.

After looking out the bedroom window, Adam put on his pyjamas with the intention of joyfully announcing to Terra that the clouds were visiting. When he opened the bedroom door she was already standing in the hall, waiting. She walked past him and crawled into bed with her sleeping mother.

"The clouds have landed, Mouse," he whispered excitedly.

Terra was unaffected by the news. Rather than responding with her usual glee she began to stroke Kayley's hair. Adam became concerned that something more than the fog was bothering her. He moved to his side of the bed and sat.

"Did you have a bad dream?"

Terra turned her head to look at Adam. She felt alone. Her emotions were attached to memories of events that were yet to pass. Sorrow and elation were bound seamlessly together. She didn't understand and couldn't explain. The final stage of a journey, long and purposeful, only made possible by the order of things, was ending and had begun. Terra shook her head and then attended to her mother. The gentle caressing awoke Kayley. Her eyes opened. Even with her back to her daughter she knew the soft touch. Kayley smiled and rolled over.

***

Terra remained silent for most of the morning. She followed her mother throughout the house, staying close and watching over her. During breakfast she sat on Kayley's lap. Adam and Kayley stopped pressing Terra for answers, though the melancholy worried them both.

PAIRS

Henry and Alexandra awoke later than usual. They had spent a significant portion of the previous night in sensual discovery. Alexandra opened the curtains of the bedroom to a grey pall through which she couldn't see to the railing of the deck. The tricky business of existence had been erased, as if in an act of amendment. She returned to bed, cuddled with Henry, and gave his penis a gentle congratulatory pat.

When they finally emerged, Adam was cleaning the breakfast dishes. He teased them with a roll of his eyes. Kayley had gone upstairs for a quick shower. Terra had become even more anxious, but didn't utter a word. She was standing close to Adam, holding onto his pant leg. Henry and Alexandra were both concerned for her.

***

When she regained her bearings, Kayley found herself staring at the floor, her torso draped over the side of the tub. In escalating panic, she deduced that she had slipped and that her stomach had taken the brunt of the fall. Everyone on the main floor froze when they heard the thud. Kayley screamed in horror. Terra shrieked and Adam picked her up. Alexandra raced down the hall, and hurtled up the staircase, three steps at a time.

"Stay here with Terra," Adam said to Henry, as he placed her in his waiting arms. Alexandra burst into the bathroom, and was overcome by the horror in Kayley's eyes. She felt cold and weak. Her thoughts scattered. It wasn't until Kayley reached an arm up toward her that Alexandra found the ability to move.

Adam heard the crying as he rushed up the stairs. He followed it to the en suite of the master bedroom. The two women were sitting on the floor. Tears streamed silently from Alexandra's empty eyes. She was holding Kayley, who wept hysterically into her shoulder.

Chapter 78

Nothing

PAIRS

Nothing matters

D. W. RICHARDS

Nothing matters any more

PAIRS

Nothing matters any more than you, my child

"Oh God, Daleesha, it's so horrible!"

"It just wasn't the soul's time and place, Helen. The universe is adjusting itself. There will be another chance. That's how we need to look at it."

"It's too real, too cruel."

"There is a reason for everything. A bigger picture."

"Please don't start. I can't think of it as anything other than tragic. You know that she had to be induced."

"Yes. I know."

"Awful. My mother gave birth to a stillborn child. The skin of its entire body was black. Could you imagine the horror? I am sick with grief. How they all must be hurting."

"It wouldn't have been that way for Kayley. It was too soon after the accident."

"Are you sure?"

Chapter 79

Without an expressed invitation, Alexandra entered Kayley's townhouse and found her sitting at the kitchen table, sipping black tea and contemplating the brown envelope that she was holding. It was a moment that had been a year in the making, and while feeling somewhat anticlimactic, still left Kayley wishing for a longer postponement.

Over the past several weeks, guilt had made initial eye contact difficult for Alexandra. Kayley sensed the awkwardness and was glad that she had arranged for their time alone.

"What's that?" Alexandra asked.

"A letter from the lawyer who took care of Gavin's estate. I'm a little nervous to open it."

"Nervous?"

"I'm worried that it might contain censure from beyond the grave. *Dearest Kayley, you destroyed me.*"

PAIRS

She quickly finished her tea, placed the envelope on the table, and walked to the sink. While rinsing her mug, Kayley became lost in the thoughts of Gavin and Alexandra that had been braiding together all morning.

"Do you want me to open it for you?" Alexandra offered.

"This may require a glass, or two, of wine." Kayley put her mug in the dish tray before leaving the kitchen.

"Bring it," Alexandra said, as Kayley was moving past the table.

Kayley hesitated. She hadn't actually concluded that she was prepared to read the contents when she found herself picking up the envelope. When they stepped out into the yard, Kayley held it under her arm and retrieved the keys from her pants pocket.

"How are you doing?" Alexandra asked.

"I'd be lying if I said I was fine. But I will be." Kayley replied while locking the door.

With the deadbolt in place, they stood facing each other. Alexandra exuded guilt and Kayley conveyed affectionate reassurance.

"I just haven't quite figured out what to say to Terra. I'm sure she knows something has happened."

"Do you think there is a book that might help?"

"A book?"

"Yeah, a children's book. When I was a waitress at the diner I overheard a conversation between two of my boys. One was the father of a little girl. Apparently, he had found a book that he could read to her that dealt with the topic of daddy choosing a man to be his life partner. If there isn't a book—there should be."

"A book," Kayley repeated, sounding to Alexandra as if the concept was a little too complicated to remember.

The comment had a ring of destiny, as if the story was already fully formed. Kayley was amused and puzzled that such an obvious answer had evaded her. There was little to do except put it on paper.

"A picture book," she mused aloud, on their way toward the front gate.

"Well, yeah! It would be a children's book."

They stepped onto the street and walked past the cars parked curbside toward the new Mustang convertible. Alexandra suppressed her desire to run to her new toy. Although remaining steadfast during their chat, she couldn't resist the occasional enamoured glimpses.

"You're right, there should be. I could write that book. First-hand. Maybe I could consult with a child psychologist."

Kayley had been too caught up in her evolving plans to take notice of the specific vehicle to which they were headed. She remained oblivious right up to the passenger side, where they stopped under Alexandra's direction. It was not until the door was opened for her that Kayley became aware of the car. Although she was generally not an automotive enthusiast, it was apparent to her that Alexandra was proud of the purchase, so she made a production of her surprise. Kayley stepped back and found that she did appreciate the raw appeal. Top down, black leather upholstery, red metallic paint, and wide, chrome rims. It was powerful and sexy, perfect for Alexandra.

"Very hot," Kayley said.

"I know. I'm sure Adam got a hard-on when he saw it."

"And Henry?"

"Not so much. He asked me why I didn't get a Hummer."

"And?" Kayley asked. She accepted Alexandra's invitation and lowered herself into the bucket seat.

"They don't come in soft-top."

Alexandra closed the door, ran excitedly around the back of the car to the driver's side, and hopped in—literally. The ignition was an aggressive awakening of stampeding pistons that Alexandra stoked with the **accelerator**. She looked at Kayley and bounced her eyebrows to express her pleasure with the engine's rumble.

"I had a little aftermarket work done," Alexandra explained. "Still street legal though."

PAIRS

Kayley watched fingers of wind brush through Alexandra's short, black hair as they drove down the street. She could almost hear John Mellencamp singing "Jack and Diane." It was inspiring for Kayley, picturesque in a wonderfully sweet way and tender as any romantic sonnet. Time had come for her to be honest with Alexandra. She couldn't hold back any longer.

"I know you feel guilty," Kayley said. "But don't. I don't want you to. I made a choice. And I'd do it again."

"What you went through, no woman should go through."

"I don't have regrets. Not about the pregnancy. I have been wondering if I could have done something different that morning, something that would have averted my fall. I knew I was having some dizzy spells, I should have opted for a bath."

"Of course not. You went to take a shower like every other day. Please don't beat yourself up. I don't know if I could survive that."

Alexandra's glanced over to her. Kayley fell into her deep brown eyes. They reached for each other. Their fingers folded together and Kayley took the back of Alexandra's hand and gently pressed against her cheek.

"Do you know why I did it?" she asked, after lowering her arm.

"Because you're an incredible, selfless saint."

"Partially," Kayley agreed, with humour. The levity fell away as she began her nervous confession. "There was a selfish reason."

"Selfish?"

"I love you." The words felt almost like a reflex to her, uncluttered and wired.

The intent of Kayley's announcement had escaped Alexandra. She had misinterpreted the romantic declaration as one of profound friendship. "I love you, too. How does loving me make you selfish?"

Kayley's grandmother was in the habit of saying words or phrases twice as a means of infusing a deeper meaning. Being a wordsmith, it had always bothered Kayley. She had never mentioned this to her grandmother and was now glad she hadn't. The irony would have been too poetic. She struggled to express herself.

"No. I mean—I *love* you, love you. Maybe selfish is exactly the right word, but it wasn't entirely selfless."

Alexandra was very cut-and-dry on matters that most would prefer to believe complex and vague. She looked at Kayley, beautiful under the tussling of her blond curls, and saw the emotions that resided within her.

"Lezzy?"

Subtleties and guarded words were of little use when talking to Alexandra. Kayley had rehearsed the conversation several times and from several angles. Through it all, the simplest fact remained inescapable—*sort of* boiled down to *yes*.

"Lezzy," she conceded. "I didn't know how deep my feelings went until I had to admit to myself that I felt like I was having *our* child—yours and mine. I had wanted that all along. I think that's why Gavin popped into my head. He was another unsorted relationship." Kayley gestured with the envelope. "You're not a Gavin to me—but these feelings are a surprise."

The wind, the engine, passing cars, and sounds along the roadside could not fill in the gap left by absence of Alexandra's voice. She squeezed Kayley's hand but had difficulty meeting her eyes. A part of her wanted to share the same feelings and rescue Kayely's vulnerability. However, it was not within her and because of that, her guilt compounded. She sank lower in her seat. Kayley sensed the weight pushing Alexandra down.

"I don't need you to feel the same way," she reassured. "It's not a possessive or jealous love. It's nice. The world is just better with you in it. That's all. And don't worry. I have no intention of leaving Adam. I love him dearly. I simply happen to love you, too."

Alexandra drew her hand free, cupped the back of Kayley's neck and tenderly reined her in for a quick, traffic-conscious kiss, after which Kayley placed her head on Alexandra's shoulder.

"I do love you," Alexandra said. "Just not lezzy. But lady, you're definitely my hero and if I was a lesbian—you'd be my kind of girl."

"You're not just sparing my feelings?"

"No really. I think you and Henry are alike."

Kayley sat upright. Amused, she was reminded of her observation the night at Adam's apartment when they had first discussed the Grand Dame and recalled all the permutations of pairs that matched, pairs that complemented, and pairs that completed.

"So you think I'm like Henry?"

"Only you're not so prissy," Alexandra replied, becoming caught up in memories of exasperation. "Sometimes he irritates me so much that all I want to do is jump his bones and screw him senseless. Weird, eh?"

"Sex him into submission," Kayley offered.

"Humble him a little, but nicely. You know, like—*you get your yah-yahs off just like everybody else, princess.*"

"Don't you think you're encouraging him to irritate you?"

The possibility stunned Alexandra. She reflected on Henry and the timing of the pretentious slivers that he pushed under her skin.

"You think?" she asked.

"He is a pretty smart guy."

Although Henry looked like a man, smelled like a man, and had the sex drive of a man, Alexandra knew that he was smarter than a smart man. He was, in no uncertain terms, a very smart woman.

"Frig! He's been playing me!"

"I bet you *really* want to jump his bones now?"

Alexandra had never been conned in her life—by anyone. The thought of being so easily outmanoeuvred annoyed Alexandra into a frenetic state of arousal—and being turned on infuriated her even more. It became very circular. She pressed down on the gas pedal.

"Frig!"

Kayley laughed when she felt the sudden acceleration. The world rushed by. She felt happy to be in love. Alexandra enjoyed the way Kayley seemed to light up whenever she laughed. She never wanted to hurt her.

"Did I lead you on?" Alexandra asked. "Was it the make out session at Daleesha's party?"

"No. You had me before that." Kayley smiled playfully. "You had me at *didactic*."

"Henry can definitely be didactic," Alexandra admitted, while drifting into a gnashing fantasy.

Kayley could read the desire. "You're really wanting him right now, aren't you?"

"It's your fault. He wasn't even on my mind." Her eyes narrowed during her plotting calculations and her voice dropped to the low, licentious snarl of the goddess. "Play me, will you?"

Kayley was pulled into Alexandra's intensity. She marginally feared for, yet curiously envied, Henry. A whip-crack, real or imagined, retrieved her from the dungeon. "So I'm *your* hero?" she asked. "How so?"

"Your bravery. Getting pregnant. You inspired me. And now I can have the child you were willing to carry. The timing, the order of things, the price—it all bothers me."

"Don't let it. If nothing else, that alone makes it all worth it for me. Maybe that is exactly how things were supposed to go. The soul I was carrying can now be born from you, as it should."

Alexandra glanced at Kayley and nearly drove off the road. She was overwhelmed by the sublime compassion and couldn't stop herself from crying. She didn't want to try. She cleared the tightness in her throat and managed to whisper her appreciation.

"Thank you. And I'm sure Henry thanks you too."

Alexandra glanced, once again, at Kayley and found buoyancy in her eyes. It released her. The penitence faded away.

"And, of course," she added cheerfully, while brushing the tears away, "Love-heart thanks you."

"Love-heart?" Kayley asked.

"My vagina. Henry felt that there really wasn't anything Kitten about me. I have to agree."

"You're calling your vagina Love-heart?"

"Trial phase."

Nothing about her friend could surprise Kayley anymore. In her own way, Alexandra was an entirely unaffected person, a prodigy of simple clarity. She was a child of the world who completely disregarded the lines when colouring. However, in all that Kayley had accepted at face value, one peculiar aspect about Alexandra had continually piqued her curiosity. As a result of their deepened bond, she no longer felt that it would be inappropriate to talk about the *Lindsay* identification.

"If you don't mind me asking, how did you get all the ID with your picture and Lindsay's name?"

"There's a bit of story to that," Alexandra replied.

"I was hoping there would be."

Alexandra grinned as she thought back to the night in the hotel room, watching television, and wondering how long that odd little man could maintain his surprisingly substantial erection.

"When I used to perform, I was a headliner. And I would travel from town to town doing my show. Well, I had a bit of a following."

"I bet you did."

"But I had this one groupie in particular that was at every show. He was a small guy. He spent scads of cash to watch me dance. After a while we got to know each other. Now and then I'd sit and talk with him for free. Clothes on, of course. Naked costs. I wouldn't chat too long. You always want to seem unattainable."

The nightclubs all shared one constant fixture in her memories: a bald man entrenched at the front of the catwalk. He was a greasy, twitchy ATM that worshiped beautiful women in sweaty adoration. And he worshiped her above all others. It was difficult not to take advantage of such a man. But she had managed.

"The long and the short of it," Alexandra said, "was that he worked for the RCMP, and when he found out what I wanted to do, he offered to help—for a price."

"Men!" Kayley scoffed.

"Hold on. It's not what you think—not exactly, anyway. He wanted me to sit, bare ass, on his face. For one hour."

"Since you had the ID—I take it you did."

"Yep. It really didn't seem like prostitution to me. Maybe it was, but face-sitting didn't bother me. So I thought, what the hell. What have I got to lose except an hour of my time? I met him at his hotel. I ordered the most expensive dinner on the room service menu. He stripped to his underwear. I tied him to the mattress, sat bare ass on his face, and watched the season finale of *Survivor*. It was two hours—so he got a bonus. Of course, I had to stretch now and then, so it wasn't a solid two hours."

Alexandra waited for a reaction, but Kayley was looking at her in wide-eyed wonder. Interpreting the silence as an encouragement to continue, Alexandra finished her tale.

"True to his word, next time we met he had a full set of Lindsay's ID. And, I guess because I gave him the extra hour, he had a fresh set of my own. I quit stripping that very night."

It took a few minutes after Alexandra had stopped talking for Kayley to fully digest the explanation and as she did so, her awe shifted to amusement. An unshakable image of Alexandra half-naked, sitting on the face of a scrawny geek took up residence in her head. She imagined her drinking beer and eating chips from a bowl that rested on his hairy, linen-white paunch.

"Alexandra."

"Yes?"

"You are *my* hero."

Kayley saw the profile of Alexandra's grin and took hold of her hand when it was offered. Alexandra squeezed gently and then returned to the steering wheel. She glanced to Kayley's lap after turning into the neighbourhood of the newly refurbished Grand Dame.

"Gavin and I also have something else in common. Beside the unsorted relationship thing."

"What?" Kayley asked.

"We were both molested," she said, and then quietly answered the question that resided in Kayley's eyes. "Adam told me. And how bad you felt. You shouldn't feel bad."

"Henry managed it so much better than I did."

"Henry knew. You did not."

The link between Gavin and Alexandra became clear to Kayley. The universe had arranged a second chance to learn the lesson that her immaturity had let slip through her fingers a decade ago. Although she had believed Gavin to be gay, she still could have permitted herself to love him. It was not a matter of all-or-nothing. To be in love, to feel love toward him could be enough. It would be enough with Alexandra.

"Open it," Alexandra said.

"The envelope?"

"No—the car door. Of course the envelope."

Kayley looked down at her lap. She glanced to Alexandra for moral support and after receiving an encouraging nod, sliced open the top corner with her fingernail, then tore open a seam across the top. She slowly pulled the papers out. There were two sheets of lined paper held together by a paper clip. A rectangular sticky note was attached to the top sheet.

"Well?"

"It's a letter from Gavin. With a note from his wife."

"And?"

"She said that Gavin wrote this to me as part of his therapy." Kayley had spoken the words before their meaning had sunk in. She stopped reading and blinked at Alexandra. "Oh my God! I put the man into therapy."

"Somebody thinks pretty highly of herself. Read on."

Kayley returned to the note. As she read, her angst subsided. "He finished the poem. He never got up the courage to send it because so many years had passed."

"Read the damn poem already!"

"I want to read his letter first."

"Fine. But out loud."

"To myself first."

"Oh for frig's sake!"

Chapter 80

The picnic had been Kayley's idea. It had leapt to mind the day they had accepted the offer on the house. She wanted to say farewell. All had input on the menu. As a result, foie gras sat next to Pogos, and bottles of Labatt Blue chilled alongside a bottle of Haut-Brion.

Henry stepped back from the blanket for a final overview of the spread, immediately noticed the omission, and returned straight away to the house to make the absent salad. Inside, hushed voices spoke indiscernible words that refracted in a prism of hard surfaces. Adam was showing Tess the fruits of his labour. As friend and mentor, her approval mattered. They were waiting at the second floor landing.

"What do you mean this was *no flip*?" Adam replied to Tess.

"You took way too long. You're lucky the *uber-bod* was bankrolling this."

"It was just me and the newbie. What did you expect?"

"Adam, I've seen the both of you work," Tess remarked. "She may not have your overall vision, but she is fast and dead-on at what she does—maybe even better than you in that regard. Fuck, the two of you could have put up an entire subdivision in less time."

PAIRS

With a single unspoken expletive Adam cursed Tess's perception. She always won at poker. She always cut the best deal. And she always called him out whenever he didn't give her the straight goods.

"I didn't want it to end, Tess."

She smiled kindly, and placed her hand gently on his shoulder. "That's so fuck'n sweet. But if you're going to be in this game Adam…"

"Less heart, more balls, I know."

The sound of a flushing toilet was heard faintly through the closed door at the end of the hall. Adam and Tess fell silent. They faced the washroom when the door opened. Terra stepped out and marched giddily toward Adam with her hands held in out in front of her, fingers spread.

"Let's see," Adam said, as he moved toward her.

He took hold of her hands and squinted as he did his playful examination. Terra giggled at the silly inspector and his exaggerated suspicion. The stamp of approval was in the form of a kiss on each palm. Terra retracted her arms and slipped between Adam and Tess to the landing.

"Lead the way," Adam said, and then followed her closely down each step.

"Fuck, you do good work." Tess's praise resonated like a gong. "Sorry, Terra. You didn't hear that."

"Yes I did."

"But you don't use those words," Adam confirmed.

"No. Mommy would be mad."

Henry followed their voices out to the hall. They were still coming down the staircase when he had reached the foyer. From behind Adam, Tess gave Henry a thumbs-up.

"Everything is good to go out back," he said.

"Adam said the layout is all you, Henry. Great eye," Tess said. "Ever consider becoming a designer or architect?"

"No, actually, I hadn't."

"You should. You're way better than a lot of the dips I've worked with."

"Really?"

"Good Lord, yes."

Adam glanced at his watch. "The ladies should be here soon."

"Are you staying for lunch?" Henry asked Tess.

"Nah. This is a family affair."

"You're family to me, Tess," Adam said.

"Adam, you silver-tongued dog," she replied, while heading toward the front door. "Get your nose out of my ass. Sorry, Terra."

"I heard that, too."

They followed Tess out onto the front porch. The comfortable rumble of the Mustang at the top of street drew their attention. Adam pointed to the car for Tess's benefit. Kayley didn't seem to notice. Alexandra rose up above the rim of the front windshield, waved, and dropped back into her seat. Tess smiled at Adam, shook her head with amusement, and descended the stairs to the flagstone walkway. She waited for the arrival of Kayley and Alexandra.

***

After settling back down behind the steering wheel, Alexandra poked Kayley in the leg. She didn't react. Tearful but happy, Kayley was too engrossed by messages from the past to be nudged into the present.

"We're almost there." Alexandra felt the need to keep her tone to a respectful whisper.

As she drove down the street, it occurred to her that this would be last time they would be at the house. The Grand Dame belonged to someone else now. She had known all along that this day would come and she had been fully aware of why they were having the picnic. But the significance had escaped her. As Alexandra began to grasp the conclusiveness, she slowed down the car and, during the slow trot, appreciated the neighbourhood around her.

When she pulled into the driveway under the cradle of fingertip shadows from the branches of Lindsay's birch tree, Terra let go of

Adam's hand and ran toward the car. Alexandra saw her coming, parked, turned off the ignition, and opened the door.

"Hey, Mouse!" She repositioned herself sideways in her seat and placed her feet on the ground.

Terra moved between Alexandra's legs. They embraced, and Terra rested the side of her head against Alexandra's stomach. Alexandra stared up at the house, processing the finality as she stroked her hand along the curly red hair. Everyone had assumed that Terra was greeting Alexandra with a welcoming hug. However, that was not the case. Things were becoming clearer for Terra as she pressed against Alexandra's belly button. She was, in fact, listening.

"Way better," she whispered happily.

Chapter 81

Dearest Kayley,

It is odd writing to you after all these years, and to think of you in such different light. I confess that I was angry for a while. But I have come to understand that it was I, my shame—not you—that let me down. You could not have known that I had been molested as a child. I never told you. And because of that, I didn't give you a chance.

I am happy now. I have a wonderful wife, Stacy, and two amazing children, Christopher and Lindsay. "Blessed" sounds so tragically suburban, but that is fine, I live in the suburbs now so I can say it. I am blessed. I hope your life is going as well.

You may be interested to know that, in a way, our daughter is named after the poem that you and I wrote together. Lindsay means "from the linden tree island" and if you recall, the birthplace of our poem was under a linden tree at the Public Gardens.

I regret that I never let you know me—all of me. I was too guarded, always fearful of the world finding out. That put up a wall in our relationship. We may not have ended up as life partners, but I am sure we could have been incredible friends. My lesson, which I wish to share with you (some things never change, Kay), was to try and live the rest of my life without regrets. Never pile up a list of should-haves. This was my inspiration for the last stanza. I've also taken the liberty to give our work a title.

All my best,

'Spaz'

PS: It is wonderful to love you.

PAIRS

Public Gardens

The clouds have landed
While I slept,

Suspended breath,
　　　All is possibility.

Nothing to purvey,
Or reveal,

Save myself

　　　And the garden path
　　　　　Down which I walk

　　　　Alone

These stepping-stones,
Moments,
Living glimpses

Riddles that I marvel
Impossible with detail
Change should I hesitate

Bridged, one to the other,
Revealed and relinquished

　　　Through turnstiles

A journey

I shall not measure

In regretful spans
Of afterthought

LaVergne, TN USA
09 November 2010
204059LV00001B/60/P